JEAN pressed close against Quint to enter the low, narrow doorway. She turned slowly to face him. An unspoken challenge seemed to show in her eyes.

"Damn!" Quint dropped the burning corn husks as they seared his fingers. As they struck the floor, he stamped out the fire in them. The room was in darkness except for the faint outline of moonlight limned on the floor by the outer door.

"Quint," Jean said softly.

They met in the center of the room. Her arms went up and around his neck as he encircled her slim waist and crushed her close against his hard body. Their lips met. He bent her backward. She struggled a little, knowing and perhaps not caring that there was nothing she could do to protect herself. She could appeal to his honor. She did not appeal; her soft mouth was closed with his hard lips.

Fawcett Gold Medal Books
by Gordon D. Shirreffs:

THE MANHUNTER   13728 $1.75

NOW HE IS LEGEND   14233 $1.50

THE UNTAMED BREED   14387 $2.75

THE UNTAMED BREED

by

Gordon D. Shirreffs

FAWCETT GOLD MEDAL • NEW YORK

THE UNTAMED BREED

Published by Fawcett Gold Medal Books, a unit of CBS Publications, the Consumer Publishing Division of CBS Inc.

ISBN: 0-449-14387-2

Printed in the United States of America

First Fawcett Gold Medal printing: February 1981

10 9 8 7 6 5 4 3 2 1

To
Alicia Buenovino

There was a mountain man before now, southbound across the land making his way from high ground to low ground and back again, through cold rain and hot sun, where the wind is a mighty nomad, by barren hills and nameless mountains, with the morning on his left hand and the evening on his right.

On a day of days, and he traveling, he came at the edge of evening to the rim of the Valley of the Rio Grande del Norte. A great golden eagle of the country flew to him, resting her wings on the wind.

"Have you got where you are going?" she asked.

"I have not," replied the mountain man. "I'm bound for the top of the country and the two sides of it. If I go up by the peaks, I'll come down by the canyons. If I follow the river far enough I'll walk by the sea. If the mountain meadows are above me, the streams will lie below. I'll go wherever the free wind blows and wild water flows, until I see the sight of all the country."

"You'd best take up your travels then," she said, "for they stretch far before you."

ONE

June 1837. The Medicine Lodge Fork of the Big Horn River.

The land was much broken by mountain spurs and deep gullies choked with brush. It was mostly destitute of timber except for an occasional bosque of cottonwoods and the intermittent green lines of cottonwoods and willows following the courses of tributary streams. The sun had vanished behind the mountains to the west. A faint pewter-colored trace against the eastern sky betrayed the rising of the new moon, but darkness still covered the land. The dry wind was shifting uncertainly before it flowed down the mountain slopes and through the canyons toward the lower ground. It stirred up a faint sweetish rotten smell.

The four horsemen with their eight-mule pack train were moving quietly through the breaks toward the unseen valley of the Medicine Lodge Fork. Each man led two pack mules apiece, both of which were loaded with two eighty-pound packs of prime beaver plews. The lead horseman caught the faint stench on the wind and instantly thrust up his right arm to halt his companions. They sat their mounts silently in the darkness, listening intently and sniffing the night air.

Quintin Ker-Shaw, Scots-Canadian known to men as Quint Kershaw and to mountain men as Big Red, dismounted from his claybank pony, tied a knot in the hackamore reins, then looped them over the saddlehorn to hold the pony in position against the pull of the reins. He treaded catlike on moccasined feet sensitive to the ground toward a small stand of cottonwoods grouped at the mouth of a shallow gully through which trickled a slim twisted ribbon of a stream on its meandering way south toward the Medicine Lodge Fork two miles away.

Quint was a veritable panther of a man, six feet two inches tall, 190 pounds of lean, sinewy muscle and bone. He was hawk-eyed and hawk-nosed and had a thick and greasy sorrel beard. His fine even teeth were pure white in contrast to the saddle-brown hue of his weathered countenance. His reddish hair had been woven into two thick braids, wrapped in shining otter skin and hung in front of his broad shoulders. A small silver ring shone in his left earlobe. His hat was a shapeless, battered creation of rough wool with a rattlesnake-skin band into which had been stuck a gray eagle feather. He wore a heavy, scantily beaded mid-thigh-length elkskin jacket over a thick woolen shirt. His wrinkled seatless full-length buckskin leggins were fringed with Blackfoot hair. His loincloth was of thick red flannel. The clothing was glazed and smutted with grease, dirt, ashes, dried animal blood, sweat and dribbled whiskey; a frosty look of absolute filth, products of a fall and winter trapping season with three months of *hivernaning*, or wintering between the seasons. The rank stench of a hard-living outdoorsman hung about him.

Quint carried a ten-and-a-half-pound J. & S. Hawken half-stocked Rocky Mountain rifle, .53 caliber, thirty-two balls to the pound. Stocked with striped rock maple and fitted with iron and pewter so as not to reflect light, its only ornamentation was a coin-silver thistle, emblematic of Quint's Scottish birthplace, inletted into the beavertail cheekpiece. The Hawken was the ultimate Rocky Mountain rifle. Quint's nickname for the weapon, with its legendary deadly accuracy was Auld Clootie, broad Scots for the Old Devil. He handled the Hawken as though it was an extension of his mind and body; a *man's* bond with his *rifle*.

Quint halted behind a cottonwood, seemingly becoming a part of the thick trunk itself. He tested the darkness with nose and ears, coupled with an indefinable sixth sense and innate wisdom of the wilds hand-honed from living on the razor's edge of peril for the past seven years. He could faintly hear the running water of the stream and scent the aroma of newly sprouted grass and leaves still warmed from the June sun. All that and more he knew and instantly classified, but it was the other scent that had alerted him; he knew it well enough from bitter past experience—the sweetish-rotten cloying smell of decomposing human flesh.

Quint glanced back over his shoulder. There was no sign of his three trapping partners—Luke Connors, the rawhide-tough Kentuckian; the quarter Cree French Canadian François "Boudins" Charbonne; and Black Moccasin, a Lenape or full-blooded Delaware, the only breed of Indian the mountain men would take into full partnership. Their pack mules were loaded with a fall and spring harvesting of prime beaver plews from Bovey's, Clark's, and Rock Forks of the Yellowstone. It represented a small fortune to be taken to the forthcoming July rendezvous, the "Fur Fair" on the Seeds-kee-dee Agie River and the fork of Horse Creek, about 150 miles to the southwest. They had been traveling nights and hiding out during the bright days, persistently trailed by "Bug's Boys," the merciless and predatory Blackfeet. Perhaps by now the Blackfeet had stopped trailing them and turned back to their own country to the north. This was a sort of mingled Crow and Shoshoni country now, an area claimed by both tribes, the Shoshonis from the south, the Crows from the north and east. They had been battling over possession of it for generations. It was prime buffalo land, and more than that, to the Shoshonis at least, it had certain spiritual values.

Quint moved on noiselessly, circling through the timber to approach from downwind of the source of the scent. He moved sideways, crouching low, bringing the heavy rifle up to his shoulder in fluid and effortless motion while full-cocking the hammer. The silver-blade front sight was centered in the buckhorn rear sight, holding on the hatted head which showed above the brush. There was something strange about that motionless head. The vagrant wind shifted, then died away, but the smell of rotting flesh still hung in the air.

Quint moved forward like a hunting cat. The odor grew to a strong stink and then to an almost overpowering stench. A faint buzzing sound came to him. He paused. The subdued light of the rising moon reached the valley of the Medicine Lodge Fork. The head seemed like a huge porcupine, so full of arrows was it. There was no body below it; the head had been forced down on to a thick stake set up in the center of a clearing.

Quint pinched his nostrils together and covered his mouth with the palm of his left hand as he approached. He stumbled over something—a human leg, gnawed through so that the thigh-bone shone a greasy, glistening white in the moonlight. A cloud of buzzing blue-green flies heavy with bloat hung over the leg and head.

As the light grew Quint became aware of other parts of dismembered bodies, including several decapitated torsos scattered about the clearing and just within the edge of the timber. One of the torsos had been emasculated and the genitals stuffed into the mouth of a scalped head resting on a stump. The torsos bristled with arrows and crawled with flies.

11

Quint approached the head on the stump. He bent a little and looked closely at it despite his revulsion. It *looked* like Jim Slocum. Quint figured from the scattered body parts that there must have been three or four men in the party.

Quint hurriedly got downwind of the clearing and looked out into the shallow valley, bare and treeless to the long broken line of willows and cottonwoods that marked the course of the river. The open area was dotted with hundreds of buffalo lying on the grassy earth or placidly grazing. To the east, toward the unseen Big Horn River he could see many hundreds more of the shaggy black forms of buffalo. It was almost eerily quiet. There was no sound except for the faint trickling of the stream and the soughing of the wind through the timber.

Quint returned to the clearing. He tipped his hat as he passed the head on the stump. "Don't bother tae get up, Mr. Slocum," he murmured politely in his clipped Scots.

An owl hooted twice from the shadowed timber. There was a short pause, and then the hooting was repeated.

Luke Connors looked back toward the dim shapes of his two partners. "All clear, mates," he said. They moved together toward the stand of timber.

"What's that stink?" François Charbonne asked.

Luke grinned. "We're downwind from Big Red, ain't we?"

"Ye couldna smell me, laddie, ower that stink o' yours," Quint commented dryly out of the shadows.

"What is it, Big Red?" François asked. He knew, of course.

"You mean *who* was it," Quint corrected. "Jim Slocum, maybe Jonas Waldo, that half-breed Etienne Barbeau, and someone else."

"Are yuh sartain sure?" Luke asked.

Quint jerked his head back toward the timber clearing. "See for yourselves. The yellowskins got to them. Likely Bug's Boys ambushed them a couple of days past."

The horses and mules shied and blew as the stench grew thicker in the quiet air. Luke padded forward, holding a hand over his mouth and nose. "It's Jonas Waldo all right." He jerked out an arrow and held it up to the moonlight. "Ain't a Blackfoot arrer, Quint. Surprised at yuh."

Quint wrinkled his big nose. "I wasn't that interested at the time."

"Crow, I'd say." Luke tossed the arrow to Moccasin.

The Delaware caught it. He nodded. "You right. *Ab-sá-ro-kee.*"

Luke looked at Quint. "Yuh warned them not to get too far ahead of us and to travel at night until they reached the Medicine Lodge Fork."

Quint shrugged. "Jonas always was careless, always in a hurry. Never listened to anyone. Guess he figured he was safe enough in Shoshoni country."

Luke spat to one side. "It's their country only as far as a Shoshoni bullet can carry and a Shoshoni arrer can fly, Big Red."

Moccasin nodded. "Shoshoni and Absarokee always fightin' over this country."

"Why?" the Canadian asked. "We've seen lots better, I think."

"Big medicine for the Shoshoni," Luke explained. "And prime buffalo country."

"Shit! They can't keep them Crows outa here."

"No," Quint put in, "but they sure as hell keep on trying."

"Should we bury them?" François asked.

Quint shook his head. "And let the Crows know there are other white men around?"

"And mebbe Bug's Boys," Luke added.

François shrugged. "I was thinking of the wolves. Etienne Barbeau was my good friend."

"He'll nae mair be a friend of yours dead, Boudins, than when he was alive if we bury him and notify the yellowskins we're passing through their country."

"They had five pack horses loaded with prime plews," Luke said. "Two seasons shot to hell."

"And four good men," François added.

"Four damned fools!" Quint spat out. "Traveling through Crow country in broad daylight most likely."

Luke scratched inside his shirt. "Christ, but this ol' coon is grease hungry. They's prime buffler meat out there in the valley. One shot, one young bull, and we'll make enough meat to keep us alive until we reach the rondyvoo."

"One shot might bring down a young bull and maybe two hundred Crows," Quint reminded him.

Moccasin grunted. "If I had my old elkhorn bow," he murmured.

Luke grinned. "Yuh ain't shot a bow in ten year, Moc. Besides, you're too good with that Hawken long gun o' yourn to fool around with a bow and arrers."

François relieved himself against a tree. "What's the plan, Big Red? We ain't had fresh meat for a week now."

"We'll wait until moonset, cross the valley to the timber

13

along the river and get into cover on the south side of it. I'll try for a young bull at dawn light."

They squatted upwind of the decaying flesh, smoking steadily to overcome the stench of decomposition, while the new moon waned and died. When it was dark Quint led the way into the open and headed for the Medicine Lodge.

TWO

Quint lay within the shallow saucer of a buffalo wallow on the south bank of the river. Here both banks of the river were clear of the usual bordering lines of timber for a quarter mile. The river was shallow, flowing over a gravelly bottom parting here and there to flow on both sides of banks of earth and gravel. Quint's partners with their horses and pack mules lay concealed in the thick stand of timber to his left. Buffalo grazed on the north side of the river to the rising slopes below the naked red sandstone bluffs. The shaggy beasts moved slowly into the wind, as they always did while grazing, using their keen sense of smell instead of their poor eyesight to alert them to any approaching enemies. A lone red-tailed hawk drifted with motionless pinions resting on the wind high over the drifting herd. Two score of big varicolored wolves had appeared with the dawn light and now trotted boldly along the flanks of the herd, seeking out the old, the disabled, or the weak.

A cow grazed off by herself directly across the river from Quint. Her gangling calf, dropped just recently, stayed close by her side. She was heedless of a trio of cream-colored wolves who moved closer from downwind. She would be the closest sure shot for Quint—a good 125 yards. The nearest bulls were about 75 yards beyond, tossing their heads nervously as they picked up the faint scent of the approaching wolves.

Quint drew out his powerful brass telescope to its full length and scanned the far side of the valley, looking for

Indian sign. He searched the bluffs and the gully-cut hills toward the east and the Big Horn River. He studied the valley. The west wind rippled the grass, giving the impression of waves beating toward a distant beach. The rising sun glinted brightly like shards of broken crystal from the ripples on the river. There were no other humans in the valley outside of Quint and his partners. He was *almost* sure of that. Still he studied the north end of the valley. He could see a lone buzzard hovering low over the copse at the mouth of the gully where the four trappers had been slaughtered and mutilated. Or had they been mutilated while still alive and *then* slaughtered? Quint put the thought out of his mind. It was not good to think about it.

Quint glanced toward the timber where his partners lay hidden. They would be sitting there, smoking and waiting for the bellowing sound of the heavy rifle report, softly cursing Quint for his caution and hesitation. They were sure enough "grease hungry," and there was only one way to satisfy that hunger—good red buffalo hump meat with the blood still running from it.

He'd drop the cow first with a lung shot to lure the bulls closer to her because of their natural curiosity. He loaded his Hawken, full-cocked the big hammer and drew back on the rear trigger to set the front trigger with a faint click. Sighting on the cow, he drew in a deep breath, then let out about half of it and rested his finger on the trigger.

The rifle drove back firmly against Quint's shoulder. The throaty thudding report echo ran along the line of bluffs opposite. Quint peered through the powder smoke. The cow had lunged a little as she was struck by the heavy ball, then moved ahead a few feet, paused and tottered about aimlessly before settling down on her foreknees. Sunlight glistened from the bright blood dripping from her mouth and nostrils. The nearest bulls raised their shaggy heads as they caught the scent of fresh hot blood. The wolves had loped away at the sound of the shot, but they hadn't gone very far, for the tantalizing smell of the blood held them close to the cow. The calf stood by its mother's side, bawling just a little. A young bull drifted close. He sniffed suspiciously and then hooked at the cow with his horns. He was more interested in her sexually than he was in her strange behavior or any possible danger.

The wiping stick drove home the second charge. Quint cocked and capped the Hawken. He sighted on the young bull. He'd want a neck or heart shot to cause sudden death. The wolves had begun to slink off, while looking back over their shoulders to the east. Something in that direction had begun to disturb the grazing herd. Quint took his finger from the trigger. Faint yellowish dust was rising far down the valley. A faint drumming sound echoed along the bluffs. The buffalo began to move westerly, toward the higher ground and into the wind in order to scent better the enemy that had disturbed them. It wasn't like them to move toward higher ground unless they were seriously disturbed. A steady tremor came to Quint through the hollow-sounding earth.

Quint sighted his telescope on the mass of the herd moving from east to west. Then he saw them—half-naked, brown-bodied centaurs riding their ponies in among the rear buffalo of the moving herd, drawing the gut strings of their laminated horn bows so that the arrow feathers rested against their jaws, to release the obsidian-, bone- or iron-pointed shafts into the lumbering beasts who almost brushed against the racing ponies. Buffalo after buffalo went down as the buffalo runners bore into the herd, riding with the speed of prairie wind, guiding their ponies by leg pressure alone. They released arrow after arrow with machine like regularity, reaching back over their shoulders to pull another arrow from their quivers, nock it, draw it to the full and then loose it. The whole act was an absorbing study in grace and efficiency.

It was beautiful to watch, and deadly as well—the thundering herd and the rumbling of thousands of hoofbeats; the trembling of the responsive earth; the sun shining on the tossing horns, the naked sweating torsos of the hunters, and reflecting from the flashing arrows. The lumbering beasts were being cut off in small bunches by the hunters and forced to circle, or to mill while still on the run into ever tightening spins.

Who were they? Blackfeet? Crows? Gros Ventres? Shoshonis?

Quint sighted his telescope on one of the closest hunters. He was rather short and seemed to be darker than the average Crow, a tall light-skinned people. He wore his hair in braids rather than in Crow style, which was usually a high crested pompadour. It wasn't likely they would be Blackfeet.

"Shoshoni," Quint murmured. He nodded in satisfaction. The Shoshoni, or Snakes as many called them, from the sign-language symbol for them—an in-and-out motion of the

16

hand to indicate the weaving of grass shelters, although the Shoshonis had forsaken the building of such shelters many years earlier once they had acquired the horse and the ability to hunt the buffalo from whose hides they made their skin lodges. They were friends to the white man, at least most of the time. Still, it was wise not to take any chances. The temptation of horses, pack mules, prime beaver plews and Hawken rifles might just be too much for them.

Quint had picked up some of their language—it was one of his skills, the ability to quickly learn tongues other than his own. He vanished over the lip of the buffalo wallow and took to the low shelter of the brush that stippled the open ground. He reached the timber and faded into it, then whistled sharply twice and heard the response of one of his partners.

When they saw the Indians they had forted up amid a jackstraw pile of timber left over from a ravaging flood of years past. The horses and pack mules were sideline hobbled and picketed as well for double security.

"Well, old hoss?" Luke asked.

"Shoshonis, I think."

"Well, by God, what do we have to worry about then?" François demanded. "Whites and Snakes get along well enough together."

"We're still not absolutely sure who wiped out Jonas and the others," Quint reminded the Canadian.

Luke nodded. "If the Snakes did it, they can take the plews down to the rondyvoo and trade 'em in. Who's to be the wiser? It's likely they'll be headin' for the rondyvoo after this buffler hunt anyways. Ain't nobody will know they killed Jonas and his partners, is there?"

"Except us," Quint murmured. "We can sit here tight as a burr under a saddle blanket and burn daylight until they're through with the hunt. If they don't spot us, we can slip out after dusk," Quint said.

"What about *our* meat?" François demanded.

"Ye want to go out there and butcher the cow I dropped?" Quint asked pointedly.

François shrugged. "Not likely. Never had any trouble with the Snakes, though. Even had a Snake winter squaw once. Prettiest squaws I ever see. Make the best damned wives too."

Luke shook his head. "Me, I like a Crow."

Flint clicked on steel. Moccasin lighted his Dublin pipe. "Shit," he said around the stem. "Cheyenne for me. Or mebbe

17

'Rapaho." He looked sideways at Quint. "Like the one you had, Big Red."

Quint nodded as he filled his pipe. "A long time ago. First year I was in the trappin'. She didn't live long."

"Yuh screw her to death, ol' stud?" Luke asked slyly.

Quint shook his head. "Smallpox," he replied quietly.

François leaned back out of Quint's line of vision and shook his head at Luke, warning him to keep off the subject.

The sounds of the stampeded herd had faded up the valley. Quint walked to the edge of the timber. The dust was drifting on the wind. The plain was dotted with many downed buffalo. Already some of the Shoshoni women were getting ready to skin and butcher them.

Quint returned to his partners. "They're starting to butcher. If any of them head toward the timber, we'll have to pull foot ahead of them and keep the timber in between them and us until we can get out of the valley."

After some time passed, Moccasin padded through the timber to where he could see the activity across the river. "Jesus Christ!" he shouted in solid Anglo-Saxon. "Come look! We got more company!"

The long line of hills and buttes had disgorged from their gullies a mass of feathered horsemen who rode leisurely out on the open grassy plain to take up position on a low ridge a quarter of a mile from where the Shoshoni men and women were skinning the fallen buffalo. The Shoshonis stopped their work and stood there transfixed, staring incredulously at the newcomers.

Quint put his glass on the horsemen. War bonnets and lance feathers rippled in the wind. The ponies were painted, with scalps and feathers at jaws and foretops. Their tails were tied up and full of feathers. The sun glistened on the fresh warpaint of the warriors, and shone on decorated shields, polished rifle barrels and lance points. War clubs and pipe tomahawks hung by thongs from their wrists. Those warriors who had not covered their heads with warbonnets or other headgear had cut their hair into a four-or six-inch bang which had been induced to stand upright with clay and other sticky substances into a pompadour, or roach, painted red. The remainder of their long hair hung down their naked backs. They were tall men, handsome and fierce, grotesquely painted and decorated for war. There was a proud and imperious bearing about them. Absarokees—the Children of the Raven!

18

Quint handed the telescope to Luke. "Crows. A big war party. They've caught the Shoshonis napping."

Luke focused the telescope. He nodded. "They're all there. The Warrior Societies—the Crazy Dogs, the Foxes, the Warclubs and the Fighting Bulls. The whole damned shitaree of 'em!"

"Why don't they charge?" François asked. "It looks lak the Snakes are gone beaver."

Quint shrugged. "Point of honor, maybe? They may want a fight, not a massacre. From the looks of them, they want the Shoshonis to *know* who they are. They're sae damned sure of themselves."

"Why don't the Snakes run?" François asked.

Quint shrugged. "Damned fool pride. They believe this is *their* hunting ground. They'll likely die here proving it."

Luke put the powerful glass on the Shoshonis. The women and children, with their mounts, travois horses and dogs, had drawn together behind a line of warriors who had formed between them and the main body of Shoshonis, who now faced the motionless Crows. A burly Shoshoni warrior had quickly donned a feathered warbonnet, stripped the covers from warshield and rifle and was riding up and down the forward line of warriors, gesticulating and crying out to his braves.

"Who's the chief?" Quint asked.

Luke shrugged. He handed the telescope to François.

François studied the chief for a moment. He turned toward his partners and stroked the forefinger of his left hand down from the middle of his nose and then to his cheek, the sign of a double scar the Shoshoni had sustained in a challenge fight with a Blackfoot chief whom he had killed. "Washakie," François explained. "Rawhide Rattle. The one called by his enemies Snake-with-Scar-on-His-Face. Subchief of the Wind River Shoshonis. The Crows will have a real shitaree on their hands now. He won't run from them."

Some of the Shoshoni women galloped forward to give their men their warbonnets and extra weapons. Warbonnets and horned headdresses were quickly put on. Warpaint was daubed on their faces. Feathered lances rose in the air. Painted shields made from the thick neck hide of a buffalo bull, well steam-shrunken to harden it, then toughened with layers of hardened hoof glue, were slung from Shoshoni arms.

The Shoshoni warriors had separated into two groups. One of them faced the waiting Crows, while the other formed behind the women, the elderly and the children, who were

19

now riding furiously toward the river. François eyed the Shoshonis through the powerful telescope. "The warrior society facing the Crows are the Oho-mu-pe, the Yellow Noses. They are the best fighters and hunters among the Snakes. Yuh can tell them by their hair being cut short with bangs in front. The warriors behind the women and children are the Wo-Bine, the Logs. Yuh kin tell them from the Yellow Noses because they part their hair in the middle and wear a braid on either side wrapped with weasel or otter skin. Their job is to protect the rear and the wimmen and children." He looked sideways at Quint. "Time to pull out, Big Red," he suggested. "Them wimmen are goin' to head for the timber on this side of the river, sartain sure."

Quint looked east along the river course. The stand of timber beyond the clear area where he had dropped the buffalo cow from was a little more than a quarter of a mile away. To the south was a series of low hills, badly cut up with gullies choked with brush. Birds were rising swiftly from the timber and winging their way to the east, away from the stands of timber. Something was disturbing them.

"This ain't the holler tree for us coons," Luke warned.

The Shoshoni women were riding hell-for-leather into the shallow river. Sheets of glittering spray were thrown up. Horses went down and were expertly forced back on their feet by the women. Quirts rose and fell. Horses whinnied and neighed in fear.

"Move the animals to the west end of the timber," Quint ordered. "Get ready to pull out if necessary."

As the trappers led their animals through the timber to the west, the Shoshoni women halted their horses in the clear area between the two stands of timber. The Logs lined the riverbank looking across the river toward the scene of impending battle.

Moccasin stayed with the animals while Quint, Luke and François catfooted back through the timber to seek a vantage point to watch the sway of forthcoming battle.

"The Foolish Ones," François said. He pointed to two Shoshois who had mounted the same horse and were now riding toward the motionless Crows. "They carry only a quirt and a buffalo scrotum rattle. They use them to count coup on an enemy."

"Loco," Luke said.

François shrugged. "If they live, they get to be made a war chief."

"*If* they live," Quint said quietly.

"They believe they can only be killed by getting hit on some insignificant part of their bodies," François added.

"Should be their brains," Luke grunted.

The Foolish Ones galloped their horse close to the line of Crows. The leader of the Crows advanced slowly beyond the line of warriors. He was a resplendent figure, stripped to his breechclout. He wore a furred headdress of buffalo hide with the polished black horns protruding from either side. His painted face and the horned headdress made him look like a devil. Even the Foolish Ones hesitated in trying to count coup on this magnificent warrior.

Midway between the two opposing lines of warriors the Crow chief thrust his lance tip into the ground and then looked expectantly toward Washakie. It was a challenge to single combat and one that Washakie could not in honor refuse. The Shoshoni galloped toward the waiting Crow while shouting at the Foolish Ones to get the hell out of the way. This was the business of chiefs, he shouted at them.

Luke lowered the telescope. "That Crow is Twenty Coups. One of their best war chiefs."

All eyes were on the two chiefs. Washakie had thrust his lance into the ground beside that of Twenty Coups. They rode apart from each other and drew their bows from their cases. They fitted arrows to the bows and slung their shields forward on their left forearms.

François came through the timber from where he had been keeping an eye on the Shoshoni women. "Big Red!" he yelled. "That other stand of timber is full of Crows!"

Quint ran lightly to the edge of the timber, trailing his rifle.

"This ain't our fight!" François yelled after Quint.

Luke spat to one side. He checked the percussion caps of his rifle and pistol. "Wanta bet, Boudins?" he asked. "That red-headed bastard can't but always help the underdog. Now he aims to black his face against the Crows or I'm a gone beaver."

The Shoshoni women, with the old people, the children and their animals, galloped toward the stand of timber where Quint and his partners were concealed. The Logs swung in behind the retreating group and formed a line with military precision, to wait the onslaught of the second party of Crows. There were over a hundred of the enemy forming along the line of timber, outnumbering the Logs by at least five to one.

21

The Shoshoni women, hunched in their high-pommeled saddles and driving the pack animals ahead of them, crashed into the timber. Some of them were knocked from their saddles by low-hanging branches. Travois were upset. Children fell from the travois or the backs of pack animals. The pack dogs barked in fright. Some of the women glanced sideways at the three trappers who stood just within the edge of the trees with ready rifles in their hands.

Quint ran lightly out from the shelter of the woods and shouted at the leader of the Logs. The Shoshoni turned to stare at the tall Sóo-yah-pe, the American who seemed to have come out of nowhere. Quint made the sign of peace. He then quickly made the sign for friend by raising his arms, then half-closing the fingers of his right hand and placing the fingers loosely separated on top of the left hand.

"Haunce! Haunce! Friend! Friend!" Quint cried.

The Shoshoni Pon-Sooke, the Otter, knew trappers were usually friends to his people and the deadliest of enemies to have. He swiftly made the sign for friend. *"Haunce! Haunce!"* he responded.

Quint worked quickly, using some sign language and his limited supply of Shoshoni. "My three friends and I will help you, but you must obey my orders."

Pon-Sooke nodded. "What do you want us to do?"

"Have your horses taken into the timber. Form a line halfway between here and the timber. When the Crows attack, fire once, and then fall back into the woods. You understand?"

When Pon-Sooke sent his horses back, he had only twelve Logs standing in the open facing a hundred mounted Crows. The Crows moved closer, with arrows nocked to their bowstrings and Nor'west trade muskets ready. Quint anticipated their tactics. They would provoke a volley from the Logs, then charge ferociously before the Logs could reload. Once the Crows were in among them their arrows and bullets would do deadly execution. The job could be finished off with lances, tomahawks and warclubs.

While the sideshow was going on south of the Medicine Lodge, Washakie and Twenty Coups were going through the formalities of their duel, dashing back and forth on their ponies while releasing arrows at each other from the backs of the mounts or under their necks, with the body of the pony as protection and only a heel exposed to their opponent. Twenty Coups must have been grinning to himself as he went through the combat, all the while knowing something that Washakie and the Yellow Noses did not—a full third of the Crow warrior strength was closing in on the Logs and the women of the Shoshonis.

Pon-Sooke looked back at Quint as the Crows began to ride faster toward the Logs.

"Ma-gunt! Ma-gunt! Shoot! Shoot! *Egit-sha! Egit-sha!* Now! Now!" Quint yelled. He closed his left hand and thrust it downward while opening the fingers at the same time for the sign to shoot.

The horses of the Logs were being held at the edge of the timber. "Get those goddam horses out of here!" Quint yelled. They were rearing and plunging about among the trees in their excitement. One of the horse-holding Logs went down beneath a flailing hoof. A set of four horses broke loose from a small Log and threatened to stampede the horses of the women. A young Shoshoni woman, hardly more than a girl, ran forward and gripped their hackamores. She got the horses under control, glancing sideways at the tall Soo-yah-pe as she did so.

"Good girl!" Quint shouted. "Now get them out of here!"

The Shoshoni women took heart at the girl's performance. Some of them took the horses from the Logs to allow the men to join the forthcoming fight.

"Stay here," Quint ordered the men.

The girl came back through the timber. She had a battered and rusted Dickert flintlock trade rifle whose ancient stock was held together with rawhide and brass wire. She took her stand beside the men. Her great dark eyes flicked sideways to look at Quint.

Moccasin came through the woods to join the line of waiting riflemen. "She's got her eye on yuh, Big Red," he said out of the side of his mouth. He grinned.

"You! Do ye want to die?" Quint yelled at the girl. "Get back wi' the wimmen!"

She shook her head. She pointed her ancient fusee toward the advancing Crows. *"Nee-ah ka-im-enunggan!"* she cried spiritedly.

François grinned. "She say she don't hear yuh, Big Red."

"She's got warrior blood in her," Luke said.

Quint spat to one side. "It may be leaking out of her soon enough," he said grimly.

"Ma-gunt! Ma-gunt! Ma-gunt!" Pon-Sooke shouted.

The Logs' muskets roared, spitting out flame and a dense

cloud of stinking powder smoke which stood between them and the advancing Crows. The Logs ran back behind the cover of the smoke, reloading as they came.

The Crows were laughing. Not one of them had been hit by the wild, erratic volley. The Snakes were like women. They were so frightened they had fired without aiming. The Crows opened fire with their muskets and loosed their arrows through the swirling, obscuring powder smoke. They cast aside muskets and bows, swung their lances to their hands from their backs and quirted their horses after the Shoshonis, eager for the kill before the Shoshonis could have time to reload.

The hard-breathing Logs crashed into the brush and timber and quickly took up positions on the side of the four trappers. They saw the heavy, big-bored Hawken rifles. They saw the cool, detached expressions on the faces of the three white men and the Delaware. They stood in awe of the ability of these mountain men who seldom, if ever, missed their targets.

The trappers had placed two or three bullets in their mouths to moisten so that they would stick to the powder and had poured a charge of powder into their left palms, ready to reload in an instant.

Quint shouted, "François, tell the Shoshonis that every second man shoots at my command! While they are reloading the others must shoot, and so on!"

The Crows came on, forty yards, then thirty and now twenty yards.

"Shoot at the horses of the leaders!" Quint commanded. "Now! Shoot! Shoot! Shoot!"

Half of the rifles and muskets flamed almost in unison. The heavy bullets struck into the leading horses of the charging Crows. Most of them went down in a wild tangle of horse and rider. Others bunched up behind the fallen horses and warriors, or ran into them, only to meet a second crashing volley through the thick cloud of powder smoke.

Quint fired. He instantly poured the loose powder in his left hand down the smoking muzzle of his Hawken. He spat a bullet into the bore, rammed it down with his wiping stick, then slammed the butt down hard on a log to better seat the charge. He raised the rifle, full-cocked it, placed a cap on the nipple, set the trigger, full-cocked the hammer and then fired all in a fluid motion exactly as his three partners were doing.

The Crows were hurled back by the seemingly endless sleet of lead boring through the thickening cloud of powder smoke.

Some of them began to sing their death songs. A halfhearted attempt to form a charge was broken up by bullets before it could get started. Half a dozen warriors were dropped from their ponies' backs. It was too much for the rest. They turned tail and fled, followed by the jeers and taunts of the Shoshonis and the trappers as they advanced from the timber and around the sides of the fallen group of dead, dying and wounded warriors and horses.

When the last of the retreating Crows had vanished into the far stand of timber, the Logs and the mountain men got in among the wounded and the dying. Rifle butts and knives rose and fell. Scalps were circumscribed by razor-sharp knives and popped off, then swung about to free them of excess gore. Red droplets sprinkled the victorious warriors and trappers. Then the triumphantly ululating Shoshoni women came out of the timber, butchering knives ready to get in among the wounded before the men had all the fun. A wounded Crow was held down by three screaming women while a fourth pulled his legs apart to sever his genitals while he was still alive and could suffer the excruciating pain and intense humiliation.

Quint stepped back from the final moments of massacre. He looked into the taut face of the young Crow who was being emasculated. The warrior was hardly more than a boy. Quint drew his pistol from his belt, cocked it and fired. The half-ounce ball smashed between the Crow's eyes. The knife-wielding woman jumped to her feet with the bloody mess of genitals in her free hand. She hurled them at Quint's face and struck viciously at him with her knife. Quint came up off the ground on one foot and kicked her in the belly, and as she went down he sideswiped her with the butt of his rifle to knock her unconscious over the body of her victim.

Quint moved away from the carnage.

The young Shoshoni girl rose from among the Crow corpses and wiped her knife on the scalp of one of the dead. She watched Quint curiously as he walked toward the river.

The Crows who had been shattered in the fight against the Logs and the trappers had crossed the river and reformed. Now they attacked the rear of the Yellow Noses, who were engaged in combat with the main body of Crows. Dust and powder smoke shrouded the flats on the north side of the river. The Crows outnumbered the Yellow Noses at least five to one. The melee had become a whirling combat on the hard ground newly sprouted with spring grass. The horses moved

25

as though on springs, their heels playing like lightning on the earth, a devil's tattoo and exhilarating although outright deadly spectacle.

Washakie and Twenty Coups had fought it out hand-to-hand until both were dismounted. Now they fought on the ground within the rings of circling, shooting warriors, oblivious to anything but their intense hatred for each other.

Luke Connors came through the drifting powder smoke to Quint. "We'd better pull foot, Quint. The Crows will make gone beaver out of the Snakes."

Washakie feinted with his warclub, thrust his shield hard against that of Twenty Coups, brought a knee hard up into his crotch, and as the Crow bent forward in agony Washakie brought his warclub down in a smashing blow to the top of Twenty Coups' head. The Crow went down without a cry. Washakie drew his knife. He plunged it into the breast of the Crow and slashed until he found the heart. He excised the heart and raised it above his head while cawing raucously like a crow, then sank his teeth into it. The blood ran down his chin, chest and hands, but he was oblivious to anything but his savage gnawings at the organ.

The combat swirled about the Shoshoni chief. The Shoshonis, outnumbered and suffering heavy losses, were forced back almost to the bank of the river. Washakie went down wounded and unconscious over the body of Twenty Coups.

Quint ran through the timber to get his horse. Placing three bullets in his mouth and a charge of gunpowder in his left palm, he kicked the claybank into action, rode to the river and splashed across it. His hat blew off. His sorrel hair and beard fluttered in the wind. The claybank struggled up the north bank. A yelling Crow raised his horn bow and drew an arrow back to his jawbone, aiming at Quint's broad chest. Quint fired the Hawken at twenty-foot range. The ball hit the Crow in the chest and the impact drove him over the rump of his horse.

Quint rode through the ranks of the Shoshonis while loading. He struck the butt of the rifle hard against the horn of his saddle, capped the weapon and fired it from waist height directly into the belly of a charging Crow.

Luke, François, and Moccasin had mounted. They charged across the river through the ranks of the Shoshonis and struck the foremost rank of the Crows. They fought hand to hand amidst the swirling dust and powder smoke. The Shoshonis gained heart and charged after the trappers.

26

Quint fired his last bullet. There was no time to reload. He reversed the heavy Hawken, swept it over the top of a Crow shield and made a red ruin of the warrior's painted face. The rifle caught behind the shield, and as the Crow fell from his horse he dragged it from Quint's hands.

Washakie had regained consciousness. He knew he was going to die. This was the way of it—better to die in glory when one is still young, face to the enemy and reddened weapons in hand, than to sit around lodge fires, toothless and dreaming of the past. His breast was slashed from right shoulder to under his left nipple. His scalp was slashed. The red track of a bullet shone on his left shoulder. An arrow had nicked his left knee, weakening it so that he could hardly stand. Sweat and blood poured down his scarred and painted face. His voice had not weakened, however; it rose strong and clear in his death song.

Quint fired his pistol into the face of a Crow. The smoking weapon was driven stinging from his hand by the blow of a tomahawk on the barrel. He threw himself to one side to avoid a lance thrust. His girth slipped and he fell sideways, still in his saddle. He kicked himself free as his horse galloped off into the ranks of the yelling Crows.

Quint rolled away from the lance thrusts. He could see Washakie, now down on his knees, fighting to the end. Quint's hand closed on a discarded Shoshoni *pogamoggan*, a fearsome primitive mace.

The Crows danced about Washakie, counting coup on him, one of the greatest of all Snake warriors. They did not notice the sorrel-headed giant who rose up behind them whirling the warclub and shouting to them in their own tongue, *"Shoda-gee!* Welcome!" Quint dealt out fearsome blows on all sides. Crow skulls were fractured. Faces were smashed. Chests were caved in. Blood flew from the end of the warclub in a red spray. Quint stood over the prone Washakie. *"Loch Moy! Loch Moy! A MacIntosh!"* he shouted the war cry of his ancestors' clan in a brazen voice. He was fey, that mystical fervor that overcomes those of Celtish blood while in battle, so that they feel no wounds or pain, and fight as though they alone will settle the outcome of battle.

The Crows were driven back, at first by the ferocity of the savage white man and then with a superstitious fear of him. Nothing could stop him; no weapon harmed him. Then panic seized the Crows. They fell back from the battle and ran, leaving their dead and wounded strewn among the dead horses and buffalo. Luke, François and Moccasin charged after them, firing into their backs, turning their precipitous retreat into an absolute rout. Soon the only trace of the fleeing Crows was the dust that rose in the distance as they fled toward the distant Big Horn.

Luke turned his horse and galloped back toward Quint and Washakie. "For Christ's sake, Quint," he yelled. "It's all over!"

Quint glared at his friend. Then he slowly looked about himself. The Yellow Noses, the Logs and many of the women stood awe-stricken looking at this tall Soo-yah-pe, covered with blood that was not his own, standing straddle-legged over Washakie, with the blood-soaked *pogamoggan* still held upright in his hand.

The flame of battle died slowly within Quint Kershaw. He lowered the warclub and dropped it. He looked about himself. He looked down at the sprawled body of Twenty Coups. He drew his Green River knife, placed a foot on the neck of the Crow, then swiftly circumscribed the scalp with the razor edge of his knife. He jerked the hair upward, freeing it from the skull with a popping sound. He whirled it around to free it of excess blood and then threw it toward the nearest Yellow Noses.

Quint knelt and wiped his knife on the scalp hair fringing the leggings of the Crow. He stood up and looked about himself, then walked a little unsteadily toward the river.

THREE

The Camp of the Shoshonis on the Popo Agie.

The Shoshonis had wasted no time in getting out of the valley of the Medicine Lodge Fork after the battle with the Crows. So many of the Crows had died there at the hands of the Shoshonis and the trappers there was no question but that the river valley would be haunted by the vengeful spirits of the Crow dead for many years, perhaps forever. It was not a good place any more.

The village of the Shoshonis was established on the Popo Agie River about 125 miles from the forthcoming rendezvous on Horse Creek. The trappers had traveled with the tribesmen to the new village, as it was on the way to the rendezvous, to which the Shoshonis had planned to go after their buffalo hunt on the Medicine Lodge Fork. They had not expected to fight a battle there.

Luke Connors, an expert in "kill or cure" frontier medicine, had treated the wounded Washakie and others of the Shoshonis who had been wounded or injured in the battle. Washakie had insisted that the trappers accept the full hospitality of the Shoshonis for at least a week before departing for the rendezvous. A large lodge had been erected for their convenience and some of the women had been ordered to cook their food, make new clothing for them and sleep with them if they required it. It was the finest Shoshoni hospitality. Why not? If it had not been for the trappers the Shoshonis would have suffered certain crushing defeat on the Medicine Lodge Fork and perhaps annihilation. Besides, as each of the trappers knew, it was the worst insult to refuse the proffered hospitality of an Indian.

The young woman was stirring bits of boiled buffalo tongue in a water-filled buffalo paunch which she had brought to a rolling boil by dropping fire-heated stones into it. She was Dotawipe, or Mountain Woman, she who had fought like a warrior at the Medicine Lodge Fork and whose eyes were constantly on Quint whenever he was near her. She was an orphan; her parents had been killed by Crows when she had been an infant. She was the niece of Zawipe, Good Woman, one of the two wives of Ba-Witch-yagat, Buffalo Bellowing, who was the *buhagant,* the medicine man, spiritual teacher and leader of that band of Shoshonis. He was considered to be a great and infallible prophet.

Quint came up from the river, where he had been bathing. He wore only his red flannel breechclout. He entered the tent and saw Mountain Woman. Her dark and glossy hair had been braided and was bound by polished brass rings. She seemed very light-skinned for a Shoshoni. It was her eyes that had attracted Quint, at least originally. They were like deep dark pools. She was as shy as an antelope, at least when she was near Quint.

"En-Hone," Mountain Woman greeted Quint. It was the name by which the Shoshonis had honored him. En-Hone, or Red Badger, because of his sorrel hair and the fact that he

29

had fought with the stubbornness and ferocity of a badger in the battle with the Crows.

Quint sat down and placed his back against a back rest. Strangely enough, his father's family, an obscure cadet branch of the Clan MacIntosh, had a badger on their coat-of-arms, although he had never questioned his father about the origin of the armorial beast.

"Where is Good Woman?" Quint asked. "She's always done the cooking here."

"She is not well."

"And you volunteered for the duty?"

She looked sideways at him. "Washakie ordered me to come."

He nodded. He knew Washakie was trying every device to get Quint to stay with the Shoshonis, at least for the winter. The retribution of the Crows might be fierce indeed. The Shoshonis would need all the help they could get.

"How old are you?" Quint asked.

She shrugged. "I think sixteen winters. My parents died when I was very young."

"Have you always been with this band?"

She nodded.

"And your parents too?"

She looked directly at him. "No. They came from the west."

"Where in the west?"

"I don't know."

"Were they Shoshoni?" he persisted.

She was getting annoyed. "Yes, of course!"

"Perhaps they were Flatheads? Bannocks? Nez Perce?"

She stood up slowly. "The food is cooked, En-Hone."

Was it possible that she was part white? Quint eyed her, as though judging a piece of horseflesh.

"Don't you think I am of the Nimina, the People?" she asked.

"Of course I do!" He grinned at her. "Or perhaps you are of the Par-Keeh, the Blackfeet?" he joked.

Her face changed so suddenly it startled him. She placed a hand across her mouth and fled from the tipi.

Quint stared after her. "Now what the hell did I do wrong?" he asked himself.

Luke came into the lodge. "Whatever it was, yuh panicked her, ol hoss. Why'd the lassie, as you'd call her, run outa here like Ol' Ephraim was arter her?" he asked curiously. He studied Quint. "Yuh didn't try to get your horny paws up under her skirts, did yuh? Frankly, I been wonderin' what's been holdin' yuh back with some of these Snake wimmen. Yuh ain't had one in the robes or out in the cottonwoods since we been here."

"Like you, eh, Luke?"

Luke looked at his black and broken fingernails as though he'd never seen them before. "Oh, I don't know," he said archly. He grinned.

"No, I didn't try to get under her skirts."

"Yuh don't have to try very hard around here. Chastity ain't a virtue among the Snakes like it is among the Cheyennes. Besides, that lil gal has a soft spot in her skull fer yuh ever since she saw yuh fightin' at the Medicine Lodge."

"She's only a child."

Luke sat down and tilted his head to one side as he studied Quint. "I'll be God damned," he said slowly. "Never knew that to stop yuh before. Mebbe yuh been out in the timber too long, laddie."

"Maybe I'm waitin' for the rondyvoo."

Luke shrugged. "I wish I knew what was in that mind o' yours, partner."

Moccasin and François came into the lodge. The Delaware sniffed the cooking meat. He drew out his knife and speared a bit of the buffalo tongue. He blew on it, then tasted it. "Good," he opined. "Woman a good cook."

They drew up around the simmering pot and speared bits of the succulent meat from it, chewing and smacking their lips, while covertly watching Mountain Woman, who was just outside the lodge. She was working over a pegged-out buffalo hide, using an elkhorn scraper to remove the bits of flesh, membrane and tissue from it, preparatory to tanning it for a robe.

Moccasin boldly eyed the Shoshoni woman. "Good squaw for a man. Can fight. Cook. Tan good robe. Maybe good fuck too, eh, Luke?" He grinned, sliding his dark eyes sideways to leer at Quint. "Mebbe yuh try her out in cottonwoods, eh, En-Hone?"

Quint shrugged. "Mebbe." He began to fill his pipe. "How do ye three lay your sights for this coming season?"

Luke chewed reflectively. "I'm for the south, Quint. That is, if ye're willin'. We been trappin' in this north country for five straight years now. Beaver is beginnin' to get scarce. The market is doin' poorly. I've had enough of these northern winters. Besides, mebbe we're runnin' out of good medicine.

31

The Blackfeet get worse every year. The Crows will never forgive us for sidin' against them on the Medicine Lodge. The Snakes don't exactly trust me because I useta live with the Crows. So, I'm damned with both tribes, seems like."

"Where to this time? The San Juan country? The Gila? Back to New Mexico? Maybe the Columbia or the Sacramento?"

Luke looked sideways at Quint. "If yuh come along with me, yuh kin pick out the place. Yuh always liked New Mexico, as I recall, though we was only there one season." He grinned. *"Taos!* That's the place that shines! Brown wimmen and white likker! A man scarcely has to shoot center in that country to live easy, and the lusty señoritas are always waitin', ripe and willin'. Them Taos wimmen and Taos Lightnin' can make a man forget he was ever born a Christian."

Quint raised his eyebrows. "By God, Luke, I didn't know that about ye. Born a Christian, is it?"

Luke shrugged. "I don't tell *everything* about myself."

François lighted his pipe. "The beaver trade is fallin' off, like Luke says. They're makin' hats from Japanese silk now instead of beaver. Beaver hats goin' out of style."

"Where we trap Japanese silkworms, Boudins?" Moccasin asked with a straight face.

"First we got to find Japan," Luke suggested.

"There's still some market for prime plews," Quint insisted. "I aim to have one more good season to stake myself for next year, wherever I'll be, and whatever I'm going to do."

Luke shook his head. "Beaver's played out."

"I was thinking of going south into the Rockies and trying once more."

"Too late, Quint."

"Five years we four've been trapping together. Three winters we've *hivernaned* together. Ye'll no break up the team now, lads?" Quint pleaded.

"Not for me," Luke insisted firmly.

"It's more than the lack of beaver. It's more than the cold winters and the murderous Blackfeet, isn't it?"

Luke tamped down the tobacco in his pipe. He reached for a twig to light the tobacco. "It's my medicine," he said quietly. "It's tellin' me to get out of this country while I still got my ha'r."

Quint spat disgustedly into the embers. "Maybe you're just getting old."

Luke's green eyes flashed. "Damn yuh, Quint! I got the ha'r of the ba'r in me! I'm half hoss and half alligator! I can outtrap, outfight, outlie, outdrink, outgamble and outfuck any child in these damned mountains, and yuh know it for a fact!"

Quint smiled a little. Luke was a touchy critter when one mentioned age. At that, he was hardly more than ten years older than Quint, say about thirty-four years.

"What do ye aim to do, Luke?" Quint asked.

"Mebbe hunt meat for Bent's Fort. Mebbe scout and hunt for one of the Santy Fe caravans. Mebbe go to Californy and marry one of them señoritas there. One whose pa owns a couple of hundred thousand acres."

"How long do ye think ye'd last in California? Ye'd be like an animal in a cage. Being a meat hunter for Bent's Fort or one of the Santa Fe caravans hasn't a hell of a lot of future in it."

"I been tellin' him that," François put in.

"So, what do *you* aim to do?" Luke demanded.

François shrugged. "New Mexico for me. I got cousin in Taos. He's got a tradin' business. Not much, but he marry a local woman. Her father he got much land. He's gettin' old. His daughter only child." He grinned. "You understand?"

"Moccasin?" Quint asked.

The Delaware looked up from his food. "My Cheyenne squaw White Bead Woman. Southern Cheyenne live along Arkansas. She with Yellow Wolf's Hevataniu, the Hairy Rope band. White Bead Woman cousin to Owl Woman. Owl Woman daughter to Gray Thunder. He Keeper of the Sacred Arrows. Big Medicine. Owl Woman married to Little White Man. That Colonel William Bent. Big man with the Southern Cheyennes. So, I go back to Cheyenne wife. Live with Hairy Ropes. Hunt meat and robes for Bent's Fort." He grinned.

"Yuh got great connections there, Moc," Luke said.

Quint nodded in agreement. Luke and he had been at Bent's Fort five years past when the adobe walls hadn't been finished yet. The combined trading post and fort was right on the Mountain Division of the Santa Fe Trail and just across the Arkansas River from Mexico. Charles and William Bent and their partner Ceran St. Vrain did a thriving buffalo-robe business with the Utes, Comanches, Kiowas, Kiowa-Apaches and Southern Cheyennes.

"Yuh recall Colonel Bill Bent offerin' us jobs when we was there at the fort, Big Red?" Luke asked.

Quint spat to one side. "I sure do. As engagees, nothing more than flunkies."

Luke shrugged. "Mebbe we shoulda listened. Good quarters. Good food. Fair pay. No more standin' up to our crotches trappin' in icewater, shrinkin' our man-parts to nubbins. Mebbe it froze our brains as well."

"At least we're free men, Luke."

Luke looked sideways at Quint. "Free men? Shit! Ain't *no* one free in this damned world any more. Yuh got to work for someone else most of yore life, unless . . ."

"Unless what?" Quint prompted.

"Unless yuh got a stake, like yuh said." Luke studied Quint. "What would yuh do with such a stake, ef'n yuh had it, Big Red?"

Quint looked out through the doorway. He watched the Shoshoni girl working industriously at fleshing the buffalo robe. He saw the curve of her thighs under the soft elkskin of her skirt. He could see the soft, full swelling of her young breasts pushing against the inside of her dress. He felt a swelling in his man-part.

"Quint?" Luke asked.

Quint looked about him. The others were grinning at him. *"Quien sabe?* I'd like to get into trading myself. Or maybe find a mountain valley where a man could make a future home for himself. A valley that has everything—good water, shelter, plenty of game and timber. A place a man could call his own."

"Where?" François asked.

"New Mexico maybe."

François shook his head. "The greasers have took up all the best land. Besides, yuh'd have to become a Mex citizen."

"So? Charley Bent married one of the good-looking Jaramillo girls and now lives in Taos."

"But he's got money and position, Quint," Luke argued. "You ain't, my friend."

"I'll have it someday, somewhere."

"Meanwhile, come along with me. Mebbe they's somethin' we can find down south. I looked for gold once, in Kotsoteka Comanche country."

"And they let ye live with hair on your head?" Quint asked.

Luke grinned. "I had a Comanche squaw then."

"Why'd ye leave?"

Luke shrugged. "I got into trouble with them. Accidentally killed one of them in a wrestling match. Just made it across

34

the Arkansas a spit and a holler ahead of them. I just never bothered to go back and see my little squaw."

"Yuh both come with me," Moccasin suggested. "Cheyenne girls pretty. Famous for chastity. Got big tits. Make best moccasins on Plains. Make good wives. Both yuh come. I got connections."

"He's got somethin' there," Luke agreed. "What do yuh say, Big Red?"

Quint shook his head. "I aim to get a stake."

"Yuh'll end up losin' your ha'r without us to take care of yuh."

"I'm still thinking of trapping further south."

"Where? Bayou Salade? The San Juans? The Heely? Beaver are poor down there, leastways with the market the way it is."

Quint shook his head. "Ye remember old Gabe Pritchett talking about that lost valley of his in northern New Mexico? Maybe two hundred or two hundred and fifty miles northwest of Taos? Somewhere in the Rockies up around the headwaters of the Rio Grande?"

"*Bullshit!* Ol' Solitary can outlie any child in these here mountains."

"Gabe Pritchett big liar," Moccasin agreed. He held out two fingers in a V-shape to indicate a forked tongue.

"I believe him," Quint insisted. "He's never lied to me that I know of. If what he says is true that valley is haunted with beaver. It ain't too far from Taos, or Bent's Fort for that matter, for trading."

"Only about three hundred and fifty miles from Bent's," François said dryly.

"Gabe Pritchett big liar," Moccasin repeated.

"They called John Colter a big liar when he told about the Yellowstone, didn't they?" Quint challenged. "No one believed him there was hot water pouring up out of the ground and mud pots bubbling like it was the floor of hell."

"Gabe Pritchett ain't John Colter!" Luke shouted. "If that damned mysterious valley of his was so great, whyn't he go back there? Tell me that! Besides, no one ever saw those packs of prime plews he was supposed to have trapped in there. Who saw them? You? Me? Anybody? Hell no!"

Quint refilled his pipe. "Ye might have a point there. Anyway, Ol' Solitary is goin' to be at the rondyvoo, and I'll get him to talk about that valley of his. If he does, and he tells me where to find it, I'm going there, partners."

"Yore brains got froze last winter along with yore ass, partner," Luke said. He rolled his eyes upward. "My God! Believin' ol' Gabe Pritchett! I've heard everything now!"

The village crier interrupted their palaver as he went among the many lodges beating on his drum and calling out for the people to get ready for the *wu-tap,* or scalp dance ceremony, to begin within the hour. Mountain Woman left her robe fleshing to go to her tipi. Quint watched her interesting hip action as she walked gracefully away. He didn't notice his partners watching him surreptitiously as he did so.

FOUR

The sun was bright on the land with only a few fleeting clouds drifting to the west like fat sheep on a bright-blue field. The big council lodge erected by the women of the Yellow Noses stood in the center of the village. There too stood the subchief Washakie, the *buhagant,* Buffalo Bellowing, the four trappers, the two headmen of the Yellow Noses, *Gweenatsie,* the Eagle, and *Purcose,* or Buffalo Leggings, along with various other dignitaries and elders of the tribe. The rest of the people formed a double line on each side of the big lodge.

Eight old men and woman appeared, singing and beating on little sticks as they went from lodge to lodge of those warriors who had been foremost in the fighting on the Medicine Lodge Fork. They received gifts of fine buffalo robes for the men and buffalo meat for the women. Through the courtesy and hospitality of Washakie the four trappers had been supplied with such gifts to give to the oldsters.

When the gift-giving ceremony was over a group of what appeared to be mounted warriors appeared near the river. Some of them wore feather warbonnets or other war headgear, and they carried long fringed lances. They rode slowly

36

and proudly toward the center of the village and the big lodge. As they reached the waiting dignitaries, Gweenatsie, the Eagle, raised the tribal oriflamme, a twelve-foot lance trimmed from top to bottom with eagle feathers tinted red next to the lance, then white and finally black at the tips.

Luke nodded toward the approaching riders. "My God, ain't they comin' out buckskin fancy?" He leaned forward a little. "Odd-lookin men," he added.

"They're wimmen," François whispered. "It's the only time they can wear men's clothing and the only time they can take a leading part in any tribal ceremony."

Six musicians began to beat with sticks on shallow hand drums. The women wearing men's dress dismounted. They carried their lances, painted buffalo-hide shields fringed with feathers, warclubs and tomahawks. The lances were thickly fringed with many scalps and had tribal totems at their tops like the standards of the Roman legions.

Quint suddenly recognized Moutain Woman. She was wearing a magnificent warbonnet decorated with white, black-tipped feathers and a pair of polished black buffalo horns. Quint almost smiled at the fierce look on the normally gentle face of the girl, until he remembered her in the thick of the fighting in the timber at the Medicine Lodge Fork, and of how she had finished off some of the Crow wounded.

The warbonneted women began to sing in time to the steady, insistent beating of the drums. They advanced toward the warriors who had been foremost in the fighting at the Medicine Lodge Fork. Mountain Woman advanced and retreated in perfect timing with the rest of the dancers, always directly in front of Quint Kershaw. Back and forth they danced hour after hour, to the monotonous beating of the drums, pausing only in their original position as each song ended, to wait for the next song to start, when they would again advance and retreat. The solemn ceremonial dance was thought to bring immense benefits to the tribe.

The beating of the drums, the lines of women advancing and retreating, the tapping of the women's small moccasined feet on the hard-packed earth, and the undulating movements of their unhampered breasts under their sweat-damp upper clothing began to arouse Quint. Now and again he would glance sideways to his three partners to see if the dancing was having the same effect on them. There wasn't any doubt about it.

Every time Mountain Woman closed in on Quint her great

dark eyes seemed to search and probe into his. There was no expression on her painted face, now glistening with sweat that ran down from under the edge of the great warbonnet. He caught her odor when she came close, a compounding of perspiration, dried crushed wildflowers, the smoky smell of the tanned elkskin garments she wore, and that indefinable and tantalizing female smell, all of them mingled together to stimulate and arouse a horny male.

"It's like castoreum to a beaver, Quint," Luke whispered out of the side of his mouth. It was almost as though he had read Quint's thought. "No wonder a beaver can't resist it. Take care, laddie. The little gal there with the big headdress is workin' on yuh."

"Is that how the Crow squaw caught ye, old hoss?"

Luke nodded. "That, and other things. Besides, I was damned near dead drunk at the time. Took me two days to get a big enough hard-on to satisfy her."

Late in the afternoon the dancing stopped. Everyone in the village attended a feast of wild carrot stew. The tired, perspiring women who had performed the *wu-tap* ceremony went to the river to bathe and then to their lodges to get ready for the big social dance that evening that was to be given by the Yellow Noses.

Quint was too disquieted and restless to take a siesta along with his partners. He took his rifle and telescope, outwardly to go hunting, but really because he wanted to get away from the confines of the village and the presence of too many people. Indians, in the main, were a highly social group, with little of the loner in their psychological makeup. Quint wanted time to think about the torrent of dreams within himself. He wanted to get away from the almost overpowering presence of the Shoshoni belles, and one of them in particular. Mountain Woman had little of the flirting boldness of the other available young women of the village. Most of them would look squarely at men, with none of the custom of looking at the ground in the presence of a male. Mountain Woman rarely looked at Quint, or at least he thought so, but there had been a number of times when he had caught her studying him from a distance.

Quint drifted through the timber on the hill beyond the village. He reached a place where the hill was capped with softly greening aspens. He dropped to the grass and filled his pipe. He could see the panorama of the river valley spread out before him like a model relief map. The village was out of

38

sight just around a low butte to the east. The river flowed along at the base of the butte, then curved to sweep past the village situated on its green meadowland. There was an eddy at the base of the butte with a pool six or seven feet deep. There was a bare patch of sand and gravel on the shore, like a miniature beach, curtained with willows, cottonwoods and greening brush. Here it was that the women of the village came to do their bathing.

Quint struck flint and steel, lighted his pipe and puffed it into life. He sat with his back against a tree idly watching a red-tailed hawk floating high overhead. Something caught the corner of his right eye—a quick, light-colored movement down at the tiny beach. He looked down. There were people on the beach. One of them splashed into the water, shrieking aloud at the impact of the cold water.

Quint stared. He drew his telescope out of its buckskin case and focused it on the beach. He whistled softly. "Don't they shine!" he said. They were the women who had been dancing the *wu-tap* ceremony.

The women splashed about in the shallow water with the late-afternoon sun shining on their glistening wet bodies. He could easily see the rounded rumps, bouncing tits, rounded thighs and dark triangles of curly hair at the crotches. He had not had a woman since the rendezvous last year.

Mountain Woman had swum out into the center of the eddy pool. She surface-dived like a seal, presenting her smoothly rounded rump to the dying sunlight as she went under. Quint watched her through the telescope. She floated on her back with her full breasts glistening wetly. She drifted with the current and then rolled over to swim back to the pool. At last she swam to the shore and left the water. For a moment or two she stood there, stretching her arms behind herself to extend those lovely, brown-budded breasts to their fullest. Then she passed her hands up and down her body as though feeling each curve and hollow.

Quint closed his eyes. In a moment or two he could have pushed himself up from the ground without the use of his hands. He sat up to ease the pressure and focused the telescope on the beach. There were only two of them left there now, Mountain Woman and another woman whom Quint recognized as Bareyagat, Elk Calling, a rather buxom, bold-eyed wench who had had her eye on Quint more than once during his stay with the Shoshonis. The two of them were talking, and then Mountain Woman turned to look directly up the long slope to where Quint sat watching them. He saw her face clearly, then suddenly she was gone. Both she and Elk Calling had snatched up their clothing and vanished in among the willows.

That evening the military society of Yellow Noses gave a dance to honor those who had fought bravely on the Medicine Lodge Fork. The name of the lodge came from Oho-mu-pe, literally Yellow Mouths or Yellow Noses, sometimes commonly interpreted as Yellow Foreheads. Members had their hair cut short and square across the forehead, then plastered with yellow clay or paint. The Yellow Noses were the bravest of the brave among the Shoshonis, and definitely the superior of the other society, the Wo-Bine, or Logs, but there was never any rivalry between them.

Memberships in the two societies were usually hereditary, although not restricted as such. If a man had an elder brother in either society, or friends there, that would be the lodge he would join. The usual method of inviting a man to join the Yellow Noses was to have a dance and ask him to join them, if he was willing to do so. It was considered to be the greatest of all honors among the Shoshonis.

Everyone in the village was there in his or her best. The firelight flashed from polished brass earrings and finger rings. It shone on the masses of pink and white beads encrusted in floral patterns on the shoulders and the outsides of the sleeves of the buckskin and elkskin shirts of the men and on the dyed quills, elk teeth and iridescent sea shells on the dresses of the women. Feathers, dyed red, black and white, rippled in the breeze. The women lined up in a great circle around the bonfire with the Yellow Noses dancing in between them and the fire. The thudding of the drums, the rasping of the sticks and the slapping of moccasined feet on the hard-packed ground had almost a hypnotic effect on those who watched the "brave" dancing.

Quint sat with Washakie, whose recent wounds kept him from the dancing, and his three trapping partners. Quint knew his partners were anxious to get on to the rendezvous, the free-flowing whiskey and the ready, willing and able squaws in the willows and cottonwoods.

When the moon rose Eagle and Buffalo Leggings danced toward Quint and the others. The two warriors wore their fringed buffalo robes denoting their rank as leaders of their proud military society, the Yellow Noses.

"En-Hone is looking," the two warriors chanted. "He is brave and shall join us, if willing." They looked at Quint expectantly. "Will you join the Yellow Noses?" they cried.

Quint knew the rules. He got to his feet. "No! I will not!" he shouted. A pleased shouting and whooping arose from the onlooking men while the women shrilled their ululations. The sound echoed back from the heights. Quint had used the formal *nanoma ponait*, or inverted speech customary on such occasions, thus signifying he *was* willing to join. Had he agreed to join he would have been turned down, with no discredit to himself, for the Yellow Noses were purely a voluntary society.

Buffalo Leggings produced a pair of trade shears and looked expectantly at Quint's shaggy hair, ready to cut it short and to form bangs over the forehead in the approved stylistic fashion of the Yellow Nose.

"Cut my hair short," Quint said gravely, "for it is my good medicine, this sorrel hair and beard of mine. If it is cut, I shall have good fortune forever."

The two leaders understood then that he did not want to have his hair cut short. They satisfied themselves by fastening the two yellow-beaded sticks one on each side of his head and then painted his forehead with yellow.

Despite his usual cynicism, Quint, for some deep-seated reason, felt proud to have been accepted as an equal by these fierce fighting men. Perhaps it sprang from his own wellspring of descent from a famed fighting race of warriors, the Celts.

When the dancing was over the bonfire was a deep bed of ashes from which thin tendrils of bluish smoke rose, the trappers went to their lodge. They sat for a time smoking.

"A great honor, Big Red," Luke said dryly.

"Ye three should been honored as well."

Luke shook his head. "No. It means nothing to us. It can mean a heap to you. Anyway, we'll be leaving for the south after the rondyvoo. Who knows if we'll ever be back up this way again? Won't do me much good to be a Yellow Nose, or a Green Nose or any other kind of nose."

"How about a Red Nose?" Quint asked with a grin.

"That comes at the rondyvoo and down south at Bent's Fort, or mebbe Taos."

"I don't aim to come back this way myself."

The three trappers looked sideways at the shadowed face of their partner. "No?" François asked quietly.

41

"What the heil is the matter with ye?" Quint demanded hotly.

Luke shrugged. "We was thinkin' of that nice plump little piece. What's her name, Moc? Mountain Willow or somethin'?"

"Mountain Virgin," the Delaware said slyly.

"Ye all know Goddamned well what her name is!" Quint snapped.

"Bet she's as tight as your fist around a whiskey glass," Luke suggested.

"Tighter," François added.

Quint shook his head. "Ye lecherous studs, ye!"

They all grinned at each other.

"We're off to the Fur Fair in the morning then, laddie?" Luke asked.

Quint nodded. "It's a deal, partners."

Later as they lay in their buffalo robes on top of soft pine boughs Quint stared up at the darkness in the top of the lodge. It was almost as though he could see Mountain Woman standing on the graveled shore of the river, drawing her arms behind herself so as to thrust out those fine, brown-nippled breasts of hers. He saw her passing her hands up and down her wet and glistening body, feeling each curve and exploring each hollow, while she seemed to be looking directly at him. Had she known he was up on the hill studying her and observing each detail of her nakedness?

"Jesus God," Quint whispered softly.

In the bright clear light of early morning the four partners rode for South Pass, to cross the Wind River Mountains to the great Fur Fair on the Seeds-kee-dee Agie. Just before they were out of sight of the Shoshoni encampment Quint turned in his saddle to look back. A slight woman figure stood on a low hilltop near the village looking in his direction. He had no need to use his telescope to identify her.

FIVE

Rendezvous, July 1837, Horse Creek and the confluence of
the Seeds-kee-dee Agie.

The ten day rendezvous, or Fur Fair, had been arranged a
year in advance. It was held in a wide open meadow along
Horse Creek and the cold, clear-green Seeds-kee-dee Agie
born along the western slope of the Wind River Mountains.
The Seeds-kee-dee Agie had been named by the Indians in
honor of the prairie chicken, who annually holds his head
low, puffs up his throat, thrusts out his wings, ruffles his
feathers and dances a thundering mating ritual along the
banks of the said river.

Here gathered the mountain men and the Indians of half a
dozen tribes, some of whom were deadly enemies elsewhere,
but peaceful on the neutral ground of the rendezvous. Here
came the traders from St. Louis with their pack mules and
mule carts heavily laden with goods ready to trade for beaver
plews and other furs and hides. There were all of three
hundred white men and triple that number of Indians—
Flatheads, Bannocks, Shoshonis, Nez Perce and a few Arapahos, along with their half-wild children and many hundreds
of ponies shadowing the ridges on both sides of the valley or
grazing on the grassy bottoms along the watercourses.

The members of the rendezvous came from the most exclusive club in the vast West—the mountain men. There was no
possible way to be an accepted member unless one could
outfight a grizzly, outdrink an alligator, outrun Indian trouble and live off one's own hide. The measure of such men was
the extent of their skills; their mountain craft. They knew
how to *survive*. These were the men who lived through
months of incredible danger and hardship during the fall and
spring trapping seasons with only two interests—staying
alive and amassing a lot of pelts in a life of perpetual risk.

There were Americans, French Canadians, Scots and Irish,
English, Dutch, a lone Spaniard and a few Mexicans, as well

43

as dark-skinned half-breeds and some Delawares who were the only Indians the white men ever admitted to full partnership in the trapping. They were men dark-hued from constant exposure to the weather at all times of the year whose hair and beards were coarse and bushy and rarely trained or trimmed. They wore their hair full, or plaited, and sometimes braids like some Indian tribes. They mostly hated the Indians, and looked down on them with contempt, but still, paradoxically they took great pride in being mistaken for an Indian. To say to one of them "I tuk ye for an Injun" was actually a compliment.

Standing tallest of all, bold and independent, were the free trappers, those who, as opposed to the company men, hunted where and when they pleased, selling their furs to the highest bidder, owing allegiance to no one and jealous of their independent status. Most of them were born Americans, with one outstanding exception—Big Red, Quintin Kershaw, the Scot-Canadian, self-naturalized American and damned proud of it.

The rendezvous was a melee, a carnival, a fair, a drinking bout and, for the first few days, nothing more than a Saturnalia, with unlimited drinking and whoring the order of the day. The area was a constant din of gun reports, braying mules, barking dogs, yelling children, bellowing trappers and screaming Indian women.

Temporary shelters with bales for counters had been set up by the traders to display their wares. There was everything and anything a mountain man or an Indian might fancy, some of it absolutely necessary, much of it useful, and a great deal positively useless. The trade goods sold at exorbitant prices that neither the risk of loss nor the high cost of transport could justify. In some cases, before deducting necessary costs, the profit was about two thousand percent. The necessities consumed more than half the beaver packs of a trapper—the rest went for booze, tobacco and trinkets and gewgaws for the squaws. Months of incredible danger and hardship suffered and endured by the trappers paid for a year's supply of powder, lead, knives, traps, tea, coffee and trinkets in addition to gewgaws for Indian wives, concubines and prostitutes, as well as for themselves.

After the first few days of trading the rendezvous developed into an orgy. The Indian men and women threw away every possession for more alcohol. The rendezvous area was filled with hundreds of drunken Indians, men and women,

44

vomiting over themselves and each other, fighting each other, prostituting their wives and daughters, or themselves if they were women, for more and still more liquor. Many of them broke up their homes with lecherous adulteries right out in public. The groves of trees were filled with fornicating couples, and many times they didn't even bother to take shelter within the trees. Stinking-drunk trappers reeled into the shadows for their humping and grunting. Squaws staggered about offering themselves, or lay on the ground pulling up their dresses and spreading their legs wide to gain a handful of beads, a hawk's bell, a few yards of cheap cloth, a knife or hatchet, or perhaps a drink of whiskey for themselves or their men.

Quint Kershaw stood with his back against a cottonwood listening to the conglomeration of sounds and din filling the valley of the Seeds-kee-dee Agie. He heard the chant and rattle of the hand players. The thin and eerie music of the Jew's harps and flutes mingled with the steady and insistent thudding of drums and the pounding of stiffened sheets of rawhide. The hundreds of fires flared jewel-like against the darkness of the night. Smoke rose and formed a rifted layer over the entire valley. The fitful evening wind brought with it the mingled odors of trampled grass, manure, hot cooking grease, the ammonia smell of the horses and mules and the astringent woodsmoke.

Quint had traded in his peltries for materials and supplies for the coming fall season. To the usual supplies he had added a double-bitted ax, a bucksaw, several augers, some chisels and an adze. They would fit into his plan when he found that mysterious lost valley of Gabe Pritchett's. It might be the very place he had thought about many times during his years in the mountains.

The rendezvous had already worn thin with Quint after the first three days. It had been somewhat enjoyable at first, after the many months of bitter hardship in the mountains, wading the icy streams, always with loaded and cocked Hawken within easy reach, keeping one eye on the traps and the other out for skulking Blackfeet who could kill so quick a man might never know what hit him. He remembered the icy, hoary breath of winter sweeping over the snow-clad mountains as he huddled in a lodge half-buried in the snow, with the wind howling its banshee call over the lodge, tearing at his guts for sheer loneliness. He remembered too well

45

the mingled stench of greasy, filthy clothing, unwashed bodies and foul breath, stale woodsmoke and the aura of old cooking grease. Four big men crammed together in a lodge hardly big enough for two of them.

There was another odor he could not seem to get rid of since he had come to the rendezvous—the subtle woman odor. His clothing was fresh and new, hardly three days old, and he had bathed twice daily in the nearby river, sometimes to the jeering remarks of his partners and friends who usually forbore such niceties the first days of the rendezvous. Still, the odor remained with him. At first he had thought it was from his contact with an Arapaho squaw, one of the four who had been hired for the night by Luke to entertain himself and his three partners. It had been one hell of a debauch, with the eight of them rolling around on the robes in the big lodge, passing the women on from one to the other so that in the dimness Quint had never known which two of the four he had really fucked. He had little memory of the actualities of the event. The liquor had been strong within him. He did remember one fact clearly—while he had been coupling with one of the women he had been thinking of Mountain Woman. Still, *she* had had a different scent than the one that seemed to cling to his clothing and even his body. The Arapahos had smelled of cheap perfume, body sweat and stale liquor.

Quint looked toward the camp of the Shoshonis at the far end of the valley. There were many rows of tipis, with the soft firelight showing through the thin tanned skins making the lodges appear like great cone-shaped lanterns. Mountain Woman must be in the camp of the Shoshonis, although he had not seen her yet. In fact, he had kept away from the Shoshonis. He had seen some of them trading. He knew well enough that he must go to their camp before the end of the rendezvous. He knew then that the odor which tantalized him, whether it was real or imagined, was that of Mountain Woman. What was it Luke had said to Quint the day of the *wu-tap* ceremony when Mountain Woman had danced back and forth in front of Quint, so close at times that he could have easily touched her without moving? He had been referring to her odor, of perspiration, dried crushed wildflowers, the smoky smell of the tanned elkskin garments she wore, and that indefinable and tantalizing female smell.

"It's like castoreum to a beaver, Quint. No wonder a beaver

46

*can't resist it. Take care, laddie. The little gal there with the
big headdress is workin' on yuh."*

Quint half-closed his eyes. He recalled the lines of young
women dancing to the beating of the drums in the *wu-tap*
ceremony. He remembered all too clearly her glistening wet
body as she surface-dived in the pool of water at the Popo
Agie and of how she had floated on her back with the dying
sunlight shining on her full breasts.

"Jesus Christ!" Quint spat out. She had almost hooked
him. It was always the ambition of these squaws to hook a
white man who would dress them up, mount them on the
finest of horses and cover their fingers with rings and their
arms with bracelets.

He pulled the pint pewter flask from within his wool shirt
and took a good solid belt of Monongahela. He wiped his
mouth on the back of a hand and looked moodily toward the
camp of the Shoshonis. Several more drinks and he'd take his
trade goods in one hand and his cock in the other and go
looking for Mountain Woman. Ah, but the next day, when he
was sober . . .

Some of the trappers were already beginning to form
hunting parties for the fall and spring. The *engagees,* those
men who worked for the trading companies, had begun to
press the many bundles of plews for transport back to St.
Louis. One party of 110 men had left for the Blackfoot
country with L.B. Fontanelle as commander and Jim Bridger
as pilot. Thirty more trappers were leaving the next day for
the Wind River country.

There was a disquieting rumor floating about the rendezvous that this might be the last year the trading companies
would bring in supplies. It was almost certain that the Rocky
Mountain Fur Company was there for the last season. For
some years the price of beaver had gone down. The drop in
beaver values had been sharp and readily apparent in that
year's trading.

Quint drank again. He felt the delayed warming explosion
in his guts as the good Monongahela whiskey reached its
proper depth. He looked toward the Shoshoni camp. What the
hell! The Shoshonis really had nothing against rape, provided it wasn't a married woman. If a woman was raped, her
rapist could take her from the camp and stay away long
enough until matters cooled off and then return to pay for
her. Trouble was, Quint wasn't sure he wanted to keep her.
He would need someone with him if he found Gabe Pritchett's

47

lost valley. It would be hell to have to do the trapping, the skinning and curing, the hunting and the cooking alone. With a squaw, all he'd have to do would be to trap and hunt for food.

He drank again, wiped his mouth, hitched up his pants and started out for the Shoshoni encampment.

"Big Red!" Luke called through the darkness.

Quint turned. "Aye?"

"Boudins has finished the cooking."

"So?"

Luke looked queerly at Quint. "Yuh been drinkin' too much?"

"Naturally," Quint said dryly.

"Yuh fergit we got a guest comin' for dinner tonight?"

"Gabe Pritchett?"

Luke nodded.

"I didn't know he was here yet."

"He came in late today with some Utes. Moccasin seen him. He told Ol' Solitary yuh wanted to see him. The old bastard said he'd dine with us this evening and to have plenty of Taos Lightnin'."

Quint looked toward the Shoshoni camp.

"She'll be there when yuh want her, Big Red," Luke said.

They walked together toward their lodge.

SIX

François Charbonne sang to himself as he hovered solicitously over his cooking at the fires beside the skin lodge. He had traded for a fine young buffalo bull that day from a drunken Flathead. Now he was preparing all of the meat and the "lights" for a gargantuan feast to be held that evening for Gabe Pritchett, Old Solitary. Old Solitary loved buffalo fixings, unless he could get strong panther meat.

The diners would have hump, ribs, tongue, fleece of back

fat, liver and kidney. The testicles had been reserved for Old Gabe. The tongue was baking deep in the ashes filling the firepit. The liver had been set aside to be eaten raw as an appetizer, with a pinch of gall from the gallbladder for piquant seasoning. The choice hump slabs, four inches thick, had been skewered on an old iron ramrod for roasting brown and "crumpy" outside, tender and juicy within. The ribs were slowly roasting over a separate fire of thick embers and *bois de vache,* or "wood of the cow" buffalo chips, dried buffalo manure.

Minced tenderloin and hump meat with thighbone marrow as sweet as butter and delicate oil blended with hump fat had been rolled into balls, then covered with thick dough to be simmered and fried in bone marrow. Best of all, the *pièce de résistance* in François' cuisine was his specialty—*boudins*. About eighteen inches of intestine was turned inside out and sketchily cleaned. Each intestine was knotted at one end and then packed tightly with a mixture of minced tenderloin, kidneys, brains, a pound or so of quarter cut close to the bone, marrow, suet, grease, wild onion juice and salt. The open end was then knotted to form a sausage about ten inches long. The *boudins* were then broiled and placed in a spider, a frying pan with legs that stood over the embers, to simmer slowly in their own succulent juices. There were none finer to be had than those prepared by François "Boudins" Charbonne.

"Where's old Gabe?" François asked testily. "By gar, I'm about ready to serve."

Luke drank Monongahela from a camp kettle. He wiped his mouth both ways with the back of a hand. "He'll be along. That old bastard can smell *boudins* fifty mile away and up wind at that."

"Or smell a jug," Moccasin added as he reached for the camp kettle.

Luke nodded. "His belly is a bottomless pit and yet he looks gant as a gutted snowbird most of the time."

"That's because everything he eats turns to shit," François said matter-of-factly. He wiped the dripping perspiration from his face with a sleeve.

"Speak of the devil," Quint murmured. He looked back over his shoulder.

Gabe Pritchett, Old Solitary, limped noiselessly through the shadows toward the fire. He paused ten feet from the fire and eyed the humps and ribs browning over the embers. He studied the fat, greasy *boudins* sizzling in the big iron spider. None of the partners looked at him. He was taciturn to an extreme, spoke only when he willed, never answered a salutation or a greeting and kept to himself. He was a solitary, usually trapped alone, drifting into the most remote and hostile areas of the mountains, and sometimes vanished completely for a year or two at a time. He was the perfect profile of the lone free trapper; a true servant of the untracked wilderness.

Gabe leaned on his twelve-pound Hawken flintlock rifle. The firelight shone on the many roundheaded brass tacks that studded the buttstock of his rifle. Some said each tack accounted for a dead and scalped yellowskin, but no one really knew. Old Gabe had never verified the rumor, one way or the other. His sharp blue eyes were hidden under craggy brows and the matted salt-and-pepper hair hid his forehead. His beard was tangled and matted with dirt and decaying particles of food. His nose curved toward his narrow pointed chin like the beak of a hawk. His long hair hung in front of his shoulders in two braids wrapped in ancient otter skin to paralyze bad luck and strengthen good luck. Gabe always wore a strip of faded and filthy calico about his brows in lieu of a hat. His heavy elkskin jacket and seatless buckskin leggings were thickly fringed with Blackfeet hair. The original coloring and decorations of his garments had long since been replaced by a black shining surface of grease and dirt that shed rain and snow and attracted flies in warm weather. A powerful effluvium of perspiration, acrid urine, sour grease, unwashed body and hair, and stale woodsmoke formed an aura about him as he moved. A gnarled big toe with a thick black nail protruded through a hole in one of his Ute moccasins.

Gabe was old for the mountains and his time, perhaps on the far side of fifty years, but no one really knew. Maybe he didn't quite know how old he was himself. He was sure his soul would come back after his death in the form of a bull elk. He was so positive of this he had told other trappers of signals and signs by which they would know it was him in the body of the elk. He had no close friends, or perhaps any friends at all, except perhaps the Eutaw, or Ute Indians, who regarded him with supersitious fear and awe more than friendship. Although Gabe usually spoke in the colorful and exaggerated vernacular of the mountain man, there were times when he lapsed into an almost

50

poetic form of speaking, in quite correct English, particularly when he was caught up in his famous yarns. It was an indication that he had a far more polished background than he ever let on. For some reason, perhaps unknown even to himself, he liked and respected Quintin Kershaw. Perhaps it was because he secretly admired Quint's book learning and deep intelligence, in addition to his famed prowess as a trapper and Indian fighter. It might have been because he saw in Quint the pattern of a man he might once have been, could have been if he had so desired, or had at least wanted to have been long, long ago.

Quint looked up at Gabe. "Set and have a horn, Gabe," he invited, "a little of the arwerdenty." He held out a camp kettle filled to the brim with good stout Monongahela and a pinch or two of dried castoreum from the sexual glands of beavers of both sexes, which added the musky, perfumish flavor Old Gabe preferred.

The four partners, powerful drinking men themselves, were fascinated as Gabe easily downed at least half a pint of the lethal brew without lowering the kettle. Gabe lowered the kettle, tucked it handily between his knobby knees, wiped his mouth both ways with the back of a clawed, dirty hand, then belched and sighed contentedly.

Gabe's strange blue eyes flicked about. "Yuh asked me to the makin's. Why?" he asked abruptly.

Quint smiled. "Just being friendly-like, Gabe."

"Bull buffalo shit!" Gabe snorted. He eyed the big spider packed from side to side with puffed and steaming *boudins*. "Them *boudins* ready?" he asked.

François nodded. He took big pieces of cottonwood bark and placed *boudins* on them, passing them out to his partners and Gabe. They stole glances at Gabe as he ate with short, incisive bites like a rodent. The hot grease ran down his chin into his matted beard. He wiped his hands on his jacket and leggings. He licked the grease from the bark plate and then stabbed at another *boudin* with his knife. He practically swallowed it whole and then washed it down with about half a pint of whiskey.

"We were talking about that lost valley of yours," Quint said conversationally.

"Where a man can harvest prime beaver plews from the bank with a club," Luke added.

Gabe shook his head. "Ain't no such place. Them ribs ready?"

51

They all ate voraciously of boiled hump and roasted ribs and then emptied the second pan of *boudins*. Gabe sucked constantly at the kettle of whiskey. He sat back and belched.

"Down south somewheres, ain't it?" Luke asked.

"North of Taos," François added.

"Yuh got tongue in them ashes?" Gabe asked.

François dug out the baked tongue and cut it into pieces. It was the crowning glory of the feast, soft and succulent, with an exquisite taste.

Gabe cleaned his knife by thrusting it into the earth a few times. "I heard ye did well along the Yellowstone this past season," he said. He wiped his greasy fingers on his matted hair and then filled his pipe.

François nodded. "Sixteen packs of plews, all about prime."

"Yuh formed your fall party yet?"

Luke shook his head. "Why? Yuh want to pitch in with us, Gabe?"

"Yuh know I travel alone, Luke."

"We ain't formin' a party this season. Boudins is headin' for Taos. Moccasin is goin' back to his Cheyenne squaw on the Upper Arkansas. Me, I aim to go along with him. Mebbe meat-hunt for Bent's Fort. Yuh know the market's droppin' on beaver. Makin' hats out of silk now. Waal, I've had enough of the northern winters anyways. What about you, Gabe?"

Gabe shrugged. "I got nuthin' to worry about. I'm the big coon with some of the Eutaws. Might go back to live with them. Gettin too damned crowded in this north country anyways."

Quint drank from his kettle. "Might ye be heading back to that secret valley of yours?"

The icy blue eyes studied Quint suspiciously. "I ain't said so, Big Red."

Luke filled his pipe. "Big Red aims to have one more good season afore he quits forever. Wants to make a stake, he says, mebbe buy trade goods and go into business. But he's got to have a stake. Me and Moccasin here, we want him to go along with us, but he wants none of it. At least until next spring."

Gabe glanced at Quint. "Whyn't yuh go with 'em?"

"I ain't aiming to spend the rest of my life wandering about in these mountains until Ol' Ephraim gets me or a Blackfoot hangs my hair on his lance."

"Reason enough. But what's to prevent a Eutaw, a Jicarilla or mebbe a Comanche doin' the same thing?"

"My medicine, Gabe."

"That sorrel hair of yourn? Hawww!"

Quint grinned. He'd got the solitary old bastard laughing, at least. No mean trick that. It was a good sign.

Gabe drank again. "I hear tell yuh got in good with the Snakes. Saved Washakie's ha'r fer him. Made yuh a Yellow Nose."

Quint nodded. "The whole shitaree, Gabe."

The old man tilted his head to one side. "Now, if yuh was to ask my advice, which yuh ain't, whyn't yuh just stay with the Snakes this winter?"

"Like ye do with the Eutaws?"

Gabe looked beyond the fire toward the unseen towering mountains to the south. "Great country there," he murmured. "Man don't have to rile up his rheumatiz no more. Plenty fat young squaws to cook, tan his hides, keep him warm under robes on winter nights. Yuh cud do the same with the Snakes. Good people. Prettiest squaws in the mountains."

A rifle shot split the quiet night. A trapper whooped. Men shouted. Another gun cracked flatly. The dogs began to bark raucously in the Indian encampment.

Gabe looked around. "Damned fools," he said harshly. "A year's killin' work for ten days o' *this*. Trade off your plews for whiskey and gewgaws for the squaws. Dead broke with a helluva hangover when yuh leave here. Then back to the hell of icy streams in the dawn light, or at dusk, half expectin' to hear a Blackfoot whoop and the drive of a flint-tipped arrer into your back, or a Nor'west fusil goin' off and takin' half yore head with it. Or, mebbe yuh just get wounded and helpless, and Bug's Boys get a chance to work on yuh with fire and knives. They stake yuh out nekkid, whilst the old squaws hike up their dresses, pry your mouth open, then squat over yuh and piss and shit into your mouth and all over yore face. Or ef'n the Blackfeet don't get yuh, Ol' Ephraim comes gruntin' out of the bushes at yuh and tears yore head off with one swipe, or guts yuh, clean as ary whistle. *Wagh!* Or mebbe an avalanche comes and buries yuh, and yore frozen carcass don't show up until spring thaw, and there ain't anyone around to give yuh a decent burial, and the wolves get at yuh. . . ." His dry voice trailed off into silence and he seemed to be looking far beyond the dark valley of the Seeds-kee-dee Agie and the shadowed mountains to something no one else would ever know.

They eyed the old trapper thoughtfully, looking at each other surreptitiously out of the corners of their eyes. It was something each of them had thought of many times, but only to themselves. They were fatalists, or thought so of themselves, or at least *wanted* to be such. It was always the bold front presented to each other.

Gabe came back to the present. "The old beaverin' days is about over. The bales of plews are small, very small this rondyvoo. Streams gettin' trapped out. Price o' plews droppin' every season. Trade goods goin' sky-high. Soon, mebbe next year even, the bottom will drop out altogether. Then what's to become of yuh? Yuh don't know anythin' else. Yuh been in the mountins too long. Yuh're more like the yellowskins than some of the yellowskins themselves. They want to act like white men and you want to act like yellowskins. Don't make any sense. What's to become of ye? *What's to become of ye?*"

"One more season, Gabe. One more stake," Quint replied.

"So, yuh make yore stake? What then?"

Quint shrugged. "Like Luke said, maybe some trading. Maybe get a place in around Taos. Maybe trade for horses with the Comanches. There's plenty chances for a man if he's got a stake."

"Loco," Gabe said sourly.

"My sights are aimed that way, Gabe," Quint insisted quietly. "I'm going, for certain sure."

They all looked at Quint. The firelight played on their weatherbeaten features and glistened in their eyes. Each of them looked at least ten years older than he really was. The mountains put their mark early on a man.

"Why hasn't this mysterious valley been trapped out by now, Gabe?" Quint asked just as though the old trapper had admitted that it existed.

Gabe scratched in his beard. "Yuh kin leave your traps in the saddle panniers," he said softly. "Yuh kin harvest beaver with a club, or shoot 'em from the bank as they swim past."

"What about the Eutaws?" Luke asked. He winked at Quint. The secretive old bastard was loosening up.

Gabe knew what they were up to. He really didn't care

54

that much any more. One winter's trapping alone in that damned valley had been enough for him. "The Utes might not bother yuh. That is, the tribal bucks. There are renegades in the mountains, though—the Cochetopa Utes. Ain't really pure-bloods. Mixture of Utes, Jicarillas, Navajos, Mexes, mebbe some whites as well. No one really knows much about 'em 'ceptin' they're mighty bad medicine."

"Chico Vasquez' bunch?" François asked.

The old man nodded. "Aye, and he's a mean one. Calls hisself 'chief.' Mixture of everything, like the Cochetopas. Some say he's even got nigger blood, but I ain't sure how come he got *that* in him. Wouldn't surprise me none. Got a hideout up thar."

"Where?" Quint asked.

"Yuh think I'm loco enough to tell yuh? If they ever found out I told anyone where they hid out . . ."

"But yuh do know where it is, hey, Gabe?" Luke asked.

Gabe sucked at the spout of the kettle. He stabbed at the last *boudin* in the pan and wolfed it down. "Fust time I seen that valley," he mumbled about a full mouth, "I crossed a pass, mebbe nine or ten thousand feet high. Early October it was. Snowed all night and day for seven days. Snow was three feet higher than my head in some places. I had to bust a way for my old hoss and two pack mules by divin' flat into the snow and packing it down, hour after hour, until I liked to have fruz solid."

"Ponchas Pass?" Luke suggested.

The gimlet eyes bored into Luke's eyes for a few seconds. "I didn't say where it was, ol' hoss, did I?"

Quint winked at Luke and shook his head slightly. It wouldn't do to make Gabe change the subject, or get suspicious, and maybe clam up altogether.

"So yuh turned back, eh, Gabe?" François asked.

Gabe shook his head. He knocked the dottle out of his pipe and then began to refill it. "Couldn't go back. I got over the peak of the pass. Warn't no way I could go back then. It was snowin' again, fillin' my tracks behind me. So I just kept goin'. Down, down, *down*, until I reached a grove of quaking aspens nigh the timberline. Found a cave there, smellin' of bear, and holed up in it with my hoss and mules for two days until the snow stopped."

The faded blue eyes were now looking far beyond the rendezvous in the valley of the Seeds-kee-dee Agie to the south, hundreds of miles, perhaps half a thousand or more, if

Luke's hints to Quint at one time were fairly accurate. "Ye remember ol' Gabe Pritchett talking about that lost valley of his in northern New Mexico? Maybe two hundred or two hundred and fifty miles northwest of Taos? Somewhere up in the High Rockies around the headwaters of the Rio Grande?" Those had been Quint's own words back at the Shoshoni camp on the Popo Agie. A country perhaps known only to the Utes, the wild animals, and maybe old Gabe Pritchett.

"Come one mornin' the sun come out," Gabe continued. "I looked down into the valley. It was all green and gold, with a light dustin' of fresh snow. Aspens in autumn gold shone above a sun-silvered stream windin' through tree-covered bottomlands and meadows, whilst high above the timberline the great grinnin' peaks were solid white with snow. There was a long narrow lake in the bottom of the valley with an inlet and an outlet. I put my old glass on that stream. By Jesus! They was one beaver dam arter another and the humped shapes o' lodges as far as the eye could see. And the stream followed the inner part of the valley somewheres into the distance, and I knew for sartain sure, there must be hundreds more lodges up that way . . . . " His voice died away.

It was quiet around the fire now, except for the popping and snapping of the burning wood, and the faint voices of trappers at other fires who were drinking and yarning much the same way. The tobacco smoke mingled with the smoke from the fire and drifted about the lean, weatherbeaten faces of the trappers.

Gabe drank deeply. He shuddered a little at the impact of the powerful liquor. "I didn't know where I was. 'Twas all new to me. I knew, of course, that ol' Abe Walker, Pawnee Jack Stearns, and Antonio, who was some kind a breed, Mex and Comanche, I think, had been in and around that country for the past two years or so, less'n they had left it to trap the San Juan, or mebbe the Heely. They was always mighty close-mouthed about where they was trappin'. It was hostile country."

Luke spat into the fire. "They never reached the San Juan or the Heely, Gabe. Fact is, no one ever saw 'em again, *anywheres*. They tuk a one-way walk into the shadows. Some say the Eutaws got 'em. Or mebbe it was Chico Vasquez' bunch. Mebbe they went east and the Comanches lifted their ha'r. That's most likely."

Gabe shook his head. "No," he said flatly.

"Go on, Gabe," Quint urged.

Gabe nodded. "Luke allus did have a big mouth."

Luke grinned. "Sorry, Gabe."

"I made my way down into the valley," Gabe went on. "The place was thick with game—deer, bear, including a few of the biggest goddam grizzlies I ever seen anywhere, and I've seen the biggest of 'em, I tell yuh! Streams and lake was full of fat trout, which I don't fancy, bein' a meat man myself, but, howsumever, they make a tasty change now and again from red meat. Waal, I turned my animiles loose arter I unloaded 'em. By that time, they was so thin yuh could read a Bible, chapter and verse, through their ribs."

"I covered that valley three days handrunnin'. I figgered this was the place I'd allus been lookin' fer. The high mountains would pertect my camp against wind and snow. There was good grazin' and plenty of cottonwood trees in sheltered places so's I could feed their bark to my animiles. I could trap all fall, hole up for the winter, then trap again in the spring. I had plenty tobacco, salt, tea, coffee, some flour and whiskey. What more could a man need or want?" His eyes drifted to look at Quint's intense expression.

"A winter squaw?" Luke suggested dryly.

Gabe shrugged. "Never really wanted one. Can't hardly stand a man *hivernanin'* with me, much less a damned chatterin' squaw."

"So, yuh stayed, eh, Gabe?" François asked.

"Worked like a beaver that fall season, runnin' twelve traps. Streams fruz early. Built me a lodge near the bottom of the pass where there was a natural cave. Butted the lodge onto it, dug the dirt down a couple feet, built a log wall, roofed it over, made me a chimney out of sticks and clay."

"Sounds like ye planned to stay longer than just a trapping season, Gabe," Quint suggested.

Gabe seemed to be lost in a world of thought of his own. His eyes seemed to be fathomless; those eyes which had seen so much that no other white man and perhaps few Indians had ever seen of the Great Shining Mountains.

Quint leaned forward as though to look into the old man's eyes. "Gabe?"

Gabe jerked his head a little as though he had been brought back suddenly from the shadowed halfworld of his own thoughts to the reality of the listening men about him, the dying campfire and the muted sounds of rendezvous life along the Seeds-kee-dee Agie.

"Were ye planning to stay there longer than one season?" Quint asked.

Gabe nodded. "I had thought of it. It looked like a good place for a man to die."

"Why'd ye leave?" Quint asked boldly.

"Jest before the winter set fully in I found a skull with a bullet hole through the back of it. In the bresh I found parts of the skiliton, where the animiles had dragged it and left it. Found a U.S. military belt buckle I knew had belonged to ol' Abe Walker. He fit in the 1812 War when he was a younker. Allus wore that belt. Might proud of it, he was. A day or so later I found what was left of Pawnee Jack Stearns. At least I *think* it were him."

"How did he die?" François asked.

Gabe pointed to the side of his head. "Hole yuh could put three fingers into. Bullet dropped outa the skull when I picked it up. .58 caliber it was."

"That accounts for two of them," Quint said. "What about the half-breed, Antonio?"

Gabe shrugged. "No trace." He looked about at the others. "Some said he useta be a Comanchero. Warn't long at the trappin'. Campkeeper for the others mostly. Curing the plews. Cookin'. Huntin'. Like a squaw."

Gabe stared into the fire. "My medicine told me to get outa there—fast! They was somethin' in that damned valley that was no good. I'd been feelin' it for days, but weren't sure until I found those dead men. I went back to my lodge to pack my gear and what plews I had. That night it snowed. It didn't stop for a week. The pass was solid with it. They was two more passes, southerly, but I knew if the north pass was snowed in, they would be too." He rubbed his jaw reflectively. "Them was good *boudins,* Frenchie," he said.

François nodded. "I got plenty more." He filled the spider and set it over the embers.

"So, ye were trapped in the valley for the winter, eh?" Quint asked.

"The winter was like I was alone on this ball of clay called Earth. The icy winds didn't come down too much into the valley, but I could hear it howlin' up on the heights. It was a marrow-freezin', bone-crackin' winter all around the valley. Eerie it was, I tell yuh, with the howlin' of that wind, but it was the silence arter the storms that was worse. Many the nights I lay awake listenin' to the silence. . . ."

They all slanted their eyes toward Old Gabe.

"They was nights I coulda sworn they was someone outside the lodge. I heerd nothin'! I saw nothin' in the mornin' except the new-fallen snow, smooth and clean, and not even an animile track on it, 'ceptin' mebbe a coupla hundred yards away, but never any kinda tracks, human or otherwise, anywheres near my lodge."

"Mebbe your stink druv 'em away, Gabe?" Luke suggested.

"More likely draw 'em to ol' Gabe, if they was wolves," François said.

Moccasin had not spoken one word all during the story Gabe was telling. His dark eyes studied the old man's face. Like Quintin Kershaw, who at times seemed to be wholly Indian himself, he was in close rapport with Gabe and his tale. There were things most white men would never know about the solitude of the woods and mountains.

"One night of the full moon," Gabe continued in a low voice, "I don't recollect when, but it was arter the start of the new year, I heerd a hissin' cry, like a giant snake. Somethin' made me get outa my robes and run outside. I stripped off my clothes and run bare nekkid through the snow, shriekin' at the new moon from the top of my lungs. It was mebbe ten below at the time. I like to fruz my hairy old ass off when I finds myself half a mile from the lodge, wonderin' how I got there. I just about made it back to the lodge and crawled into my robes, scared to within an inch of my life."

The hair raised on the back of Quint's neck. "Why, Gabe, why?"

"I don't know. I don't hardly remember leavin' the lodge. I heerd that hissin' noise, wuk up outa a sound sleep, and had to go, is all."

"To take a leak?" Luke asked slyly.

"Shit, Luke! In that winter I never left the lodge sometimes durin' the night for anythin'. *Anythin'*, I tell yuh!" His voice rose high and cracked.

François placed wood on the fire and turned over the *boudins*. "That hissing noise, Gabe. Yuh sure yuh heard it?"

Gabe shrugged. "I think so."

"Yuh see anythin' at all outside?"

"Like what?"

"Mebbe a man, or what look lak man. Twenty feet tall, mebbe, eh? Yuh see somethin' lak dat?"

Gabe tilted his head to one side. He slewed his eyes sideways, both ways, then reached for the kettle.

"Gabe? Yuh see somethin' lak dat?" François repeated.

"I dunno, Boudins. Why'd yuh ask?"

"Where I come from, up nort', dey got spirit condemned to wander wilderness forever. Some say he outcast who once ate human flesh. Always he near water—river, lak, pond mebbe. All night long, winter and summer, he prowl woods lookin' for victims who wander away from campfires into darkness. No one in dat country travel by land or water after dark."

Quint eyed the dead-serious Canadian. "The windigo? The demon spirit that haunts the woods?"

François nodded. "The same. Horrible forest demon. Twenty, thirty feet tall. Never wear clothes. Mak loud cry, lak hissing snake. Hear for miles."

"Jesus God," Gabe murmured. "What's he look like, Frenchie?"

"Big mouth. No more lip than snappin' turtle. Mouth full of jagged teeth. Eyes stick out lak great frog, rollin' in blood, what drips when he spies victim. Feet a meter long, yuh understand? Mebbe more dan tree feet long. Only one toe on each foot wit big sharp nail and pointed at the heel. Hands lak giant claws, lak lobster, mebbe."

Quint grinned a little. "Ye ever see one, Boudins?"

François was horrified. *"Sacré Demon! No!* Yuh see one windigo and not kill heem, you become one too, but still look lak human. Feed on rotten wood, swamp moss, stump mushrooms, but mostly human flesh!"

Moccasin shifted about uncertainly. He looked back over both his shoulders and then drew closer to the fire.

"Some say, yuh eat human flesh, windigo come look for yuh," François added.

Gabe stared narrow-eyed at the Canadian.

Vague stories about Gabe drifted through Quint's mind. There was a shadowy legend about Gabe's wintering up on the Yellowstone, years past, when few white men had ventured into that land. There had been a partner with him. They had been snowed in for months. In the spring, old Gabe had appeared, gaunt and hollow-cheeked, but alive. His partner had never been seen again. No one had ever partnered with Gabe again.

Luke stirred up the fire. "What the hell we got to worry about, mates? None of us ever et human flesh."

No one spoke. Old Gabe seemed to have shrunken into himself.

"Ye all right, Gabe?" Quint asked.

Gabe nodded. "How yuh kill a thing like that, Frenchie?" he asked hollowly.

"By fire. But, heart made outa ice. Yuh got to pound it in little pieces, or else it bring back windigo body. Then melt little pieces in fire."

"I mean, what about one of them *human* windigos?"

"Stun wit big rock. Burn him up wit all his possibles."

"What happened in the spring, Gabe?" Quint asked to get off the subject of windigos.

"Worked like I was loco. Settin' traps. Waitin' for the passes to clear of snow. I skinned the plews and cured 'em, and all the time lookin' back over my shoulder like someone was watchin' me."

"Eutaws, mebbe?" Luke suggested.

Gabe shook his head. "Won't go near that goddam place."

"Chico Vasquez?" François asked.

"I don't know!" Gabe replied testily.

"Tsoaps," Moccasin said wisely in Shoshoni. "Ghosts."

Gabe nodded. "I thought so too. Changed my mind later that spring, though. I got ready to leave. Figgered I might be able to get through the north pass, but it was full of snow. I left my lodge and my plews and struck out to the south to check them passes down there. Figgered I might be able to make it to Taos, or mebbe Bent's Fort. One day I see smoke at the north end of the valley. When I got back there my lodge was burned to the ground. Everything was gone—traps, plews, pack mules, two full seasons' work, gone like the melted snow on the ground when the chinook wind blows. No signs of anyone there. No tracks, horse shit, nuthin'."

"Tsoaps," Moccasin repeated. He hiccupped.

They cleaned out the last of the *boudins* and refilled their pipes.

"What then, ol' hoss?" Luke asked.

"I found some hoss tracks later on at the south end of the valley. Hoss was loaded with something heavy. Mebbe *my* hoss and *my* beaver. I started trailin' it. Run into Ol' Ephraim in the thick brush. Never seen him until I was right on top of him. Didn' know which of us was the most surprised." He grinned crookedly. "I give him a half-ounce Hawken ball right through his belly at one-foot range. Got another one into him with my pistol. Drew my knife afore he got to me. . . ."

"Then?" Quint asked.

Gabe laid down his pipe and lifted the hair at the right side

61

of his head, then shrugged his right shoulder out of his jacket. Where his right ear had been was a ragged, tattered appendage with parallel scars from above the ear, down to the neck, missing the jugular by half an inch, then tracing a deep course across the shoulder to the right biceps.

"Jesus," Quint breathed.

Gabe let the hair drop and shrugged back into his jacket. "Bruk my right shoulder. Draped my scalp over my eyes, somethin' no Blackfoot had ever done. Chewed partway through my right arm. Bruk my Hawken in two at the small of the stock." He placed a hand on the rawhide and brass wire that bound the forestock and the butt stock together at the small of the stock. "Threw me ten feet away with another swipe. Cracked my left leg. I got my knife in him up to Green River a dozen times afore I passed out. I knew I was goin' to die. But that ol' grizzly, he left me alone, mebbe because he was bad hurt hisself. He left and I became unconscious. Musta laid there half a day. Stopped the bleedin' with moss and dirt. Wolves come around at night. I got to my pistol, loaded it and fired at 'em whenever they got too close.

"I got to a stream. Figgered I set my leg, but don't remember. It ain't never been the same. Crawled to my hoss, got aboard somehow, rode to my lodge and fell off. Found some charred food in the ruins and some possibles I kept cached near the lodge—jerky, spare powder and ball, flints and suchlike. I fixed my old Hawken like yuh see here. Knocked over a deer and had enough meat for a week and to get outa there. By then the pass was open. So, I got to hell outa there and *I never went back!*"

Quint stared at the old trapper. "Ye didn't go after the men that stole your plews and pack mules?" he asked incredulously.

Gabe shook his head. "I had enough of that goddamn place!"

"But, mon!" Quint cried. "Ye had maybe several thousand dollars' worth of plews!"

Gabe looked away. " 'Twarn't losin' the plews as bothered me, Big Red."

"I would have tracked those damned thieves to hell and back if they had taken *my* plews!"

Gabe shrugged. "The money didn't mean enough to me for me to stay in that accursed valley."

"It's no the idea of the money itself, Gabe. It's the principle of the thing."

Luke grinned. "That's my partner talkin'. To hell with the money. It's the *principle* of the thing. Waal, that's the Scotch for yuh."

"Scots!" Quint snapped.

Luke grinned again.

Quint drank deeply and then leaned forward. "And, even so, Gabe, forgetting about the plews and the mules, was it not in your mind to stay there in that fine valley? Was it not the place ye had been looking for all these years? Rife with beaver, game, shelter, water and beauty?"

Gabe looked up. He nodded.

"Can ye gang back there, my friend?"

Gabe shook his head.

"Perhaps it would not happen again, eh, Gabe?" François asked. "The stealin' of your plews, eh?"

"The place is bad medicine, Frenchie. The Eutaws had told me that afore I went there. Other mountain men had warned Abe Walker, Pawnee Jack Stearns and that breed Antonio not to go there, and if they did, to keep one eye always behind them. In those days beaver was bringing eight to ten dollars a plew. They had to go." Here Gabe looked at Quint. "They wanted a stake to take them to Californy, and they was willin' to do anythin' to get it. Waal, they paid the price, and I did too. I was lucky enough to get out of there payin' the price I did. But, yuh'd go there anyway if I showed yuh the way?"

Quint nodded. "They'd no get the plews from me, Gabe."

"He'll try to find the place whether or not yuh show him the way, Gabe," Luke warned.

"*Toaps,*" Moccasin said. He shook his head.

"Ain't no place for a man alone. Got to have someone to watch his back," Gabe reminded them.

"No good against windigo," François said.

Moccasin nodded. "*Tsoaps.*"

Luke slanted his eyes sideways to look at Quint. "He's thinkin' of a winter squaw, Gabe."

"Good enough for the loneliness of some men; not good enough for safety in that damned place."

"I fear nothing!" Quint boasted loudly. The liquor was getting to him.

"Nuthin' yuh kin see," Gabe corrected dryly.

"*Tsoaps,*" Moccasin hiccupped.

Gabe drank again. The liquor seemed to have little effect on him. "I'll be headin' south come August. Mebbe spend the

63

winter with the Eutaws. Mebbe keep on to Taos. If yuh must go, Quint, I'll ride with yuh most of the way. Yuh'll have to go on alone. I won't go within twenty mile of the place."

"Fair enough, Gabe."

"I ain't doin' yuh any favor, Quint."

Gabe looked thoughtfully into the dying fire. "What kinda winter squaw was yuh thinkin of?"

"Who said I was thinking of a winter squaw?" Quint demanded.

Gabe looked guilelessly at Quint. "Why, ain't yuh?"

There was no reply from Quint.

Gabe scratched inside his jacket. "Next to a Eutaw I'll take an Arapaho. I like the way they go ridin' around nekkid to the waist with their tits bobbin' up and down. *Wagh!*"

"Crow," Luke put in. He hiccupped. "Best-lookin' women. Damned near white, specially under their dresses. Best beadworkers, tanners, cooks, and they can keep a man happy all winter long laughin' and chatterin'."

"Haughty as hell," François said sourly. "Like they got somethin in between their legs lak no other woman got."

Luke grinned. "Mebbe they do, Boudins."

François grinned back. "Mebbe I'll tak a long look into it! Look into it? Yuh unnerstand? Look into it! *Wagh!*"

"My God," Quint murmured.

François drank, wiped his mouth and looked slyly sideways at Quint. "Me, next to Shoshoni, I lak 'Ree squaw. Tall. Got long legs. Pertty. Fuck like hell all the time."

Moccasin solemnly shook his head. "Shit! Cheyenne best. Me know."

"Some punkin's that little Shoshoni kitten," Luke said. "Cost a lot of ponies, that one. What's her name? Mountain Top, or somethin'?"

"Mountain Bottom," François corrected. He blinked his eyes as he swayed back and forth.

"Mountain Woman," Quint said. He closed his eyes.

"That's old Buffalo Bellowing's niece, ain't it, Big Red?" Gabe asked. "Nice little piece, as I recall."

Quint nodded gravely. "Aye, that she is." He hiccupped.

"Might not cost Big Red much," Luke opined wisely. "He's in solid with the Shoshonis. Saved Washakie's scalp for him when the Crows was about to let his spirit out through it."

"And made him a Yellow Nose," Gabe added. "Man, yuh ain't got much sense throwin' all that aside jest to find that damned valley o' mine. I still think yuh oughta stay with the

Shoshonis, at least for this winter. Yuh could live like a king."

"No," Quint said firmly. "I'm going to that valley, Gabe."

Gabe got stiffly to his feet and ran his gnarled hands up and down his thighs. "Damned rheumatiz has about crippled me. Waal, that's the price yuh pay for beaverin' when their fur is prime. Twenty year in the mountains and I'm old before my time." He picked up his Hawken and leaned on it. "Whar kin I find yuh in August?"

Quint drank from the kettle.

The others looked expectantly at him.

Quint looked up. "At Washakie's camp on the Popo Agie. It won't be out of your way?"

Gabe shook his head. "I got nuthin' else to do. Wait for me there, then. Come time for us to ride south I'll come fer yuh." He was gone into the shadows as noiselessly as he had come.

"Yuh think he really saw somethin' in that valley?" Luke asked at last.

Quint shrugged. "Who knows? Old Solitary spends too much time alone. Maybe the loneliness finally got to him; what some men call the Folly of the Woods. Besides, remember he's about the best yarn spinner in these mountains."

Moccasin shook his head. "He not lie. Ol' Gabe like Delaware. He *never* lie. Not easy to believe, but not lies."

"Yuh'll be goin' south for sure then, Quint?" Luke asked.

Quint nodded. He looked from one to the other. They were the best in the business. He knew he'd never find another set of partners like this trio. Still, all good things must come to an end.

Luke reached for the kettle. "Never took a shine to them Eutaws. Mebbe I'll eye yuh, come spring, Quint, if'n yuh can hold on to your ha'r that long." He hiccupped loudly.

The fire was almost out. The faint dry wind stirred the ashes and formed a swirling wraith over the heads of the trappers. One by one they got up and swayed rubber-legged into the lodge, leaving Quint sitting alone with the almost empty kettle beside him. He emptied the kettle, wiped his mouth, then stood up and looked off into the darkness toward the south.

The wind suddenly shifted and soughed through the rustling cottonwood leaves.

Somewhere in the darkness on a hill a wolf howled once.

SEVEN

August 1837—Moon of Black Cherries.

The way of life among the Shoshonis might be much the same as it was among Quint Kershaw's Highland ancestors in ancient Caledonia. It was almost an idyllic life, for a male at least. There was hunting, feasting when there was plenty and the way of the warpath to war and glory, and perhaps the ultimate reward of a Happy Hunting Ground—the Gaels called it Tir-na-n'-Og, -West-over Seas, the Beautiful Land of Youth where there is no pain, disease or death. Where a warrior may feast and drink, fornicate and fight to his heart's content throughout eternity.

The air was growing cooler day by day. The leaves were beginning to turn. The days had drifted past with Quint hardly noticing the passage of time. Soon Gabe Pritchett would come for him. It was then that he'd have to make up his mind what he wanted to do. He had one of two choices—stay with the Shoshonis for the winter, or travel south to the valley he had already begun to think of as his own without ever seeing it. *Kershaw's Valley*—it had a soul-satisfying ring to it!

During the latter days of Quint's sojourn with the Shoshonis he had started to become restless. He had begun to idle the days away sitting in the lodge of Washakie, watching the busy life of the village and yarning with the tribal elders.

The lodge of Buffalo Bellowing was next to that of Washakie. Quint could see that Mountain Woman was finishing a new saddle for herself, as though preparing to leave for a long journey. She was helped on this project by her friend and confidante Elk Calling. Hardly a day had gone by in the making of the saddle that Quint hadn't watched Mountain Woman at her work. She bent over it with her young face intent, never looking up in his direction, but it seemed to him that she always made sure he was watching her before she brought it out of the lodge to work on it. He saw the swelling of her young full breasts against the elkskin of her dress as she bent over the saddle. He noticed her tiny feet encased in exquisitely beaded moccasins. He watched her shapely hands as they deftly fashioned the saddle. When Elk Calling helped Mountain Woman the two of them would chatter away, quite often surreptitiously glancing toward Quint when they thought he wasn't looking toward them. Or did they *know* he was watching them? One thing Quint did notice—when he looked directly at them, it was always Mountain Woman who modestly looked downward, as a woman should do when in the presence of a man. Elk Calling would boldly return his gaze until it was Quint who turned away.

It was Washakie who finally took the bull by the horns near the last part of August. "Have you decided to winter with us, En-Hone?" he asked.

Quint shook his head. "No, Washakie."

"Your partners have left for the south. Do you plan to follow them?"

Quint slowly filled his pipe while eyeing the young, full body of Mountain Woman.

"En-Hone?" the chief said.

Quint looked quickly at the Shoshoni. "Eh? Did you say something?"

The chief studied Quint. "If you plan to leave for the south you should be getting ready. The snow will be falling in the high mountains by the time you get there."

Quint nodded absentmindedly.

"Stay with us. In a few weeks we raid the Crows for horses. Perhaps you can find something among their herd that will suit you."

Quint shrugged. "I have good horses, Washakie."

Washakie looked casually at Buffalo Bellowing. "Including that paint horse you traded for at the rendezvous, En-Hone? He is too blocky to be beautiful, and he is not as fast as your sorrel, but he has endurance."

Quint looked sideways at the two Shoshonis. "Ah, but he interests you, Washakie?"

The chief shook his head. "I wasn't thinking of myself. I have all the horses I want, or need."

Quint grinned. "Is that why you plan to raid the Crows?"

Washakie was not to be taken in. He waved a hand. "Oh,

67

that!" he said loftily. "Just to irritate the Crows, to add to their anger for the defeat we gave them at the Medicine Lodge Fork."

"I see. I thought that might have something to do with it." They grinned at each other.

"We could use you on the raid," Washakie suggested.

Quint shook his head. "I should be on my way south by that time."

"Alone?"

Quint lighted his pipe while studying Buffalo Bellowing out of the corners of his eyes. The medicine man was, of course, the guardian of Mountain Woman, and Quint would have to deal directly with him for the woman—that is, if he really wanted her. It should be simple enough. What troubled him was that he wasn't sure he really wanted a winter squaw. Still, if what old Gabe had said was true, he'd have his hands full with the trapping and hunting alone, without the bother of stretching and curing the plews, and doing his own cooking and taking care of the lodge.

Buffalo Bellowing glanced toward Mountain Woman. "She has been working hard on that new saddle to get it ready in time."

"Why?" Washakie asked. He knew, of course.

Buffalo Bellowing shook his head. "I don't know. She acts strangely these days. I see her often looking through her clothing selecting certain things as though she meant to travel soon."

"Maybe on the horse raid?" Washakie asked slyly.

"At that she'd be a good one," Buffalo Bellowing said. "She can shoot well and rides almost as well as a man. But if she goes on the horse raid with you, she won't need that fancy saddle or those fine clothes."

Washakie nodded. "Is it possible that she's thinking about a *man?*" Washakie said archly.

"Am-mi-soits, the Spider, has his eye on her. Some say he plans to steal Mountain Woman from my lodge. Others say he is gathering goods and robes for his lodge to ask Mountain Woman to come and live with him."

"A good man. He has already counted first coup on two Crows. He wears the necklace of grizzly bear claws. Wasn't it a year ago when he met Aw-ha-pit-woodha while hunting? He was on foot, with but one arrow left in his quiver but he stood his ground. Before the huge bear attacked him he counted coup on him, then wounded the great beast with his last arrow, and finished him off with his knife."

Quint eyed the two Shoshonis. Such a deed counted more with them than killing an enemy in hand-to-hand combat or counting coup on an enemy in the midst of hostile warriors.

"And he is not the only young man who has eyes for Mountain Woman," the medicine man continued remorselessly. He held up a hand and began to tick off the names of other suitors on his fingers. "There are Elder Brother, White Robe, Rabbit Tail, Hairy Leggings, Red Sun, Big Toe, No Hands, Lynx and Porcupine. There are . . ." His voice trailed off and died away at the look on Quint's face.

"You'll be running out of fingers first, and then the men of the village," Quint suggested dryly.

Washakie filled his pipe. "I have great respect for you as a warrior and hunter, En-Hone, but in some ways you are not too clever."

"Get to the point," Quint said.

"Mountain Woman."

"She's only a child!"

"For your people? Perhaps. But not for ours. She is sixteen years old, En-Hone!"

"You think she is too young?" Buffalo Bellowing asked. "She should have a man now. Already, since you've come to stay with us, I've turned away three suitors."

"Why?" Quint asked.

The medicine man leaned closer to Quint. "Since she saw you at the Medicine Lodge Fork she has eyes for no other man."

Among the Shoshonis, as among many other tribes, the man was considered to be the sole proprietor of his women-folk, his wives and daughters, and he had the right to dispose of them or barter for them if he so chose to do so.

"How many ponies do you want for her?" Quint asked abruptly. It wasn't quite polite, but he was tired of the involved maneuvering the two Shoshonis were doing.

Buffalo Bellowing waved a hand. "That is not necessary, at least for you, En-Hone. If a man wants a woman he can steal her from the village long enough to make her his, and then bring her back in time, and no questions will be asked. Or if a man wants a woman, and she is willing, he can take her to his lodge where he has stored a good supply of skins and robes, porcupine quills, beads, chains of sea shells and an extra horse for her."

"Strangely enough I have no skins and robes, porcupine quills, beads, chains of sea shells and so forth."

"Ah, but you have an extra horse!"

Washakie puffed at his pipe. "A man such as yourself, who is honored here among our people, would have no trouble in getting a lodge and those other things."

Mountain Woman looked up from her work. She had heard most of the conversation among the men, but she pretended otherwise. She had a tight feeling in her chest and a loose moist feeling between her legs. She was a virgin. No man had ever penetrated her. Some of the boys had fooled around with her in the cottonwoods, but none of them had fornicated with her. That was not to say that plenty of them had not tried.

"I think he really wants you," Elk Calling whispered into Mountain Woman's ear. "Some say he is bigger in his man-parts than any stallion they've ever seen."

Mountain Woman had seen him bathing in the river several times. She had seen other men naked, of course. She and some of the other younger women and girls had sometimes hidden in the willows and cottonwoods to watch the men and boys bathe, as the men and boys sometimes did to watch the girls and women. None of the men she had seen had such a big man-part as En-Hone. If he put that in between her legs would that mean that he loved her? No one, not even wise old Good Woman, her aunt, and wife to Buffalo Bellowing, had quite been able to tell her what love was. She had asked Good Woman a number of times.

"To be with a man always," Good Woman had said thoughtfully. "And not to get tired of him and his ways. That's not easy, I tell you! Do not look at other men. Raise your husband's lodge, prepare his food and always make him comfortable. Welcome him home from the hunt and the warpath. Bear his children. That is all I know."

But, supposing the Soo-yah-pe had a different meaning for love? Perhaps it would be something mysterious and thrilling she might learn from En-Hone, when and if he took her to his lodge. She had seen some of the women of the Soo-yah-pe at the rendezvous that summer. They were the wives of men who wore black and were called missionaries. The women had been horse-faced, with flat chests, and always wore black as though they were on the warpath. They never painted their faces or the parting of their hair with red to make themselves look more attractive. They had looked with disapproval on the young, unhampered Indian women. She wondered idly if

70

there were any white women as attractive as she was. How would those horse-faced, skinny women be in bed under the robes with a man?

"Will En-Hone stay with us this winter?" Elk Calling asked.

Mountain Woman shook her head. "He means to go south into the mountains to trap beaver."

"Alone?"

"I don't know. His friends have left without him."

"Then he'll need someone to clean his pelts and take care of his lodge."

"I suppose so," Mountain Woman said carelessly.

Am-mi-soits, the Spider, rode his fine calico pony toward the two young women. Suddenly he urged the pony into a full gallop. The sharp tattoo of the hooves rang on the hard-packed earth. He shot past the women, so close he could have reached down and touched them. He drew his pony up in a hoof-pawing rear not far from the lodge of Washakie. The sun glistened from the necklace of polished grizzly bear claws he wore. He wore two feathers in his hair. They were cut at a sharp angle, indicating he had counted coup on two enemies of the people.

Am-mi-soits turned the pony and returned toward the women at a fast run. As he neared them he suddenly threw himself over the side of the mount, hanging by one heel over the pony's back, while he clung to a horsehair rope braided into the pony's thick mane. His own long braided hair swept the ground. He raced to the far end of the village and then returned at top speed, throwing himself alternately from one side of the pony to the other in a dazzling exhibition of horsemanship.

Neither of the two young women looked up. They kept on chatting as though Spider and his fancy pony did not exist.

"Do I have to do that to win the lass?" Quint asked between puffs on his pipe.

"Could you do it?" Washakie asked with a grin.

"I don't like to make an exhibition of my skills as a rule, Washakie."

"That we all know, but when you do . . ."

Quint looked steadily at the chief. "I kill, my brother. War is a cold-blooded business at best, and it should be gotten over with at once."

Even the tough-minded Shoshoni felt a little uneasy at the glacial look in the white man's hard gray eyes.

After a time Spider rode his foam-flecked pony toward the

71

river. Mountain Woman had paid no attention to him. He joined some of the other young men, who were fishing. None of them, and most of them had tried, had ever been able to make an impression on Mountain Woman. At least, not since she had seen En-Hone, the big sorrel-haired Soo-yah-pe, fighting like a Wi-ag-gait, a Foolish One, at the Medicine Lodge Fork.

Elk Calling watched Spider ride toward the river. "He's really after you, Mountain Woman. He'll be a big man someday."

"He's only a boy," Mountain Woman said scornfully.

Elk Calling shrugged. "Certainly, he's not as big in his private man-parts as En-Hone." She grinned a little.

There was no comment from Mountain Woman.

"En-Hone only wants a winter squaw anyway," Elk Calling added. "You wouldn't like that."

Mountain Woman shook her head. "If he goes south and takes me with him, as I think he wants to do, he'll come back here in the spring and live here with the People."

"I wonder? The trappers are *tibos,* barbarians. They are like wild animals. You've seen them at the rendezvous rolling about drunken in the cottonwoods with those cheap women who sell themselves for a handful of beads or a hawk's bell. They don't care *where* they plant their seed. But then it's true many of our women want a child that is half white." She slanted her great dark eyes toward Mountain Woman. "They seem to think it's a great honor," she sneered.

Mountain Woman began to gather her materials and tools together.

"You'll see," Elk Calling persisted. "He'll take you to his lodge and get in between your legs like a breeding stallion. Then he'll take you to the south away from your people, and into enemy country. He'll make you work your fingers to the bone, cooking, curing his hides, cleaning, making his clothes and keeping him warm at night under the robes while he makes free with your body and maybe fills your belly with fertile seed. Then, when the ice melts on the streams and he can trap again, he'll keep you only long enough to clean and cure his pelts so that he can take them to the traders. Then he'll send you back to us with a swollen belly and a handful of beads, while he gets drunk with the rest of the *tibos.* You'll never see him again after that."

Mountain Woman held Elk Calling eye to eye. "You are a liar," she said firmly.

"I do not lie!"

"I don't want to hear any more about it!"

Elk Calling stood up. "I warn you, Mountain Woman. He doesn't want a wife at all. He's like all the other white men. How many of them do you know who have actually married one of our women and stayed with her? He will use you and work you to death and then get rid of you before you become old and fat!"

The open-handed blow caught Elk Calling alongside her head and staggered her. She went down on one knee and then came up again like a bent sapling that has been released. She closed with Mountain Woman, clawing for her eyes. They rolled shamelessly on the ground, their dresses rising high about their thighs.

"Fight! Fight! Fight!" a little boy shouted.

The villagers came running and stood about the two embattled young women. They shrieked with laughter and encouraged one or the other of them.

Good Woman came running from her lodge. She dragged the two combatants apart. "Shame on you!" she shouted at Mountain Woman. "Would you go to En-Hone's lodge all scratched and bloody?" she demanded.

"She'll be bloody enough when he gets through with her their first night under the robes together!" Elk Calling shrieked.

This time it took four of the older women to separate Mountain Woman and Elk Calling.

The excitement was broken up by the camp caller beating on his drum as he walked about announcing there would be a social dance that evening and everyone was invited. The women scattered to their lodges or the river to get ready for the big event.

EIGHT

Mountain Woman prepared herself with extra care for the dance. She bathed thoroughly. She rubbed crushed dried wildflowers between her palms and then rubbed them between the smooth inner parts of her thighs well up into her crotch. She applied them under her arms and between her breasts. She painted her cheeks and the parting of her hair with vermilion. She braided her black glossy hair into two thick braids and enclosed them in heavy brass bosses. She fastened large brass hoops to her ears and covered her fingers with many tiny brass rings, as many as ten to a finger. Her dress had been made by herself with the help of Good Woman and Elk Calling after the rendezvous. It was made of two *grossecorne* skins as the French Canadians called the *took-utt-se*, or mountain sheep. The skins had been tanned almost milk-white and were as soft as velvet. The dress was ornamented with rows of elk's teeth, porcupine quills and highly prized coast abalone shells. The shoulders and outer parts of the sleeves had been sewn with close-set masses of French Canadian trade beads in colors of pink and white forming intricate floral patterns. The tail ends of the skins were uppermost and the hoofs and tails had been left for ornaments. She wore elkskin leggings and the tiniest of moccasins trimmed with pink and white beads in floral patterns.

Quint Kershaw sat in front of the council lodge with Washakie, Buffalo Bellowing, Eagle, Buffalo Leggings and some of the elders to watch the social dancing. Quint kept an eye on Mountain Woman as she danced back and forth to the pulsating monotone cadence of the drums and rasping of the sticks. She made a living picture that Quint found almost irresistible.

The elders idly discussed various tribal matters as they

watched the dancing. They avoided talking about the one matter that interested them the most—would En-Hone stay with them that winter? They needed him. He was good medicine; a great warrior; a mighty hunter. The Blackfeet knew him of old and feared him. The Crows knew him as well, and feared him too. With En-Hone in their band, even the white men would be impressed, for all of them either feared or respected him. They were hoping against hope now that he would stay with them. Word had passed quickly through the village that En-Hone had filled a lodge with skins and robes, porcupine quills, beads and a chain of expensive and highly prized abalone shells. He had tethered a fine paint horse outside of the lodge, for the woman he meant to take as his woman. Still, no one really knew whether or not he would make the move that night, or possibly ever. He was a strange and moody man at times.

"Must you still go to the south, En-Hone?" Buffalo Leggings asked.

Quint nodded. "As soon as the one you call Caw-Haw, the Crop-Eared One, gets here to guide me to the south."

"Why must he guide you?" Eagle asked. "You know those mountains well."

"Most of them," Quint admitted. "But there is a valley there, full of great beaver, much game, shelter and timber. I may make it my home in the future."

"But that's in the land of the Eutaws!"

"They don't go to that valley."

Buffalo Bellowing, the *buhagant,* was a man wise in spiritual matters. He was famed as a seer and prophet. He had seen the sacred gray buffalo arise from under the waters of Bull Lake to stand on the water shaking his mane and tail while he bellowed like thunder. Buffalo Bellowing had gone there to spend the night so as to become endowed with magic and spiritual power. He had been a gifted wolf dancer in his youth, with their uncanny ability to see enemies on the darkest nights. He knew much, but usually said little unless it was of grave importance.

"Do not go to that valley, En-Hone," Buffalo Bellowing said quietly.

"Why, old one?"

"It is not a good place."

Had he heard Gabe Pritchett's yarn?

"Have you been there?"

The *buhagant* shook his white head.

75

"But he *knows*," Eagle whispered to Quint. "He is never wrong. Stay with us here, En-Hone. You've been warned."

Buffalo Bellowing closed his eyes. He seemed to become rigid. "There is a madness in Caw-Haw's eyes," he murmured. "His valley is not a good place. It is a place of blood and death. Do not go there, En-Hone. You will lose everything, perhaps even your life."

Quint felt an uneasiness. He wanted to laugh off the old medicine man's foreboding prophecy, but he could not. But he knew he would not stay with the Shoshonis. He also knew he might never return there.

"Caw-Haw is a *buhagant* among my people," Quint assured his friends. "He would not guide me to such a place if it meant misfortune and death for me. He, too, has his medicine."

Washakie looked sideways at Quint. "Ah, but is it *good* medicine?"

Quint shrugged. "It has kept him alive in this country for twenty years."

"I meant good medicine for *you*, En-Hone."

"He's guiding me there, isn't he?" Quint demanded.

Buffalo Bellowing opened his eyes. "He does not want to guide you there. He wants you to stay with us."

"Now, if yuh was to ask my advice, which yuh ain't, whyn't yuh just stay with the Snakes this winter?" old Gabe had asked Quint at the rendezvous. *"That valley ain't no place for a man alone. Got to have someone to watch his back,"* he had warned. And again, *"If yuh have to go, Quint, I'll ride with yuh most of the way. Yuh'll have to go on alone. I won't go within twenty mile of the place."*

"The Eutaws say that valley is the place of a devil, or devils, like our dwarf NunumBi, 'Little People' who roam about shooting invisible arrows of misfortune into any one who goes there," Buffalo Leggings said quietly. "They will follow a man through life causing illness, horse laming and wife desertion, perhaps even death."

"Some say it is the home of the Great Brown Bear of the Mountains," Washakie added. "He who dwells among summit snows and whose howls mingle with summer thunder and winter wailings of the storms."

"Fairy tales," Quint said.

"Then there is the Big Beaver," Eagle added relentlessly. "He who it is said lives in the marshes. His breath can split the hardest rock. His fiery eyes can melt the thickest ice."

"My God," Quint murmured. He rolled his eyes upward.

76

The dancing was still going on, but some of the dancers had quit and gone to their lodges. Now, even as Quint watched them, several other couples left, until only Mountain Woman and Spider remained. The fires had burned low. The shadowy pair moved back and forth, slowly and gracefully, even though the musicians had finally stopped playing and gone to their lodges. Now, the only sound to be heard was the slapping of the moccasins on the hard-packed earth of the dancing area.

Conversation had died out among Quint and the Shoshonis. They sat silently watching the dancers. The wind had turned cool. It blew through the valley bringing with it the hint that the summer season had drawn to a close and that soon it would be the time of September, When the Plums Are Scarlet, and the Shoshonis must start their fall hunting.

"It will be a hungry winter with much snow," Buffalo Bellowing prophesied. "The Great White Giant of the North will spread his white robes over all the land and blow his icy breath across it. The streams will freeze to the bottoms. The trees will crack from the cold and sound like rifle shots. By the Time of the Moon of Falling Leaves nothing will move across the land. The people in the lodges will be cold and hungry. Even the animals, those who do not sleep through the winter, will cry out from the cold before their voices are stilled forever. Nothing will live in the high country."

Quint eyed the prophet speculatively. Buffalo Bellowing had a great reputation for such prophecies. He had never been wrong.

Washakie nodded. "He *knows,* En-Hone."

Quint shook his head. "When Caw-Haw arrives, I'll go with him."

"With a woman?"

"I don't know."

Washakie inclined his head and pursed his lips toward the closely dancing figures of Mountain Woman and Spider. "Spider has placed extra skins in his lodge this day."

"And many porcupine shells," Eagle added.

"With chains of sea shells from the great salt water far to the west," Buffalo Leggings said.

"He means to take Mountain Woman to his lodge this night," Buffalo Bellowing warned.

"You are sure of this?" Quint asked.

"The whole village knows it," Washakie replied.

"There is not much time," Eagle suggested.

Quint shrugged. *"Ka-shoon-banah!* I don't know! Caw-Haw

77

hasn't come, so I don't know if I will go south." If he did not find the valley he'd have no use for a woman that winter.

The wind was colder. The hills were dark humps against the night sky. Somewhere out in the darkness a coyote howled.

Buffalo Bellowing raised his white head. "Caw-Haw comes."

The couple had stopped dancing at the sound of the coyote's voice. Spider stood close to Mountain Woman, but she had no eyes for him. She was looking toward the dark hill whence the crying of the coyote had come.

Hoofbeats echoed hollowly from the earth. The shadowed shape of a mounted man came out of the dimness. He was hunched in his saddle with a heavy rifle across his thighs. His coal-scuttle stirrups almost dragged on the ground.

The rider dismounted stiffly from his horse. He cradled his rifle in the hollow of his left arm and walked slowly toward Quint and the Shoshonis.

"It's time, Big Red," Old Gabe announced hoarsely.

The wind blew harder, swirling ashes up from the dying fires. Little leaping flames flickered back and forth across the thick beds of embers and ashes. They lighted the faces of Mountain Woman and Spider.

Quint stood up, towering over the hunched figure of old Gabe. He walked slowly toward the woman.

Spider looked uncertainly toward the approaching white man. There was a superstitious fear of this Soo-yah-pe among his people. It was said to be so among other tribes. Even the white men had a fear of this man. He had seen him fighting at the Medicine Lodge Fork as though he feared nothing and almost as though he welcomed death.

Mountain Woman trembled slightly. The top of her head was hardly lower than that of Spider, who was not very tall himself, but En-Hone towered above them both. Her head barely reached to the top of his deep chest.

It was very quiet except for the whispering of the night wind.

Spider looked up at En-Hone. He knew well enough why he had come to them. He slyly slid his right hand to the middle of his back and rested it on the handle of his knife. Yet he knew if he attacked this man, blood brother and friend to Washakie and a Yellow Nose to boot, he would be banished from his people.

Quint shook his head at the young Shoshoni, as though to

warn him not to try anything desperate. He looked down at Mountain Woman. "Come," he said quietly.

Mountain Woman hesitated, modestly of course. It wouldn't look too good if she seemed in a hurry to get under the robes with him.

"Come," Quint repeated.

Still, she hesitated. She wanted to go with him, of course, but there was some fear of him deep within her. Perhaps he wasn't truly human at all.

"Egit-sha! Now!" Quint snapped. He turned on a heel and walked toward his lodge.

Mountain Woman hurried after him. She did not look back at Spider.

The young Shoshoni did not wait to see Mountain Woman follow her new master into his lodge. He walked to his own lodge near the river, got his rifle and other gear and threw a light robe about his shoulders. His aged mother had prepared a fire in the lodge and had banked it in anticipation that her only son would be bringing home a wife. Spider kicked the fire apart, scattering the burning embers over the pile of firewood and the new robes piled on top of a layer of fresh evergreen branches. He left the lodge and mounted his horse and took the lead rope of the horse he had tethered there for Mountain Woman. He touched the calico with his heels and rode toward the dark hills. He did not look back. There was no one to watch him leaving his village, perhaps forever. The steady drumming of unshod hoofs echoed hollowly back through the valley.

The coyote howled once more. Then the night was silent except for the dry voice of the wind.

NINE

The tipi was dim except for the faint flaring light of a buffalo-fat candle fixed in a deep clay bowl so that its illumination was cast upward against the underside of the tipi top. The lodge was small, but it was a new one, well made of eleven summer-taken buffalo-cow hides, a gift to Quint from Washakie. A gentle draft of cool air came down from the vent flap.

Quint sat on a winter-thick, soft-haired reddish buffalo-cow robe, a real "silk," with his back against a rest. A full jug of Monongahela was on the floor beside him. Mountain Woman sat across from him. The faint light brought out the planes and shadows of her rather broad face and glistened from her large dark eyes. He had not spoken to her since the peremptory command he had given her to come to his lodge.

Mountain Woman had prayed to Tamapah, the Sun-Father, Father of the Day and Father of them all, for further good fortune in this marriage. Good fortune was with her. She had seen the old man Caw-Haw riding from the darkness after the crying of Coyote just a few moments before Am-misoits would have been certain to ask her to come to his lodge. The crying of Coyote during a full moon was always good luck. But there had been no moon that night. Would that make any difference? She would have to ask Buffalo Bellowing. Perhaps it meant bad fortune instead of good. Coyote was the father of the Shoshonis, but he was also the Father of Lies. The old man Caw-Haw was much like Coyote. Perhaps it had been he who had cried out from the darkness, before changing his shape from that of a coyote into that of a hunched old man with dirty gray hair, smelling always of rotting teeth, piss, stale perspiration, tobacco smoke, grease and bad whiskey. Who *was* he really?

Quint slowly filled his pipe. He felt misgivings about what he had done. There could be no going back now, not in front of her people, at least. She would be the laughingstock of the village and fair game for any lecherous young buck eager to get his balls off into her. Even if Quint did not consummate this temporary union with her and did not speak of it to anyone, the first man who did penetrate her would know at once that Quint had failed to do so.

When his pipe was filled she came across the lodge to him and held a glowing twig over the bowl. Her great eyes looked deep into his. The mingled odors of her—the smoky smell of the tanned *grossecorne* skin, crushed dried wildflowers, faint perspiration and that indefinable Indian-like smell of mingled woodsmoke and sweet grease—tantalized him, but he put the thought from his mind. Some of the mountain men claimed each tribe had its personal smell, but Quint had never thought so. It was all the same to him. Perhaps he had not been with enough Indian women to differentiate between them. There had been that Arapaho child, of course. Her name escaped him at the moment.

Quint puffed at the pipe. The sweet-smelling smoke drifted about the woman and him. He could see her shadowed face and felt the weight of her breasts against his shoulder as she crept close beside him. The pipe was drawing well.

After a time, when there was no response from him, she went to her place on the women's side of the fire. Her face was impassive. Now and again he looked at her, but it was as though he did not see her at all but instead was looking through her and beyond her to something that was troubling him. The thought came to her that his mind was always traveling alone. She never really knew what he was thinking, but then it seemed to be that way with everyone who knew him. Sometimes he was like Buffalo Bellowing, who hardly seemed to commune with the people of the village, so engrossed was he with the spirit world. Was that also true of En-Hone? She wondered fearfully what *his* spirits must be like, they haunted him so.

Quint sipped from the mouth of the jug. It was good, he argued with himself. All was good. He had a good lodge within the village of a people who admired and respected him, though he wasn't quite sure they *loved* him. He had a good woman, a fine supply of robes and dried meat. He had five good horses in the village herd.

81

The candle flared up and died low. The village seemed to be asleep.

After a long time Mountain Woman pulled the heavy dress over her head. She stripped off her moccasins and leggings. She did not speak. Her heart was too full. She was naked now, shivering a little in the cold air. She looked over at the shadowed figure of her man. He sat motionless as though he had fallen asleep. Then he raised the jug to his lips and drank deeply.

The draft whispered down from the open vent. There was a smell of rain in the air. Mountain Woman sat down on the thick robes of the bed. She looked at Quint again. There was no response. She knew he could see her there in her nakedness. After a time she lay down and drew the thick covering robe over herself. She rested her head on the rolled-up hide that served as a pillow and looked up into the dim top of the lodge, watching the fanciful candlelight shadow figures flickering back and forth.

Mountain Woman awoke after a long time. She peered over the edge of the robe. The candle was almost burned out. Quint sat still. His cold pipe was in his left hand resting on the floor. His right hand was clasped about the neck of the jug.

It was warm beneath the robe. She had thought by this time she would have been thoroughly penetrated by that stud of a man. She remembered, with a scary delicious feeling, the sight of his limp man-part as he had bathed in the river, and speculated how much it would swell to hardness and stand erect.

Mountain Woman fell asleep again.

Rain pattered on the lodge skins. The wind had shifted. A draft blew down the vent and scattered the cold ashes of the fire, furring the floor and the bed robes with a light and fluffy down.

Quint opened his eyes. He raised the jug and drank deeply. He grunted as the liquor hit his gut. *"Wagh!"*

A spit of rain came down the vent. Quint looked across the lodge and saw the humped shape beneath the bed robes. "Jesus Christ," he murmured. *He had forgotten all about her!*

Quint padded outside in the cold pattering rain. He shifted the vent poles and then returned within the lodge. He shivered from the cold wetness. He flint-struck a fire steel and kindled a fire, adding twigs and bits of wood until the lodge was filled with the crackling brightness. Still the girl slept.

82

Quint looked down at her shape and the dark glossy hair at the top of the robe. By Jesus! She was *his*, wasn't she? He had paid for her. He had brought her to his lodge. She had come willingly.

Quint stripped off his clothing and kicked off his sodden moccasins. He took another solid drink and then slowly pulled back the covering robe. She lay there in the rising firelight like a luscious pearl in a shell with the golden firelight playing on her soft brown skin, full breasts with their brown buds, and the soft black triangular patch of curly hair where her rounded thighs met her belly.

Quint stroked his rising organ. It thrust out proudly before him. He stepped onto the bed. Mountain Woman opened her eyes. They widened at the sight of him and his proud erection. She raised her arms up to him. He virtually fell on top of her, almost driving the air from her lungs. He felt for her soft mouth with his. The smell of the whiskey sickened her for a few seconds. He was more than half drunk, she realized. She wasn't used to kissing, but she tried. She had little or no knowledge of foreplay, but it was well that she did not, for Quint was in no mood for the niceties that night. He forced her legs apart and thrust a rough hand into her crotch, pushing the callused fingers up within her. She winced and tried to withdraw from him, but it was no use. He held her fast like a rabbit in a snare.

Quint placed her hand on his cock. "Stroke it, damn you!" he snarled at her. "Make it grow!"

Her eyes widened. How big did he want it? Then she remembered how her roan mare had been bred by a giant of a sorrel stallion rearing up behind her, thrashing his fore hooves in the air until he managed to drive his huge organ into her.

She widened her legs and raised her knees. She didn't know what to do and he wasn't in the mood to be tender or understanding and to teach her. Oh, she had been told by some of the older women what to expect on her wedding night, but this seemed to be a different matter altogether.

"Guide it in!" he growled at her.

She held the tip of it across the slit of her vagina, just enough so that it penetrated the soft moist lips. Then he leaned full and hard against her, reaching down with his hands to raise her knees up high so that he could push in deeper and deeper, and even deeper until she thought she would have to scream out for mercy. He would burst her

83

asunder and penetrate into the very bottom of her belly. He stroked in and out, roughly at first and with little timing, while she clung to him staring up into his sweat-dripping contorted face. At last something gave deep within her. She felt a flash of tearing pain and then a great feeling of mingled pain and relief. Later, as he continued his relentless savaging, he suddenly shuddered spasmodically and she felt a flooding within her. He fell sideways, withdrawing himself from her, dribbling warm fluid over her belly and thighs. He lay still.

After a time she raised her head. She passed her trembling hands down to her crotch and then rubbed them gently back and forth. She raised her hands to look at them. The dark blood shone in the dying firelight. She looked sideways at him. He was asleep with his mouth wide open and snoring like the Thunder Beings of the West before they bring the rain.

The rain stopped sometime before the graying light of the dawn reached the valley of the Popo Agie. A cold damp wind prophesied the coming of the day. Mountain Woman stirred. She opened her eyes to look up into the gray eyes of En-Hone. She saw something in them that she now recognized. He sat up and drew the robe from her body. She saw his erection. She turned her head aside in feigned modesty.

Quint kissed her lips. He toyed with her breasts. He passed a hand down to her tender crotch and thrust his fingers into it, pushing them in and out until she became aroused. Spreading her legs, knees raised, she groped eagerly for his man-part and gripped it as hard as she could.

"Take it easy," he said with a pained smile. "You'll get it soon enough."

She winced with the pain of the penetration, and then felt the growing ecstasy of the act. He drove it in with rhythmic strokes until in a little while they worked together like a well-oiled machine. They were good together. At last they exploded in unison. He lay down beside her and drew her into his arms.

She looked up into his shadowed face. "You make my heart big, En-Hone," she whispered shyly.

TEN

September 1837. Kershaw's Valley—Moon When the Plums Are Scarlet.

The first translucent light of dawn began to swallow the cold darkness. The serrated tops of nameless peaks around the high pass stood out against the mother-of-pearl light like gigantic sawblades, incredibly close and yet equally remote. The snow-veined peaks to the west were touched with the soft half-light. The wind began to blow tentatively down the dark mountain slopes and through the pass.

The faint moaning of the dawn wind awoke Quint Kershaw. He stirred under the low-hanging branches of a spruce tree at the top of the timberline. The snow fell from the branches as he moved. He cursed under his breath. Quint dug out the snow that had fallen within the hood of his Hudson's Bay blanket capote and down his neck. He was stiff-limbed and his blood seemed as cold as a mountain crick. He withdrew his buckskin-sheathed Hawken from under the spruce and dusted the snow from it. He raised his head and stood there with it tilted slightly backward testing the dawn with his nose, eyes and animal-like hearing. The pass seemed deserted. Old Gabe Pritchett had left Quint and Mountain Woman twenty-five miles to the north and east, heading for the Uncompahgre River after giving Quint directions on how to find the pass.

Old Solitary's last warning came back to Quint. *"There is something evil about that place, Big Red. Somethin' that is not for men. Stay away from it. Go and trap Bayou Salade or the San Juans, but not that valley."*

Gabe had shrugged his shoulders in resignation at Quint's refusal to turn back. He had ridden a short distance from them and then stopped to look back. *"Vaya con Dios,"* he had said. *"Go with God."* It was unusual for Gabe to speak so. If he believed in God no one had ever heard him say so. He had ridden on a little farther, a strange hunched figure dark

85

against the pristine whiteness of the newly fallen snow. He had turned again. *"Acaso!"* he had called out. *"Maybe..."*

Quint said softly to himself, "Go with God. Maybe..."

There could be no turning back. Quint's stubborn mind was fixed.

He drew his robe from under the tree and made a pack of his extra possibles within it. He stripped the cover from his loaded rifle and capped the nipple, drew out his massive North pistol and capped it as well.

The pass and the surrounding mountains had an absolute and crystalline loneliness about them. Everything was greatly magnified. There was no sign of human or animal life. In some ways Quint liked it so—himself against Nature, trying to become part of it, in the great mystery of all life, earth, the mother of us all. A wild thing that could not bear civilization.

It had been so for the past ten days as Gabe, Mountain Woman and Quint had traveled to the south from the Popo Agie. The high country seemed empty of human life. It was Ute territory, but the travelers had not seen any of them. Still, an Indian is not seen unless he wants to be seen. It wasn't likely the Utes had not seen the three of them passing through. Maybe the early snowfall had kept them to the lower, more sheltered valleys.

Quint sipped from his flask as he looked up toward the summit of the pass. The Monongahela made him cough. His eyes watered. He felt the warming glow in his guts. *"Wagh!"* he grunted hoarsely. He grinned to himself.

He had only his necessary possibles with him—rifle, pistol, sheath knife, whetstone, hatchet, .53 caliber bullet mold and two powderhorns with their brass measures, one for fine glazed DuPont powder and the other for the best English Diamond Grade. He had his bullet pouch with balls, percussion caps and bar lead, wire worm, awl, firesteel and flint, pipe and tobacco. His treasured German brass telescope was in its buckskin case. His food consisted of a buckskin bag of pemmican and some jerky. Mountain Woman had charge of the rest of the stores and gear in her hideout down in the remote valley at the foot of the pass.

Quint slogged upward through the knee-deep snow. The sun crested the mountains to his left just as he reached the summit of the pass, out of breath and panting deeply from the exertion and the thinness of the air. He figured the altitude was above nine thousand feet.

The summit was bare of snow, windswept and icy cold.

Quint looked back down the way he had come. He had told Mountain Woman to return to her own people if he did not come back within three to five days. But he knew she'd come looking for him if he did not return before that time.

Quint took cover behind a ledge of naked rock and looked down the long steep pass. A great valley spread out before him. He whistled softly. He knew the place for what it was, although he had only old Gabe's description to go by. It was far larger than he had anticipated, however, and he could see areas where branch valleys and canyons trended away from the central valley. A wide convoluted stream that bisected the floor of the pass was fed by smaller streams flowing down the thickly wooded slopes on both sides of the valley. The massed close-set aspens gleamed like pure gold against the dark-green mantle of the gaunt pines and the lighter green of the cottonwoods down along the watercourses.

It was a place of lonely and magnificent beauty, surrounded by towering mountains that sloped back on all sides. The sun shone down on it, giving the herbage a soft velvety appearance.

Quint focused his telescope. Wild flowers covering the lower meadows still bloomed in variegated shades of purple, red and gold. At the far end of the central valley he could see what looked like the end of a narrow lake. The morning mist was rising from it after the first blush of the early-fall sunrise. Closer at hand he could see the stumps of trees where Brother Beaver had gnawed through the trunks. The beehive shapes of lodges showed along the beaver-dammed streams.

"Yuh kin leave your traps in the saddle panniers," Old Gabe had said softly. "Yuh kin harvest beaver with a club, or shoot 'em from the bank as they swim past."

"The old bastard was right after all," Quint murmured.

The morning mist had burned away from the lower parts of the great valley when Quint reached the timberline and passed down through the timber. The raucous jays and scolding squirrels became silent only when they saw him, for they could not hear his passage. A deer, startled at the sight of the noiseless, swiftly moving man figure, bounded from the woods and across an open meadow, veering to one side to avoid a young lumbering grizzly. Mergansers on their way south for the winter tarried to dive on trout in the streams, pursuing them in their hopeless twisting flight from certain capture.

"I made my way down into the valley," Gabe had related.

"The place was thick with game—deer, bear, including a few of the biggest goddam grizzlies I ever seen anywhere, and I've seen the biggest of 'em, I tell yuh! Streams and lake was full of fat trout, which I don't fancy, bein' a meat man myself, but, howsumever, they make a tasty change now and again from red meat."

The high sides of the valley would shut off much of the icy winter winds. There was plenty of grazing for the horses and acres of cottonwood trees, whose inner bark, stripped and chopped up, was also good forage. Quint could work the streams during the fall, *hivernan* for the winter, and be on hand for the early-spring thaw. He could set twelve traps per day instead of the usual six per man, by having the squaw dress and cure the pelts instead of having to take the time off from the trapping to do it himself. All he'd have to do, fall and spring, would be to trap beaver and hunt for meat. Between the seasons he'd have the winter lodge, with plenty of food, tobacco and whiskey, this last rationed, of course, but enough to keep a man fairly satisified. He grinned to himself. Then, of course, there was the young squaw. She was fairly well broken in by now, and always eager. She knew her way amid the buffalo robes on cold nights, with a trick or two of her own devising.

The rising sun warmed the valley. The thin snow on the flats and lower slopes began to melt and trickled in braided fashion down to the rushing streams swollen by the melting snow.

By noon Quint had reached a point where a naked shoulder of rock thrust itself out toward the center of the valley. He gnawed on a piece of jerky while he studied the dams and lodges as far as he could see.

Before the arrival of rapacious man, the only true enemy of the beaver, they had been diurnal, working by day and sleeping by night. Increased hunting pressure over the past twenty years had forced a change in their life habits, so that in the heavily trapped areas they spent their days in the lodges and the nights working on the dams and lodges and storing up their winter food supply. Here, in this remote valley, now seemingly shunned by Indians and white men alike, only a few white men had done any trapping, and that some years past, so the established habits of the big rodents had not changed.

A whiskered nose came gently to the surface on a large pond near Quint's hidden point of observation, followed by a hump of glossy black. The beaver swam toward a nearby lodge, moving ahead of a spreading V of ripples that eventually lapped against the banks of the pond. He waddled up on top of the lodge. He was close to four feet long and would weigh in at about fifty pounds.

Quint whistled softly. "My God," he murmured. "How many brothers and sisters do ye have, laddie?"

In a few moments Quint had his question partially answered. More beaver emerged from the still dark pond and clambered upon the banks. They disappeared into the quiet woods. Faint snufflings and rustlings came to Quint's acute ears, followed by soft sounds of shaking as the busy rodents gnawed away at saplings. Then there came the slow, crashing fall of a tree. In a little while the broad tail and rump of a beaver appeared from out of the underbrush as it dug into the soft ground with its hind feet to drag the sapling toward the pond.

The huge beaver on top of the lodge was meticulously grooming his coat by the use of a split claw located on the inner side of each hind foot, drawling it like a fine-tooth comb through the hair to remove all the parasites, tangled hair and accumulated grit.

Quint could not contain himself. "Clean well your coat, my bucko!" he cried. "Save my squaw that dirty work!"

The beaver slid into the water and smacked his broad flat tail against its surface with the sound of a dry, splitting board. Sleek rounded forms came scuttling through the underbrush to plunge into the pond one after the other, forming overlapping concentric rings on the surface of the water. Before long the surface of the pond was as flat as a sheet of dark metal.

Quint could work the higher-level streams first before the onset of the really cold weather, then work down toward the lower levels until the streams became ice-locked. He anticipated no competition in this remote place.

By late afternoon Quint knew he had found his bonanza. The streams in the adjacent valleys and canyons were alive with beaver, muskrat and otter. There were many bear, deer and foxes. He did a little mental arithmetic. Four or five beaver packs, eighty plews per pack, and prime at that or he was a Dutchman, would bring in about three thousand dollars in cash and trade goods at Bent's Fort, as close as he could figure. There were other furs he could acquire—bear, otter, fox and muskrat and maybe wolf, if there were many of them in his valley. By Jesus, with the woman to help him, there was no reason he couldn't clean up. He could leave the trapping in the spring then, if he had a mind to. With the beaver trade declining, the big money was in trading anyway. Maybe he'd take a crack at it.

There was something else that had been plaguing him the past few years. He had seen men scarcely ten years older than he was, crippling around with rheumatism after only a few years of wading in the icy waters of beaver ponds. If he could get a stake in the spring from the sale of his furs, and invest that stake in trading say, in Mexico, in a few years he could come back to his valley and start a small kingdom for himself there.

The sun passed beyond the western heights and the cold descended immediately. Quint was miles from the foot of the pass by which he had entered the valley. He decided to camp in the branch canyon where he found himself at dusk. He would not risk a fire that night. He had not thoroughly checked the web of valleys and canyons for signs of other humans.

He made his camp amid a jackstraw tangle of fallen timber in a hollow which had filled deeply with fallen leaves from years past. He had his capote and robe for shelter. He gnawed at the last of his jerky and drank cold water from a nearby stream. A light dry snow had begun to fall once the downslope winds stopped blowing for the night. Quint lay bundled in his capote, buried in the leaves, with his robe over the top. Once in a while he nipped at his flask. There would be a gibbous moon that night, peering through low-moving, scattered clouds, but at the moment it was dark as Erebus. These were the times that were hardest mentally on him. There was absolutely nothing for him to do—no cleaning of his weapons, or reading of his father's few trail-worn books he always carried with him, but which were now back in the parfleches on the pack horses where Mountain Woman waited patiently for his return. He wondered idly how many times he had read and reread his tattered copies of the Bible, Scott, Burns, Milton and Shakespeare, not only to himself but to Luke, François and Moccasin as well during the long winters they had *hivernaned* together.

The feeling came slowly and insidiously over him just before the rising of the moon. He had dozed off a little. A man hardly slept sound in unknown and possibly hostile country.

90

He opened his eyes and placed a hand on the cold wood and metal of his Hawken.

Quint sat up, threw back the robe and peered over the top of one of the logs.

Nothing moved except the rising moon, the drifting clouds and falling snow, the trickling stream and the rising and falling of Quint's chest.

The deep-throated howling in several keys came out of the darkness up the canyon. Quint raised his Hawken and cocked it. The howling came again, this time closer. It died away in faint echoes. The hairs prickled on the back of his neck.

Minutes ticked past as the moon rose.

The howling came again, this time behind him, toward the mouth of the canyon.

Cold sweat ran down Quint's sides. He crouched low, peering over the tops of the logs to see if he could skyline the source of the howlings. He set his trigger.

They *must* be wolves. Still, there was an eerie quality about the howlings that didn't seem quite wolflike.

The moon topped the heights to set the peaks agleaming and bathed the valley in a pale-bluish light between the moving clouds.

Quint thought he saw something move in the thick woods across the stream. He wasn't sure; perhaps it was but a shadow compounded of moonlight, falling snow and the lower branches of the trees.

"*The windigo,*" a faint hoarse voice seemed to say just behind Quint.

Quint whirled and fired blindly all in one motion. There was no one there. The crashing discharge of the shot echoed and reechoed through the woods and died away against the heights.

Quint reloaded in a matter of seconds. "Damned fool," he accused himself. It wasn't like him to go off half-cocked like that. The place must be getting to him. Maybe it was the beginning of the feared Folly of the Woods which worked insidiously from within to steal a man's mind, boring away until reason was forever lost and the victim went screaming through the woods to howl at the moon.

Quint cocked and capped the Hawken. He raised his head. Something seemed to move just beyond the outer corner of his left eye. He turned his head to look across the stream to the edge of the dark timber. He wasn't sure of it then, or ever afterward, but whatever it was it vanished into the timber like a puff of thin wind-driven smoke. It wasn't a wolf, or any

91

four-footed creature. It had seemed to stand erect like a man, but partly crouched over as though trying to conceal itself.

"Where I come from up nort', they got spirit condemned to wander wilderness forever," François had related. *"Some say he outcast who once ate human flesh. Always he near water— river, pond, lak mebbe. All night long, winter and summer, he prowl woods looking for victims who wander away from campfires into darkness. No one in that country travel by land or water after dark."*

The valley was now flooded with the beautifully subdued illumination of a moonlight night. The shadows moved gently in a faint wind. The tall silhouettes of the pines and outstanding rock formations stood out gaunt against the light as though cut out of black paper and pasted against a light-colored background. The snow had stopped falling. There was an ethereal quality about the night. An awesome silence enveloped the valley and the canyon. It was a ghostlike landscape frozen in bluish moonlight.

"Tae hell with ye!" Quint shouted.

"Tae hell with ye! Tae hell with ye! Tae hell with ye!" the echoes cried. They died away down the valley.

Quint grinned crookedly. He drank, wiped his mouth and spat to one side. "I'm a bad man to meet in the woods! Shit! There's some would bet I'm already a windigo myself!"

He burrowed down into the leaves and pulled the robe over his head. In a few minutes he was asleep.

He awoke at first dawn light, stiff and cold, and crawled from his bed of leaves. He jumped up and down, shadow-boxed and ran back and forth until his circulation increased. He took a stiff drink to hurry it along.

As the light grew he stepped up on one of the logs and then jumped to the next log, and so on, without touching the ground, scanning the freshly fallen snow on the ground for signs of tracks. Many wolf tracks dotted the snow, some as close as fifty feet from his sleeping place. Wolves had completely surrounded the place while he slept. But had they been there the night before? He hadn't seen them then despite the howling chorus from the shadows.

Quint started down the canyon to the valley when the sun was fully up. Once he stopped in the timber downwind from a young grizzly who was standing up on his hind legs in a meadow boxing with the vapor from his breath. Finally, tired of the game, he dropped to all fours and ambled off across the clean white snow.

92

Thin needles of ice had formed on some of the smaller beaver ponds, pushing out across the still surfaces. Even as Quint walked noiselessly past a pond covered with scum ice a whiskered snout broke through the thin crust and a fine beaver cruised leisurely about breaking it up. In a little while several more beavers appeared. They waddled clumsily out on the shore, dragging their flat tails behind them. They were completely unaware of the man who watched them with delight from behind a nearby tree. They began to harvest aspen and alder branches, taking them to the pool and then diving down to the bottom to implant the branches in the muddy bottom in front of their lodges, to keep the bark green and soft for the winter. Already they had a thicket of the branches implanted in a row almost forty feet long, to be sunk below the deepest ice in the wintertime.

The afternoon of Quint's second day in the valley he found the place where Gabe Pritchett had located his winter lodge. There was a cave behind it, where Gabe had abutted his roof to make an extra room for the lodge. Rock ledges thrust out from the steep slopes to form protecting arms about the lodge area. There was thick timber on both sides of the lodge and a meadow thick with good grass for grazing. The main stream was one hundred yards down the slope, with a waterfall which had eroded a deep pool at its foot. It was a good place. The old man knew his business, Quint thought. There was something else, though. When Quint scraped at the newly fallen snow in the hole about which the lodge had been built he saw that the ground was ominously blackened from fire, and he turned up bits and pieces of charred wood.

He camped there that night. In the early morning he started up the sun-bright pass. He paused halfway up and looked out over the valley. It was as it had been the first day he had seen it. Bright, with clear sunlight and sparkling blue water. The wind was cool and dry and fragrant with the odor of the pines. Deer grazed in open meadows. Here and there bears waddled about. Red-tailed hawks soared high above the tallest trees, resting their motionless pinions on the wind. An eagle sailed the wind currents close against a sheer escarpment.

Quint Kershaw nodded. "This is the place," he murmured.

He cradled his Hawken in the crook of his left arm and started up toward the summit of the pass.

The nomad wind murmured after him—Kershaw's Valley.

ELEVEN

The terrain out beyond the lower reaches of the pass was thick with crusted snow. The sun reflected from it and hurt the eyes. Far out on the snowfield some dark dots moved slowly toward the pass.

Quint focused his telescope on the dots. The sharp clear lens picked out Mountain Woman. She was leading the two saddle horses and had lead-roped the three pack horses to the saddle of one of the riding horses. She was making slow progress breaking a path for the horses through the snow.

Quint raised his rifle and fired it. The heavy discharge boomed along the moutain wall and died away in the distance. He aligned the glass on the woman and her horses. He grinned. She seemed to have vanished until he saw her rifle resting on one of the saddles with her head just behind it pointing the weapon in the general direction of the rifle report.

Quint raised his rifle over his head and moved it back and forth. "Dotawipe! Dotawipe! Dotawipe!" he called. The mountain dutifully backed him up by echoing his voice, "Dotawipe! Dotawipe! Dotawipe! Dotawipe! Dotawipe! Dotawipe! Dotawipe! Dotawipe! Dotawipe!"

Mountain Woman swung up into the saddle of her paint horse. She lashed it with her quirt, forcing it to move against the crusted snow.

"No! No! No!" Quint yelled. "Break a path for the horses!"

It was no use. She kept lashing the paint horse through the knee-deep snow. By the time she reached Quint the knees of some of the horses had been badly cut so that blood ran down their legs to their hoofs and stained the snow.

"Goddam ye!" Quint shouted. "Ye should not have driven the poor beasts through the sharp crusts of the snow! Look at them! Could ye not have broken a path for them?"

She was hurt. "En-Hone! I thought you needed me."

"Ye damned yellowskins don't know how to treat good horses!"

Quint raised a hand as though to strike her. She did not cower away from him. The women of her people were used to brutality from their men. In a sense, they were little more than animals to them.

Quint lowered his hand. He turned away from her. She had meant well. In the weeks they had been together she had developed a devotion to him. He had not wanted that devotion. He hadn't figured on more than a winter squaw for convenience, assistance, self-protection and companionship of a sort. Love had never entered his mind. He had never been sure he could love any woman, even a white woman.

"I thought something had happened to you," she explained.

"Beat her well and often, En-Hone," Buffalo Bellowing had advised Quint. *"She tries to have the spirit of a man at times. That is not as it should be."*

"You've found the place?" she asked hopefully.

He nodded and pointed up the pass. "There."

Her face fell a little. Her hope had not been that he had found it but rather that he had not. At the same time she knew this man well enough to know that if he had not found it he would keep on until he did.

"There are no *tsoaps* there," Quint added. He would not tell her of the wolves that had closed in on him his first night in the valley. Of course they had been wolves! The Shoshonis firmly believed the *tsoaps* haunted the meadows and forests and were ever ready to give warning of the time and departure to the spirit land of those who heard them. In that case no one but the doomed themselves would hear them.

"What did you see or hear?" she asked.

He shook his head. "Nothing."

She held his eyes with hers for a moment and then shrugged. She turned away from him to take up the lead ropes of the pack horses.

Quint led the two saddle horses up into the pass. The sun had melted some of the snow so that thin rivulets of water coursed down the steep slopes and spilled over miniature falls. Mountain Woman looked up often at the broad back of her man. She felt that he had seen or heard something. She knew the valley was not a good place. Buffalo Bellowing knew of the valley although he had never seen it. He had warned En-Hone against it. She looked up at the drifting clouds, shaping animals from them in her mind. She hoped to see one of them like Hoo-Ja the Sage Hen, the Spirit of Good Medicine, but she had no luck.

The sun was slanting far to the west when they reached the crest of the pass. The western side of the valley was already veiled in long shadows while the eastern side was still softly lighted by the sinking sun, which gilded tiny waterfalls of melted snow that ran down the eastern slopes.

Quint turned to Mountain Woman. "This is the place," he said. "Kershaw's Valley."

It was a beautiful place, in some ways like Mountain Woman's homeland, but even more lush and beautiful. En-Hone had told her it was full of game and the many streams were choked by the dams of beaver while the ponds were dotted with their lodges. She shivered a little, although the wind was not cold.

"Well, little one?" Quint asked.

She looked up into his gray eyes. She could never get quite used to them. They were like the ice that covered the streams and ponds in the wintertime, and yet she had seen a warmth in them at times that probably few other people had ever seen, or perhaps recognized.

She had to be honest. *"Ka-shoon-banah.* I don't know."

"Do you want to go back?"

"With you?"

He shook his head. "I stay."

"Then I stay with you."

"I'll give you your freedom if you want to go back."

They stood there for a few moments, the young Shoshoni woman and the tall red-haired Scot, the very epitome of a mountain man who knew the land almost as well as and in some cases maybe better than her people—poles apart in birth, breeding and in ways of thought except for perhaps one thing they did have in common—a love and respect for the land for what it was, not for what it could and would be.

"You are my man now," Mountain Woman said. "I go where you go."

"Perhaps only for the winter?"

There was no expression on her broad face.

"You understood that when you came to my lodge on the Popo Agie," Quint reminded her, not unkindly.

She nodded. "I go where you go," she repeated firmly. She looked up at the sky. "It will soon be dark. The descent of the pass might be dangerous. Shall we camp here for the night or shall we go down, En-Hone?"

Quint led the way down. Once he turned and looked back at her, a slight, short figure bundled in the blanket capote he had given her. He smiled. She would be a good one. She was only sixteen years old, but already a real woman.

The sun was gone when Quint pointed out the place where old Gabe's lodge had been. They would camp there that night. He left her to set up the camp and rode farther into the valley. Half a mile from camp he saw a deer moving through the shadowed timber. He dismounted and approached from downwind. The wind suddenly shifted with the coming of the darkness. The buck scented Quint. He bounded off. The Hawken was raised in a velvety motion. It spat flame and smoke as the sights were aligned on the fleeing quarry. The gun report boomed hollowly through the valley. The deer went down.

By the time Quint got back to the camp Mountain Woman had set up the small eleven-skin lodge and laid out the sleeping robes. She had started a fire and gotten water from the stream. The water was already boiling in the camp kettle.

Quint gutted the deer and hung it in a tree to cool. While Mountain Woman prepared the evening meal, Quint cleaned his Hawken. He drew the load from her new Leman trade rifle and cleaned it too. The sun was long gone and a cold wind swept down from the dark heights.

Quint watched Mountain Woman as she worked about the camp, never idle for a moment. Once she looked sideways at him and smiled. He could not know of the gnawing fear she held pent up within her. She was deathly frightened of this beautiful and remote valley, but she would not let him know by word or expression. This was what *he* wanted; that was enough for her.

TWELVE

The weather warmed the first three days Quint and Mountain Woman were in the valley. They worked from dawn until dusk building their winter lodge. They had not been able to find a better place to site it than the place Gabe Pritchett had used for that same purpose.

Quint's first task was to clear out the hole Gabe had dug and over which he had constructed the lodge. The passage of years had filled the depression with loose earth washed down from the overlooking heights and then covered with dead leaves. He had reached the hard-packed earth at the bottom of the hole and was neatly squaring away the sides.

Mountain Woman came up the slope dragging pieces of branch. She dumped her load and wiped the sweat from her forehead as she surveyed the work Quint had done. "No, En-Hone," she said, shaking her head. "The hole must be circular, as in a tipi."

"What the hell are you talking about?" he demanded. "Every house, shelter or shebang I've ever lived in has been square or rectangular."

She shook her head. "That's a bad way to live. There is no medicine power in a square or rectangle. Everything the People do is done in a circle. That's because the power of the world always works in circles and everything in nature tries to be round."

Quint got out of the hole. He sat down on one of the trees he had felled to use in framing the lodge. The good sun was warm on his back. The air was fresh and cool with a winy pine-scented odor to it. The dry wind cooled the sweat on his forehead.

She placed her hands on her hips and studied him. "Well?" she asked at last.

Quint shrugged. "Show me," he suggested. "I've done all the digging I'm going to do in that damned hole."

She took the spade and attacked the sides of the hole to reform it into an oval—as a tipi truly was, rather than circular.

"You're giving yourself a lot of extra work," he said.

She shook her head. "It's the *right* way. Everything the Power of the World does is in a circle. So Buffalo Bellowing teaches us. The sky is round. Your people have taught us the earth is round like a ball. The stars are round too. Just look at the sky at night. The wind in its great power whirls about destroying everything in its path. Birds make their nests in circles, for theirs is the same religion as ours. The sun comes forth and goes down in a circle. The moon does the same, and it and the sun are round.

"Even the seasons form great circles in their changings. They always come back to where they were. The life of a man or a woman is a circle from childhood to childhood, for when they get old they get childlike again. So it is with everything where power moves. Our tipis are round like the nests of the birds, and these are always set in a circle within the village, like a nest of many nests, where the Great Spirit Tamapah, the Sun-Father and Father of us all, even *you*, En-Hone, meant for us to hatch our children."

Quint eyed her as she again attacked the sides of the hole to round them out. "Well, I'll be goddamned," he murmured. He had never thought of it that way. Coming from a *woman* too, and she hardly more than a girl.

They revetted the sides of the oval-shaped hole with branches and staked them into place. Forked uprights were planted in the ground just outside the circumference of the hole. Quint cut lengths of saplings to build the outer walls resting against the forked uprights. Saplings were laid from the forked uprights to a central pole planted in the center of the hole. Smaller saplings were placed across those that ran from the uprights to the central pole. A thick layer of grass was placed on top of the saplings, followed by a sheet of old tent canvas Quint had brought from the rendezvous. The canvas in turn was covered by a layer of puddled mud covered over with a thick layer of dried leaves which were pressed down into the mud.

The rear of the shebang, as Quint called it, rested against the undercurved front of the cave, which was under the steep slope above the lodge. Quint cut several trees and staked them out above the junction of the lodge and the front of the cave so that water would run off to the sides.

Mountain Woman had no knowledge of a chimney, so Quint constructed one of sticks and clay. The top of the chimney was close to the ledge over the cave, so that the smoke would rise close to the face of the towering rock wall above the lodge site, making it practically invisible to anyone looking that way from a distance.

Quint cut several small windows into the side and front walls and covered them with sheets of thinly scraped hide for panes. The windows were made purposely small to keep out any animal marauders, particularly bears. He built a wide bunk by resting crosspieces on forked sticks driven into the floor. Mountain Woman then laced and crisscrossed strong bark cord from one side to the other and then from top to bottom to provide a springy surface. She layered this with pine branches, butts down, for a mattress and covered them with two buffalo robes sewn together.

Quint built a peeled-pole corral for the horses and then extended saplings from the rock overhang to form a shelter for them during the bitter weather. He spent hours cutting firewood, which Mountain Woman stacked thickly on each side of and against the front of the lodge as added protection against the wind. She stored their baggage parfleches filled with dried meat, pemmican, staples, extra clothing and other necessities back in the cave.

Once the lodge was finished Quint left the final touches to Mountain Woman and started out on a more detailed exploration of his valley. Every day he was further amazed at the richness of it. Everything he needed or would ever want was there in great plenty—beaver, other furbearing animals, game of all kinds, wood for fires and for building, water and pasturage. There would likely be buffalo, at least in the milder weather, in the lower country to the south and east.

Here, in time, he could make his own little kingdom. It was only a matter of time before a great westward movement would begin in the United States. The young and bustling nation would need room for expansion and development. Men had long been talking about something called "Manifest Destiny," the God-given right of the Americans to press on to the west and southwest and take it for their own. When that time came the day of the mountain men would be over; the passing of an era.

"And then what?" Quint asked himself as he rode the

sorrel through his valley. He was only twenty-four years old, with a lifetime of experience behind him, but experience mostly in beaver trapping and fighting Indians. The trapping had seen its best days. He knew, deep within himself, that he was not quite ready for personal exile yet, even in this seeming earthly paradise.

"What did you see or hear?" Mountain Woman had asked him the day he had met her at the foot of the pass. He knew she had not believed him when he had told her he had not seen or heard anything. Oddly enough, the first night he had spent in his valley had been the only one during which he had heard those howlings. That didn't mean that wolves were not about. At least he *hoped* they were about. He grinned wryly. If they were not, what was it he had heard, and vaguely seen? He put the thought from his mind. It was a natural habitat for wolves. He had seen their tracks. Therefore, they had to be wolves. It was as simple as that. And yet . . . he forced the eerie thought from his mind.

Quint rode toward the lodge after two days of exploration at the southerly reaches of the main valley and the adjacent smaller valleys and canyons. It was dusk. He scented the woodsmoke long before he saw the lodge. The faintest trace of smoke lay against the rocky heights behind and above the lodge. The horses grazed in the meadow. Quint unsaddled his sorrel and turned him loose. He carried his rifle and saddle toward the lodge and as he did so scented the odor of cooking food. He paused on the slope between the stream and the lodge and looked down his valley.

"En-Hone," she said quietly from behind him.

Quint turned. She was wearing the beautiful mountain-sheep dress she had worn the night he had taken her to his lodge. Her hair hung in two glossy braids in front of her shoulders. She had painted her cheeks and the parting of her hair with vermilion. He noticed the scent of crushed dried wildflowers about her, warmed by her body.

Quint shook his head in admiration. "Ye're aye the bonnie lassie, Dotawipe."

"Do I please you, En-Hone?"

He nodded. "Aye, lassie. Greatly."

They had not had intercourse with each other since a night on the trail at least ten days past. They had been too busy and too tired the following nights for anything but exhausted sleep.

Quint smiled. "Tonight?" He nodded. He turned and looked

down the long valley. "For tomorrow I set my first traps."

She fell asleep in his arms that night like a tired child after a busy day. He lay awake for a long time staring up at the low ceiling thinking about her and her place in his future. It would depend much on what he planned to do. If he stayed in the valley and made it his home she would be the greatest of assets to him. If he left the valley in the spring with his packs of plews for trade at Taos or Bent's Fort, it would be to seek his fortune elsewhere, preferably in New Mexico. In that case she would be a deterrent to him. He knew her own desire. She wanted to return to her own people in the spring, with him, of course, there to spend the rest of his life. That would never be. He wondered now, as he had many times in the past weeks, if he had made the wisest of decisions in taking her into his lodge.

Once during the night he woke up suddenly. He threw aside the warm robe. He shivered in the damp chill as he picked up his Hawken and opened the door. He stepped outside. The moon was on the wane. The valley lay quiet with an almost unnatural stillness. He wondered why he had awakened. There seemed to be nothing to be alarmed about. Nothing. Still . . . He shook his head and went back to bed.

The beaver, *Castor canadensis,* had an almost perfect domain in the great valley Quint Kershaw had decided to make his own. Countless generations of beaver had constructed complexes of main and secondary dams and canals all bound together in a masterpiece of aquatic engineering. This was where Quint was to begin his fall trapping season.

Quint reached the trapping area in the cold darkness before dawn. He had one of his lead horses carrying two hide parfleche panniers each containing six folded beaver traps. The beaver were ready for the icebound winter. Their lodges had been sealed, leaving only a small air vent in the top. Their winter larders of aspen, alder, poplar and willow stalks were stored underwater by means of spearing their ends into the muddy pond bottom and weighting them down with rocks to form thickets as much as thirty to forty feet long and five feet high on the average.

Quint rapidly cut a supply of trap stakes, or float sticks, from hard dead wood and a like number of still-succulent willow wands for bait. He stood on a trap to depress the powerful springs so that the catches held them down. He stripped off his buckskin trousers and rubbed his legs well with beaver grease to mask the man scent and ward off the chill of the water. He set the trap about three inches below the water surface by scraping the icy mud together to get the right height for the trap required for freedom of action of the jaws. He left a hollow place under the trip, or pan, to allow for its fall, then covered the trap iron, including the pan, with soil sifted from his fingers and allowed to settle naturally. He ran out the six-foot trap chain, passed a trap stake through the ring at the end of it and made it fast to the ring with a piece of strong cord, thus making sure the stake would act as a float stick still attached to the trap if a trapped and struggling beaver managed to pull it loose from the bottom. He thrust the end of the stake into the bottom mud and hammered it down with his hatchet. The use of such hard wood for the trap stake would prevent a stray beaver from gnawing on it for food.

Quint thrust the butt end of a peeled willow wand into the bank and arched it back over the trap. He opened his bait bottle, a buffalo horn tip scraped thin, and smeared some of the sticky, granular castoreum from within it on the small end of the willow wand hanging ten to twelve inches or more just above the water-covered trap.

The trap would be sprung when the beaver stood on the pan as it lifted its nose toward the lure. Once the jaws snapped shut, the frightened pain-stricken animal would plunge for the safety of the deeper water, taking the trap with it. The weight of the trap would hold the animal under-water for the two or three minutes it took for it to drown.

Quint worked steadily and efficiently setting his traps. Now and again he would curse softly under his breath. Christ, the water was cold, and this was only his first day of the fall season. Before the streams and ponds were ice-locked he'd have to go through the same chilling, agonizing ordeal hundreds of times, only to start all over again in the early spring when the beaver winter plews were at their thickest and finest. By the time it was fully daylight he had set his first six traps. He was chilled to the bone and soaking wet from the waist down. His hands were blue and wrinkled with the cold, and his privates seemed to have shrunk and shriv-eled up into his groin. Most of the older trappers he knew were badly crippled with rheumatism and arthritis from the thousands of hours they had spent wading in such icy streams. That would not be his fate. After the spring season he would be through with beaver trapping forever. Of course, he had said that every fall and spring season handrunning for the past four or five years.

He rode south to set his second set of six traps. In years past, like most trappers, he had always set six to eight traps. Six was about the average for a man working alone, who had to skin and dress the pelts as well. With Mountain Woman to do the dressing and curing, as well as the other menial chores, while he did the trapping and the hunting, he could afford to run two traplines of six traps each. That meant he could likely double the usual season's take.

When his last trap was set for the day he spent the rest of the time exploring, poking into places he had not fully scouted as yet. He wanted to know every aspect of his valley and its potential; he was looking for a site for a permanent home should he decide to settle in the valley—Kershaw's Valley.

In the dying light of the late afternoon he started back toward the lodge. It was well after dusk when he reached it. He sat on the floor, with his back against a willow-withe rest made by Mountain Woman, and ate well of venison haunch. After he had eaten she filled his Dublin pipe for him and lighted it. She then sat down opposite him and returned to her work of making a backrest for herself.

Quint idly watched her deft fingers as she wove the backrest. "I saw no *tsoaps* this day," he said. "There's nothing to fear in this valley."

"None that you saw," she corrected.

He would not admit to her that more than a few times that day he had had the feeling that he was being watched. He had heard things for which he had no accounting. Nothing greatly out of the ordinary, of course, but still that for which he could not account. There was always the feeling of a *presence*. A wolf, or bear, perhaps, but not a human. Still, he wasn't sure of that either.

He studied Mountain Woman. She seemed tireless, but then she had the boundless energy of her extreme youth. He himself never felt tired no matter how hard and long he worked. He had never questioned this ability of his. It was sufficient that he did have it. Without it, he would not have survived long in the mountains.

"How was the trapping?" she asked.

"Who knows yet? It should be good. I'll find out later on this evening."

"You're going out again?"

He nodded. "There will be a moon. I'll check the first trapline and return here with the beaver."

"And the second line?"

"I'll leave here long before dawn and reset my first line, then check the second line and reset that."

Her great eyes seemed to slide sideways as she looked toward the door of the lodge. She always kept her loaded rifle close beside the door next to an improvised spear she had made from a butcher knife and a stout sapling.

"Ye'll be all right alone, lassie," he soothed her.

"Let me ride with you."

Quint shook his head.

"Why not?" she demanded. Her fear of being left alone was making her bold.

"Damn ye! I don't want to be encumbered wi' a woman!"

"But you said there was nothing to fear in this valley."

"No!" he roared.

"Please, En-Hone."

"A woman's place is in the lodge. It's not that there is anything to fear out there. It's just that ye'd be in the way. If ye won't obey me, woman, there is still time for ye to leave before the pass fills with snow."

Quint shrugged into his capote and slid his flask of whiskey into a pocket. He turned toward her. "And I'll no be coming back this night now!" he snapped. From the pile on the bed he took a robe for the night, picked up his rifle and left the lodge.

The moon was up when he checked the first set of traps. They yielded five prime beaver. The sixth trap had been sprung. The jaws had closed on a beaver's leg, but the desperate animal had chewed through its own leg to free itself. It always gave Quint a bit of a turn when he saw such a thing.

Quint took the six traps to the next pond over and reset them. He skinned his five beaver by the light of the moon, first removing two fat tails for future roasting.

When Quint had finished skinning the five beaver he rode south to his second trapline. It yielded three big beaver. By the time he finished resetting his traps and skinning the three carcasses the moon was almost gone.

Rather than return to the lodge and a silent woman he decided to spend the night amid another jackstraw pile of fallen timber. He bundled in his capote and burrowed into a thick bed of dry leaves and drew the robe over on top of himself.

Once during the night the paint pony snorted. Quint rose quickly and silently from his bed of leaves with his Hawken cocked and ready. He stood there scanning the dark timber, scouting with his eyes, nose and ears. He saw nothing, smelled nothing, heard nothing and felt nothing out of the ordinary. He was letting the bloody story of the valley get to him.

He was up before the dawn and returned up the valley in broad daylight, bypassing his first set of traps. Mountain Woman had little to say when he reached the lodge. She roasted the beaver tails before she set to work on the eight plews he had brought back. She had set up a graining block. She scraped the pelts of all fat, blood, membrane and tissue and then worked them on the graining block. She then stretched the plews on willow hoops and hung them from tree branches to dry.

Within two weeks the lodge was surrounded by dozens of the reddish-brown circles of drying plews. Deer hides had been pegged out for cleaning and drying. Meat dried on racks in front of the lodge where Mountain Woman could easily keep an eye out for four-footed predators and thieves.

Each time Mountain Woman was alone at the lodge was a time of terror for her. She could not define her terror, but that only made it worse. A known enemy is feared less than one that is unknown. She hated the place. It was as beautiful as, and perhaps in its own way more beautiful than, some of the mountain meadows and valleys in the country of the Seeds-kee-dee Agie and Wind River Mountains, but she had a lingering horror of the place. She wondered about En-Hone. He was absorbed in his work and did it with a discipline she found hard to believe. No Shoshoni male would have worked the way he did.

There was something else that worried Mountain Woman. It added to her terror and gnawed at her, especially on the long dark nights when she was alone in the lodge. It was with her always; during the day she kept so busy she sometimes forgot about it, but it was always there lingering in the back of her mind waiting for a chance to haunt her. The more beaver he trapped that fall and in the spring, the quicker he would be gone from the valley, and the less would be her chances of staying with him, or having him return with her to her people. She had not deluded herself when she had left her people to go with him. She, herself, could be welcomed back alone; there was no dishonor in what she had done. It was true that some mountain men—not too many perhaps, out of the majority of them—had taken Indian wives of various tribes and then had come to live with her people as one of the tribe. It was a slender sprout of hope she had always nurtured, ever since she had known she meant to become En-Hone's woman, one way or another, for better or for worse.

THIRTEEN

November 1837—Month of the Freezing Moon.

It was the middle of November. Snow thickly mantled the peaks and sheathed the slopes down below the timberline. The mornings were sharp with frost. The streams and ponds were covered with thin and brittle ice through which Quint had to break his way to set his traps. He was working farther afield every week. He usually stayed out the nights in order to save time. He had taken to adding his four spare traps to the usual twelve to gain as many plews as he could before the valley became winter-locked. It was murderous, bone-chilling work, but the working time of the fall season was running out.

He thought often of the old-timers as he worked, those veteran trappers whose joints were stiff with rheumatism. Old-timers? Some of them were still in their middle thirties, and few of them were over forty years of age. As yet Quint had no great problem in that respect but there were mornings out in the field when he awoke in the predawn darkness and felt the beginnings of stiffness. He had to work it out before he began his trap setting only to aggravate it still further when he waded into the streams.

One dark and dismal dusk he set his last trap and then waded to the bank. Cold mud and icy water dripped from his hands and ran down his buckskin-clad legs. He placed his hands in the small of his back and stretched himself. If the weather held as it was and didn't get colder, and if the heavy snowfalls held off, he should reach his estimated quantity of fall plews within two weeks.

A cold, searching wind swept down the darkening valley from the snow-mantled heights. Quint shivered in the blast as he shrugged into his thick capote and pulled the hood up about his head. He opened his flask and drank deeply. He stood there, a lean lath of a man, looking about his domain. He felt good, despite his arduous work and the chilling cold of water and air.

The first dry flakes of snow touched his face. Soon they came swirling out of the darkness and began to cover the ground and settle on his capote. The valley was quiet except for the faint moaning of the wind.

Quint emptied his flask, belted his capote tighter, slid his Hawken into its buckskin cover, then swung up into his cold saddle. He touched the sorrel with his heels and rode north.

The sorrel splashed through the thin ice of the shallow stream and got out of the water on the far bank amid a thick stand of timber. He began to trot eagerly toward the camp in anticipation of forage and shelter. He suddenly reared, half unseating Quint, and neighed in sheer fright. The huge dark shape burst out of the brush with a ferocious grunting and growling, intent on instant murder. One swipe of the grizzly's nine-inch-wide paw knocked Quint from the horse and sent his Hawken flying into the brush. The next blow caught the horse alongside the head and staggered him. The shaggy fury closed in on the horse, striking at it with curved, six-inch razor-sharp claws.

Quint rolled aside out of the way of the uneven combat. He thrust his right hand inside his capote and drew his pistol. He cocked it and fired up into the bear's belly. He drew his knife, but before he could use it the bear shifted its stance and planted one of his feet on Quint's right calf, crushing it to the ground. Half a ton of ravening beast pinned him helplessly. Blood from the horse's wounds sprayed through the air and struck Quint. He could not free himself from under the grizzly's foot, which was forcing the leg down into the thick mat of leaves.

The horse fell sideways, lashing out with its hooves at the bear. The bear shifted to renew its attack on the sorrel and in so doing removed its foot from Quint's leg. Quint gripped a sapling and pulled himself to his feet. He struck out with the

108

knife at the dim shape of the grizzly, driving it home anywhere he could. Each time the keen blade sank through the thick coat, tough hide and iron muscles covered with layers of fat, the bear roared insanely, but he kept on savaging the sorrel.

Quint closed in on the bear, sinking the blade up to Green River with each powerful stroke. The bear turned toward him. The sorrel struggled to his feet and crashed away through the brush and timber, heading for the camp. The grizzly's first murderous swipe at Quint went just over his head as he ducked and struck a tree. Bark flew. Quint crouched and stabbed the knife upward into the thick muscular layer and fat of the bear's belly. He felt it strike and grate against bone again and again.

Quint was hurled back by a paw blow which caught him on the left shoulder. The claws tore through the capote, buckskin jacket and wool shirt to score deeply into the flesh. Quint rolled from under the bear and into thick brush. The bear lunged toward him but did not see him right away. The knife came up into his belly and he staggered a little, spewing a spate of blood down over Quint.

Quint got to his feet. The grizzly was on him instantly. One paw swiped out. The tips of the claws bit into his left cheek just below the eye and scraped the cheekbone as the razorsharp talons raked down to the point of the jaw. A half inch closer and the grizzly would have excised the left half of Quint's face with the precision of a surgeon's scalpel.

Quint fell back, half stunned from the force of the blow and the excruciating pain. His back met a tree, and before he could slip sideways the roaring beast closed in on him again. Old Ephraim's short, powerful forelimbs went about the tree in an effort to hug Quint to his chest in an embrace that meant certain death. Quint managed to present his knife at belly height. As the bear closed his grip he forced the knife into his own belly, aided by Quint's pushing in on the handle.

Quint began to black out. This was the end.

The rifle roared just behind the grizzly where Mountain Woman had placed the Leman's muzzle hard against the beast's spine. The bear jerked spasmodically. A moment later Mountain Woman fired Quint's Hawken into the bear's back. Blood poured from the grizzly's mouth and nose as he staggered back and swayed sideways.

Quint closed in on the beast, as savage in his atavistic fury as the bear had been in his attack. Again and again he plunged the bloody knife deep into the bear wherever he could find an opening. Old Ephraim shuddered and then toppled sideways to land with a crash at Quint's feet.

Quint looked across the fallen giant. Half of his face was a mass of blood and torn flesh. His white capote had been dyed blood red.

"En-Hone!" Mountain Woman shrieked.

He grinned crookedly. "Aye, lassie! Am I no a bonny fighter?" he cried. He fell forward unconscious over Old Ephraim.

Mountain Woman dropped the smoking Hawken. She knelt beside Quint and wiped the blood from his face. She pressed her head against his chest to listen for his heartbeat. He was still alive.

Mountain Woman ran back through the timber to get the paint horse. She rode it bareback to where Quint lay. The horse shied and blew in fright at the odor of the grizzly and the blood splattered all over the area. She struck the frightened horse alongside his head with the butt of her rifle to quieten him and then dragged Quint to his side. She shook Quint to enough consciousness so that he managed to get to his feet with her help, and then drop over the horse's back. She ran back through the timber leading the paint and dumped Quint on the ground in front of the lodge. She dragged him inside inch by inch out of the thickly falling snow.

Mountain Woman rolled Quint over on his back and cut the coat, jacket and shirt from his body. There was no expression on her face as she saw the bloody havoc the grizzly had created on his face and left shoulder. She packed matted beaver hair on the wounds to staunch and absorb the bleeding and bandaged it in place.

Mountain Woman rode back through the timber to retrieve the rifles and Quint's knife and pistol. She stood for a moment, held in awe, looking down on the dead giant, and then she rode back to the lodge.

Quint opened his eyes and looked up into Mountain Woman's face. He smiled faintly. "Have I died and gone tae heaven, lassie? Is it an angel I see?"

She shook her head. She had no idea what an angel was but she knew it must be a white woman.

"Get the medicine, like a good wee lassie," Quint whispered hoarsely. He pointed to the oval-shaped keg of Monongahela. She filled a cup and was about to pour it on the bandages when Quint stopped her. "I'll admit 'tis antiseptic,

110

lassie, but it will do me far more guid inside of me than on this tough skin of mine." He drained the cup and shook his head a little at the powerful impact of the whiskey. He held the cup out to her. She refilled it. He drained it again. He crawled to the bunk and clambered up on it. He fell back heavily and passed out again.

FOURTEEN

December 1837—Night of the Wolves.

The snow was falling thickly. The stream was a trickle of water through early winter's quiet shroud of ice and snow. Three drowned beaver lay in a stiffening pile on the snowy bank. Two of the six set traps had been empty and unsprung. The sixth trap was not in position but its stick floated on the dark still surface of the pond.

Mountain Woman piled the five traps on the bank. She was soaking wet from the hips down and soon the water would freeze on her leggings and moccasins, encasing her legs and feet in a crust of ice. The light was beginning to fail. The trap under the water was the last of the twelve she had set the day before. She had tallied three beaver from the first setting of six traps, for a score of six in all, unless there was a beaver in the trap out in the pond. She had been working the traplines alone for the past ten days while Quint recovered from his wounds and the great loss of blood he had suffered.

Mountain Woman stepped into the water and felt her feet sink into the stiff icy mud. Halfway to the float stick she sank down almost to her knees. A flash of panic went through her mind. If she got mired there would be no one to pull her free.

At last she broke free from the mud. She half waded and half swam toward the float stick. She was stiffening all over her body almost to a state of numbness. She caught the float stick at last and drew it behind her as she swam toward the nearest bank. It dragged heavily, so she was sure there was a beaver in the trap. She crawled out onto the bank and drew the trap out of the water. It held a small beaver, but it was better than nothing, and in any case she would not have dared return to the lodge without the valuable trap. She did not have the skill of En-Hone in setting the traps. He had a mysterious extra sense which he used. He called it a sixth sense; she called it good medicine. It was probably a combination of both of them.

She pried the trap open and removed the beaver. She would cross the pond by means of the dam. She didn't have the courage to enter that almost frozen water again. She looked across the dark still surface of the pond to the far bank. She started and got quickly to her feet. Something obscured by the falling snow had moved through the timber beyond her tethered paint horse.

Something moved again, this time closer to the horse. *Wolves!* She snatched up the trap and the beaver and ran to the dam. She had left her rifle leaning against a tree beside the pile of beaver. All she had with her was her sheath knife.

A wolf appeared farther down the bank. He trotted toward the horse. He hardly glanced toward Mountain Woman, just as though he felt no harm in her. The horse reared back and snapped its tether. He plunged into the timber with two wolves close at his heels. One solid kick from his hind legs flung one of the wolves sideways into the snowy brush. The paint disappeared into the timber, neighing in fear, accompanied by a vicious snarling of the wolves.

Mountain Woman dumped her traps into the pannier, then slung the pannier over her shoulder. She grabbed her rifle. Quint had taught her to keep the hammer at half cock with a cap on the nipple ready for instant firing. She checked the cap.

The paint horse crashed through the brush back into the clearing where Mountain Woman stood. She raised her rifle and full-cocked it all in one motion. She squeezed the trigger as the sights lined up on one of the wolves. The heavy slug struck the snarling beast in the head. He fell sideways into the brush. His mate turned and ran. Mountain Woman grabbed the paint's hackamore. His left flank was bleeding from some superficial clawings, but he seemed more frightened than badly hurt. She slung the trap pannier over the horse's rump opposite the other pannier. She tried to mount, but the animal was too skittish. The wolves were still close by in the timber waiting for another chance.

Mountain Woman reloaded her Leman. Her fingers were stiff and cold, but she managed to ram the load well home.

112

She placed two extra bullets in her mouth as Quint had taught her to do, and led the horse along the back, keeping a wary eye back over her shoulder as she did so. The wolves were still back there, shadowy and elusive. They would not give up. They had drawn hot blood from the horse and the taste had been good.

It was very dark in the timber. The snow was now falling thickly, obscuring Mountain Woman's vision. Once a wolf howled fifty yards behind her, and then it was quiet again.

The snow was cold against her face. Her feet were like chunks of ice and her legs were stiff and wooden. Fear rode her back. How many wolves were there? Were there enough to corner her and the horse and bring both of them down? Wolves liked to eat from quarry that was still alive. . . .

How far was it to the lodge? Three miles? Perhaps four? The snowfall was dying away almost as quickly as it had begun. The woods looked all alike and the snow effaced any landmarks. The moon would soon be rising.

Mountain Woman halted. She stood there listening. The night was deathly still.

She hurried on. Each step was a torment but she could not stop. Her only safety would be in reaching the lodge. She could release the horse and let the wolves have him in order to gain time for herself, but then she'd have to abandon the valuable traps as well. En-Hone would not like that.

She began to feel exhaustion. She had hardly slept, or even rested, in the past three or four days. They had run together, day and night, so that she hadn't been sure just how much time had passed. Now the strain, coupled with hardship and the cold, was going to bring her down.

She slogged her way across a wide meadow which she thought she recognized. It was only half a mile or perhaps less from the lodge. At least she *thought* it was . . . "hoped" might be a better word.

The moon was rising.

Mountain Woman staggered and went down on one knee. She stayed there for a few moments and then used the rifle to aid her in getting up. She had to rest. There was a tree that had fallen and now rested at an angle against another tree. She reached the tree and then slapped the paint pony as hard as she could across the rump with the buttstock of her rifle. The horse buck-jumped and then plunged into the timber accompanied by a raucous jangling of the traps in their panniers. In a little while the sound died away in the direction of the camp.

Mountain Woman turned. Her breath caught in her throat.

Three dark low shapes were moving stealthily across the meadow toward her.

She scrambled stiffly up the snow-covered tree trunk and perched with her numbing feet against a branch stub six feet from the ground. She rested her rifle across her lap and full-cocked the big hammer.

The moon rose, slowly bathing the valley in pale cold light. By its light Mountain Woman saw six wolves sitting in a crescent shape not fifty yards from her with mouths open and tongues lolling, almost as though they were grinning at her predicament.

Quint awoke to the tattoo of hoofs on the frost-hard ground and a metallic jangling sound. Mountain Woman had returned.

"Thank God," he murmured.

He had not wanted her to go out and work the traplines, but she had been insistent and finally adamant about the matter. His conscience had bothered him then, although he did not tell her why. It was painful enough to admit to himself. He didn't want to take her from the valley in the spring when he went to Taos or Bent's Fort with his harvest of plews. They were *his* plews, not *theirs*. Was she persistent in running the traplines because she wanted to secure her position in the matter? On the other hand, perhaps she had already secured herself more than he cared to admit to himself by her hard unrelenting work in the camp and in dressing the pelts. He could never have amassed as many plews as he had now without her help.

Quint sat up suddenly. Where was she? He stifled a groan as his healing wounds drew up. Christ, but it was cold! He no longer heard the thudding of hoofs on the ground. She should be on her way from the corral to the lodge by now. He listened. It was deathly quiet.

"Dotawipe!" Quint called.

He thrust his legs out from under the robes and reached down for his moccasins.

The faint howling of wolves came from somewhere just south of the camp.

Quint grabbed his Hawken, bullet pouch and powderhorn. He thrust his pistol and sheath knife under his belt and limped outside. The snow had stopped and a pale moon was

114

rising over the mountain to the east. He went to the corral. The paint pony stood trembling at the gate, the trap panniers hanging over his back. Blood stained his left flank.

Quint dumped the panniers on the ground and swung up onto the paint's back. He drummed his heels against its sides but it wouldn't move.

"Goddam ye! Move!" Quint roared. He brought his right fist smashing down atop the pony's head and dug his heels into its sides at the same time. He *moved!*

The wolves had moved closer to the trees. The first of them suddenly launched himself upward. Mountain Woman reversed her rifle and smashed the metal-shod butt down on the wolf's head. It was only a glancing blow. The wolf flung himself sideways. The next wolf leaped. She fired at short range and missed, but it was enough to make the wolves more cautious. They began to circle the two trees, moving easily and swiftly around them so that Mountain Woman had to constantly look to her rear and then to either side to make sure none of them was attacking.

She reloaded slowly and clumsily. She rammed the bullet home on top of the powder charge and then fumbled for a percussion cap. She dropped two of them before she managed to seat one on the nipple. She full-cocked the rifle and aimed it at one of the wolves. She didn't see the wolf who had worked his way under the tree on which she was perched. He leaped upward and dragged his fangs down one of her dangling legs, ripping through the frozen moccasin and scoring her ankle. She dropped the rifle. It discharged as it struck the ground and the bullet sang thinly off into the air.

Mountain Woman drew up her legs and perched on the slippery surface of the slanted tree. She drew out her knife.

The valley was now completely moonlit.

The wolves drew back into their waiting circle. They seemed to know she was virtually unarmed now, except for the knife. They watched the bright blood drip from her ankle to the white snow on the ground. One of them, the boldest of all, crept close to the tree and then lapped at the bloody snow, keeping one cautious eye on Mountain Woman as he did so. Then he backed away, watching her steadily.

The rush came so quickly she did not expect it. They all charged toward the tree. Suddenly a rifle cracked flatly. The ball struck one of the wolves in the head, killing him instantly. Quint rode out of the timber. He fired his pistol to wound another wolf. The butt of his Hawken smashed the head of a third wolf. He turned the horse and rode in among the remaining wolves, swinging his heavy rifle, crushing a skull here and breaking a bone there, until the last two wolves began to run for shelter across the open meadow. That was a mistake. Quint swiftly reloaded the Hawken. He fired. The leading wolf went ass-over-teakettle in front of the other. The second wolf could not stop. He crashed into the first wolf and went down, then regained his footing. By the time he reached the edge of the meadow the rifle flatted off again and he died there.

Quint finished off the wounded wolves with his knife. He looked up at mountain Woman and grinned. She fainted dead away and fell into his arms. He lifted her across the back of the paint pony and then quickly reloaded both rifles.

The night was quiet again. The snow started to fall again through the soft moonlight.

Quint brought her back to the lodge and staunched the wound in her ankle. He stripped her to the buff and rubbed her down with beaver grease, then placed her in the bed and covered her with all the robes they had. He built up a roaring fire, took a hefty belt of the Monogahela and then left the lodge bundled in his capote and fur cap.

Quint got the three pack horses out of the corral and rode one of them, leading the two others, back to the meadow where the wolves lay dead on the snow. They were already stiffening. He loaded them onto the skittish pack horses and then returned to the lodge. He dumped the carcasses in front of the lodge and then put the horses away.

One by one he hauled the wolves into the lodge and began to skin them as rapidly as he could. He dumped the first naked carcasses down the slope near the stream. When he returned to the lodge Mountain Woman was out of the bed and sharpening her skinning knife.

"These are some of the finest and thickest wolf pelts I've ever seen," Quint said conversationally. He eyed Mountain Woman as he spoke.

Mountain Woman nodded and made her first incision. After a time she looked up at him. They smiled at each other.

FIFTEEN

December 1837—Moon of the Popping Trees.

The snow had fallen thickly for three days and nights. It lay on top of the frozen streams and beaver ponds and mantled the dark evergreens, bringing their laden branches low to the ground. The slopes and heights of the valley were covered in white, with here and there windblown shoulders of pinkish-red rock standing free from the snow in dark contrast to the universal whiteness about them. When the snow had finally stopped falling the freezing cold had set in like a grip of steel. An awesome quiet came over the land with a stillness that should bring peace until spring.

Quint Kershaw lay alone on the bed in the lodge. He watched the play of firelight on the low ceiling overhead. A raging fever had struck him down after his exposure, weak from his wounds as he had been, during the night he had fought the wolves to save Mountain Woman. Old Ephraim's thick brown-yellow pelt lay over Quint's legs. Mountain Woman had skinned the huge beast alone, using a rope and horse to turn him over. Mountain Woman had cut out the six-inch claws to fashion a necklace for Quint. He hadn't wanted it, but she had insisted that he wear it. Had he not killed one of the greatest killers of all? Aw-ha-pit-woodha, the grizzly bear? He protested that he alone had not killed the animal, but she declared that her people would never believe that she, a mere *woman,* had done such a remarkable deed as killing a grizzly.

It was cold. Jesus, it was cold! And she was out in the dusk feeding the horses and putting them into the shelter. She covered each of them with a robe lest they freeze to death that night. She had been gone a long time. Since the night she had been attacked by the wolves she had been more careful with the horses. She had raised the sides of the corral and strengthened it. At night she drove the horses into the stout shelter against the rock ledge and then closed and barred the door. If, during the day or night, she heard wolves, no matter how far away they were doing their lonely howling, she'd go outside and fire her rifle to keep them at their distance. Twice she had made clean hits, wounding one wolf and killing another. They could not afford to lose the horses. They were indispensable for getting the packs of plews out of the valley and to the traders.

Quint dozed off. A gun cracked flatly somewhere outside the lodge and not far from the corral from the sound of it. Quint was out of bed in an instant. He staggered a little in his weakness as he snatched up his rifle and cocked it. He yanked the door open and stepped out into the bitter cold.

"Dotawipe! Dotawipe! Dotawipe!" Quint shouted.

There was no answering call.

Quint cursed savagely as he limped through the crusty snow toward the corral. Another shot split the quietness.

Mountain Woman came running from the corral. "What is it, En-Hone?" she cried. "What are you doing out of bed?"

"What were ye shooting at?"

She stared at him in surprise. "I wasn't shooting."

"Dammit! Someone was! Are ye deaf?"

She studied him uncomprehendingly for a moment and then she burst into that merry tinkling laughter of hers that always sounded like tiny silver bells to Quint. *"Wi-ag-gait!* Foolish One! It is the Great Brown Bear of the Mountains breathing his icy breath on the trees to split them."

He shook his head. He should have known that it was the bone-chilling cold, splitting the trees. "Does he have to do it at night?" he demanded. He grinned.

"Get back into bed! Do you want to die out here?"

"Have ye fed the horses?"

She nodded. "Of course."

"Then I'll go back to bed if ye come with me."

She turned her head, a little modestly. "I will after I cook the supper," she promised.

"Ye had better, else we might not survive this night of bitter cold."

Quint got back into bed and watched her while she cooked. She chattered away about how well she had taken care of the horses and of how good they looked. She did not know when Quint dozed off.

He lay with his head resting against the back bar of the bed, with a buffalo robe across his shoulders and the thick pelt of the grizzly across his legs. She remembered how many knife holes she had sewn up in that same pelt. But if En-Hone had put his mark on the hide of Ah-ha-pit-woodha, the great beast had marked En-Hone for life, for starting just under the left eye and running down his left cheek into his reddish beard was a raised, angry red scar which time would never erase. He would wear that scar to the grave.

Quint opened his eyes as she placed a bowl of stew in front of him. She leaned over and kissed him. He could feel the pressure of her full breasts against his chest. He began to get interested. He tried to draw her to him, but she laughed and returned to her fire, looking coyly sideways at him as she did so.

She was a marvel, Quint admitted to himself. She was a tireless worker and an avid lover. She had managed to keep the camp going when he had been trapping. She had taken over the trapping when he had been injured. She had tended his wounds and treated him with remedies she had learned from her people. In her "spare" time she cured the hides and worked them into suppleness, from which she made moccasins, clothing and robes.

"Get in here with me," he ordered when he finished his food.

"There is work to be done, En-Hone." It was her usual ploy in the game they sometimes played.

He scowled at her. "Do ye want me to get out of this bed in the cold?" he demanded.

She added wood to the fire Indian-fashion, by placing the butts into the flames. She swiftly dropped her elkskin dress, kicked off her moccasins and ran to him. She pulled back the robes and crawled in, placing her arms around his neck and drawing him close to her so that he might kiss her in the white man's fashion. He passed his hands down her firm full body. She opened to him and he stroked her gently until she was fully aroused.

She looked up into his shadowed face. "Shall we have a child, En-Hone?" she asked.

He shook his head. "I will be leaving here in the spring to go south to the traders."

"We can still have a child."

He stopped stroking her. It was not the first time she had mentioned having a child. Each time she was a little more insistent.

"En-Hone?" she asked.

119

"I can't be bothered with a child. There is no one here to help ye with childbirth."

"I need no one."

"No! I am going south in the spring."

She lay quietly in his arms as he penetrated her, and then she gave fully of herself as she always did.

When she was asleep he raised himself on an elbow and looked down at her. What was her game this time? Love of motherhood? A souvenir of his time with her to show the women of her people that she had been a white man's squaw if only for one winter and that the child was the result of that temporary liaison? Or did she know well enough that if she did have a child he could not, in good conscience, send her back to her people?

He lay on his back for a long time with his hands locked at the nape of his neck, staring up at the dim ceiling. He listened to her gentle breathing and felt her warm softness against his side. Finally the dying fire and the intense creeping cold forced him to get fully under the thick robes with her.

The valley was awesomely silent under its thick mantle of snow and the penetrating cold. Now and then a winter-split tree cracked sharply in the quiet. Once a wolf howled, a rising crescendo of deep-throatedness in several keys which died away in the distance. It was deathly quiet for the rest of the night.

SIXTEEN

January 1838—Moon of Frost in the Tipi.

"In the beginning God created the heaven and the earth," Quint began.

"And the earth was without form, and void; and darkness was upon the face of the deep. And the Spirit of God moved upon the face of the waters.

"And God said, Let there be light: and there was light.

"And God saw the light, that it was good: and God divided the light from the darkness. And God called the light Day, and the darkness he called Night. And the evening and the morning were the first day.

"And God said, Let there be a firmament in the midst of the waters, and let it divide the waters from the waters.

"And God made the firmament, and divided the waters which were under the firmament from the waters which were above the firmament: and it was so.

"And God called the firmament Heaven. And the evening and the morning were the second day.

"And God said, Let the waters under the heaven be gathered together unto one place, and let the dry land appear: and it was so.

"And God called the dry land Earth; and the gathering together of the waters called he Seas: and God said that it was good."

Quint's voice died away. He had been reading from the Bible in a curious and yet pleasing mingling of English, broad Scots and Shoshoni and with a little help now and then from sign language.

Quint looked at her. "That is the Creation, Mountain Woman," he said.

She sat on the floor sewing together a deerskin shirt for him. She shook her head. "Who is this God?" she asked as she threaded her needle with a strand of moistened split buffalo sinew she had taken from her mouth.

Quint shrugged. "No one has ever seen him."

"How can that be? Wasn't he a man?"

"Not exactly."

"What was he then? You said he created man in his own image."

Quint scratched his head. "Well . . ." He stopped. "He was a god," he said simply. "Like your Dam-ap-wa, your Father-God, the Creator of your world, as your people say."

"And he created your world too?"

He smiled. "There is only one God. All peoples were created by the one God."

"Your God?" She shook her head. "No. Not my people. Not the Shoshoni."

"I am afraid that it is so."

"No," she insisted.

"Who created your people then?" he asked patiently.

"Coyote," she replied simply. "Out of clay."

121

Quint couldn't help but grin at her. "Bea-idg-apwa? The Father of Lies? You're joking, lassie. A *coyote?*"

She was annoyed. "He did it when he was a man! It is so! Sometimes he is a man and sometimes he is Coyote!"

"Where does it say so?"

She shrugged. "We don't have a black book of paper leaves like yours to tell us where we came from. Buffalo Bellowing and the elders taught us, and we in turn must tell it to our children. My people speak with a single tongue. They don't lie like your people. Therefore, if they don't lie they must be telling the truth." She bit off a piece of sinew thread with a sharp snap of her white teeth as though to end the argument.

Quint began to fill his pipe. "Ye've a bit of indisputable logic there, lassie," he agreed dryly.

During the long nights of winter, evening after evening, the two of them had become involved in the deepest of subjects. For a female who had never been to school and could not read or write, Mountain Woman had a remarkable grasp of many things. She learned quickly and was completely capable of forming her own thoughts and opinions. It would have been a risky proposition among her own people to speak back to a man as she did with Quint. She came from a completely male-dominated society, but with Quint she had early recognized that he was altogether different from the males in her tribe, and in many ways, quite different from the males in his own race, at least those with which she was acquainted. A squaw to the latter, at least a "winter squaw," ranked about third in their estimation of values, after their rifle and horse in the order named. They could get along fine without a woman, and even without a horse, but never without a rifle.

Quint lighted his pipe. "Did Coyote create the world as well as creating man, or was it your Father-God?"

She shook her head. "Did your people have a time when great rains fell for many days? When the flood waters covered everything and there was no dry place left to stand?"

Quint took his pipe from his mouth and looked at her strangely. "The Great Flood?" he asked, as though to himself.

She nodded. "That is so. What did your people do then when water covered the earth and there was no land to live upon?"

He reached for his cup and took a nip of whiskey. "Why, there was a very wise old man by the name of Noah. The Lord, our God, told him to make a great *sac*, in your language, a great canoe of wood. In this *sac*, which was called the Ark, he was to place his family and two each of all the animals on the earth, male and female. Then the rains came for many days until the entire earth was deeply covered with water. The Ark floated for many days on the flood while every living thing not within the Ark was drowned.

"After a time the waters receded. The Ark landed atop a great mountain. In time the waters fell away and the land dried. The animals and the people came forth from the Ark and repopulated the earth. That is the world as we know it today." He drank from the cup, feeling very wise, but also very foolish at the same time. He, himself, had never quite believed *that* whopper. Still, it was possible.

She smiled at him as though he were a little child who did not know the truth. "En-Hone, how can you always be so wrong in such matters?"

Quint shrugged. " 'Tis easy for me, lass, but perhaps not so in this case—that is, the Great Flood and Noah's Ark. That is the truth, according to the Bible. How does your belief differ from that?"

Mountain Woman picked up a skein of bark string. She unreeled a length of it from the skein and twisted the ends about her fingers. "When the Great Flood came," she said confidently, "Har-ne, Beaver, the wisest of all creatures, was called upon to make a world again for all living things." She began to form designs in the bark string, as white people do in the game they call cat's cradle. "Har-ne dove deep beneath the flood waters, scooping up mud and sticks with his forepaws, to make a great mound much as he does today while building his lodge and his dams. He worked long and hard, never ceasing, until the job was done. There was a dry-land part of the world again, with plains, forests and mountains for all the other animals. *Of all the animals in the world, only Har-ne could have done it.* He always creates a world of his own wherever he wants to settle, with wisdom and dedicated effort. He builds his dam and pond, builds a lodge that is virtually impossible to assault, and stores food where only he can get it. He creates a small world suited only to himself, although many other animals also found it a fine place to live and breed. There!" she cried triumphantly.

"I'll be damned," Quint murmured.

She stood up and held the deerskin shirt out to him. "Try this for size," she said.

He pulled the shirt over his head. It fitted perfectly. "You're a master tailor," he said.

"*Tsoh?* Well?"

He grinned at her. "It's perfect!"

She held out a hand for the shirt.

"Are ye taking it back already?" he asked in mock surprise.

"It needs decorating and beading."

"I like it as it is."

She shook her head. "It has to be beaded," she said firmly.

He pulled the shirt over his head. "It means nothing to me, Dotawipe."

She took the shirt. "It does to me," she said quietly. "Do I want my man to appear before the women of my people in such a plain and ugly shirt? What would they think of me?"

She sat down beside the fire and reached for her bark containers of seed beads. She knew he had little intention, if any at all, of returning with her to her people. He would go south to Taos or Bent's Fort. She knew there would be no place for her there. She had heard tales of the Mexican woman of Taos. They were bold creatures who exposed their breasts and showed their bare legs without shame to any man. They were said to be as shameless as the women of the Crows, or those squaws who hung about the rendezvous, lying down in the grass with any white man who came along and who had her price of a knife, a hawk's bell, a string of beads or a square of cloth. Worst of all were those of them who bargained for drink, for themselves and their men. Some of them had a sickness between their legs that didn't bother them, but gave any man who had intercourse with them a "crying in the pants," as the white men called it.

Quint filled and lighted his pipe. "Would ye like to hear of God's creation of the animals?" he asked.

"If that is what you want."

"Ye won't correct me on this one, will ye?" he asked with a perfectly straight face.

She bit off a piece of thread. "Not if you are right, En-Hone."

She looked up at him as he bent his red head over his black book. The precious winter weeks alone with him were fast slipping away. The scar on his face had healed. His shoulder and leg were as good as new. He had been getting restless of late, now that he had begun to feel his great strength and stamina return. Every day he would put on his capote and walk outside to check the horses, then he'd look at the sky and the streams, as though he was mentally ticking off the time when he could set his traplines.

The cycle of life would soon begin under the ice-locked ponds during the months of January and February. The mating urge would overcome the beaver. In the winter lodge the mated pair would oversee the activities of the young who were two years old, as well as the previous year's kits. When the ice melted in the spring and the streams ran free again, the female, feeling her time coming, would drive the two-year-olds from the lodge and the pond. The food resources of the pond were limited, and not enough for all, so the two-year-olds must look for a new home. Just before the time of birth in May the female would chase the male and the kits out of the lodge to find temporary residence in abondoned lodges or bank holes. There would be four to six kits in the litter, weighing about a pound apiece. In a few years' time after Quint's ravishing of the ponds they would be fully replenished, but then, according to his plan, he would no longer be there. Likely there would be no one there to trap, for the market was dying even now.

Quint relighted his pipe. "And God said," he began, "Let the waters bring forth abundantly the moving creature that hath life, and the fowl that may fly above the earth in the open firmament of heaven.

"And God created great whales, and every living creature that moveth, which the waters brought forth abundantly after their kind, and every winged fowl after his kind: and God saw that it was good.

"And God blessed them, saying, Be fruitful, and multiply, and fill the waters in the seas, and let fowl multiply in the earth."

She was listening intently as she sewed on the first of the beads.

"Do ye understand?" Quint asked.

She shrugged. "Do *you?*" she asked pointedly.

He was nettled. "Dammit! I'm reading it for your own good!"

She looked up at him. "*Are* you, En-Hone?"

She always had such a neat way of disarming him.

"Would ye like to learn to read?" he asked, to change the subject.

"In your language?"

"There is no written language of yours."

"Then I don't need to learn to read."

125

"It would be of help in later years," he suggested.

"Why? If I'm going back to my own people in the spring, there will be no need to read your language."

She had him there.

Minutes ticked past. At last she looked up at him. "Why do the footprints of the white man lie so heavily on the land?" she asked quietly.

"Why do ye ask?"

"You've told me so yourself. They build great lodges many stories high. They build hard trails all over the country. They build bridges across the rivers and make dams like beavers. They put stinking big canoes on the rivers and fill the air with smoke. They bring war and death to anyone who gets in their way. They bring disease and liquor to the Indians and kill them off that way if they don't shoot them, or try to starve them off their land. You've told me yourself they will cover the entire earth within a generation or two."

"I've no argument against that," he admitted.

"But you are not like those other white people. Your ways, like the Indian, become part of the land. You live with the country and not just in it. Your moccasin prints are shallow, leaving no permanent scars, as with the animals who share our world. Why are not the rest of the white men like that?"

He shrugged. "It's a disease, I suppose. People like myself, and a few others, are small in numbers compared to the vast multitudes who are slowly moving west. We few don't want to own the land as much as to live in it, or enjoy it." Immediately, as he spoke, he knew he was speaking hypocrisy. He wanted to trade his plews for trade goods, with which to amass further goods and property. He wanted to make this valley his, in time, and only his. Even now he was planning to despoil the beaver population as soon as the weather permitted.

How could he tell her? The pristine wilderness the Indians had once ruled, and which had hardly been marked by the mountain men, was already slowly being filled with strangers. They were only the first tiny tricklings of a forthcoming flood. Both Mountain Woman and himself would live to see it. It was only a matter of time, and very short time at that.

Mountain Woman smiled up at him. "But you, En-Hone, need not worry," she assured him. It was almost as though she had read his mind. "There will always be a home for you among my people. If we have children they will be raised as Shoshonis. You will be a man of honor. En-Hone, the Red

126

Badger who saved the life of Rawhide Rattle on the Medicine Lodge Fork. En-Hone the Yellow Nose! En-Hone, who fought a great grizzly bear and killed him only with his knife."

Quint shook his head. "The whites will come to the valley of the Seeds-kee-dee Agie. They will settle along the Missouri and all its tributaries. It is a good land, rich with grass and game. They will settle there and build many lodges. They will put boats on the rivers and roads across the land. Someday they will reach the Great Salt Water far to the west and settle the land there too."

"But will they not honor you as we do?"

How could he tell her what a squawman was? She didn't know the opprobrium that was attached to that name, more of an epithet among his people than a name. What would he do with half-breed children and a fat and aging Shoshoni wife? He looked down at her. She was slim and strong and fresh. But with that damned too vivid imagination of his he could forsee how she would be in years to come—a shapeless, toothless bag of decaying flesh.

"You didn't answer me, En-Hone." She searched his scarred face.

"Would ye like to hear of the creation of man?" Quint asked.

She nodded, almost as though in resignation, and bent over her sewing.

Quint took a drink of whiskey. He cleared his throat. "And God said, Let us make man in our image, after our likeness: and let them have dominion over the fish of the sea, and over the fowl of the air, and over the cattle, and over all the earth, and over every creeping thing that creepeth upon the earth.

"So, God created man in his own image, in the image of God created he him; male and female created he them.

"And God blessed them, and God said unto them, Be fruitful, and multiply, and replenish the earth, and subdue it: and have dominion over the fish of the sea, and over the fowl of the air, and over every living thing that moveth upon the earth."

Mountain Woman exploded into laughter.

"What's the joke, Dotawipe?"

"So, God created man in his own image?"

"So?"

"In the image of Coyote, the Father of Lies?" she asked incredulously.

Quint shook his head. He laughed as hard as she was

127

laughing. He reached out for her and drew her closer to him so that she rested her dark head against his knee. He passed a hand over her lovely hair. She looked up at him with a devotion he found hard to believe. He kissed her. He slid a hand within the bosom of her dress and fondled her breasts. She threw the shirt to one side and stood up. She bent over him, forcing him to lie back upon the bed with her pressing down hard upon his crotch.

"Again?" he asked her.

She nodded. "Always."

He stripped her to the skin and placed her in the bed. He cast his clothing aside and got in beside her, drawing the heavy robes up over them.

Outside in the wintry valley the icy wind howled through the snowbound pass.

SEVENTEEN

April 1838—Moon of the Grass Appearing

The warm days reached the valley. The ice on the streams and ponds stretched, popped and rumbled. Water showed in the cracks and openings of the melting ice. The cottonwoods, poplars and quaking aspens were beginning to turn a soft green, although there were still patches of snow among them. The temperatures rose higher, although the nights were still cold and at times there were late snowfalls. But it was spring and time to harvest the prime winter-thick beaver plews.

Quint began to trap the ponds and streams farthest away from the lodge, working the southerly parts of the network of branch and side canyons and valleys. He had thought of moving the camp closer to the center of the main valley, but it would have taken too much valuable time away from the trapping. Therefore he spent two or three days at a time away from the lodge, not counting traveling time. Mountain Woman came every second or third day to take the plews back to the lodge for curing.

It was simply greed that kept Quint working the long hours and setting as many traps as he could. It was exhausting, mind-dulling work, but the rewards would be great. The beaver were larger than those he had trapped in the fall and early winter. The plews were prime. The skin underneath the fur was firm and whitish, with all the blue transparency of the summer thinness gone. The fur was dense, soft and silky under the long glistening king, or guard, hairs.

March had been a Norse hell in the melted snow and ice of the ponds. Often Quint had to break through the rotting ice to set his traps. He clambered out of the water on stiff and aching legs. The calf of his right leg, crushed almost to the bone by the grizzly, ached incessantly whether he was in the water or not, and often kept him partially awake the few hours he allowed himself for rest. But the plews accumulated by the dozens and the lodge was surrounded by the reddish-brown discs as they cured and dried. He increased the lure of his bait by pounding the castoreum together with the fresh aspen buds appearing on the trees, a combined lure of both sex and food, a lure irresistible to man and beaver alike. Sometimes he cut shallow breaks in the tops of some of the dams to catch the older beavers when they came out lured by the trickling water to repair the leak and thus stepped into a trap set about two inches below water level.

There was nothing but hard, exhausting work for Quint and Mountain Woman. There was no time for anything but their labor. They spoke mostly in monosyllables, if they talked at all. But that was the way of it after the soft living in the dead of winter. Mountain Woman grew thin with her work of curing the pelts, taking care of the horses, and even hunting the game while Quint worked relentlessly toward his goal. She knew she might be working toward her own great loss, for the more plews Quint trapped, the more money he would accumulate toward making his new start in life in Mexico. He never spoke about it. He had made no promises to her in the past and even now in the present. He had never given her the slightest hope that he might take her with him.

One day the sun was pleasantly warm on Quint's back as he emptied his traps. The water was still cold about his legs, but the sun promised warming weather. The streams and ponds were being worked out. Only the wariest of the beaver still survived in the farthest reaches of his trapping domain. There might be only a few weeks of trapping left. Each day Mountain Woman grew more persistently in his thoughts.

He had learned to fully appreciate her that fall, through the winter and now in the spring. It wasn't love, at least as he thought of it. Come to think of it, he had never fully defined the meaning of the word, at least in relation to himself.

Quint waded out of a remote pond after he had set his last trap for the day. He filled his pipe and lighted it. He had a full day ahead of himself until he must return at dusk to empty the traps. He looked about the quiet and peaceful valley. What had bothered him so his first day there? It seemed so long ago. He grinned a little wryly as he thought of his first night, alone in the timber, with the wolves prowling through the darkness and the falling snow.

He picked up his rifle and mounted the paint pony. There was one area he had never fully explored. It was the approach to what he thought was a pass that should allow access to the lower land south and east of the valley.

It was a truly beautiful day with a mild temperature and the sun sending down golden shafts of light through the newly leaved trees. He rode through an extensive meadow edged by trees and bordered by a swiftly rushing stream. He tamped down the tobacco in his pipe and sucked in on the pipe to get it to draw better. He looked casually ahead of himself, toward the far side of the meadow.

Quint was off the pony in a flash with his Hawken thrust over the saddle and cocked, aiming to the south. Thirty feet ahead of him a pile of fresh manure steamed in the sunlight. A hawk was floating above the timber to the south. Suddenly it tilted up on a wing and veered swiftly downwind and out of sight.

Quint led the pony back into the woods. He tethered it to a tree and then ran noiselessly through the woods to the edge of the stream. He waded across it and then followed the course of it until he was even with the trees that edged the south side of the meadow.

He stood there a long time, watching the shadowed woods and listening to the soughing of the wind through the pines. He heard nothing else. Nothing moved.

Quint moved into the woods, drifting from tree to tree like a forest shadow itself, and just as silently. There was a clearing to one side of a flat, slightly tilted shield of rock at the foot of the pass. He found damp marks on the rock as though someone, or something, had hurriedly crossed the surface to reach the shelter of the trees that filled the upper slopes of the pass to the timberline.

Quint backtracked to the meadow. He found track marks, those of a horse whose hooves had been covered with hide boots, for silence. . . . Whoever had been riding the horse had been moving fast, from the distance between the hoof marks. He had evidently crossed the meadow a few minutes ahead of Quint, from the fresh condition of the manure.

Quint focused his telescope on the upper reaches of the pass. Foot by foot and yard by yard he studied the pass all the way to the top. Nothing moved. Maybe the elusive rider had backtracked through the woods on the far or eastern side of the meadow while Quint had been advancing on the western side of it beyond the stream.

Quint rode back to where he had set his last traps. He poked about in the brush and timber. He found a place where someone had been standing for quite a long time, moving about a little, and where he could easily see Quint at work setting his traps.

Suddenly he thought of Mountain Woman. Supposing there had been more than one of the unknowns? Supposing one or more of them had been watching Mountain Woman while Quint was being watched?

He mounted the pony and rode swiftly to the north. Half a mile from the lodge he found horse tracks on a gravel bank in the center of the stream that coursed at the foot of the slope below the lodge.

A thin bluish streamer of smoke rose from the lodge. The ringing sound of an ax cutting into wood echoed from the heights.

Mountain Woman turned from her woodcutting as Quint approached. She wiped the sweat from her forehead. Her eyes searched his face. She had noted the foam flecking the coat of the paint pony. He should not be back at this time of the day, or on this day at all, according to her calculations.

"Everything all right?" Quint asked casually as he dismounted.

She nodded. "But you've seen something."

It was no use lying to her. She knew something was wrong.

"Horse droppings. Tracks in the woods."

"Where?"

He jerked his head. "South. At the far end of the main valley." There was no use in alarming her by telling her about the tracks he had seen near the camp.

"Indians?"

He shrugged. "Utes maybe."

131

"Maybe a white man?"

"I don't know."

"Maybe Mexicans? We're not far from Mexico."

"We might even be in Mexico."

"Then it could be Mexicans."

"How the hell should I know?" he snapped. "He or they were wearing moccasins. They had boots on the horse, or horses, which means they didn't want to be heard. Moccasins don't mean they were Indians. *I'm* wearing moccasins and I ain't no God damned yellowskin!"

She watched him as he strode to the lodge. She heard the cork come out of the whiskey jug. In a little while he came out of the lodge and sat down on a log. He eyed her.

"We've got plenty of plews. The pass must be open by now. We can leave any time," she suggested timidly.

"Goddammit! No! That's just like a woman! Do ye think I'll run from a pile of fresh horseshit and a few moccasin tracks?"

"No, En-Hone," she replied quietly. "You will not run from anything." It was not intended as a compliment.

She knew he had come back to the lodge because he was worried about her. That in itself was something to think about. Or was it because he was worried only about his precious plews?

"I can take care of myself," she assured him.

"I know that! I was thinking of the plews!"

"What will you do now?"

He began to unsaddle the paint pony. "I'll take one of the pack horses and go back to see if I can find out anything more. I might be gone overnight, as I've got to empty my traps at dusk."

"You'll go alone?"

"There may be only one of them."

She shook her head. "There are more. I didn't want to tell you this, but I saw two men two days ago, right after you left to go to the south."

He gripped her by the arms. "Where?" he demanded.

"You're hurting my arms!"

He released her. "Where?" he repeated.

She pointed to the towering escarpment across the stream. The lower slopes glistened from melted snow. " There, En-Hone."

"You're sure? Perhaps it was bears. They look like men at a distance."

She shook her head. "They were not bears. They were men.

132

At first I thought they were *tsoaps*, but then I knew they were men."

"Do ye think they knew ye saw them?"

"I gave no sign of it."

"Were they whites or Indians?"

"They were too far away to see."

"I'll take a look up there before I ride south. Ye'll be all right?"

She looked up into his face. "I always have been when I'm alone here," she said simply.

Quint mounted the pack horse. He looked down at her. "Get into the lodge at dusk. Bar the door. Keep your rifle and pistol always at hand. If I hear any shooting I'll return at once."

"If you're near enough."

Quint looked away from her. "Take care," he said.

She watched him ride across the shallow stream. How could she tell him of the crawling fears she had when she was alone in that place? Of how each succeding day was a worse horror than its predecessor? Of how many times she had hoped he would say that he had enough plews and that they could leave the valley? Of how each day she felt that it might be the last time she might ever see him, even as this day? This day. She watched his broad back as he urged the pack horse up the slopes beyond the stream. A curious, lingering foreboding took possession of her. She shivered. She hurried into the lodge and barred the door behind herself.

Quint dismounted high on the slopes below the escarpment. He took his rifle and prowled about amid the huge talus pieces that had scaled off from the towering facade high above him. He found a shallow pocket of soil behind a damp earth. There were fairly fresh footprints in the damp earth. He found some gnawed bones and a crust of hard biscuit. He picked up corn shuck tobacco wrappers, half a dozen thin cigar butts, *cigarritos* the spics called them. Fifty feet from the soil pocket he found two piles of human fecal matter. Whoever had been hiding there had been there several days at least. He looked over the ledge. There was a clear view of the stream, the lodge and the corral, as well as the approach from the south. Maybe they had been there when he had arrived that day. He could see the horses moving about in the corral and the packs of plews on the platform he had constructed to keep them off the wet earth.

Quint drew out his telescope to its full extent and focused it

133

on the lodge. Mountain Woman came out of the lodge. She was carrying her rifle. He could see her clearly. Once she turned and looked directly up toward where he was, shading her eyes with her free hand. She waved.

There could be a good haul at the camp—four horses, five packs of prime plews, the good robes and pelts within the lodge, the tools and the woman's weapons. Profit enough for anyone in that country.

"And, the *woman*," the voice seemed to say in his ear.

"Aye, the woman," Quint repeated. He was ashamed that he had not added her to the potential loot.

He stood there undecided for a long time. Should he gamble that nothing might happen? Maybe the strangers were just curious, but then they would hardly have lingered around that long without making themselves known, or slipping quietly away. He wanted to hunt them down, and yet he was reluctant to leave the lodge area, the valuable plews and other possessions, *and* the woman.

Mountain Woman wanted to leave. Christ, how she wanted to leave! But there were still beaver in the ponds, at least for that season. It was his last season. He wanted to make it the best he had ever had.

He'd have to gamble that, if they meant to raid the camp. they'd wait until he returned with fresh plews, his valuable traps, horse and good Hawken rifle. Aye, that was it! As long as he was out in the field trapping, they'd bide their time. Then he could have time to track them down, or make sure they were gone, then return in haste to the lodge, pack up and haul out of there as swiftly as he could. It was easy enough to convince himself of that course, because it was really what he wanted to do all along.

Quint found further tracks when he reached the lower slopes. Far back in the timber in a small branch canyon he found the remains of a rude camp—a concealed fireplace of blackened rocks, a scrap of blanket, an improvised latrine well used and a worn-out moccasin. The sole of the moccasin was worn through but it once had had a thick sole, thicker than that usually worn by Plains or Mountain Indians. Likely Apache, Jicarilla, or, on a longer shot, Kiowa-Apache. Probably Ute, though. It meant little. Many Americans and Mexicans wore such moccasins.

Just before dusk he was at the far southern end of the main valley. He had found no further signs of strangers. There

134

would be a new moon that night, enough light for him to be able to finish emptying his traps.

Quint worked swiftly through the dusk and the pre-moon darkness. There was no use in trying to put the possibility that there was no fear or danger from whoever it was in the valley, or whoever *had* been there. They might be watching him even now as he worked. It reminded him too strongly of working up along the Yellowstone, with the possibility of one of Bug's Boys hiding in the brush.

The moon rose and flooded the valley with clear cold light. Quint quickly skinned his catch, cut out the castoreum glands and took two of the bigger tails for roasting. He bundled the plews together and tied them to the cantle of his saddle. He took the hackamore of the horse and turned to lead it back to the camp. He stumbled over something at the edge of a small natural clearing. He looked down. A skull lay at his feet, staring up at him with vacant eyeholes. He moved it with a big toe. It rolled sideways and he saw the ragged black hole in the back of it.

"Jest before the winter set fully in I found a skull with a bullet hole in the back of it," Gabe had related.

A cold uncanny feeling crept through Quint's body. The valley was deathly quiet. The wind had died away with the rising of the moon. Nothing moved. Not a leaf stirred.

Quint looked slowly behind himself. The woods were shadowed and still. The faint trickling sound of the stream came to him.

Quint led the horse through the clearing and entered the woods on the far side. A human thighbone rose a little as he stepped on one end of it. Quint wasn't interested or curious at that moment to look around in the brush for any more grisly relics of the first white trappers in the valley.

When he reached the lodge at moonset it was as it had always been—quiet and serene, surrounded by plews drying on their willow hoops, smoke rising from the chimney and the good smell of cooking food.

Quint sat on the bed and filled his pipe after eating. "Whoever it was is gone now, Dotawipe," he assured her for at least the fifth time since he had returned.

"Did they use that south pass?"

"I don't know."

"I don't think they used the north pass."

He shrugged. "You don't know that."

"I *know*," she insisted.

135

He lighted his pipe, eyeing her over the bowl.

"We can be out of here in two hours under cover of the darkness, En-Hone."

"By the north pass?"

She nodded. "It's the best and safest way. It's close at hand. If we wanted to leave by the south pass we'd have to travel the whole length of the valley."

"You know I don't want to go north."

She instantly retreated into the clamlike silence he hated when she would not argue with him, or discuss anything further. A womanish ruse if there ever was one, and one almost impossible to contend with.

"We stay," he said at last. "There are still some beaver left in the south part of the valley."

"But En-Hone!" she protested. "Maybe we've used up our good medicine."

"*Enough,* woman! That's my final decision!"

After a time he spoke again. "It will be only a matter of ten days to two weeks, lassie," he placated her.

She nodded dutifully. "Yes, En-Hone."

During the next week he stayed away from the camp while he continued trapping at the far south end of the valley. He did his own skinning and curing. He set his traps before dawn, then emptied them and reset them at dusk. Keeping twelve traps going was a man-killing task, and every day the take was less. It was really only his damned Scots stubbornness that kept him at it. Besides, he meant to show her he could get along without her. It was a false premise and he knew it, but he could not admit to himself that he was wrong.

One beautiful day he emptied the last of his traps. Out of twelve traps he had taken only two beaver, and small ones at that. It was time to leave. He had had enough of it. She was right after all. They should have left the valley while their medicine was still good. Then again, she had wanted to leave by the north pass, and *that* he did not want to do. His destination and future was in the south, in New Mexico. One part of him wanted to keep her with him; the other part wanted to get rid of her. Others of the mountain men had taken Indian women for wives, or at least winter squaws. Luke Connors, Bill Sublette, Kit Carson, Joe Meek and many others had taken such women, and somehow without compunction or conscience they had gotten rid of them. It was the custom among the breed; no shame was attached to it. Luke Connors had taken two of them, a Crow and a Comanche, at one time or another. Quint had never heard him say he had missed either one of them. He had missed their usefulness, however. "Used," that was the word. Quint didn't like to think about it, but it was surely true.

EIGHTEEN

May 1838—Moon When the Ponies Shed.

Mountain Woman bathed herself within the lodge. The warming sunlight streamed in through the open doorway. She soaped herself, using the water she had brought from the stream and heated over the fire. She had laid out her fine elkskin dress. It was the one En-Hone had so admired the night of the social dance when he had asked her to come to his lodge. She had secretly completed a pair of new beaded moccasins which she would wear with the dress that day to welcome him home. She stood on a square of tanned deerskin, feeling every curve and hollow of her body. She thought of the day she had done that while on the bank of the Popo Agie, knowing that En-Hone was on a nearby hill studying her through his telescope. She wondered idly if that had caused him to make the final decision to ask her to his lodge. Perhaps today he would agree to leave the valley with her and return to her people.

She began to notice the faint sour body odor. She washed the soap from her body and passed her wet hands up and down her skin, then sniffed at them. She was puzzled. There was no odor noticeable on her hands, but she could still smell something disagreeable. At first she wasn't sure where she had noticed such an odor before, and then it came slowly to her. It was like the rank body odor of the mountain men after a wintering in the mountains.

Mountain Woman turned slowly and looked toward the front of the lodge. A broad-shouldered swarthy man wearing filthy clothing and a huge battered sombrero stood in the doorway. His dark eyes were on her full breasts and then slowly traveled down to look at her legs and particularly her crotch. Her pale-brown skin glistened with a wet sheen making it all the more enticing.

Mountain Woman moved swiftly. Her rifle and spear were near the doorway, right beside the intruder. Her Deringer pistol lay capped and half-cocked at the head of the bed. She leaped toward it, snatched it up and pointed it toward the man while sweeping back the hammer to full cock with her left hand as Quint had taught her to do.

The shadow of another man darkened the doorway. He pushed in beside the first man. The first man smiled ingratiatingly. "Put down the *pistola,* woman," he said in Spanish. "We won't hurt you," he lied.

The second man smiled, revealing even white teeth. His cold blue eyes studied Mountain Woman. "She don't maybe speak spic, Antonio," he suggested. He smiled again, looking like a winter-hungry wolf. "You speak American?" he asked. "Me, American. Jake Stow, at your service, ma'am." His smile was one of the facial muscles only; a mechanical action without any warmth from his cold eyes.

If En-Hone showed up and they didn't see him, he'd kill them both in a matter of minutes. But if they surprised him, as they had surprised her . . . She forced the thought from her mind.

Antonio moved a little closer to Mountain Woman. "Me Comanchero, you understand?" he asked in English.

She shook her head. "Not Comanche. Stay back!"

Jake smiled. "She does speak American. He don't mean he's Comanche *Indian,* ma'am. He means we're Comancheros. Understand? You savvy? *Comprende?*" It was as though both of them meant to frighten her into submission, although she hadn't the vaguest idea at that moment what a Comanchero was. A feeling of cold fear crept through her. Something came back slowly to her. Something En-Hone had once told her about such men. It was not good. They traded with the Comanches and Kiowas and one of their principal activities was slave trading, the selling of women and children.

"My man comes home soon," Mountain Woman said in halting English. "Better get out. He shoot. Kill fast."

Jake raised his eyebrows. "That so? You hear that, Antonio? Her man comes home soon. He shoot. He kill."

Antonio shook his head. "He not kill us. We kill him."

The two men grinned at each other.

"He's got no business trapping here," Jake said. "He's an American, ain't he? This is Ute country and part of Mexico

138

anyway. This is *our* valley. Anything that comes in or out of here belongs to us—horses, guns, traps, plews and furs, *and* women. Come to think of it, weren't any women around here until that red-headed sonofabitch brought you here."

The two men moved slowly apart. Mountain Woman's eyes darted back and forth trying to watch both of them at the same time. She moved the pistol back and forth in an arc to cover them.

"You got only one shot in that *pistola*," Antonio said.

"I kill one of you anyway," she threatened.

Jake smiled "A woman after my own heart."

They moved farther apart. Jake made a quick movement toward her. She turned a little to face him. Antonio yelled. Jake dropped to the floor. Antonio drew his knife and cast it in such a way that the heavy stud at the top of the bone handle was foremost. He dropped to the floor as he threw the knife. The stud struck Mountain Woman in the center of the forehead. Reflex action tightened her finger on the trigger of the pistol as she fell. The pistol flamed and the bullet struck the doorpost next to Jake Stow.

Jake was through the swirling smoke in an instant. He kicked the empty pistol aside and reached for Mountain Woman. "Jesus!" he yelled. "Lookit them big tits!"

Quint Kershaw heard the distant gun report. He kicked the pack horse in the ribs and slapped it on the rump with the buttstock of his rifle.

The Comanchero known to men only as Kiowa lay concealed behind a fallen tree at the edge of a sunny meadow. His left eye, partially sightless, was askew and of a dirty milky-blue color, while the right eye was a pale blue. Both eyes were in startling contrast to his dark, pockmarked face, a "rough-face" with flattened nostrils and thick negroid lips. The man was part Indian, part Negro, and part white, with not a single redeeming virtue of any of the three of them. His heavy Hawken rifle lay across the tree in the direction he was looking. Fifty yards to his left was Jose, the Jicarilla Apache, standing behind a tree with cocked rifle in his hands.

Jose whistled softly. Kiowa looked toward him. Jose pointed across the meadow to the south. The sorrel-headed trapper was coming. They could hear his mount crashing through the brush, the jangling of the traps in their panniers and the soft thudding of the hoofs. Kiowa grinned. To hurry in this deadly game was to make a mistake. To make a single mistake was to die.

Quint burst into the meadow and galloped the horse close along the edge of the stream that bordered the meadow on the west. The rifle flamed and cracked from the far side of the meadow. The half-ounce slug slapped alongside Quint's head, cutting a shallow furrow through the skin. The horse flung himself sideways in panic. Quint took a header off his back. He struck the ground and rolled over and over, still having enough sense left to hang onto his rifle. He rolled over the bank and plunged into five feet of icy water. He struck the bottom. The shock of the water helped him partially regain his senses.

Quint did not try to surface. He held his rifle with his left hand and swam awkwardly underwater, helped by the rushing current. He surfaced when he saw the shadow of an overhanging bank above him. He stood up with his head just under the bank and grabbed an exposed tree root to keep himself from being floated out into the open by the strong current. He thrust the butt of his rifle into the thick mud at the bottom of the stream and used it to support himself.

His senses still reeled from the smashing shock of the bullet. He looked out from under the bank and thought he saw the shadow of a man cast upon the surface. Whoever it was, he was standing on the bank right over Quint's head. After a time the shadow vanished.

Quint held his rifle between his knees and passed a trembling hand along the right side of his head to feel the furrow made in his flesh. He promptly vomited.

Minutes ticked past. The icy water was numbing Quint's whole body and his head felt as though it was going to explode. He let go of the root and pulled the rifle from the mud. He bent his body and pushed with his feet to propel himself out from under the bank and below the surface of the stream. The current carried him downstream until the water shallowed about a gravel bank. He crawled out onto it and looked upstream. There was no sign of anyone.

He backed into the stream and wiped out the marks he had made on the gravel. He waded to the shore and crawled out on the bank, then wormed his way into the brush to where he found several fallen trees not far from the edge of the meadow where he had been ambushed. He could go no further. He burrowed into the leaves and passed out.

Jake Stow had been forced to have Antonio hold the woman

still while he raped her. Even so, she fought like a wildcat until he knocked her out, breaking off her front teeth in the process. He stood up from her. She moved and opened her eyes. He kicked her alongside the head and knocked her out again.

"She's all yours, Antonio," Jake said. "By God, she's still fairly tight."

Antonio unbuttoned his pants and took out his stiff organ. He hooked a boot toe under the woman and threw her over on her belly. "Maybe for you," he said over his shoulder. "I like virgins. I'll try her from the rear."

Jake rooted around in the parfleches while Antonio thoroughly sodomized the unconscious woman. Jake waited outside with a whiskey jug in his hand until Kiowa and Jose appeared, leading the paint horse with its full trap panniers.

"Well?" Jake asked.

Kiowa nodded. "Dead. One shot. Mebbe hundred and fifty yards."

"Two hundred," Jose corrected. He eyed the whiskey jug.

"Dead? You sure?" Jake asked.

Kiowa nodded again. "He fall into stream."

"Where's his Hawken rifle?"

"He take it with him," Jose said.

Jake narrowed his eyes. "What the hell do you mean? He take it with him! What the hell does *that* mean? He's dead, ain't he?"

Jose shrugged. "He fall into stream. Hold onto rifle. We look in stream. No man. No rifle. Gone."

Jake looked toward the timber. "Gone where? The streams ain't that deep. He must have washed ashore somewhere."

Kiowa spat. "Downstream somewhere."

"You stupid bastards! He's a man with the bark on! When you shoot a man like that you got to *kill* him! You got to make sure! How do we know he ain't alive in them woods waiting to get a crack at us?"

Kiowa grinned. "With a hole in his skull?"

Mountain Woman cried out sharply from the lodge.

Jose looked toward the lodge. "My turn soon?"

Jake shrugged. "You and Kiowa argue it out. She ain't going anywhere."

"I ain't in no hurry," Kiowa said. He grinned. "When me get trew with her no one else want her."

Jake sucked at a tooth. "I know you like to leave 'em dying or dead, you murderous bastard, but maybe we could take her

141

out onto the Llano Estacado and sell her to the Comanches."

Kiowa fixed his one eye on Jake. "No. Too much trouble. Leave her here."

Jake nodded. "Have it your way. She won't be worth much anyway when you get through with her. Let's get the furs loaded."

Antonio came out of the lodge buttoning his trousers. "They kill that trapper bastard?"

Jake jerked his head at Jose. "Go on, Jose. She's all yours. Leave something for Kiowa here." He grinned. He looked at the quiet woods. "They say Kiowa did. A head shot."

"They get his rifle?"

"No. They claim he fell into the stream with it."

Antonio stared at him. "He gets shot in the head and falls into the stream and takes his rifle with him and they couldn't find it? A good Hawken? They're worth their weight in gold to a Comanche. You take me for a fool?"

"I told them you got to kill a man like that. If they didn't and he's somewhere in them woods with that rifle of his we've got trouble on our hands."

Antonio nodded. He looked up at the sun. "We'd better get out of this damned valley by dusk. I never did like this place."

Mountain Woman screamed hoarsely. In a little while Jose came out of the lodge. "Good," he grunted in deep satisfaction. "Kiowa finish her now." He grinned loosely.

They watched the mixed breed enter the lodge.

"I'm almost sorry for her," Antonio said. "She was nice. Young too. Maybe we should take her along. She could keep us satisfied until we got out of this goddam up-and-down country."

"How long do you think she'd last?" Jake asked.

They passed the whiskey jug from one to the other of them as they loaded the packs of plews. Now and again one of them would look toward the quiet lodge.

"She ain't crying out none," Jake said.

"Wait until he gets at her with his knife," Antonio said.

A scream like that of a wounded mare came from the lodge.

"I told you," Antonio said with self-satisfaction.

She was still screaming when they finished loading the pack horses. Kiowa dumped the parfleches outside the door, followed by all the robes and Mountain Woman's fine *grossecorne* dress and beautifully beaded moccasins. He loaded them on a pack horse.

142

"Go get our horses, Jose," Jake ordered. "We'd better get to hell out of here before full darkness."

The Jicarilla brought the four saddle horses and the one pack horse back through the timber. By that time, the camp had been thoroughly looted.

Kiowa struck fire and touched off a handful of dried grass. He threw it into the lodge.

They rode from the place in the swiftly gathering shadows. A wisp of smoke trailed from the doorway of the lodge.

The camp and the lodge seemed abandoned. The Comancheros had vanished into the thick timber. A gush of thick smoke poured from the doorway of the lodge.

Quint Kershaw heard the soft thudding of many hoofs on the surface of the meadow. He crawled to the edge of the timber just as the four horsemen crossed the open. They were leading Quint's horses and pack horses, all of them heavily laden with his five packs of plews.

He was still very weak. His rifle and pistol were water-soaked. He drew out his telescope and quickly wiped the water from the lens. He rested it on a log and focused it on the ghostlike horsemen. There was nothing he could do now but etch their indistinct features on his memory.

NINETEEN

The moon rose serenely over the valley. A wolf howl broke the quiet. Then, like a belated echo, another wolf howled. They were in the timber near the meadow. The howling died away. The valley was quiet as before.

Quint Kershaw opened his eyes at the baying of the wolves. The silver moon hung high over the valley. The light was on his ghastly pale face, darkly streaked with dried blood. He felt for his rifle, then remembered that it was temporarily useless. He drew his knife. Something was moving stealthily

143

through the woods toward where he lay hidden among the dry leaves.

The wolf's head rose above the log close in front of Quint. A forepaw was placed on the log, and then another. Quint launched himself. The razor-edged knife swept across the throat muscles of the wolf, severing the jugular. The wolf fell backward, kicking spasmodically. Swift movements in the timber faded away into the distance. Silence moved in again.

Quint reached for his rifle and used it to help himself to his feet. "Get back to your dens, ye skulkin' bastards!" he yelled. "I'm no this nicht's meal for ye!" He passed a hand across his eyes. The incessant beating of dull sickening pain within his skull was almost unbearable.

He swayed back and forth as he made his way across the meadow until he reached a tree. He leaned against it to regain his strength. It took the utmost of willpower in his system to start out again for the camp.

He scented the odor of woodsmoke before he was within sight of the lodge. He left the timber and splashed across the stream. Where the lodge had once humped itself in a mushroom shape above the ground level was now a blackened pit from which stinking tendrils of smoke still rose.

"Dotawipe! Dotawipe! Dotawipe!" Quint yelled hoarsely.

Her name echoed back from the heights. There was no answering cry.

Quint poked through the thick bed of ashes in the lodge pit. There were no charred human bones. He had not seen her with the raiders. He raised his head and looked about himself. Perhaps she had seen them coming and had hidden herself, but why hadn't she answered his call?

"Dotawipe! Dotawipe! Dotawipe!" he shouted.

The echoes died away down the quiet valley.

Something crunched under his feet as he walked toward the corral. He picked up the necklace of grizzly bear's claws she had strung for him. He hung it about his neck.

Quint hunted through the woods and up on the bare rocky slopes of the mountain. She was nowhere to be found. He searched along the bank of the stream looking down into the clear moonlit water for her. She wasn't there.

The moon was on the wane when Quint went to his hideout cache on the high slope behind the lodge. He removed the possibles he had hidden there—a pound can of gunpowder, bullets, percussion caps, an extra Green River knife, a bag of

144

pemmican and some jerky, a little tobacco and, of course, a quart of whiskey.

He sat on a stump and thoroughly cleaned and dried his firearms while gnawing on a piece of jerky. Luckily he had not lost his hatchet. His powderhorns and the smaller horn where he kept his percussion caps had not leaked.

At last he was done and ready. He stood up and looked about himself. He was irresolute until he finally realized there was no longer any need for him to stay there. There was the look of a hunting wolf about him—tall and lean, with the dying moonlight on his scarred face and the dried blood alongside his head. It was his eyes that were the most terrible to see.

"Dotawipe! Dotawipe! Dotawipe!" he shouted.

Surely she would hear him this time if she was still alive. There was no answering cry.

Quint strode down the slope toward the stream. He waded across it and entered the timber on the far side. Several times he called her name as he moved to the south; each time the call was fainter than that which had preceded it, and then it was heard no more.

An abysmal quietness and a feeling of utter loneliness seemed to come over the darkening valley.

When Quint Kershaw vanished into the timber and the sound of his voice no longer rang through the woods, something stirred high on the slope behind the camp. Mountain Woman crawled painfully from the hollow behind a rock ledge where she had hidden since she had crawled out of the burning lodge after the Comancheros had left. She had heard En-Hone calling to her. She had watched him searching for her. Once he had passed within fifty feet of her. She had watched him as she cleaned his rifle. She had heard his receding calls in the timber.

She lay still for a time on the naked rock trying to regain her strength, and more, the will to live. It would have been better if they had killed her, but mercy was a virtue of which they knew nothing. It had been terrible enough when the first three of them had ravished her and sodomized her. It had been the one-eyed man who stank worse than any animal she had ever known, and far worse than the filthiest mountain man, who had damaged her internally. No man might ever want her again. She knew something else—she might never be able to respond to a man again, even her beloved En-Hone.

She crawled down the slope. She probed into the cooling ashes in the lodge pit. She found a butcher knife with the handles burned off. She bound the haft with a buckskin thong to make a substitute handle. Here and there amid the charred ruins at the rear of the lodge and under the overhanging cave roof she found some old clothing and a pair of En-Hone's worn-out moccasins. She found a half-burned elkskin robe. There was some charred meat and a bag of pemmican. She hung the elkskin robe about herself after she had dressed.

Mountain Woman did not look back at first as she slowly climbed up the pass. When the moonlight was almost gone she rested. She looked down into the quiet shadowed valley. It had been a happy placed despite her constant misgivings about it. The happiness had been because of En-Hone, not because of the valley itself.

She put an exploring hand down about her ravished crotch. Before the Comancheros had come, she had suspected that En-Hone had impregnated her, but that had only been a few days before she had been attacked and raped. Each of the four ravishers had shot their evil seed into her. They were lusty men. En-Hone would have called them studs.

She sat there for a time. She had not responded to En-Hone's calling her because she believed he would have nothing to do with her after her ravishing and injuries. If she became pregnant, whose child would it be? She bent her head and placed her work-worn hands against her eyes, feeling the hot tears trickling from them.

It was fully dark when she began the final ascent of the pass. By midnight she had crested the pass and had started down the northern approach to it.

Mountain Woman wasn't sure how far it was to the Seeds-kee-dee Agie. Caw-Haw, the Crop-Eared One, old Gabe Pritchett, had once said the valley was about three hundred and fifty miles from the camp of the Shoshonis on the Popo Agie.

By dawn's light she was a tiny figure plodding her way through a mountained vastness across the open country below the grinning peaks and through the haunting valleys, unpeopled and still.

She was seventeen years old that day.

TWENTY

June 1838—The Time When the Ponies Get Fat.

Quint Kershaw loped on steadily and tirelessly, a lean lath of a man with a stained bandage about his head concealing the shallow healing scar of a bullet track alongside his skull. His grizzly-claw necklace rose and fell with the movement of his chest. His bullet pouch and both powderhorns slapped against his left hip in the rhythm of his mile-eating stride. He carried his heavy Hawken rifle arm's length at his side. His worn moccasins slapped the hard earth. On and on, hour after hour, day after day, with his eyes on the horizon once he left the mountains behind him, and started across the piedmont hoping always to see the moving shapes of four horsemen and the pack horses they led. From their route, once they had left the course of the Upper Rio Grande and crossed the San Luis Valley toward the Spanish Peaks, they should be heading for Bent's Fort on the Arkansas.

Quint had come down from his valley to follow the course of the Upper Rio Grande southeasterly into the San Luis Valley. He had passed through thick forests of fir and aspen where icy streams frothed in steep canyons. The air was sharp and dry and still cold at night, for it was still late spring.

He had trailed his quarry through the shaggy foothills bordering the high plains, a country of stark hogbacks, gaunt buttes and long pine ridges separating meadows of grass spotted by willow thickets. He had climbed a nine-thousand-foot pass just to the north and west of the Spanish Peaks—the Indian Huajtolla or Wah-To-Yah, the munificent stone teats, the Breasts of the World. Rocky ribs radiated from the Spanish Peaks, and in the gullies were pockets of grass and berry bushes. Bear, deer and flocks of wild turkeys inhabited the great descending slopes. Once there had been many beaver in this land, but its proximity to Taos had caused the area to be trapped out.

From the Spanish Peaks the land sloped to the northeast and became increasingly arid. Hills barren as grindstones shimmered in a growing heat haze, seemingly suspended above the earth. Oak brush and then black junipers and scrub piñon replaced the tall upland trees until the arid soil could support no trees. Instead the rolling plain was dotted with sage, greasewood, cacti and blade-leafed yucca. Dry streams gullied the land in drab, boulder-strewn canyons that gradually crumbled away and leveled off into the flat plains bordering the Arkansas River.

Quint had stayed relentlessly on the trail of the thieves. He moved on and on from late spring into early summer by day and by night, resting only a few hours at a time. Sometimes he ate as he ran, gnawing at the last of his pemmican. He would not take the time to hunt. He would not fire his rifle in any case, for fear of warning the thieves or alerting any yellowskin within hearing distance. It was Ute country on the higher lands, Jicarilla Apache more to the south, and to the south and west, the domain of the fierce Lords of the Plains—the Comanches.

Two days from the valley he had come across the carcass of a deer, hardly dead twenty-four hours, from which his quarry had taken only the choicest cuts, leaving the remainder for the coyotes and the wolves. The carcass was black with flies when Quint came upon it. He had risked a fire that night to bake the deer's head in a stone-lined pit of ashes covered with a thick layer of dirt. When he had awakened the head was done. He had taken it hot from the ashes and gnawed on it as he continued on his trail.

Thirst came with him once he passed the Spanish Peaks. It was a brooding land; a land of little rain. Fresh water was impossible to find. He had no time to hunt for it and had little faith that he'd find any. Sometimes he found water in hollows, and once he waded into a buffalo wallow in the darkness just before the dawn. The wallow had evidently been filled by the occasional thundershowers that swept those barren plains so suddenly and swiftly they left little water behind themselves. The surface of the water was speckled with tiny pink-and-white floating bladders. It was real "buffalo tea," a mingling of stale water, buffalo piss and droppings. All Quint could do was to strain the smelly water through the dirty bandage he wore on his head to eliminate the more obvious odds and ends in it. It might have been better if he had passed on without touching it. Hours after he had drunk it, he was suddenly doubled over with severe cramps. If he went down, and stayed down, he'd be found before long by the wolves and coyotes that haunted those barren plains feeding off the vast buffalo herds.

He passed between the Rattlesnake Buttes and then trended northeasterly to pick up the course of the Apishapa, which flowed into the Arkansas about thirty-five miles west of Bent's Fort—that is, when it flowed. It wasn't flowing now.

The nights were cold. Quint was about done. His legs felt as though they were made of wood. His shoulder wound and the bullet track alongside his skull drew when it was cold. His guts cramped and then loosened, and several times he couldn't get his leggings down fast enough before the bottom dropped out altogether.

Where in God's name was the Arkansas?

All he could see ahead of him through the darkness was the next low ridge dim against the dark-blue sky. He wanted to lie down and rest. But if he did, he wasn't sure he'd be able to get up again.

The faint pungent sweetish smell of burning buffalo chips came to him. He hit the dirt immediately. He peered toward the next ridge. Something moved along the top of it. The smell of horses came to him—many horses. He closed his eyes and rested his head on his forearms. It was a hostile land. A sort of no-man's-land used by the Kotsoteka Comanches, the Buffalo Eaters from the Canadian River country, about two hundred miles south and their allies the Kiowa-Apaches. The Utes came down from the mountains and hunted buffalo there, but they were cousins to the Comanches. The Jicarilla were friendly with the Comanches too. Still, the unseen fire burners might be *ciboleros,* the New Mexican buffalo hunters, who had hunted buffalo in that area for generations.

Thirty-five miles from Bent's Fort. He'd have to have water before he attempted to get there. The fire burners were in between him and the river. Even if he did get to the river, he knew he'd never make it to the fort on foot.

His guts twisted into a hard knot and an involuntary groan escaped from his dry cracked lips. Cold sweat broke out on his forehead.

There would be a late moonrise that night. If he didn't get into cover before then he'd stand out like a stiff cock on that barren ground. Cover? He grimaced. There wasn't any.

149

He studied the dark ridge. The whole dark top of it seemed to move; grazing horses, maybe hundreds of them. He knew well enough that no *ciboleros* would have that many horses in their *caballada*. He'd need two horses anyway. If those were Comanches beyond the ridge he'd be up against the finest horsemen in the world if they pursued him.

Quint sat up. He pulled off his worn leggings. He wrinkled his big nose at the stench coming from them. He cut the leggings into long strips and then cut off the bottom part of his hunting jacket and cut that into strips too. He quickly braided two long hackamores from the leather. Now and again he'd look to the east hoping to God he wouldn't see the first traces of moonrise against the dark sky. He made a sling for his rifle and hung it over his back. He catfooted toward the ridge.

The wind was blowing toward Quint. There would be herd guards. It was a cold night. They might be hunkered down about a buffalo-chip fire. He worked his way up a gully and looked down the long slope on the north side of the ridge. He blinked his eyes and swallowed. He could see the conical shapes of tipis, many tipis, *hundreds* of tipis surrounded by the dim shapes of meat-drying scaffolds hung with much meat and back fat. The village, then, was that of a large hunting party.

How many guards?

The wind shifted a little. Quint crayfished back along the gully in order to approach from downwind of the herd. He bellied up the reverse side of the ridge and peered toward the herd. The closest horses were not more than fifty yards away. Quint moved, a noiseless, ghostlike figure, toward two horses that stood apart from the rest of the herd.

He whispered softly to the nearest of the two horses. "Hoh, hoh, hoh . . ." The mare raised her head and looked directly at Quint, slanting her split ears forward and wrinkling her nose. Knife-split ears marked a buffalo runner, the elite of the herd. Quint grinned at her. "Hyah, lover," he murmured. She nuzzled him. He had the improvised hackamore about her lower jaw and doubled-knotted before she could pull away.

The wing shifted again. A dun horse shied and blew as he caught Quint's scent. The mare whinnied softly and the dun came over to investigate. He'd had his speculative eye on her for the past few days. Quint doubled up with a sudden gut spasm. The mare got skittery. Quint spoke softly to her and quietened her. He got a hackamore on the dun with little trouble. His horse-stealing medicine seemed good that night. He took the leads of the hackamores and started catfooting down the reverse side of the ridge. The dogs in the village began a racketing barking.

Quint didn't see the stalwart young horse guard who rode slantways along the other side of the ridge until he topped it and stood up in his stirrups peering into the dimness toward Quint and the two horses. The brave narrowed his eyes. The other herd guards were almost a quarter of a mile away and closer to the camp. As far as he knew, he was the only guard that night.

The warrior raised his Nor'west trade shotgun. "*Niva tato?* Who is that?" he challenged.

Quint swung himself up onto the back of the mare from the right-hand side, Injun-style. He dug his heels into her shapely flanks and she reared, pawed the air, then buck-jumped as she dropped her forefeet to the ground. She started running as though shot out of a howitzer. Quint bent low over her neck. He looked back over the dun. He caught a faint glimpse of his pursuer. Just one of them, but others might have been alerted.

Quint raced to the south at first and then swung in a great arc to get back toward the river, hoping he'd outdistance his pursuer. Slowly he began to realize he could see somewhat better. The moon was rising. He let the eager mare out to her limit. He'd made a good choice from the feel of her. She was a little bay of perhaps fourteen hands, stout-backed and nimble-legged, with a tapering muzzle and a proud concave head indicating her Arabian origin.

Quint looked back at the dun. He was broad-chested and blocky. "Ain't this little lassie a beauty?" Quint asked the dun. He grinned. The dun was small and tough-looking, big-barreled with mulish hocks and slanting quarters. He'd likely be "hard-stomached" for an incredible amount of hard riding—a real stayer. It was a characteristic of most duns he had known.

The thought came to him that he'd likely have to break the mare, founder her and maybe kill her to get away from the vicinity of the Indian encampment. Horse stealing was a big thing to a yellowskin. One might steal his squaw and get away with it, but to steal one of his best horses and a prized buffalo runner at that . . .

A sharp cry came from Quint's pursuer as Quint was

151

skylined for a fraction of time on top of a ridge. Quint plunged down the slope, crossed a grassy shallow valley and then looked back. He saw the buck top the ridge and ride hell-for-leather down into the valley.

The moon came up to bathe the land in clear pale light, softening the harshness that was so apparent under the bright sunlight. Quint and his two mounts stood out clearly against the light-colored ground. No chance to elude his pursuer now. It would be a chase ending in the foundering or death of the mare, and—he hoped—of the buck's mount as well.

Quint crossed an area as flat and open as a gigantic billiard table. He let the mare run free. She would wear out soon enough. She was a sprinter, not a stayer like the dun. The brave was about two hundred yards behind Quint, not gaining much ground but not losing much either. Quint would have to get a greater lead on him before he reached the river.

The mare stumbled and went down. Quint clearly heard the sound of snapping bone. He hit the ground running, and as the dun surged up alongside, Quint gripped him by his mane and swung himself onto his back without the dun's breaking stride.

Quint's guts tightened. The violent act of changing mounts had aggravated his condition. He doubled up as an agonizing spasm shot through him. He became faint and swayed dizzily, and gripped the dun's mane to steady himself as he leaned perilously sideways. He turned the dun toward the river. He knew he'd never outride that damned persistent yellowskin.

The dun crashed into a dense tangled thicket of brush and vine-hung willow and cottonwood trees. The dun's forefeet plunged into a pothole. Quint was catapulted over the horse's head. He sprawled flatly, buoyed up by the thick and springy tangle beneath him. There was no use remounting. It would be difficult enough for Quint himself to get through the tangle to the river. He rolled sideways to get his feet on the ground and then forced his way recklessly through the thorned brush while dozens of tiny hooked needles tore at his clothing and flesh. He looked back. The thicket seemed deserted. Then his feet splashed into water.

The Arkansas was there before him, placid and silvery in the soft moonlight. There was a low island of sand and gravel stippled with low brush about sixty yards in front of Quint, with the main channel of the river beyond that, about a quarter of a mile to the north bank. A forsaken-looking sandhill crane stood on the low sandy island. The big bird's body was partially concealed by the brush, with just his long neck and angular head and bill protruding above the tangle.

Quint waded out toward the island. If he could cross to it and get into the cover of the brush before he was spotted by his pursuer there was a chance he could reach the main channel unseen. He plowed on, realizing with an uneasy feeling that quicksand was sucking about his ankles.

The warrior's horse crashed into the brush. He dismounted as he saw the dun standing quietly in the tangle. He crashed recklessly through the brush until he saw the horse thief wading out toward the island, then raised his shotgun and cocked both hammers. He could hardly miss at that range. He centered his sights on the broad back of the fugitive. The raucous cry of a sandhill crane echoed along the river. The warrior lowered his shotgun. The strong alarming cry came again. Among the brave's people the sandhill crane was believed to have strong protective powers. It was a bird that took pity on everybody. If a man imitated the call of the sandhill crane he could not be hit by any bullet. The bird was known to be a fearless and powerful war helper.

The thick-bodied rattlesnake had first been aroused from a chilled torpor by the sound of Quint thrashing through the brush. The reptile had half coiled ready to strike and then had uncoiled as the sound receded. It was alerted again by the sound of someone else approaching. The thick body coiled; the flat head weaved back and forth ready to strike; the many rattles sounded dryly like pebbles shaken in a gourd. The rattler struck from one-foot range, sinking its extended fangs into the warrior's left forearm just above the wrist. The warrior shrieked in intense fear and agony.

His shouts and cries came to Quint from the far edge of the brush thicket. Quint knew the lone warrior would have been followed by some of his tribesmen. If the other bucks heard the shrieks and were drawn in their direction, Quint would never be able to make it to the island and then across the main channel without being seen. Quint waded laboriously back to the bank. He shifted his rifle to his left hand and drew his knife for a quick and silent kill.

The young buck was down on his knees, his face drawn into a contorted mask of pain and fear. Somehow he had managed to draw his knife and slash through the body of the rattlesnake, but the loathesome head still remained fastened to his arm. The buck thrust his knife out defensively toward Quint.

Quint waved aside the knife. He placed his rifle and knife

153

on the ground and swiftly made the sign for peace by clasping his hands in front of his body with the back of the left hand down. He plucked the knife from the young man's hand and threw it to one side. Stripping off his belt, he made a tourniquet above the wound in the hollow of the elbow, where he placed a rounded stone to apply pressure on the artery. He plucked the snake head from the wound and then rapidly slit the flesh about the puncture wounds to make the blood flow freely. Then with an upward rolling of his eyes and a silent prayer to what ever god or gods might be listening he began to suck the venom from the wound.

Quint spat out the blood and venom. He kept at the wounds until they sucked dry. He applied firm pressure on each side of the cuts to make the blood flow more freely. As he raised his head from the wounds he heard the tattoo of pounding hoofs on the hard earth to the south of the thicket. He poured a thick pinch of gunpowder from his horn onto the wounds and looked questioningly into the young warrior's eyes as he raised flint and steel over the wounds. The young man was mystified, but the *veho*, the "yellow-eye," had done him no harm and seemed to know what he was doing. He nodded. Quint instantly struck sparks into the gunpowder to ignite it in order to cauterize the wounds. The buck did not cry out. Quint nodded in approval of his courage.

Quint squatted back on his heels and tilted his head to one side. "Ye'll have a swollen arm for some time, laddie, and ye'll be almighty sick for a time, but ye'll not likely die from the venom. Ye might never get back the full use of that arm again, but it will be better than dying such an undignified and ignominious death for such a young buck as ye are." He grinned. "But ye don't understand a word I'm saying, do ye now?"

Quint loosened the tourniquet to allow a fuller flowing of the blood and then tightened it again. He stood up and thrust his left hand palm forward with the fingers spread, then fluttered the hand sideways and rubbed the finger tips of his right hand over the back of the left hand between the knuckles and the wrist with a circular motion, then pointed to the warrior, meaning, "What tribe are you?"

The young man made a slashing or chopping motion of his right forefinger against his left forefinger indicating hand choppers or finger choppers, a sign of mourning among his people. "Tsis-tsis-tas, the People," he added proudly.

Quint whistled softly. He quickly picked up his knife and

Hawken. "Sha-hi-e-na," he said haltingly in the Dakotah or Sioux tongue. "Cheyenne," he added in English.

The Cheyenne dubiously eyed Quint's beaded hunting shirt. He had recognized the style of it for what it was. He held out his right hand at waist height and moved it about a foot forward with a wavy motion to indicate the sign for Shoshonis. "Sus-son-i," he murmured. The Cheyennes were deadly enemies to the Comanches and considered the Shoshonis as nothing more than Mountain Comanches. His eyes widened in awe as he noted the necklace of grizzly-bear claws Quint wore about his neck.

The sound of pursuit came closer to the inland edge of the thicket. Warriors called back and forth to each other as they dismounted and pushed into the tangle with ready weapons. Quint doubled over with a cramping spasm. Sweat broke out on his forehead, and he gasped a little. He turned and hobbled to the riverbank. He used the rifle as a prop as he began to wade out toward the island. His feet sank into the sucking sands and slowed his already laborious progress.

"*Nonotox!* Hurry now!" the young Cheyenne shouted at Quint.

Quint nodded. He paused, leaning on his rifle, hardly able to keep on. His feet and rifle butt sank deeply into the sands.

Pushing Ahead had led the pursuit party from the Cheyenne village. He heard the urgent cry of Little Hawk, "Hurry now!" There was no time to lose. He led the way as fast as he could toward the sound.

The sorrel-bearded white man stood crotch-deep in the shallow water between the riverbank and a low island. He was ashen faced, and dog-sick.

The Cheyennes raised their rifles. Hammers clicked back to full cock.

"No!" Little Hawk shouted. "He saved my life when I was bitten by a rattlesnake! See?" He snatched up the thick body of the deadly reptile and then thrust out his left arm to show the cauterized wound. "He could have escaped if he had not come back to save my life! I claim him as my friend and brother!"

Three of the warriors stepped quickly into the water and waded toward Quint. Quint saw the three black feathers each of them wore on the back of their heads. "Jesus," he murmured. He had heard of their far-famed military society. "Hotamitaniu—Dog Soldiers . . ."

A mounted man forced his pony along the shoreline until

he reached the Cheyennes. He swung down from his pony and eyed Quint as he was being helped toward the bank. He wore a wide-brimmed white man's hat with a white eagle feather stuck into the rattlesnake-skin band. He was short, broad of shoulder, bandylegged, and had a pair of piercing blue eyes that seemed to be able to look right through a man and count the knuckles on his backbone.

"Howdy, friend," Quint murmured weakly.

Blue-Eyes grinned widely. "Howdy, Big Red," he said, thin-voiced.

Quint wearily shook his head in utter disbelief. "I'll be goddamned! Kit! Kit Carson! For a minute or two I thought I was gone beaver here."

"Yuh almost were, old hoss," Kit agreed dryly. "Stealin' hosses from the Tsis-tsis-tas. My God!"

Quint fell face forward onto the riverbank. It was the last thing he knew.

TWENTY-ONE

The buffalo-hunting village of the Tsis-tsis-tas was pitched in a broad level bottom beside the Arkansas River. There were about three hundred and fifty lodges of the Cheyennes and one hundred of the Arapahos, allies to the Cheyennes, a slim people with the look of eagles. The tipis were pitched facing east in a great circle half a mile across. The village was surrounded by racks and scaffolds of drying buffalo meat and *dépouille*, or back fat. Pegged-out buffalo hides were spread out all around the lodges. The Cheyennes were the Hevataniu, or Hairy Rope band, chieftained by the customary four chiefs equal in authority, who were at this time Yellow Wolf, Little Moon, Walking Whirlwind and the aged White Bull, grandfather to Little Hawk, whose life had been saved by Quintin Kershaw.

Quint had been received with great honor by the Cheyennes and Arapahos. Great respect was due such an accomplished horse thief, and moreover, had he not great medicine to save the life of Little Hawk? Did he not wear a necklace of grizzly-bear claws about his neck signifying that he had killed such a great beast in hand-to-hand combat? Black Moccasin, the Delaware who was married to the Cheyenne woman White Bead Woman, knew this great man well, for he had trapped with him many years and had told many stories about him the past winter long before the white man had appeared along the Arkansas. Too, he was the great friend and blood brother to the highly respected Little Chief, whom the whites called Kit Carson. It had been a great honor for Roan Bear, a Cheyenne medicine man, and his wife and partner She Bear, an Arapaho, to treat this Quintin Kershaw for the badwater sickness.

When Quint was cured of the sickness he moved from the lodge of White Bull into that of Black Moccasin and his pretty young wife. That same evening Luke Connors rode into the village from Bent's Fort hoping to talk Quint, Kit and Black Moccasin into accompanying him to New Mexico or, for that matter, any other place they had a mind to go. A fall and winter meat-hunting job at Bent's Fort had been quite enough for him. It was early summer now; walls and a roof were for wintertime.

"Did ye see four men at Bent's before ye left?" Quint asked. "They would have called themselves trappers. A white man, a Mexican, and possibly two breeds or Indians."

Luke nodded. "They said they came from the Bayou Salade country. They brought in five packs of some of the finest plews I ever seen, as well as some wolf pelts, deer hides and the pelt of one of the biggest grizzlies I've seen in some years. Their plews and pelts were the talk of the people at the fort."

"Mine," Quint said bitterly. "No doubt about it. What did these 'trappers' look like?"

"The leader was an American. Light-colored hair like dirty sand. Cold gray eyes like a huntin' wolf. Beautiful set of teeth. Smiled a lot, but never with the eyes. One of them was a Mexican with a lot of Injun blood in him, mebbe a half-breed. Broad-shouldered and very strongly built. Shifty-eyed. Never looked a man square in the face if he could help it. One of them was *puro indio*. Slight build. Moved like a cat. Grinned a lot for no good reason. Didn't seem like he was quite right in the head. Could have been a Ute, but I lean toward Jicarilla Apache. Hard to tell. The last of the four was the one I noticed most. Would give a man quite a turn if he come up against him some dark night 'thout expectin' it. Dark face, pox-marked, a real 'rough-face.' Flattened nose with wide nostrils. Thick lips like a nigger. No pupil to the left eye, just a whitish color like dirty milk. It was his right eye that wud startle a man, leastways in that dark face of his. It was a pale cold blue like a winter sky on a clear day. I can't say what *he* was. Might have been a nigger, or part nigger and part white, a mulatto, or maybe a quadroon, or maybe Kiowa Injun and part white. God alone might know *what* he was, and *He* might not even be sure."

Quint pulled on the new Cheyenne moccasins that had been made for him. "What were they called?"

"They didn't use names with each other except once. I got the feeling they didn't exactly trust each other."

"Why did ye think that last one ye mentioned was part Kiowa?"

"Like I said: They didn't use names with each other except once. The Injun called the dark-faced one Kiowa."

Quint stood up. "That's all? Just Kiowa?" He shrugged into a deerskin jacket Moccasin had given him and reached for his Hawken rifle and sack of possibles.

"Where do yuh think you're goin', Big Red?" Kit asked quietly.

"To Bent's, after my plews."

Kit shook his head. "Yuh ain't fully cured yet, sonny."

"I'm going after my plews, and aim to do a little bloodletting in the process," Quint insisted.

Luke shook his head. "Yuh won't find them there now, Big Red. They was in an all-fired hurry to trade their plews, other peltries and traps for trade goods and whiskey. They were still there when I left, but aimed to leave Bent's that same day."

"Where were they going?" Quint asked quietly.

"They didn't say. There was talk around the fort that they were Comancheros, and might be headin' for the Cimarron River country to trade for horses from the Comanches."

"No matter! Those are still my plews! Not theirs! Not Bent's! They're mine, godammit! I froze my ass off getting them! They damned near killed me and likely killed my squaw as well!"

"Did yuh mark the plews?" Luke asked.

"No! But they're mine!" Quint started for the door.

Kit stood up. "Wait, Quint! Listen to me!"

Kit's thin voice had hardened with the ring of authority. Men much older than Kit was usually stopped and listened when he spoke in that tone of voice. Quint turned and grounded his rifle. He leaned on it and eyed Kit.

"Yuh know as well as we do that Bent, St. Vrain and Company are fair traders," Kit explained. "Their equals in honest dealings were never in the mountains. They'd never buy or trade for stolen goods if they were aware of it. But their word is law in that fort of theirs. If yuh go there all riled up like yuh are now, and start a ruckus about them unmarked plews of yourn, and mebbe slip the sear on that hairtrigger Scots temper of yourn and throw some Galena pills around inside that fort, yuh may end up full of lead yourself or take a dive off the walls with a rope around your neck. That's as sure as my rifle's got hindsights and shoots center! If yuh had marked them plews with your mark like yuh shoulda done, and could prove it, then mebbe yuh could make a deal with them. Just remember there ain't no law around these prairie parts except the law of the strongest, and the law at the fort is Bent's law. They're judge, jury and executioner.

"Besides, the Hairy Rope band and the 'Rapahos are movin' to Bent's Fort in a few days. They got enough meat and robes for tradin'. Seems as though last spring about forty Cheyenne Bow-String Soldiers started out to horse-raid the Comanches and Kiowas. Their medicine was bad. They got ambushed. The Comanches and Kiowas wiped out every goddam one of 'em like piss ants. The Cheyennes been cryin' about it all winter. The widow wimmen been cuttin' themselves and wipin' their bloody hands on the faces of the members of the soldier societies askin' them for revenge and justice on the Comanches.

"Now that the grass is up for grazin' it's time for the warpath. The whole kit and caboodle of Cheyennes and 'Rapahos aim to paint their faces black and hit the Comanches and Kiowas with everything they got. But they need guns, powder, bullets, lead, flints and percussion caps. That's why they went on this big buffler hunt. They aim to trade in their meat and robes for what they need to bring war to the Comanches and Kiowas."

"And plenty whiskey," Moccasin added.

"Naturally," Kit said dryly. "Now, Big Red, yuh let me and

159

Luke here go on ahead tonight, and yuh can come on with the Hairy Ropes. By that time, mebbe we can get a lead on where your thieves are, and if they ain't gotten too far south, we can give yuh a hand goin' after them."

Quint shook his head. "A waste of good time. I can't afford to burn daylight. I'll go after them alone."

It became very quiet in the big lodge.

Quint looked from one to the other of them. "Well?"

Kit looked sideways at Moccasin. "Yuh figger the Hairy Ropes will let Big Red Badger have a hoss?"

"Not if we tell them not to," the Delaware replied.

"I'll go on foot," Quint blustered. "I got all the way here afoot, didn't I?"

Luke picked at a long tooth with a dirty fingernail. "The Comanches will be movin' north now that the grass is up for grazin'. Yuh aim to take *them* on too?" He stood up. "Little Chief, we'd best get on to Bent's."

Kit stood up and then squatted in front of Quint. "One more thing. Break a little now and then, Big Red, or you'll go under. *Comprende?*" He stood up and looked down at Quint.

Quint looked up at his two friends. He finally nodded. *"Comprende."*

Moccasin glanced sideways at Quint after Kit and Luke had left. "Good friends, eh, Big Red Badger?"

"Aye, Moccasin."

"Yuh ride with us. Cheyenne good friends. Ain't no better friends than a coupla hundred fightin' Cheyennes when yuh need 'em, eh?"

Quint grinned a little. "Or a drunken Delaware. Pass the brandy."

Moccasin drained his cup and stood up. "Now, give me that Shoshoni shirt. Let me git rid of it. Yuh do yourself no good wearin' it around here, no matter how good yuh stand with the People."

Quint looked down at the shirt. It was filthy now, covered with dirt, grease and bloodstains. Some of the beads and quills were missing. Seams gaped. The skirt was missing, cut off to make hackamores for the Cheyenne horses he had stolen.

"What the hell is the matter with yuh?" the Delaware demanded. "Yuh know how the People are. They lost many Bow-String Soldiers to the Comanches. To them a Shoshoni ain't nothin' but a Mountain Comanche. If we get to Bent's

160

Fort and the warriors get into the likker, which they sure as hell will, some of 'em might decide to count coup on yuh."

Quint clearly remembered that cold night in his valley when Mountain Woman had made him try it on for size. He had wanted to wear it then as it was, without the beading and quilling that meant nothing to him.

"It does to me," Mountain Woman had said quietly. *"Do I want my man to appear before the women of my people in such a plain and ugly shirt? What would they think of me?"*

"One of these Cheyenne or Arapaho wimmen will make yuh another shirt as easy as eatin' *boudin*," Moccasin suggested slyly.

"What's the catch?"

"Just make sure any of the single ones ain't got the *nihpihist*, the virgin rope between their legs and wrapped around their thighs. Leave *them* kind be! If yuh don't you'll have all her menfolk after yuh. There are plenty men-hungry widows in this camp. Just take your pick."

Quint peeled off the shirt and handed it to Moccasin. "No thanks. I can get a wool shirt at Bent's. I like them better anyway."

Moccasin studied Quint. "What do yuh suppose happened to the Shoshoni woman?"

"Dead, most likely."

"Then yuh kin forget her."

Moccasin left the lodge and walked through the gathering dusk light to the river. He hurled the bundled shirt into the river as far as he could. It floated downstream, slowly sinking as the water soaked into it. The last he saw of it was the wet masses of pink and white beads shining, and then it sank from sight.

TWENTY-TWO

The River of Lost Souls in Purgatory.

The Hairy Rope band of Cheyennes with their allies the Arapahos moved en masse along the north bank of the Arkansas toward Bent's Fort. Their intention was to join other bands of Southern Cheyennes, there to prepare for moving the Four Sacred Medicine Arrows against the Comanche-Kiowas who had ambushed and slaughtered forty-two Bow-String Soldiers the previous spring. For this they would need many guns, much powder, ball, flints and caps. Their travois and horse packs were heavily loaded with good winter buffalo robes for trading.

Quint Kershaw, somewhat pale and still not quite up to snuff, rode with the Cheyennes mounted on a fine mouse-gray California riding mule given to him by White Bull for saving the life of Little Hawk.

A far-flung fringe of scouts mounted on the fastest ponies ranged ahead of the main body, behind it and on either flank, including a detachment on the south or Mexican bank of the river. Each lodge had its own band of horses, presenting a strange appearance, for there were many bands of them walking together yet separated into their own individual groups. Each group followed its own leader, usually a mare, or sometimes a woebegone scrawny mule hardly worth the powder to kill it.

The widespread cavalcade moved along accompanied by a cacophony of thousands of thudding hoofs, barking dogs, whinnying and neighing of horses, crying out of children, and the young people shouting and calling back and forth to each other. The continuous din and seeming confusion belied what in reality was the orderly procession of a Plains Indian band on the march.

They were a handsome and dashing people, these Chey-ennes and Arapahos. To Quintin Kershaw, a fascinated observer, they had far more of a flair for the dramatic than he had seen among the Shoshonis, the Nez Perce, Utes and other mountain tribes.

The young women and budding girls were superb riders. They dashed furiously about on half-broken horses while riding astride and secure in their colorful, high-pommeled saddles.

The Cheyenne women brushed their hair to a glossy sheen and let it hang down their back in two braids, or bunched it behind and above the ears in buns wrapped in ornamented buckskin. Their fine complexions and hair partings were painted with vermilion. Gleaming, iridescent shells of great value from the Pacific coast hung from their pierced ears. They wore highly polished bracelets on their arms and many tiny brass rings on their fingers, which glittered in the bright sunlight.

Moccasin rode up alongside Quint. "Gettin' interested, Red Badger?" he asked.

Quint looked quickly away from a young woman who had raced back and forth in front of Quint quite a few times showing off her superb horsewomanship as well as one hell of a figure. She could hardly be more than sixteen years old.

"You big man with Cheyenne now," Moccasin reminded Quint. "I told yuh back on the Seeds-kee-dee that Cheyenne women pretty. Got big tits. Make best moccasin on plains. Make good wives."

Quint looked over his shoulder. White Bead Woman was riding decorously behind her master as she should. She was a real Cheyenne beauty. He turned to look forward. A quick cameo came into his mind—Mountain Woman bending over the beautiful beaded hunting shirt she had made for him. Now it was lying torn and bloodstained at the bottom of the Arkansas.

"She gone, that Snake woman," Moccasin said. "No use thinkin' about her. Look around yourself. Plenty good wimmen here for the askin'. Take your pick. I can lend yuh the horses for tradin'." He grinned slyly. "They run about ten to a virgin, Big Red."

Quint shook his head. "Not right now."

"Forget Snake woman. Forget plews. They both gone forever. Stay with Cheyennes. Better than Snakes. Hunt buffalo. Live like chief."

Quint shook his head. "Maybe, after I get my value back out of those stolen plews."

Moccasin shrugged. "Luke and me talk about mebbe goin' to New Mexico. Mebbe trade for horses and mules and sell to Bent's. Bent want lots of Navajo blankets. Sell good out here to Cheyenne and Arapaho. What do yuh say?"

"I'll think about it."

"My brother Black Beaver and his son Buffalo Droppings come to Bent's. Good Delawares like me. The best. Want to go to New Mexico, mebbe Californy. Me, Luke, my brother and nephew all go. Need one more good man." Moccasin slanted his eyes toward Quint. "Need a leader bad. Like we had up north."

"I *was* thinking of going to New Mexico at one time."

"Mebbe we can ride through Kotsoteka Comanche country. Comancheros go there with your trade goods they got from Bent's with your plews. We kin use them trade goods if we go to New Mexico. Them Comancheros mebbe tradin' for Mex horses and mules with Comanches, then sell to traders, or mebbe take to New Mexico. If them trade good yours, then horses and mules are yours too, eh?"

Quint nodded. "Damned right they are! Ye've a business head on your shoulders, Moc. Ye realize, of course, that it will be damned dangerous."

Moccasin looked slowly around the empty landscape and off to the hazy horizon. "Big Red, *everythin'* we do in this country dangerous." He glanced sideways at Quint. "That Shoshoni squaw—are yuh sure she's dead?"

"Of course! Would I have left my valley without knowing for sure?"

"I don't recollect yuh sayin' yuh found her body."

Quint's face was set and grim. "What the hell difference does that make?" he demanded angrily.

There was no reply from Moccasin.

Some miles from Bent's Fort a party of horsemen could be seen driving a *caballada* of horses and mules. Two men mounted on riding mules detached themselves from the group and rode toward the approaching Cheyennes.

"Kit and Luke," Moccasin said.

The two mountain men rode alongside Quint and Moccasin. "Yore four Comancheros headed for the Kotsoteka Comanche country all right, Big Red," Luke said. "Took five packloads of trade goods with them. Those men driving the *caballada* up ahead are *ciboleros* from New Mexico. They were finishing up their spring buffalo hunt when most of their horses and mules were run off by what they think was a

164

band of Pawnees. Yuh remember Federico Casias from Taos? He's their leader. They left their companions and the meat and hides near Cañon Chacuaco and came to Bent's to get more horses and mules. Casias says when they were on their way here they met four Comancheros driving five pack mules loaded with trade goods."

"I'll ride back with them," Quint said quietly.

"Yuh loco?" Luke demanded. "Those Comancheros are known in Comanche country, or they wouldn't be danglin' five pack loads of trade goods in front of the Comanches, along with their weapons and scalps. They're accepted for what they are; the Kotsotekas sure as hell won't accept you for what yuh are. Yuh known better'n to go into Comanche country alone! The country around the Cimarron and the Canadian will be swarmin' with 'em at this time of the year! The grass is growin'—time for the warpath and horse stealin'. Any Comanche buck would love to have that sorrel scalp o' yourn danglin' from his lance or fringin' his leggings!"

Quint quirted his mule and galloped toward the *ciboleros,* who were now diverging from their course to get out of the way of the oncoming Cheyennes. Likely they were a little worried about losing their horses and mules to the Cheyennes. They headed for a ford of the Arkansas to cross the wide, shallow river.

The *ciboleros* were a wild and colorful lot, clad in leather trousers or buckskin leggings, leather jackets and flat straw hats. They hunted the buffalo from horseback with lances, or bows and arrows. The long handle of the lance was set in a leather case and suspended from a strap about the pommel so as to hang along the side of the horse or mule they rode. A tassel of gay particolored stuffs dangled at the tip of the case. A leather *carcage,* or quiver of bows and arrows, was suspended in like manner beside the lance. An *escopeta,* or fusil, hung on the other side of the mount. Its muzzle was stoppered by a wooden plug, which likewise sported many colored streamers.

Quint caught up with the *ciboleros* as they prepared to ford the river. "Federico Casias!" he called. "A word with you!"

The leader of the *ciboleros* reined in his half-broken *grulla* mustang. "The Montero Americano, Quintin Kershaw," he said, with a flashing of as perfect a set of pure white teeth as Quint had ever seen. "Federico Casias, *servidor de Ustedes.*"

Quint nodded. "Quint Kershaw, your servant, señor," he said in kind. "You remember me then?"

165

Casias was a handsome devil, with olive skin and black mustache, and a pair of eyes like moist black velvet. "How could I ever forget you?" he asked in rather good English. "How can I help you?"

"Luke Connors just told me ye saw four Comancheros on the way to Bent's Fort."

The *cibolero's* face changed. "Friends of yours?" he asked, a little coldly.

Quint quickly shook his head. "They are thieves, *ladrones*. They stole five packs of beaver plews from me, and killed my woman to boot. They traded the plews in at Bent's for trade goods for the Kotsoteka Comanches."

The New Mexican nodded. "It was to be expected with those *ladrones*. I am sorry for you."

"Can you describe them to me?"

"Easily. You see, my friend, I recognized them."

"You knew them before?"

"To my sorrow. They are known in my country. They have never been caught in committing a crime, although there is no question but what they have committed many crimes, singly and together. There is an Indian, one Jose, a Jicarilla Apache ." Here Federico twirled a forefinger in a circle at his temple. "He's not right in the head. Loco. A New Mexican, one Antonio, who goes by many names. A quarter-breed Comanche, from what I've heard. A strange one, perhaps a demon walking the earth." Here Federico quickly crossed himself. "Dark of face, what the Indians call a 'rough-face,' one who had the pox and yet survived. His left eye was askew, a dirty white in color, while the right eye was a pale blue. I think he is called Kiowa. The fourth man was American. I don't know his name, and knew him least of all. I am not even sure he was the same man wanted in my country. Light sandy-colored hair. Cold blue eyes. Have I been of help?"

"Yes, of course. Those are the thieves all right. Did they say where they were going?"

Federico shook his head. "My friend, lawful men do not speak with such *ladrones,* and give them plenty of room to pass, and do not take their eyes off of them until they are out of the range of a bullet, you understand? However, they would have had to find water, and the closest water in that area is beyond the Cañon Chacuaco. That is where the rest of my people are camped, waiting for us to return with the mules and horses we need to haul our *carreta* loads of meat

166

and hides back to the rancho of my *patrón*." He smiled, a little wryly. "I hope my people see those damned Comancheros before the Comancheros see them."

The other *ciboleros* had driven the *caballada* of horses and mules across the river and were waiting on the south bank for Federico to join them. One of them still halfway across the river cupped his hands about his mouth and shouted, "Hurry, Federico! If the Comanches come to Cañon Chacuaco and find our people there without horses and mules with which to escape there will be no need for us to go there at all!"

Federico nodded. He waved a hand. "Go on then, Pablo! I will be with you in a moment!" He turned to Quint. "We were almost done with the hunting when our horses and mules were stolen by the Pawnees. We had hoped to be on our way back to the rancho by this time."

"Pawnees? That far south and west?"

"Sometimes they tail the caravans bound for Santa Fe on the Cimarron Cut-off, hoping to snap up some of their horses and mules. Next to the Comanches, I think they are the worst of all horse thieves."

"Or best, eh, *amigo*, depending upon how one looks at it." Quint smiled as he extended his hand to shake that of the *cibolero*. When he had been in New Mexico some years past he had formed an instant liking for Federico and had sensed a reciprocal feeling from the New Mexican.

Federico touched spurs to his mustang. "If you return to New Mexico, *amigo*, my house is your house."

"*Gracias. Vaya con Dios, compañero.*"

Quint watched the *cibolero* as he rode across the river. When Federico reached the far side he turned in his saddle and waved at Quint. The hunters drove the *caballada* through the willows and cottonwoods lining the bank and were soon lost to sight, leaving only a faint film of dust to mark their passage.

Luke and Kit reined in their mules beside that of Quint. "God help them if the Comanches get to Cañon Chacuaco before they do," Kit said quietly.

"Or *I* do," Quint said.

Kit looked sideways at Quint. "Yuh aim to go there too, then?"

"The sooner the better. Tomorrow."

"Yuh might run into a coupla hundred Comanches in the process, old hoss."

Quint spat to one side. "Let them look out for themselves."
He quirted his mule and rode after the Cheyennes.

Kit rested an elbow on his saddle pommel. "Yuh think he
means it, Luke?" he asked dryly.

Luke nodded. "Sure as hell does, Kit."

They shook their heads as they rode after Quint.

TWENTY-THREE

Bent's Big Lodge on the Arkansas

Bent's Fort was the headquarters of Bent, St. Vrain and
Company, Indian and Mexican traders. The squat mud fort,
grayish-brown in color, stood on a benchland just north of the
Arkansas River. Far to the southwest could be seen the
dull-gray twin breasts of the Spanish Peaks, seemingly only
fifteen miles away but in reality more than 120. To the
northeast, about the same distance away, one might see on a
clear day the faint outline of a truncated mountain—Pike's
Peak. Farther to the west was the dim blue bulk of the
Rockies. Somewhere in their fastness, up beyond the headwaters of the Rio Grande del Norte, was a hidden, haunted
valley—Quint Kershaw's Valley.

Although the fort was only ten years old it was already a
legend. It had been founded by the Bent brothers, Charles
and William, traders from St. Louis, with Ceran St. Vrain as
partner. It was situated close to the buffalo-hunting grounds
of the Southern Plains tribes—the Southern Cheyennes, Arapahos, Utes, Comanches, Kiowas and Kiowa-Apaches. The
fort had been started in 1828 but the difficulty of obtaining
workmen, had delayed the completion until 1832.

The fort had originally been called Fort William in honor
of the younger of the two brothers, but the mountain men
who traded there had rechristened it Bent's Fort and the
name had stuck, although some also called it Bent's Big
Lodge on the Arkansas. It was a main stop on the Mountain

Branch of the Santa Fe Trail 530 miles from Independence, 180 miles from Taos, 280 miles from Santa Fe.

William Bent was Charles' junior by nine years. Both men were small in stature but large in physical courage, even in a trade where physical courage was a staple trait. They were both as tough as oak knots. William was dark-haired and dark-eyed. His face was lightly pocked from an attack of smallpox years earlier. The Bents were offshoots of Massachusetts Puritans, but could quite easily be mistaken for Louisianians or French Canadians as they both spoke fluent Mississippi River French as well as a number of Indian dialects. When in the fort William usually wore fringed buckskin clothing and beautifully beaded Cheyenne-style moccasins made for him by his wife, Owl Woman. His Indian name, given to him by Yellow Wolf of the Hairy Rope Band, was Little White Man. Charles Bent had made his home in Taos, New Mexico, to handle the trading firm's business there, and married a New Mexican woman.

Ceran St. Vrain, or Ceran de Hault de Lassus de St. Vrain, to give his full name, was a partner of the Bent brothers. He was a round-faced, square-hewn block of a man with thick black hair and beard. He had wide-set eyes which were always quick to crinkle in humor or occasionally to flare in sudden anger. Missouri-born, of aristocratic French descent, he had been at San Fernandez de Taos as early as 1825 and had recognized it as a natural spot for trade. He had joined the Bents in partnership and taken out Mexican citizenship in 1831 to facilitate the firm's business ventures in New Mexico. He too had a Mexican wife and a fine home in Taos. He was known to the Cheyennes as Blackbeard. The Kiowas, noting his strong beaked nose, called him Hook Nose.

The tribesmen had already turned aside as Quint, Luke and Kit rode on toward the fort. Lodge markers were quickly put down. The squaws began to unload the travois in order to use the poles to erect the lodges. Buffalo hides, dried buffalo meat and tongues were piled together to be brought into the fort for trading purposes.

The plaza area within the fort was roughly eighty by one hundred feet in size. It had been thickly laid with gravel to hold down the dust. A brass fieldpiece stood near the gateway, ready to be quickly wheeled into action if required. There were about twenty-five rooms on the ground floor of the fort. They had whitewashed walls facing inward to the plaza. A timber-supported arcade had been built on all sides

169

except the front, or north, side. A heavily timbered fur press stood out from about the center of the east side of the plaza. A dark mound of buffalo robes, the swarthy wool matted and stuck with ticks and burrs, stood next to the press ready for baling for shipment back to the States. There were piles of other hides and furs there as well, and what looked like five packs of beaver hides. Quint started toward them.

"Even if they *were* yore plews, Quint," Kit said, "they're the property of Bent, St. Vrain and Company now."

"And, if yuh were stupid enough not to mark 'em," Luke added dryly, "yuh can't prove they *were* yore plews."

"They were taken in good faith here," Kit said. "Yuh can talk to Colonel Bent about it, but he's not obligated to owe yuh anything."

Two Indians dressed in mountain-man-style clothing came forward with Moccasin as Quint, Kit and Luke led their mules to the corral. The Delaware introduced them to Quint as his elder brother Black Beaver and Black Beaver's seventeen-year-old son who had been rechristened Joshua by a missionary. The boy preferred his Christian name to his Delaware name, Buffalo Droppings, which, although socially acceptable among his own people, was not looked upon in quite the same light by the white men with whom he came in contact.

"Yuh want to go to New Mexico, Big Red?" Black Beaver asked.

Quint nodded. "Maybe by way of Cañon Chacuaco."

"Kotsoteka country."

"Right."

"Yuh want partners?"

"I can use them," Quint admitted.

Black Beaver jerked his head sideways toward his son. "Him too? Smart boy. Damned good shot. Better than me. Better than Moccasin. Mebbe as good as you, Big Red."

Quint looked at the boy. "That so, Josh?" he asked.

Joshua looked at Quint's famed Hawken rifle. "That 'Auld Clootie'?" he asked.

Quint held the rifle out to the young Delaware. "Here. Take it outside and try a few rounds through it." He lifted the straps of his powderhorns, bullet pouch and possibles sack over his head and handed them to Joshua. "Use my powder and bullets, eh, lad?"

The Delaware studied Quint's scarred face. His eyes lowered to look at the grizzly-bear necklace hanging about Quint's neck. He looked into Quint's eyes. "Your powder make it shoot any better, Big Red?" he asked dryly.

Quint was solemn-faced. "Try it and see," he suggested.

They watched the sober young Delaware march from the plaza, followed by his father. He carried the famed Hawken rifle as though it were the Ark of the Covenant.

"I'll be damned," Quint said quietly.

"He's been waiting for yuh," Luke explained. "People around here been tellin' him about yuh and Auld Clootie ever since they knowed yuh was in the Cheyenne camp." He looked sideways at Quint. "That's the first time I ever saw yuh let a stranger take that rifle out'n yore hands."

"You've made a friend for life," Kit said.

Quint looked at Kit. "I know, Kit." He turned to Luke. "Where's the drinking liquor?"

Luke and Kit bunked in a second-floor room in the northwest corner of the fort. It was about fifteen feet by twenty-five and had a low, heavily beamed ceiling. A Mexican-type beehive fireplace was in one corner. The walls were whitewashed. The floor was of hard-beaten clay carpeted with buffalo robes. Navajo blankets and mattresses were rolled up and piled along the walls for seats during the day.

Luke placed a jug of amber Pass brandy on a low table. "Yuh bunk in with us here, Big Red. Plenty of room. Useta have a roommate, me and Kit did. French Canadian by the name of Etienne, but everybody called him Boudins, like we call François, and sometimes Guts for short. He was a meat hunter like me and Kit. But he insisted on hunting alone with no one to watch his back. Shot an antelope and forgot to reload right away. He was squattin' over the antelope skinnin' it when a Skidi Pawnee come up behind him quiet-like, sunk a pipe-ax into his neck and then lifted his ha'r." Luke shook his head sadly. "Etienne was a nice fella, but a mite careless. This was his full half-gallon jug of prime five-year-old Pass brandy. Part of his estate now, I reckon, but he didn't leave a will. Died, what do yuh call it, Big Red?"

"Intestate, Luke."

Luke nodded. "Dig out the cups, Kit."

There was a small newspaper clipping framed and hung on the wall beside the beehive fireplace. Quint read it;

Missouri Intelligencer, Franklin, Oct. 6, 1826: Notice —To Whom it may concern: that Christopher Carson, a boy about sixteen years, small of his age, but thick set, light hair, ran away from the subscriber, living in Franklin, Howard Co., Mo., to whom he had been bound to learn the saddler's trade, on or about the first day of Setember last. He is supposed to have made his way to the upper part of the State. All persons are notified not to harbour, support or assist said boy under penalty of law. One cent reward will be given to any person who will bring back said boy.

David Workman.

Kit was sitting Indian-fashion on a buffalo robe shuffling a greasy pack of cards. Luke and Black Moccasin were sitting with him with the brandy jug between them.

"Anyone ever collect that powerful big reward for ye, Kit?" Quint asked casually.

Kit shrugged. "Seems like no one had that kind of ambition."

Luke nodded. "Lot of money for the times."

"Mr. Workman thought a lot of ye, eh, Kit?" Quint suggested.

"Obvious, ain't it? Want to sit in on a hand or two before supper?"

Quint shook his head. He watched his three friends as they played Old Sledge. The three of them had the marked stamp of self-reliance, energy, force and great physical courage struck on their weathered features like that of a newly minted coin. The beaver trapping was about done for them, as it was for Quint, François "Boudins" Charbonne and all the other men of the mountains. What was to be the future for them? New Mexico seemed the best bet. Luke, Quint and Black Moccasin had trapped out of Taos one season. Kit knew New Mexico well. It was likely to assume his future would be there.

In the spring of 1835 Kit had trapped the Snake River and the Green River and fought his famous "duel" with the French Canadian bully Shunar, a member of Captain Drips company of the American Fur Company. It had been at the rendezvous that year at the Seeds-kee-dee Agie when Quint had witnessed Kit's fight with Shunar and had become friends with him. Although Kit was only about five and a half feet tall, maybe a little less than that, he had, pound for pound, the fighting aggressiveness of a bobcat. His gentle blue-gray eyes, silky flaxen hair and soft, thin voice, coupled with his small size, belied the fighting man that was part and parcel of his soul.

After the 1835 rendezvous, Kit had trapped the Yellowstone and the Big Horn, and in 1836 had trapped the Yellowstone, the Otter and Musselshell rivers while Quint, Luke, François and Moccasin had been trapping Bovey's, Clark's and Rock Forks of the Yellowstone that fall and in the spring of 1837. Kit had told them at the rendezvous that he was heading for Bent's Fort. He had a responsibility—Adaline, a small daughter, product of Kit's union with an Arapaho woman Waa-Nibe, Grass-Singing-in-the-Wind. Waa-Nibe had died, and rumor had it that Kit was considering a Cheyenne belle as a stepmother for Adaline. Once that liaison was settled Kit would be free again to follow his star, wherever it would lead him. Quint hoped it would be New Mexico. There was a great affinity between Quint, Luke and Kit, nothing spoken outwardly, but it was there just the same.

To the Cheyennes and Arapahos the storerooms and trading rooms of Bent's Fort were treasure houses of the white man's ingenuity and incredible material wealth. The trading rooms had low-beamed ceilings and whitewashed walls lined with shelving. Wide counters had been placed across the centers of the rooms so that the Indians couldn't reach across them to pilfer from the shelves. The Indians were allowed about twenty-five cents in goods for a prime buffalo robe which would sell in St. Louis for five or six dollars.

The biggest business that day was in armaments and munitions to use against the Comanches and Kiowas, and, of course, liquor. Bent's could supply an almost inexhaustible quantity of spirits—flat kegs designed to fit a pack saddle and filled with rum, Pass brandy or the corrosive and mind-blowing Taos Lightnin'. A good part of the trading was in the liquid-refreshment department; so much that just before dusk the bell rang in the belfry atop the gatehouse and the clerks and other employees began to shoo the Cheyennes and Arapahos out of the trading rooms and the plaza. When the last of them were outside the gate was closed and double-barred. The brass cannon in the plaza was wheeled to face the inner portal of the gateway, ready, loaded and primed. Armed sentries were posted to the bastions and along the wall walks.

The coming of dusk brought with it the thumping of drums and the steady beating of stiffened hides, coupled with the shaking of rawhide rattles and the shrill tooting of eagle bone and sand crane bone whistles from the sprawling Cheyenne and Arapaho encampment outside the fort walls and covering the bottomlands along the river.

Moccasin had been in the Cheyenne camp until the braves had painted their faces black and the heavy drinking and war dancing had begun. Then he had wisely vanished inside the fort. He was a pureblood Indian himself, of course, but he was still a Delaware, and to a drunken Cheyenne or Arapaho any man who wasn't of his tribe or an allied tribe might just be fair game that night. All scalps looked pretty much alike once they were removed from an Indian's head. That ground rule covered Moccasin's wife's Cheyenne relatives, and White Bead Woman as well. As Moccasin had ruefully mentioned a few times, when she got drunk she fancied she was still a *nutuhkea,* a female soldier of the Wohksehhetaniu, the Fox Soldiers, and although her duties as such had been chiefly social, that is to be present at meetings of the band, to take part in the singing, the dancing, occasionally cooking for the soldiers, she sometimes thought of herself as a fighting soldier. During those times Moccasin wisely got out of the way. White Bead Woman never could hold her liquor.

Moccasin joined Quint, Kit and Luke where they stood on the southwest tower with full cups of brandy in their hands, while looking down on the encampment. The many tipis looked like huge Chinese lanterns from the soft mellow firelight showing through the skins. Hundreds of fires had been kindled in the open. Shadowy figures danced constantly back and forth to the incessant beating of the drums and hides, the *shish-shish-shish* of the rattles and the piercing sound of the whistles, mingled with the war whoopings and the women's eerie ululating cries. The evening was almost windless so the drifting woodsmoke hung in slowly undulating layers above the encampment.

"Colonel Bent and Ceran St. Vrain down there now," Moccasin said. "Bent talkin' to Yellow Wolf, Little Moon, White Bull and Walking Whirlwind, along with all the elders and the soldier-band chiefs. His wife there too, Owl Woman, daughter of Gray Thunder, big medicine man and keeper of the Sacred Medicine Arrows. He wants them to forget this madness of going after the Comanches and Kiowas for what they done to the Bow-String Soldiers last year."

"Yuh think he'll convince them?" Luke asked.

Moccasin shook his head. "Yuh know how they get with a bellyful of whiskey."

"Just like we do," Quint commented dryly.

Luke spat over the wall. "Trouble with them yellowskins is that war is like a religion to them. They're mad for glory and honor."

Kit nodded. "And we fight just as hard for power, land and wealth. *Their* land, if the truth be known."

Luke shrugged. "And we'll win too, in time."

Quint looked at Kit. Something of understanding seemed to pass between them. "No question about it, Luke," Quint agreed.

Dinner that evening was at the personal invitation of William Bent and Ceran St. Vrain, and was to be served in William's quarters rather than in the main dining room of the fort. The traders were waiting for Kit, Quint and Luke in the billiard room. Black Andrew, one of William Bent's two black male servants, presided over the tiny bar in one corner of the room.

"How'd yuh make out, colonel?" Kit asked.

William Bent shook his head. "About as I expected. You can't deal with my people when they have their danders up and are fired up on whiskey." He extended his hand to Quint. "Quint Kershaw! Big Red! It's been quite a long time since we've seen you here at the fort. Good to see you! I heard you reached here the hard way, so to speak."

Quint smiled ruefully. "The report wasn't exaggerated, colonel."

The trader gestured toward the bar. "Name your pleasure, gentlemen. Ceran and myself are having mint juleps, with *ice*. . . ." He slyly slanted his eyes sideways at Quint.

Quint stared incredulously at Bent. "I don't believe it!"

Luke nodded. "They built an ice house down by the river since we were last here, Quint."

Bent eyed the new scars on Quint's left cheek and on the right side of his head. "We heard of your misadventures in the Rockies and the loss of your Shoshoni woman and a full season's prime beaver plews."

"Plus some other furs and hides—wolf, grizzly bear and deer." Quint drained his glass. He ignored the warning in Kit's eyes. "Those are my five bales of beaver plews and other furs and hides down there beside your fur press."

Ceran nodded. "We've heard about that. They were ac-

175

cepted in good faith by one of our senior clerks. If there had been any reason to suspect they had been stolen we would have held those four men here until the origin of the furs had been verified. We deal honestly here, Kershaw." There was a touch of stiffness in the trader's tone.

"I meant no implication otherwise," Quint said quickly. "I apologize for my abruptness."

Ceran waved a hand. "That's not necessary. We know how you must feel. But the furs were not marked." He smiled a little. "If we were to track down the origin of many of the furs that were brought in here I'm afraid we'd be out of business in a very short time."

"Besides, they could have gotten them from the Indians," William added. "They, as a rule, do not mark their furs, as you know. There were five packs of beaver plews and some other furs and hides, you claim?"

Quint nodded. "Five packs. About four hundred prime plews of beaver. Six prime winter-thick wolf pelts. At least ten deer hides. A big grizzly hide. I figure about two thousand dollars' worth minimum, and another two to three hundred dollars' worth maximum."

Ceran whistled softly. "You trapped all that yourself?"

"Aye," Quint agreed.

"But there was a woman with you?"

"A Shoshoni squaw. She did but a small amount of the trapping when I was disabled for a short time. They murdered her when they stole my furs."

"And you trailed them here?"

"Aye, but they slipped away, Ceran. They're headed for the Cimarron country now, aiming to trade with the Kotsotekas for horses and mules, most likely, with *my* goods."

William drained his glass and held it out to Andrew. "And you figure on tracking them down alone? If the Cimarron country doesn't kill you, or those four Comancheros don't kill you for your horse and rifle, or maybe just for the hell of it, the Kotsotekas will surely do the job."

"Still, I'm going after them."

Ceran shook his head. "It's not good business."

Quint looked quickly at the trader. "I wasn't thinking of business alone."

"Vengeance, then? Why? Because of the Shoshoni woman? Nothing you can do now will bring her back, and you might lose your life into the bargain."

"I planned to trade in those furs here or sell them for cash to get a start in New Mexico. I've been there. I liked it there. Beaver trapping is about done for. I had figured on last fall and this spring being my last season."

Dick Green, the other black slave of William Bent, came to the doorway. "Dinner is ready to be served, colonel," he announced.

"We could use a man like you here," Ceran suggested to Quint over dinner. "You're a different cut of cloth from most mountain men. Most of them live for today and to hell with tomorrow. They know nothing outside of trapping, and now that the beaver trapping is in a decline, there will be little future for them."

"What future is there here?" Quint asked. "I don't fancy meat hunting at a dollar a day and expenses, that is to say powder and ball, caps, a riding mule or horse, food and lodging for me when I'm here at the fort. There's not much future there, Ceran."

"Is there a future for you in New Mexico if you're broke?"

Quint shrugged. "I've got my health, a good rifle and riding mule as well as youth on my side, plus seven years' experience on the frontier. That's all I'll need, *if* I don't regain my losses from those damned Comancheros."

Ceran smiled a little. "I would have given the same answer myself at your age, Quint."

Colonel Bent sipped at his wine. He studied Quint. "Are you so certain that you want to go to New Mexico for your future? I must remind you that there is nothing worse than an American pauper there. You could do worse than remain here as an employee of Bent, St. Vrain and Company. We can get all the meat hunters and clerks we need. We do need leaders; men who can take charge of trading parties we are constantly sending out on the prairies. You seem to be a born leader, Quint. You could consider leading such a trading party for us. Say to the Utes, or perhaps the Northern Cheyennes now that you stand so well with their brothers the Southern Cheyennes."

Quint shook his head. "You want me to roll the 'hollow woods' out on the prairie to get a bunch of drunken yellowskins to trade their furs for a mere fraction of their value?" he asked bluntly. The potent and fiery mixture of Pass brandy, mint juleps and French wines was making him overbold.

The trader shrugged. "If Bent, St. Vrain and Company don't do it, some other trading companies will, and in most cases would take greater advantage of them. There could be opportunity for you here. By the way, are you an American citizen now?"

"I've not been naturalized, if that's what ye mean. Why do ye ask? I'm here in this country by choice, if that's any help."

"It might be to your advantage now. Were you born in Canada?"

Quint shook his head. "I was born in Scotland—Quintin Douglas Ker-Shaw. I was but a lad when my people were driven from their ancestral lands and replaced by stinking sheep!" There was a ring of steel in his voice. It was something he rarely, if ever, talked about.

"The Highland Clearances?" Ceran asked.

Quint nodded grimly. "The Highlanders were deserted and betrayed by the chiefs of their ain clans. Famine and pestilence began to decimate them. The chieftains became rich from wool and mutton; the clansmen died of starvation and cholera. My father chose exile for himself. He was a Shaw, a man of dignity and pride. He wanted to preserve our identity and dignity as Scots and human beings. He didn't have to leave Scotland. He was a man of some little position, and well educated, a dominie—a teacher, that is. My mother was a Ker, of good family that had fallen on hard times. Together they could have well made their way in society. But my father felt that the people who had been driven from their lands and would emigrate to Canada would have need of him." Quint's voice died away. He drained his wineglass quickly, to quell the break in his voice.

"And so your family came to Canada?" William prompted.

The hard gray eyes looked up. "Aye, to the settlement founded by the Earl of Selkirk in the Red River Valley there. My younger sister died of the cholera on the stinking ship that brought us to Canada. She was but a babe. My mother survived, but her health was broken. It was a harsh land, colonel. She did not survive a year. We carried muskets in our hands as we walked behind the plow. We fought Métis and Crees to defend the young Red River Colony. My father's health failed. Farming was not for me. I hunted meat for the colonists and trapped for myself and my father. He died when I was sixteen. I buried him myself beside my mother. I took a few of his beloved books as my legacy. That, and my good name, was all he had to leave me. It was all I needed, them and my rifle. I closed the door to our cabin behind me and I never looked back. There was a great demand for beaver. I became a trapper and have been such up until this spring."

"And you consider yourself as an American now?"

"Absolutely! There was nothing left for me in either Scotland or Canada."

"Good! Before you make a final decision on your future, I want you to listen to me. Have you heard of the term 'Manifest Destiny' in relation to the United States?"

"Some," Quint admitted. "It deals with the possible future of the United States on this great continent."

"Let me paint a picture in words for you. This mud fortress of ours is the center of a primitive empire that spreads across the watershed of the Upper Arkansas River. This vast territory, as all of you well know, is virtually uninhabited by white men—Americans, to be specific. Over one hundred and seventy thousand square miles of valuable trading country; a veritable empire! The Upper Arkansas marks the northern boundary, that vaguely defined forty-second parallel between the United States and the Republic of Mexico. This stretch of the Arkansas is the heartland of the Great Plains, the uneasy border between the Cheyennes, Arapaho, Prairie Apaches, the Utes, Comanches and the Kiowas, and roving bands of Gros Ventres, Crows and Shoshonis.

"The Mexicans claim Bent, St. Vrain and Company deal in contrabrand trade, supplying arms and ammunition to most of the Plains tribes, many of whom raid into New Mexico. There is another reason we are feared by the Mexicans. They think of Bent's Fort as an American spearpoint for the invasion and eventual conquest of the Mexican Southwest. It is without basis, I can assure you."

It was very quiet in the room. The distant, muted drums of the Cheyennes sounded in the background.

"Texas declared her independence from Mexico two years ago," William continued. "I think it is only a matter of time before the United States will annex Texas. Many Americans believe we should push on to the West Coast and own Oregon outright, and perhaps eventually the entire Pacific Coast, including California."

"Which would, of necessity, include New Mexico," Ceran added quietly.

"How can all this be accomplished, short of war?" Quint asked.

"I mentioned the fact that it was only a matter of time before the United States would annex Texas, and certainly with the complete approval of the Texans, from what I've heard. The Republic of Mexico claims that the western boundary of the Republic of Texas is the Nueces River. The Republic of Texas, on the other hand, claims the Rio del Norte as its western boundary. See here!" The trader pushed back the plates and glasses from his end of the table to clear the white tablecloth. He took a charred bit of firewood from the beehive fireplace and rapidly sketched in a rough map of Texas and New Mexico, delineating the Nueces and Rio Grande rivers. "It is more than two hundred and fifty miles difference between these two rivers, east to west. Perhaps one hunderd and seventy-five thousand to two hundred thousand square miles of territory."

Luke whistled softly. "A sizable back lot," he murmured.

Bent drained his wineglass and refilled it. His dark eyes glistened moistly in the candlelight. "If Texas *is* annexed by the United States as far west as the Rio Grande del Norte, Bent, St. Vrain and Company will have virtual control of the largest trading empire in the United States, if not the world."

"And, if not, what then?" Quint asked.

Willian Bent shook his head. "There can be no other way. It is the Manifest Destiny of the United States."

"How many years?" Kit asked.

William looked at Ceran. "Well, Ceran?"

"Quién sabe? Five years? Seven? No more than ten, I'd say."

Quint studied the crude map on the tablecloth. Charles and William Bent and Ceran St. Vrain were adventurous, hardheaded businessmen and shrewd, aggressive traders. They had already pushed out beyond the roughly delineated western frontier of the growing, bustling United States into a virtually unknown land where there were no cities, no towns, and only a few rough frontier posts such as Bent's Fort. There were few roads in that land, no bridges to speak of, and only a half-dozen or so known passes by which to cross the stupendous mountain ranges that barred the way to the West Coast. Bent, St. Vrain and Company hadn't gotten this far without a sound perspective of the future and an excellent sense of prophecy.

Quint looked up at William Bent. "Why have ye told me this, colonel?" he asked quietly.

The trader smiled. "For a number of reasons. First, to convince you there can be a future here at Bent's Fort for you; second, there can be a future for you in New Mexico by working there for Bent, St. Vrain and Company, but then, of course, you must become a Mexican citizen."

"With the thought that before too many years New Mexico

will become part of the United States anyway," Quint put in. "And Bent, St. Vrain and Company will be sitting in the catbird's seat."

William looked at Ceran. "See? The young man can think ahead." He smiled.

Quint leaned forward. "Is there a *third* reason ye told me all this, colonel?"

"Whether or not you work for the firm here, or in New Mexico, it will still be to your advantage privately to know these things, Quint," the trader replied.

Quint leaned back and studied the two traders. "Sharp," he murmured. "Sharp as a Barlow knife, the both av ye."

"How so?" Ceran asked.

"Maybe the Mexicans are wrong in thinking Bent's Fort is an American spearpoint for the invasion and eventual conquest of the Mexican Southwest, but they may be overlooking something else," Quint explained. "It will be to *your* advantage as well as that of the United States to have men such as myself, and Luke and Kit as well, established in New Mexico before your prophesied war comes to pass."

"And will it not be to your advantage as well?" William asked quietly.

Everything had neatly fallen into place in Quint's quick-thinking mind. He felt as though he had, by some alchemic means, been transmuted from a wandering trapper living from season to season with no thought other than to trap as much beaver as he could to finance the next season and the season after that, so on, *ad infinitum*, into one of the probing tentacles of the prophesied conquest and occupation by the United States of the Mexican Southwest. What was it William Bent had said it was?

William Bent looked at Quint. "Manifest Destiny, Quintin Ker-Shaw." It was as though he had read Quint's mind. "You are a part of that destiny now. Use it to your advantage. Do not let the opportunity presented you be lost forever. *The time is now.*"

"How will your stick float now, Quint?" Ceran St. Vrain asked.

"New Mexico," Quint replied. "*After* I find those Comancheros."

"Madness," William Bent said. He stood up. "Wait here a few moments, gentlemen." He left the room.

Dick placed a box of Havana cigars on the table. Everyone lighted up. The tobacco smoke drifted about the candles. The drums were still pounding in the Cheyenne encampment. These men whose hearing and sensitivity were like those of the hunting wolf could feel as well as hear the vibrations of the drumbeats and the steady thudding of hundreds of moccasined feet on the hard-packed ground.

Ceran blew a smoke ring and watched it lift and waver in the updraft from the candles. "They *will* have their revenge on the Comanches and Kiowas," he said quietly. "If they succeed, then it will be the turn of the Comanches and the Kiowas to seek revenge on them. If *they* fail, they will try again until they succeed, and then it will be the turn of the Cheyennes again, *ad infinitum*. Never satisfied."

"Amen," Luke said.

"Like us whites," Quint added dryly.

They all looked at him.

William Bent came back into the room carrying a small wooden case under his arm. He placed it on the table in front of Quint. "Open it," he invited.

Quint lifted the brass hasp on the case and opened the lid. The candlelight reflected from a pair of slim, long-barreled pistols without triggers, or trigger guards. The breech end of the barrels had round cylinders fitted into the frame. In addition to the pair of pistols there was a brass powder flask, a bullet mold, a brass container for percussion caps, a brass oil can, a nipple wrench, a brass cleaning rod, a quantity of cast bullets and two extra round cylinders such as were fitted at the breech end of the pistols. Quint looked up curiously at William Bent.

"A new invention, Quint," the trader explained. "Colt's Patent revolving pistols. Repeaters. Caliber .36. Five shots each without reloading. Nine-inch barrels. Take them out and get the feel of them."

Quint took out the pair of Colts and hefted them in his big hands. There was a good feeling to them; a feeling of deadly power and efficiency. "They've no triggers," he said.

"Cock them," Bent suggested.

Quint cocked the big spur hammers and the triggers dropped out from within the frames. Quint looked quizzically at Bent.

"Sheathed triggers," the trader explained. "Each time you cock the hammer that cylinder revolves, presenting another charge to be fired. You can fire that weapon as fast as you can cock the hammer and pull the trigger. Ten shots in less than a minute, firing both pistols at the same time, one from either hand. In a matter of a few minutes you can remove the
182

empty cylinders and replace them with those spares, which you can keep ready-loaded."

Quint whistled softly. "Aye," he murmured. *"That's* the ticket."

William watched Quint as he handled the deadly handguns as though they were extensions of his powerful arms. "You like them, eh, Big Red?"

Quint nodded. He let down the hammers and carefully placed the pistols back in their spaces in the velvet-lined case. "I've no the price of these beauties, colonel."

The trader shook his head. "They're not for sale. They're yours. Accept them as a gift from Bent, St. Vrain and Company."

Quint starad at the trader. "But why? Ye owe me nothing, colonel."

"You took a great loss with the theft of those beaver plews of yours. I feel no responsibility for that, but I do feel a responsibility for the fact that you aim to go after those thieving Comancheros, certainly at the risk of your life and the men who plan to go with you. If the gift of these pistols can make the difference in your survival, then they should be yours. Agreed, Ceran?"

Ceran nodded. "By all means." He smiled a little crookedly. "Furthermore, Big Red, if you are successful in surviving your pursuit and apprehension of those Comancheros, and the pistols aid in that, the story will spread by moccasin messenger all over the Southwest, and your possible further use of them in New Mexico might just create a legend about you and the pistols in your time." Ceran scratched in his beard. "Then, of course, people will want to know *where* you happened to pick up that pair of Colts."

Quint grinned. "Bent, St. Vrain and Company."

William Bent waved a hand. "That was not my only intention, Ceran, but a little publicity in that respect won't hurt, while at the same time perhaps we can salve our consciences on the matter of taking in trade Quint's prime beaver plews."

Quint nodded. He passed a big hand over the twin pistols. "Perhaps these beauties will help me regain what is rightfully mine."

"You'll be leaving soon then?" Ceran asked.

"Tomorrow," Quint replied.

"Would you mind telling us where you trapped those plews?"

183

Quint slanted his eyes sideways at the trader. "I would that," he replied.

Ceran shrugged. He blew a smoke ring. "Nothing ventured, nothing gained," he murmured. He smiled slyly, with a sideways flick of his dark eyes.

Later, in their quarters, Quint, Luke and Kit closely examined the pair of graceful, deadly-looking Colts by the light from the beehive fireplace. Moccasin, Black Beaver and young Joshua entered the room. Joshua silently handed Quint "Auld Clootie."

"Set and have a horn, brothers; a little of the arwerdenty," Kit invited. "You'll stay the night with me."

The three Delawares sat crosslegged on the floor. They passed the jug of brandy from one to the other of them, back and forth, hardly without stopping, under the fascinated eyes of the white men.

Moccasin wiped his mouth and belched. "Cheyenne crazy," he opined.

"Yuh ain't fixin' to jine them then?" Luke asked with a grin.

The Delaware shook his head. "I already tole yuh. No! I don't have to look into the pooled blood in a dead badger's belly to know my future if I go along. I can figger out ahead of time what kin happen to me on that drunken warpath."

"Yuh think they'll cut up the Comanches?" Kit asked.

Moccasin shrugged. "They think so. They got old Gray Thunder drunk as owl. He run around with sacred Medicine Arrows. Promise great victory. No Cheyenne get killed. All Comanche get killed. *Bullshit!*"

"So, ye know better?" Quint asked.

Moccasin nodded solemnly. "My medicine tell me for sure."

"What medicine?"

The Delaware drank deeply from the jug and then held it up. *"This* medicine! Always tell truth."

Quint nodded. *"In vino veritas."* He grinned.

"That Shoshoni? What that mean, Big Red Badger?"

"In wine there is truth."

The jug was passed from one to the other of them.

Quint wiped his mouth. The spirits were getting to him, like Moccasin's "medicine." "I'm still leaving in the morning. Who rides with the Big Red Badger?"

"I been with the Cheyennes all winter and spring," Moccasin said. "Too long this time. Me, Beaver, Josh will ride with yuh."

Quint looked at Luke. "Well? Have ye had enough of meat hunting?"

Luke lowered the jug from his mouth. "I'm ready, Big Red Badger. Always wanted to go back to Taos. Got a hankerin' for white likker and brown wimmen. *Wagh!*"

"Kit?" Quint asked.

Kit shook his head. "Not this trip. The colonel might want me to ride back to St. Looey for him. Howsumever, mebbe I'll be along to New Mexico later on this year."

Quint nodded. "Fair enough." He reached over to his gear and took his North single-shot pistol from it. He thrust a big finger through the trigger guard and twirled the heavy two-and-a-half-pound weapon about it as though it were a feather. He presented it butt first to Joshua. "Won't have any further need for this old smokepole, Josh. It's yours, lad. On the prairie."

The young Delaware's eyes widened. He had heard stories about *that* pistol. He took it as though it were made out of solid gold.

Quint grinned. "What do ye say, Buffalo Droppings?"

Joshua looked up. He grinned. *"Wagh!"* he bellowed.

"We'll go by way of Cañon Chacuaco," Quint said as he looked about at his companions. "Any objections?"

They looked at him, wise as owls.

"We leave at dawn tomorrow," Quint added.

The half-gallon whiskey jug was dry empty by the time they went to bed.

TWENTY-FOUR

The arid plain undulated, one roll of ground after another like great waves frozen into position as far as the eye could see in the fading light of late afternoon. The plain was desolate and waterless with not a tree, bush or rock to break the monotony of it. A maze of buffalo trails, both old and new, furrowed the surface. The mountains far to the west were just a bluish-gray hint against the sky. The only outstanding feature on the drab sameness of the plain was a truncated hill flanked on either side, east and west, by two low, dikelike ridges. The hill and ridges were much magnified and elevated beyond their actual size and height in the rarefied, transparent atmosphere. The air was constantly in heat motion and fanned by the perpetual, searching wind.

Five men mounted on riding mules moved slowly toward the elevations to the south of them. Tiny black specks like scraps of charred paper caught in an updraft soared high over the hill and ridges.

Luke shaded his eyes. *"Zopilotes."*

Moccasin nodded. "Somethin' dead or dyin' over there."

The wind shifted a little. The sweetish rotten odor of decomposition came along with it.

Quint reined in his mule and dismounted. He rested his telescope on his saddle and focused it on the area about the foot of the hill and ridges. The elevations waved and writhed sinuously in the distortion of the heated atmosphere, seeming to loom closer and then retreating to shimmer and sway as they rose in height. The powerful lens picked up the black shapes of a number of buffalo carcasses littering the level ground about four or five hundred yards on this side of the elevations. Six high-wheeled Mexican *carretas* rested their tongues on the ground. Nothing moved except the heated air and the great *zopilotes,* or land buzzards circling slowly high overhead with motionless black, white-tipped wings resting on the wind.

"Buffalo carcasses, some skinned and gutted, others not, and some Mexican *carretas,"* Quint said over his shoulder. He straightened up and handed the telescope to Moccasin. "How long, Moc?" he asked.

The Delaware studied the scene. "Mebbe yesterday for some. Mebbe the day before. They swell quick with the heat."

Luke took the glass. "Mex *ciboleros,* of course. But where are they? Where are the hides and meat from the skinned buffler?"

The only sounds to be heard were the faint wind-rustling of the short grass, the occasional stamping of a hoof and the chinking of a bit.

"Where's the next water, Luke?" Quint asked.

"Coupla miles south beyond that hill. Down in the canyon."

"And the next water?"

186

"Waterhole?"

"*Any* water."

"Southeasterly, about thirty miles. McNee's Creek, useta be called Louse Creek until about ten years ago when a man by the name of Sam McNee was killed by Pawnees there. It's not far north from the Cimarron Cut-off of the Santy Fee Trail, around the Rabbit Ears Mountain area. The creek is usually dry, but the water level is close to the surface, *most* times. . . . Yuh have to dig a *pozito,* a waterhole down a coupla feet to get seep water."

Quint looked at the Delawares. "Check your water."

Each man had two large canteens, one for himself and the other for his mule. Their water discipline was good. Each canteen was about a quarter full; enough for about half a day more at most, with strict discipline of course.

Joshua was looking through the telescope. "*Zopilotes* startin' to land."

The efficient scavengers were swinging lower and lower. Some of them seemed to vanish from sight right into the ground, evidently into an arroyo or a depression beyond the farthermost buffalo carcasses.

"Mebbe the *ciboleros,*" Black Beaver suggested.

"We were goin' to take a look-see at Cañon Chacuaco," Luke reminded them. "Besides, we need the water there."

The mules snorted and shied as they neared the stinking buffalo carcasses. Quint and Luke dismounted and handed the bridle reins to the Delawares. They walked toward the place where the *zopilotes* had landed. They paused on the lip of the shallow depression.

"Jesus God," Luke murmured as he clamped a thumb and finger about his nostrils.

The bodies were difficult to see because of the crowding, pushing, squawking buzzards as they fought for eating position, while foot-scraping up thin dust from the hard ground. Now and again a body, or parts of a dismembered body, could be seen under the dusty feathers and curved beaks as the *zopilotes* tore at the decomposing flesh. Here and there a feathered arrow shaft thrust itself up from the corpses.

Quint walked down into the depression. He held his big nose clamped tight shut as he kicked his way past two of the squawking birds to yank an arrow from a swollen carcass. He ran back to Luke and handed him the arrow.

Luke studied the shaft. "Comanche, Big Red. No doubt about it. How many bodies?"

Quint shrugged. "Maybe ten or twelve. Hard to say. I didn't stick around long enough to take an accurate census."

Luke threw the arrow toward the *zopilotes*. "We can always count the skulls after they're through with their meal." He looked sideways at Quint. "That is, if you're interested," he added dryly.

Quint shook his head.

They walked together back to the Delawares and the mules.

"Comanches," Quint announced.

Moccasin nodded. "We know where the *ciboleros* are. Now, *where are the Comanches?*"

Luke leaned against his mule. "Mebbe they went north, or west, most likely, for a raid on New Mexico." He looked at Quint. "Yuh copper that bet?"

Quint scratched in his beard. He narrowed his eyes. "We saw no dust to the north or west. They might have already come back from a raid on New Mexico. If that's true, then they would have to have water. The closest water from here in any direction is at least thirty miles or more. Odds are they came this way for water and found the *ciboleros* finishing up their hunting, skinning and butchering. These may be the *ciboleros* Federico Casias spoke about, those for whom he was bringing back the horses and mules so that they could return to New Mexico before the Comanches showed up around here." His voice died away as he saw the expressions on the faces of his companions.

"Amazing," Luke murmured.

Moccasin studied Quint. "Good medicine."

Quint casually studied the fingernails of his two hands. "Oh, I don't know," he said archly. He grinned. "I calls it logic, partners."

"It ain't quite *that* humorous," Luke said. "If you're right, Big Red Badger, then the Comanches are at the waterhole in Cañon Chacuaco. We need that water."

Quint nodded. He took the reins of his mule from Joshua. "*And* my Comancheros, Lukie."

"So, we go to Cañon Chacuaco."

"Aye." Quint looked to the west. "It will be fully dark in a few hours. There will be a moon tonight. We'll close in on the waterhole. We can scout it in the darkness before the rising of the moon. If the Comanches are not there, we can get our water after moonset."

"And if the Comanches are not there, and the Comancheros are?"

The grin on the scarred face of Quint was like that of a winter-hungry wolf.

Quint and Luke left the Delawares with the mules while they went ahead on foot. They were no more than half a mile from the waterhole by Luke's calculations. There was no trace as yet of the rising moon. The wind had shifted about dusk and then died away altogether, leaving a hushed quietness about the land.

Quint stopped suddenly. He reached back and placed his left palm flat against Luke's chest. They stood there in the darkness, testing the night with eyes, ears and nose. Quint turned to face Luke. He turned again and pointed toward a flat-topped boulder on the canyon side that thrust itself up like a stiff man-part above its smaller mates on the thick layer of talus that had scaled off from the canyon wall looming darkly high overhead. Luke nodded. Quint pointed downslope. He drew Luke close and whispered, "On top of the boulder. Get downslope. Attract attention. Goddammit, don't get yourself killed."

Luke vanished into the darkness.

Quint catfooted upslope, treading gingerly on the loose rock. He reached a point where his eyes were on a level with the flat top of the boulder. Something humped and motionless was there, something not a part of the boulder itself.

Minutes ticked past. Stone clicked against stone downslope from the boulder. It was deathly quiet again. The clicking sound was repeated. Something moved atop the boulder. A head was raised.

Quint placed his Hawken flat on the talus. He drew his Green River knife and eased downslope.

The clicking sounded again, inordinately loud in the stillness.

Someone dropped from the boulder top to land on the talus directly in front of Quint and not more than ten feet away. Quint moved. He wanted the man alive, no matter who he was, at least until he found out who he was and what he was doing there.

A stone slid from under Quint's right foot.

The man whirled and came in low and fast with outthrust knife. Quint leaped to one side, hoping to God the man would not cry out. A voice cry would carry half a mile or more in that echoing canyon. Quint shot out his left hand and gripped

189

his attacker's left wrist, while at the same time he thrust out his left leg and yanked hard on the wrist. The man fell heavily over the leg and sprawled on the talus. The steel of his knife rang dully on the stone. A hard heel hit him just behind the left ear to half-stun him, while a foot slammed down on his right wrist to hold it there, still clutching the knife. Quint planted a knee between the man's shoulder blades and clamped a big hand over his mouth.

Luke came around the side of the boulder with ready knife in hand. "He dead?" he asked.

Quint shook his head. "Not yet. Take his knife. I want him to talk. Look around. See if there are any others."

The fallen man shook his head. Quint gripped him by his hair and pulled his head back to look into his face, while at the same time he placed the razor edge of his knife across the taut throat.

"Madre de Dios!" the prisoner gasped. *"Inglés?* Americano?"

His voice was vaguely familiar. Quint looked closely in the dimness. "Goddammit! Federico Casias! What the hell were ye doing up on that rock?" He released the *cibolero* and pulled him back so that his back rested against the base of the boulder.

Federico gingerly felt the swelling lump behind his left ear. "You kick like a mule. What are you doing here? Are you after your four thieving Comancheros?"

Quint nodded. "The same." He handed his brandy flask to Federico. *"Una copita?"* he asked.

"Gracias, mil gracias!" Fedrico drank deeply, then wiped his mouth and mustache both ways with the back of a dirty hand. He passed a hand across his eyes. "Before God, my friend," he said brokenly. His voice died away.

"Drink again," Quint suggested. He squatted back on his heels. "Take it easy. Get a grip on yourself, eh?"

Luke came catfooting through the dimness. "No one around here, Big Red."

Federico lowered the flask. "I am alone," he offered.

"Anything else, Lukie?" Quint asked.

Luke squatted beside Quint. He tilted his head to one side, watching Federico drink again. *"He's* a thirsty one. I looked down the canyon. Caught the flare of fires agin the canyon wall 'bout a mile or so down thataway."

"Fires? More than one?"

Luke looked slowly sideways at Quint. *"Many,* Big Red."

Federico lowered the flask. "The milk of my mother," he murmured in appreciation.

Luke grinned. "A real drinkin' man. Where's yore *compañeros* and *animiles*, Federico?"

"We were on our way back here. We stopped for nothing. We used up most of our water. The night before last three of the mules broke loose from the *caballada* to look for water. We need every one of those mules to haul our meat and hides back to Taos. I sent my three men with the remainder of the *caballada* while I hunted for the strays, praying all the while that my men would get the mules and horses back here in time. It was important, you understand, that not a moment should be lost. If the Comanches got here before my men got back with the animals . . ."

"How come yuh was so sure the Comanches might be around?" Luke asked.

Federico looked surprised. "We had seen the Comancheros riding toward Cañon Chacuaco to trade for horses and mules with the Comanches. Besides, with so many horses and mules, the Comanches would have to have water. Plenty of water. Cañon Chacuaco is the only good waterhole for many miles."

"Go on," Quint urged. "We're wasting time here."

"My horse broke a leg," the *cibolero* continued. "I reached the area south of here late yesterday afternoon. First I saw the *carretas*, then the slain buffalo. I reasoned then my people had continued hunting while waiting for us to return. I saw no horses or mules. . . ." His voice died away.

"And you found the bodies where the Comanches had left them," Quint prompted.

Federico nodded. He closed his eyes and shook his head.

"All of them?" Luke asked.

"All but one."

"Not a man then," Luke said. "They never take men prisoners. They will take young boys they think they might be able to raise as one of them."

"So a young boy is missing?" Quint asked.

It was very quiet. Federico drank from the flask. He wiped his mouth with the back of a hand and looked sideways at Quint. "Not a boy. It was a young woman, hardly more than a girl." There was agony in his dark eyes. "Guadalupe, whom everyone calls Lupita. She is my second cousin and the only daughter of my *patrón*, Don Francisco Vasquez. Hardly

191

more than a girl, as I have said, but *Madre de Dios!*—What a woman! She has always tried to take the place of a son in her family. Her elder brother is Don Bartolomé, a drunkard, a wastrel, a chaser of women!"

"Sounds interestin'," Luke put in dryly.

"Don Francisco is getting old and his eyesight is failing. He has fallen on hard times. Don Bartolomé spends most of his time in Santa Fe, wasting his substance in the gambling *salas*. Someone had to lead the *ciboleros*. Lupita insisted on going. Don Francisco asked me to accompany them on this last trip, for me, at least, for I had left his employ. I agreed." He shrugged. "It was a mistake."

"A *woman* leading a party of *ciboleros?*" Luke asked incredulously.

"She is a woman, but she has the spirit and courage of a man! She can ride and shoot as well as any man!"

"How old is she?" Quint asked.

"Sixteen. A beautiful creature." The *cibolero* rolled his expressive eyes upward. *"Alma de mi alma!* Soul of my soul, Lupita! But she is not for me, because of our blood relationship."

"My God," Quint said quietly. "Ye surely don't mean that skinny, big-eyed kid who used to tail me around Taos years ago?"

Federico nodded his head vigorously.

"Lupita! To see her is to adore her! To know her is to love her! In the years since you left Taos she has blossomed like the rose!"

Quint looked at Luke with raised eyebrows and shook his head. Federico, no doubt, was exaggerating in true New Mexican style.

Luke spat to one side. "Well, right now your soul of souls has got a great future among the Kotsotekas, if she's still alive. My God, once the Kotsoteka women get their hands on her . . ."

Federico paled. "That's why I am here. To rescue Lupita or die in the attempt!" he cried dramatically.

Quint shook his head. "Alone, *hombre?* Madness!"

Federico scrambled to the top of the boulder and then dropped back to the ground. He held an ancient *escopeta*, a bullet pouch and powderhorn in one hand, and in the other his *carcage*, a leather case which held his powerful hunting bow and steel-tipped arrows. "I can't return to Don

192

Francisco without Lupita. He would have me killed on sight."

"And you'd rather die than live without Lupita," Quint said dryly.

Luke looked sideways at Quint. "Yuh ain't seen her growed yet, Big Red. Mebbe you'll think the same way once yuh see her." He grinned crookedly. "There'll be a fine moon tonight," he added.

Quint looked toward the east. There was no sign yet of the rising moon. "Go back for the Delawares, Luke. I want to get as close as possible to the Commanche camp before the moon rises. We can take up position in the darkness and sit out the moonlight."

Luke vanished into the darkness as noiselessly as a hunting cat.

"You plan to attack the Comanche camp, eh?" Federico asked.

"Not unless we have to."

"To rescue Lupita?"

"We need water. Besides, the Comancheros may be there."

Federico nodded. "How many Delawares do you have?"

"Three."

The *cibolero* stared at Quint. *"Three!* Is that all? Five men in all? Mother of God!"

Quint grinned at him. "We've got the element of surprise. If there's one thing any yellowskin hates worse than anything else, it's to be surprised."

"But only five men?"

Quint shrugged. "You were going to attack them alone, *compañero.*"

"Or die in the attempt! Besides, I had it in my mind to kill Lupita before they killed me."

Quint shook his head. "Dramatic, but hardly practical."

"There is a madness in you Montero Americanos."

Quint half smiled. "If there was not, my friend, we'd not be mountain men at all."

They picketed the mules in a small pocket canyon and went forward on foot along the canyon rim, staying well back so as not to skyline themselves. The smell of woodsmoke and cooking meat drifted through the canyon below them. When they were even with the site of the waterhole they went to ground and bellied up to the very brink of the canyon, hiding their heads behind the clumps of coarse grass that stippled the harsh ground.

The camp was sprawled about the waterhole. Here the

spring flowed from under the side of the canyon and collected in a depression several feet deep. Someone in the ancient past had constructed a rude dam across the lower end of the depression, over which the water flowed into its original channel along the center of the wide canyon only to sink into the sandy soil. The Comanches had sited their camp in the area about the waterhole. The tipis were small, the type used when the Kotsotekas were on the trail, and there were not enough of them to accommodate most of the people. There were many fires scattered along the canyon floor, casting their flickering light up against the reddish-yellow sides of the canyon, through which moved the gigantic shadows of the people who passed back and forth between the fires and the canyon walls. A thin, rifted scarf of smoke hung and wavered in the quiet air. The murmuring of many voices from the camp and the sounds of the horse herd further up the canyon mingled with the barking of the dogs.

"How many, would ye say, Luke?" Quint asked.

"Quién sabe? Two hundred fifty, mebbe."

Moccasin spat over the rim. "Three hundred anyway. Mebbe more."

The moon pewter-tinted the sky to the east.

Quint focused his telescope on the camp, studying it foot by foot, until he found the camp of the Comancheros, close beside the spring. They kept their animals picketed at their camp, and had piled their trade goods—Quint's trade goods—in the center of the camp. There were four men moving about the fire as they cooked their meal. Three wearing hats, one hatless, the white man, the Mexican breed Antonio, the one called only Kiowa, and the Indian Jose.

"That them, sure enough, Big Red?" Luke asked.

Quint handed him the telescope. "Sure enough," he said quietly.

"Did you see Lupita?" Federico asked Quint.

Quint shook his head. "There are women down there. All Comanches, from what I could tell. Unless they've made your Cousin Lupita wear Comanche dress. A little early for that, provided she is still alive."

Moccasin rested his chin on his cross-folded arms. "We could stampede that horse herd right through the camp," he suggested. He grinned. "Raise holy hell down there."

"We need water more than a good time, Moc," Luke reminded him.

Moccasin nodded. "How long yuh think them Kotsotekas

194

goin' to stay down there? They look comfortable. They in own country. Plenty water. Plenty food. Plenty grazing. Hell! Why they move? We stampede herd. Some of us get water. We drive off their horses. Take back to New Mexico. Sell back to their owners."

Luke spat over the brink. "Shit, yuh crazy Indian bastard! Yuh'd do just that too, eh?"

"Shit too, yuh crazy white bastard," the Delaware retorted. "Yuh got any better ideas?"

"Come to think of it, I ain't."

They grinned at each other.

Quint took the telescope and studied the camp again. Odds were hopelessly high that he'd not be able to get his trade goods out of the camp. If the Comancheros had been alone, that would have been quite another matter. Vengeance was also probably out of the question at this time. To wreak bloody vengeance and then to lose one's own life in the bargain was insane. Even if one survived, there was the overpowering fact that survival would surely place one into the hands of the Comanches. Few tribes had the notorious reputation of the Comanches for perpetrating the most horrible and unmentionable atrocities on their captives. It was said the early explorers found them a kindly folk, but when the Spaniards came in force, they brought with them the cruel methods of the Inquisition. What women captives suffered at their hands was better left unimagined.

"We'll have to make our move soon, Big Red," Luke suggested. "The moon is rising."

"Sixteen. A beautiful creature," Federico had said. *"Alma de mi alma! Soul of my soul, Lupita!"*

"Quint?" Luke said. He looked curiously at Quint.

"Lupita! To see her is to admire her! To know her is to love her!"

"He's asleep," Federico suggested.

Quint looked at the sky to the east. It had paled significantly since last he had looked at it. But the canyon was still in darkness beyond the reach of the firelight.

He moved back from the brink of the canyon and sat up. "Luke, ye take Federico down the canyon, and cross it to the other side, taking position about five hundred yards from the camp. Moccasin, take the canteens and your relatives up the canyon beyond the horse herd. Wait until moonset and see if you can fill those canteens. Sit tight until an hour or so before dawn light. If ye don't hear from me, or a ruckus doesn't start

195

in the Comanche camp, return to the mules. If I'm there with the woman, well and good. If not, I've not made it and I probably won't make it. If a ruckus starts, kill the herd guards, take some Comanche horses and stampede the rest of the herd right through their goddam camp. Shoot hell out of the camp as ye pass through. Luke, ye and Federico stay in position until an hour or so before dawn light, then return to the mules. If I can get the woman out of the camp I'll come by your way. If not, like I said to Moccasin, get back to the mules and get to hell out of this canyon. If the Delawares do stampede the herd through the camp, wait until they pass ye, then open a covering fire on any pursuers to slow them down, and then get back to the mules, or take horses, whichever is best, and get out of here. Is that clear to all of ye?"

"We're to play it by ear then," Luke said.

Quint nodded. He handed his Hawken to Luke. "Ye'll have more need of this than I will, Lukie." He opened his bullet pouch and removed the two spare loaded cylinders for his Colt Patersons. He placed them in his jacket pockets. He checked the caps and loads in his two revolving pistols.

It was very quiet on the canyon rim.

"Where will you be?" Federico asked after a time.

Quint pointed down into the canyon. "There."

"Alone?"

Quint stood up. "Someone has to go in after Cousin Lupita. Besides, there may be a chance to make gone beaver out of one or two of those damned Comancheros who stole my plews."

"But you yourself said it was madness for me to go alone to rescue Lupita," Federico protested.

"For *you, compañero*. Mind, you said you would try to rescue Lupita, or die in the attempt. Myself, I have no intention of dying in the attempt."

Federico hesitated. "But if there is no hope of rescuing her . . . surely . . ." His voice died away.

"I'll not leave her alive in their hands," Quint promised. He looked about at his companions. "Take your posts, gentlemen. The shitaree begins sometime after moonset and before the dawn. *Vaya!*" He vanished noiselessly into the darkness.

TWENTY-FIVE

Cañon Chacuaco

The moon rose high, flooding the land with a pale, cold luminescence that etched shadows sharply on the light-colored ground. Soon the canyon was illuminated fully by the moonlight. It cast wavering patterns on the waterhole and on the short length of the slowly running water that flowed inches deep over the clear white sand only to sink out of sight several hundred yards up the canyon.

The men of the Kotsotekas were interested in the trade goods the Comancheros were putting on display for them. They had plenty of horses and mules for trading. The camp held only twenty of their women, for this was a combined hunting and raiding party, who usually made their base camp in Cañon Chacuaco because of the never-failing water supply, the proximity of buffalo, and grazing for the horses and mules. Further, it was a place of security, safe from surprise from an enemy. Who would dare attack the great Kotsotekas in their own country? Three hundred warriors would be more than a match for double that number of Mexicans, who were women in battle, in any case. The Cheyennes and the Arapahos were camped at Bent's Fort on the Arkansas. They feared the Comanches and Kiowas. Had the Cheyennes not lost many of their famed Bow-String Soldiers in battle with the Comanches and Kiowas just the year before? The few Pawnees that came into that country were there only to steal horses, if they could get away with it.

This was Kotsoteka country! Were not the Kotsotekas Lords of the Plains? Their medicine was good. They were invincible. They were led in battle by Isa-nanica, Hears a Wolf, whose famed warshield had the power to turn aside arrows and bullets. Their medicine man was Pe-arva-akup-akup, Big Red Meat. He too had the power to turn aside arrows and bullets with the power of his buffalo-scrotum rattle. Whom did the Kotsotekas have to fear with such leadership and spiritual power?

Quint had worked his way down the canyon side concealed by the darkness, even as the moon began to lighten the sky to the east. He took up his position amid a jumble of slabs of fallen rock that had scaled off the heights behind him. Some of the Kotsotekas had worked up an impromptu victory dance after their successful horse and mule stealing raid, and the later slaughtering of the Mexican buffalo hunters. They had gained many horses and mules, and fifteen scalps as well as much meat and many robes. The drummers beat on stiffened hides while hard-soled moccasins slapped the ground as the warriors danced about one of the fires.

The Kotsoteka women were busy about the cooking fires, boiling the cooking water by dropping heated stones into buffalo paunches suspended from stick supports. They dropped the captured buffalo meat into the boiling water. The odor of the cooking meat drifted through the canyon.

Quint focused his telescope on the people moving about the camp. The women were all Comanches. There was no sighting of a Mexican girl. Was it possible that she was already dead? After all, she had been a captive since some time the day before. Or was she held captive in one of the small travel tipis dotting the canyon, fair game for any Comanche stud who wanted to get his balls off into her?

The separate camp of the Comancheros was below Quint and between him and the waterhole. They had picketed their horses and mules in an area of coarse grass behind their camp. Their trading goods had been spread out for inspection and bargaining. The firelight reflected from the polished barrels of Nor'west-type fusils, the iron and brass buckles of leather belts, glass beads and abalone shells, prized brass kettles and looking glasses. There was a pile of frying pans which the Comanches used for making excellent arrow heads rather than for cooking purposes. There were brass finger rings, brass and steel bracelets and a pile of hawk's bells. Blood-red Nor'west blankets were stacked beside bold-patterned Navajo blankets. There were many knives of different styles, bullet lead, flints and boxes of percussion caps.

"Bastards," Quint breathed. They had done right well for themselves in their trading at Bent's Fort, with Quint Kershaw's prime plews—at the price of a woman's life and two seasons' killing labor for Quint in the icy streams of Kershaw's Valley. Quint's left hand closed tightly about his telescope; his right hand gripped the haft of his Green River knife so hard his knuckle skin turned white.

They were all there—the American, with light-colored hair like dirty sand; the *puro indio*, Jose, whom Federico Casias had described as being a Jicarilla Apache and not quite right in the *cabeza*, a loco one; the New Mexican Antonio, a quarter-breed Comanche, or so Federico said, who went by many different names as the occasion required. He was a broad-shouldered and strongly built man. It was the fourth and last of the Comancheros Quint studied most. He was the one known as Kiowa, a pox-marked rough-face, who moved like a cat about the camp, and once he turned to look over the backs of the mules and horses on the canyon slope directly up to where Quint was concealed, almost as though he could feel the hatred emanating from Quint as he studied the Comanchero's dark face. The firelight might possibly reflect from the lens of the telescope, a dead giveaway, unless the breed mistook it for the eye of an animal. Then the breed turned away and Quint removed the telescope from the rock top where it had been resting. If Kiowa suspected a *man* was behind that faint spot of reflected firelight . . .

The moonlight was almost daylight-bright in the canyon. Two of the Comancheros would go together to inspect the horses and mules the Comanches wanted to trade and then have them separated from the remainder of the huge herd that filled the canyon far up beyond the camp. The remaining two Comancheros would stay at their camp guarding the trade goods, aided by a few Comanches they had hired as guards.

The drumming and dancing were ceaseless. It was a joyous time for the Kotsotekas; everything was good—horses, and mules, scalps and fine trade goods.

The women had finished their cooking. Now was the time for a little pleasant relaxation. The men had their dancing. The women would have the Mexican woman prisoner. They dragged her stripped to the waist from the tipi where she had been kept bound and helpless, without food or water since the time of her capture. She had been the butt of some coarse practical jokes by some of the younger men until they had grown tired of the fun and had joined the dancers. Now it was the turn of the women with her. They kept her hands bound behind her back and looped a horsehair reata about her neck. They kept her moving up and down the camp street by poking her in tender places with sharpened sticks, or by touching the ends of smoldering brands against her fair skin. One of the Comancheros, the black-faced one who looked like an evil spirit, with his one milky-colored eye, had seemed interested in her, as well as in the captured horses and mules. Perhaps he'd pay a good price for her.

Quint put the glass on Lupita. Her lustrous black hair hung in front of her face, so that it was difficult for him to see her features. Her naked upper body was fully revealed in the clear cold moonlight, while the warm firelight played on her flesh. The powerful telescope lens picked out each detail of her body, as well as the numerous bruises, scratches, cuts and burns she had suffered during her short captivity. Most of her injuries were superficial. It was possible that the Kotsoteka women had been warned by the men to go easy on the girl. Quint had never seen the results of a real working-over the Comanches could give to a woman captive, or any captive for that matter. But he had heard stories. Luke had lived with the Kotsotekas for a time, and he had told of some of his experiences witnessing such tortures. It had not been through choice, of course, but as Luke himself had said, "When yuh live with the yellowskins, *any* yellowskins, yuh got to act as much like one of them as yuh can, or else. . . ."

The girl turned her head sharply and swung her heavy mass of hair back from her face. Quint whistled softly. Federico had not exaggerated. *"Lupita! To see her is to adore her! To know her is to love her!"* Federico had cried fervently. Her face was heart-shaped. Her eyes were immense. Her mouth was a red treasure, full-lipped and bee-stung. Then the heavy mass of hair fell across her face again as she stumbled and went down on one knee. An ancient crone began to beat her across the back with a thick charred stick.

Quint lowered his free hand to the butt of one of his Colt pistols. The distance was too great for a killing shot. He was not, as yet, skilled in the use of the revolver. If he killed the crone, in any case, he'd have nine rounds left in the two guns to hold off pursuit, but he'd never make good his escape. Besides, it would be of little help to Lupita. He turned his head away from the cruel sight. He prayed to whatever god might be listening, Christian or Comanche, that the girl be spared mayhem or death until he could somehow contrive to rescue her.

When Quint looked again, she had regained her feet. A burly buck held her by one arm and was beating the crone with the same stick she had used to beat the girl. He knocked

200

the screaming woman to the ground and then kicked her repeatedly in the belly until she crawled away.

The warrior dragged Lupita after him as he strode toward the camp of the Comancheros, striking out with his free hand or kicking out with one or the other of his feet to drive back the screaming, gesticulating women who tried to get at the shrinking girl. The women had all turned back by the time he was almost to the waterhole. He cut loose the bonds about her slender wrists, fully stripped her and shoved her into the shallow pool, but kept hold of the end of the reata which was looped about her neck.

Lupita came up gasping and streaming water. She stood up knee-deep in the water and looked from one side to the other as though seeking a way of escape. Quint had the glass on her. There didn't seem to be any fear on her lovely face, just a set and determined look.

Federico had put it well. *"Hardly more than a girl, as I have said, but,* Madre de Dios!*—What a woman! She is a woman, but she has the spirit and courage of a man! She can ride and shoot as well as any man!"*

The buck squatted by the side of the pool, but he kept the reata in his hand. Lupita got the idea. She drank deeply and then laved her lush body with her tapered hands. Her breasts were full, her belly flat, and a man could span at least half the width of her waistline with his two hands. Her legs were beautifully turned, long and slim, and her ankles, as Quint had noticed before she had been cast into the pool, might well be encircled between his thumb and forefinger. Her thighs were twin swellings molded to tempt any man.

"Alma de mi alma! Soul of my soul, Lupita!" Quint murmured.

Was she worth risking his life, though?

Why had he *really* put his life into the balance by coming down into the Comanche-haunted canyon?

Quint closed his eyes. His vengeance on the Comancheros did not have to be wrought this night. That could wait. One way or another, over the passage of time, perhaps years, he'd find them again, one by one, if not all together, and make them pay with their life's blood for what they had done to him and Mountain Woman.

This Guadalupe Vasquez, this lovely child Lupita, had crossed his trail again after some years for some reason of which he now had little understanding, if any understanding at all. But somehow he knew, deep within his mind, that she would have a greater meaning to him in time to come. He didn't know how he knew this, but he was almost positive of it.

He opened his eyes. The girl had left the pool and was standing at the edge of the pool dressing herself while the Comanche was walking slowly around her, eyeing her from hock to head, appraising her, evaluating her, likely before he used her as a means of trade.

Quint put the glass on the Comanchero camp. The American and the Mexican breed had gone to the horse herd. The Jicarilla, Jose, was opening a flat-sided keg of trade whiskey. The man called Kiowa was standing at the edge of the firelight looking toward the Comanche and his girl prisoner.

The Comanche led the girl to the camp of the Comancheros. The firelight shone on her lustrous damp skin and glossy hair. The Jicarilla filled tin cups with the powerful trade whiskey and brought them to Kiowa. While Kiowa offered a cup to the Comanche, the Jicarilla drained his own cup and refilled it.

Then the trading negotiations began. Quint kept the telescope on Kiowa and the Comanche, with now and then a glance at the girl. A few Comanches gathered about the traders, interested in the bargaining. Despite the trade whiskey with which Jose kept the Comanche's cup filled, it was obvious that the warrior was a hard and shrewd bargainer. He kept pointing to certain items among the trade goods, while Kiowa would shake his head most times, and then reluctantly place one of the desired items to one side.

A small herd of horses and mules was driven through the camp to the area of the Comanchero camp. The American and the New Mexican Antonio dismounted from their horses and joined the group about Kiowa, Jose, the captor of Lupita and the girl herself.

Quint didn't need to be within earshot to learn what was going on down at the camp. It was fairly obvious that the American and Antonio, the New Mexican, were damned upset about the mixed breed, Kiowa, dealing on his own with the Comanche for Lupita. The Jicarilla, Jose, was in on the whiskey again, standing about with a loose and foolish grin on his stupid face. The American picked up the trade items Kiowa had put aside for the Comanche and started to replace them on the pile of goods. Kiowa quickly drew his sheath knife. The American turned and revealed a cocked pistol in his right hand. The burly Antonio stepped in between them, at the risk of his life, or so it seemed to Quint. The sound of the arguing voices came up to Quint, but the words were incomprehensible.

All eyes in the area were on the Comancheros. Quint took advantage of the situation by working his way down the rock-and-slab-studded talus slope until he was close behind the small herd of horses and mules for which the Comancheros had traded. Several young bucks loitered near the herd, obviously hired help to watch the herd, at least as long as the traders remained in the Comanche camp.

The horses and mules were a great deal more valuable than one woman. The amount of trade goods Kiowa had been offering would have brought at least four, five or more horses and/or mules. That would be the argument the American and the New Mexican would present to the mixed breed, Kiowa. They knew their man—a woman lasted perhaps only once with him; if she wasn't dead, maimed or severely injured, no other man would want her after Kiowa got through with her. *"I ain't in no hurry,"* Kiowa had said in reference to the Indian woman they had captured late that spring along with the five packs of beaver plews. *"When me get trew with her no one else want her."* The others had heard her screaming like a wounded mare when he had been working her over. After he had had his way with her he had set fire to the lodge with her still in it, perhaps dead or dying, perhaps not.

"They didn't use names with each other except once. I got the feeling they didn't exactly trust each other," Luke had told Quint in reference to his seeing the four Comancheros at Bent's Fort.

"You damned fool!" Jake Stow snarled at Kiowa. "Dickering with *our* trade goods for that woman! We're walking on eggs around here as it is! If these Kotsotekas wanted to, they could wipe us out and take everything we got, including our scalps!"

Kiowa spat to one side. "Shit! They ain't goin' to take our goods! How else they goin' to get goods? We bring 'em the goods, they give us horses and mules. They'd be damned fools to cut off with traders like us. We deal with 'em before, ain't we? Never had no trouble."

"Because we *were* dealing for horses and mules, damn you! Who knows what kind of trouble can start with that Comanche who owns the woman, if you don't give him a good enough deal? By God, maybe he wants the whole stock for her! He was asking enough, wasn't he?"

Kiowa looked away. "I wasn't goin' to give him too much."

Jose laughed. "Goddam woman ain't worth that many horses and mules."

"Sonofabitch!" Kiowa snapped. "Ain't one quarter them goods *mine*? If I want woman instead of horses and mules, I trade for woman!"

Antonio shook his head. *"After* we get our horses and mules. With the profit we can make from them in New Mexico you can buy all the women you want."

Kiowa shook his head. "Only for a while. Whores. Besides, whores won't let me get near them." He grinned, but it was a fixed grin with no joy apparent in it.

Jose drank from his tin cup. "Indian woman neider," he said. He hiccupped. "They don't like Kiowa. No woman like Kiowa. He got to steal or buy woman."

Kiowa turned slowly. He fixed the Jicarilla with his one good eye. Jose looked from one side to the other, dropped the cup and scuttled out of the way, heading for the Comanche camp.

"One of these days I cut the man-parts off that loco sonofabitch," Kiowa threatened.

Lupita's captor had led her away from the Comancheros while the argument was going on. Splashing the Mud figured he knew his man. The rough-face really wanted the woman. Why, he didn't know, because she was young, a poor thing compared with the women of the People, and hardly worth keeping. Not when he could get fine trade goods for her—a brass kettle, maybe, an item prized among the People; perhaps a blood-red blanket, and a fine knife; or a frying pan from which to make war and hunting arrow heads. He needed lead from which to mold bullets for his old musket. He had no use for the white man's whiskey; few Comanches did for that matter. He did like their "black soup," that which they called "coffee."

"If you take me back to my people," the woman said in Spanish, speaking in a low voice, "my father will pay ransom."

Splashing the Mud had thought of that prospect. Still, he had never trusted the Mexicans. One day they would be friendly, and willing to trade; the next day they would meet Comanche overtures with bullets and arrows.

"What do you want?" she asked. "Horses? Mules? A gun? Blankets? You can have anything you want."

He jerked his head as he reached the small tipi his woman

204

had set up, indicating that the captive should stay beside the lodge. He tied her wrists in front of her, leaving enough scope in the rawhide bonds so that he could thrust a stick through the hollows of her elbows behind her back. He tied the end of the reata to the bottom of one of the lodgepoles.

"Will you take me back to my people?" she asked.

He shook his head. "Too far. Not know what happen to me there. Here you worth much to Comanchero. Here I get trade goods for you. There, mebbe get bullet or arrow. Who knows?" He grinned and went into his lodge.

The moon waned. Dark shadows crept down the western wall of the canyon and across its floor. Many of the fires had been allowed to die. A cool wind blew down the canyon and stirred the ashes of the fires, revealing a secretive red ember eye now and then peeping through the ashes. Most of the Comanches sought the shelter of their lodges against the cool of the evening. Most of the lodges had a favorite horse or two tethered just outside of it for emergency use, or to safeguard their being stolen, although there was little risk of that happening in Cañon Chacuaco.

The Comancheros had stored their trade goods in the small tipi they had borrowed from the Kotsotekas. They would keep a guard that night, nonetheless. Their horse and mule herd was being guarded by the young warriors they had hired for that purpose. For their comfort against the chill of the night they had built a fire beyond the herd; beyond the fire there was nothing but the dark trough of the canyon trending to the north and west until it debouched out onto the open plain some little distance south and east from the truncated hill, with its twin dikelike ridges on either of its flanks. Beyond those low heights was the place where the Mexican *ciboleros* had died under Kotsoteka bullets and arrows.

Guadalupe Vasquez had been thrown a ragged, stinking scrap of a horse blanket for shelter against the cold. She huddled under it, with her buttocks on the hard cold ground and her long hair draped over her naked shoulders. The stick that had been thrust through the hollow of her elbows forced her fine breasts outward and the cold had raised the nipples of them. She was cold, stiff and horribly frightened. Try as she would she could not erase the scenes of the surprise attack by the Comanches on her party of buffalo hunters and the merciless slaughter that had followed their surrender. Some of them had wanted to fight it out, to the death, if necessary, rather than to fall into the hands of the Comanches. They knew what would be in store for them. There had really been not the slightest chance that they might hold the Comanches at bay. Groups of many more men better armed than hers had been defeated by them. They were the most savage and warlike of all the Shoshonean tribes. They were always magnificently mounted as a result of their constant raids on the great Mexican haciendas to the south and west of their range. They were absolutely invincible.

She looked across toward the small tipi where the Comancheros slept. The wind fanned the ashes of the fire they had left to burn out. Tiny flames flickered and danced and then died away, leaving the area in darkness again.

Lupita closed her eyes. The face of the strange-looking man called Kiowa, who had wanted to trade for her, seemed to approach through a swirling mist. Try as she would, she could not force that gargoyle face from her mind. It was his eyes that terrified her, seen in frightening contrast to his dark, pox-marked skin—the left eye askew and clouded, the right a startling pale blue. *Madre de Dios!* If she was traded to that two-legged animal she knew what would be in store for her. It would be more, far more, than rape of the most violent kind.

The camp was quiet now except for the soft soughing of the wind. Only the young bucks guarding the horses and mules were awake, and all of them were enshrouded in their blankets and huddled about their fires.

Lupita began to pray, *"María Santísima,* Holy Mary, hear me." Her voice died away.

Something had moved between the dying fire and the small lodge of the Comancheros. Perhaps it had just been a shadow, but then, a shadow of *what?*

Kiowa had taken the last two hours on guard. He gathered his possibles and took his rifle. The other three were sound asleep. He looked down on them. It would be easy to kill all of them and they'd never know who had done it, he could be so quick with the knife. Then the trade goods would be his and he could deal with the Comanches as he willed to do. But then, perhaps the Comanches, realizing that he now stood alone in their midst, could kill *him,* and keep their horses, mules and the trade goods as well. He didn't give a shit about trading for horses and mules. It was the Mexican woman he really wanted.

Kiowa walked behind the lodge and saddled his blocky

roan. He took the reins and the lead of a hackamore on one of the pack mules and led them beyond the camp to a scant *bosquecito* of cottonwoods. There was nothing beyond the trees but the empty canyon and beyond that the open plains. He returned to the camp and took three large canteens he had filled before he had gone to bed. He carried them to the roan and hooked their straps over the saddlehorn.

The breed returned to the edge of the *bosquecito* and looked toward the tipi of Splashing the Mud. The Mexican woman sat beside it with her wrists bound together, and a reata noosed about her neck, which was tied to the butt of one of the lodgepoles so that if she attempted to pull back on the reata the noose would tighten about her smooth white throat and choke off her breath, meanwhile disturbing the pole and alerting those who slept in the tipi. But she had not been gagged. If Kiowa approached her with the intention of freeing her from the noose, and she recognized him, she'd scream, preferring a brutal captivity among the Kotsotekas to being taken away by him. He knew that fact well enough. No woman ever wanted to go willingly with him. It wasn't only his appearance, they sensed something about him that turned them away from him in terrifying fear. He grinned in the darkness. He had learned to like seeing their fear before he had his way with them.

The Comanche horse and mule herd was restless in the deep darkness an hour or so before the coming of the dawn. The mules had been those who had sensed something in the darkness up the box canyon, and their restlessness had carried to the horses. The herd was of many hundreds, practically filling the canyon from one side to the other. They blocked the way between the dead end of the canyon and the thin thread of water from the spring that vanished beneath the white sands after a course of a few hundred yards.

Moccasin, Black Beaver and Joshua had not been able to get near the water to replenish their canteens. If Quint Kershaw had not been somewhere in the blackness of the canyon, perhaps right in the Kotsoteka camp itself, the tough Delawares might have risked approaching the water. If discovered in the act, they *might* be able to retreat back up the canyon and scale the walls of it to escape the Comanches and return safely to the mules. It was a long shot, any way one studied it.

"It will be dawn within an hour or so," Black Beaver

whispered to Moccasin in their own tongue of the Lenape, the Delaware.

Moccasin nodded.

"Shall we risk trying for the water?"

Moccasin shook his head. "The herd is too restless. The guards are between the herd and the water to keep them from it. Besides, Big Red is still somewhere in their camp."

"Unless he got away with the Mexican woman."

"We don't know that."

"Perhaps they caught him?"

Moccasin shook his head. "Not alive."

"It's possible."

Moccasin looked at his brother. "You don't know him. He's Lenape at heart, a *man*. They'll have to kill him to defeat him."

"We wait then?"

Moccasin nodded. "We wait."

They were still waiting when the first and faintest trace of pewter light tinted the sky to the east.

Kiowa catfooted through the fringe of cottonwoods close against the canyon wall and behind the lodge of Splashing the Mud. He paused behind a tree, sensing the pre-dawn with eye, nose and ears. Everything should be all right. The Comanche camp was still asleep. There were no guards within hundreds of yards. He unsheathed his knife and catfooted toward the woman.

Lupita was half asleep. She was not aware of the reata being severed. A hard hand was clamped over her mouth. Her wrist bonds were cut through. The stick was pulled out from the hollows of her elbows. She was pulled to her feet. The hand was released, but before she could cry out a gag was passed across her mouth and tied tightly behind her head. She was picked up and slung across the broad shoulders of a man. He ran noiselessly into the dark shelter of the cottonwoods and through them toward the camp of the Comancheros.

Kiowa reached his roan horse. He dropped the woman to the ground and swiftly tied her wrists together in front of her. He lifted her up into the saddle and tied her wrists to the saddlehorn. The body stench of the man was sickening. Lupita looked down into the face of her captor, and a feeling of sheer horror swept over her. He grinned up at her in the dimness. He reached for the bridle reins to lead the roan from the *bosquecito* into the sheltering darkness of the lower canyon.

"Kiowa," the quiet cold voice said from the shadows. Quint Kershaw wanted the mixed breed to know who had killed him.

Kiowa whirled, whipped out his knife and crouched into a fighting stance. He saw the tall man moving slowly toward him. He sensed immediately that this was no Comanche. He charged.

There would no outcry; no alarm. Neither man wanted to alert the Kotsotekas or the Comancheros. They closed. Quint gripped the breed's knife wrist with his left hand and forced the arm upward, while at the same time he drove a smashing blow to the midriff. Kiowa grunted in savage pain. He brought his left knee up into Quint's crotch, but Quint turned to one side, took the knee on his left leg, dragged down on the right arm of his antagonist and smashed it across his left thigh with such force that Kiowa dropped his knife.

Kiowa was strong, seemingly built of wrought iron and rawhide. He threw Quint back. He was sure now who this man was. He had watched him from a distance in his valley high in the Rockies. He slashed the edge of his left hand across the bridge of Quint's big nose and his eyes, and reached for the corded throat with his other hand. Quint staggered back. His eyes welled with tears from the blow. He came up off the ground and kicked out with his right foot, catching Kiowa in the chest. Kiowa closed in again. They grappled, and then fell back toward a tree. Quint's head struck the tree, half stunning him.

One of the young Comanches guarding the horses and mules that had been traded to the Comancheros had gotten up to relieve himself. The light was subtly paling over the canyon. He heard a faint thudding noise coming from the small stand of cottonwoods up the canyon toward the main camp. He pissed up against a tree while looking toward the timber over his shoulder.

Kiowa dropped on top of Quint and felt for his eyes with his powerful thumbs. He wanted to maim this man before he killed him; it was in his blood; it was his way of marking anyone before they died, so that they should know by whose hand they had died. He forgot anything else in his insane obsession.

Lupita pulled free from the saddlehorn. She flung a long, slim leg over the pommel and slid to the ground. She ran toward the two struggling men. She didn't know who was fighting with her captor, but whoever he was, she was on his

209

side. She kicked out as hard as she could and blind-sided the breed alongside his head with her boot heel. He fell sideways but didn't release his grip on the man beneath him. Lupita raised her clenched fists and brought them down with all her force on top of his head. He let go of Quint to rid himself of this damned stinging gadfly of a woman. Quint brought a knee up into Kiowa's crotch and smashed it into his privates. Kiowa grunted. The woman kicked him again. Quint got up on one knee and slammed a left into Kiowa's gut and a right cross against his jaw. Kiowa sprawled backward. His right hand rested on his knife hilt. He gripped it and swung his arm outward in a sweeping stroke toward Quint's crotch. Quint leaped up over the arm and kicked out his right foot with full force. The heel struck with vicious force against Kiowa's left eye and smashed it back into the socket, destroying its partial sight forever. The breed screamed hoarsely like a wounded animal.

Quint drew his knife, cut loose the bonds about Lupita's wrists and shoved her toward the roan horse. "*Vamonos!*" he snapped at her. "Ride!"

Lupita reached the roan. Quint gripped her by her left arm and leg and hoisted her upward to plump her down into the saddle. He didn't see the Comanche horse guard running directly toward him. The light was clear enough now so that the Kotsoteka could see who it was disturbing the dawn. He raised his musket and fired it at Quint. There was no time for niceties. Quint drew one of his Colts as he dropped belly flat on the ground. He fired upward. The .36 caliber slug hit the buck in his chest. The shot echo slammed through the canyon.

Moccasin, Black Beaver and Joshua ran toward the horse herd. Whooping and hollering in blood-curdling Delaware style, they mounted the nearest horses and then lashed about with their rifle butts to stampede the herd down the canyon. The herd began to move, slowly at first and then with increasing speed as fright and panic seized control of them.

The Kotsotekas awoke in their lodges and shelters. They grabbed their closest weapons and ran out into the chill air of the dawn just as the mass of the herd thundered down the canyon, crashing into the tipis and brush shelters, knocking warriors right and left and carrying along with their stampede the night horses always kept tethered beside the tipis. Those Kotsotekas who managed to evade the thundering herd suddenly found themselves under pistol and rifle fire from three mounted men who rode hell-for-leather behind the herd.

Quint slashed the barrel of one of his Colts against the rump of the roan as he mounted behind Lupita. The roan buck-jumped and then ran toward the few Kotsotekas who formed the guard for the horses and mules of the Comancheros. They stared incredulously at the half naked woman who rode toward them with a yelling red-bearded, red-headed giant behind her firing twin pistols that never seemed to run dry. Behind them came the herd, smashing a violent swath of destruction through the whole Comanche camp.

The herd guards raised their weapons to fire. Quint reached into one of his jacket pockets and grabbed one of his spare revolver cylinders, fully loaded and capped. He cast it into the thick bed of embers of the herd guard's fire. The roan was in the clear and streaking out for the open country when the revolver cylinder exploded right under the feet of the guards as they aimed at the retreating horse and his two riders. Then, before they recovered from the surprise and terror of the exploding cylinder, the stampede was on them in a cloud of dust and the hammering of more than a thousand hoofs.

A handful of Kotsotekas managed to get horses and mount. They lashed their horses after the stampede, crying out for vengeance and blood. They raced through the unsettled dust of the stampeding herd. Five hundred yards from the camp five rifles spat flame and smoke and five horses went down. Pistols cracked a spiteful echo to the heavier echo of the rifles. The Kotsoteka pursuit was effectively broken up, for the time being at least.

Luke Connors reloaded his Hawken and slammed the butt down on the hard ground to settle the charge. He looked about at the Delawares and Federico. "Time to pull foot, partners! Big Red got the Mex woman out'n their hands. I told yuh he would!"

They ran through the dust cloud trailing their heavy rifles as the dawn light began to fill the canyon.

TWENTY-SIX

The pale light of dawn covered the plain. Quint looked back over his shoulder as he rode beside Lupita. There was no sign as yet of the Kotsotekas, but dust moiled up from behind the hill and ridges to stain the pearl gray of the sky.

The hoofs of the mules and captured horses hammered on the hard ground. The abandoned *carretas* and buffalo carcasses stippled the plain just ahead. There was no sign of the scavenging *zopilotes*.

Lupita looked back over her shoulder. "Perhaps they won't pursue us," she suggested hopefully, but not very convincingly.

Quint shook his head. "No."

"Can we outrun them?" she asked.

Quint looked sideways at her. "Where? The nearest water is at least thirty miles away. These mules haven't had their fill of water for over two days. The Comanche horses are fresh and well watered."

Luke looked back at them. "And the Kotsotekas are cryin' to drink our blood out'n a moccasin. They'll run their hosses to death to get us, missy."

"Look back!" Federico shouted.

The skyline above the hill and ridges suddenly had sprouted a long line of feathered lances waving like wind-driven grass. Then a mass of mounted warriors rose to the crest of the heights as though manipulated by a giant marionette master. Two other groups of feathered horsemen surged over the tops of the ridges on either side. The massed horsemen thundered down the slopes in a wide crescent shape, every warrior eager to count coup on the living before they scalped the dead.

Quint drew up his mule in a hoof-pawing rear beside a *carreta* and a swollen, unskinned buffalo carcass. "Fort!" he shouted. "We make a stand here, partners!" He whipped out his knife as he slid to the ground, hanging onto the bridle reins of his mule. The mules sensed the excitement. They threw their angular heads about as they brayed to the heavens. Quint pulled the head of his mule hard to one side, dragged his knife edge forcibly across the distended throat and then yanked hard on the reins to drop the struggling animal beside the buffalo carcass. Luke and the Delawares followed suit, dropping their mounts to form a rough circle, leaving a space for the horses of Lupita and Federico and the two spare horses they had captured at the canyon.

"Dismount!" Quint yelled at Federico, as he dragged Lupita from her horse. He cut the throat of the roan and dropped it beside a mule. In a matter of minutes the five mules and four horses had been formed into a fort composed of a dead buffalo, a *carreta* and some still-quivering mule and horse flesh. The short grass and the leggings and moccasins of the mountain men were dyed red with blood.

Quint pushed Lupita inside the fort. He checked the percussion cap on his Hawken and dropped behind a mule, thrusting the heavy rifle across its dusty flank to bear on the approaching Comanches. In less than a minute Luke and the three Delawares followed Quint's example.

The Kotsotekas had halted just beyond the base of the hill. There was no hurry now. Their quarry had gone to ground behind their slain animals like frightened women. How many of them were there? Only six men and one woman. One charge would go right over them and their pitiful fort.

Time seemed to stand still. The sun came up in a vast silent explosion against the eastern sky. The dry wind flowed up the slopes, waved the short grass and animated the many feathers of the motionless warriors and the manes of their mounts.

Luke studied the Kotsotekas through Quint's telescope. "They sure enough got their hosses' tails tied up for war. That big buck in the center of the front line with the warbonnet is Isa-nanica, Hears a Wolf. He knows me. When I lived with the Kotsotekas his younger brother threw his weight around me. Kept after me, taunting me, challenging me, until one day I had enough. We fought. I didn't mean to kill the sonofabitch, but it happened. By Kotsoteka law I was safe enough, but I knew I had better get out of there." He looked sideways at Quint. "Hears a Wolf never cared much for me after I killed his brother."

"And he sure doesn't now, from the looks of him and his boys," Quint said dryly.

"They used to call me Isa-conee, that's Wandering Wolf in

213

their lingo. Seems like I wandered into their life and then out again," Luke said thoughtfully.

Quint nodded agreement. "Trouble is, old Wandering Wolf, ye didn't wander far enough away and stay there."

Quint looked about at his companions. "Ye Delawares shoot at the first charge. Aim for the lead horses. Save your pistols for hand-to-hand if they come over the mules. They'll likely break around the fort if they don't come right over it with the first charge. Once past the fort they'll reform as quick as they can and make a repeat charge, figuring our rifles are empty. Ye all know the way of it. While ye Delawares reload your rifles, the rest of us, all *three* of us, to be exact, will shoot at the return charge." He grinned wryly. "If they don't go right over the top of us on the second charge ye Delawares will be reloaded by then so ye can get them in the back using both your rifles and pistols. *Always shoot for the horses!* By the time they reform for a third charge we should all be reloaded."

The trappers poured about half the powder in their powder horns into their left jacket pockets. They placed extra bullets in their mouths and shook out a charge of powder into their left hands for swift recharging of their pieces. They placed their cocked single-shot pistols close at hand, hunched down behind the barricade of mules and horses and full-cocked their rifles. The crisp metallic clicks of the engaging hammer sears sounded inordinately loud in the tense stillness.

Federico stared uncomprehendingly at Quint. His handsome face was taut. "You mean there will be some of us left to shoot after the first charge? Six dismounted men and a woman against perhaps three hundred mounted Comanche warriors? *Dios mio!* They are the most valiant of all the border tribes. *They are invincible!*"

Quint shrugged. "Our hearts are big and we're all center shots. See that yours is the same and that ye shoot to kill. Look about ye! Look about ye!"

Federico looked at the calm, composed faces of the trappers. He shook his head in despair. *"Madre de Dios!* You are the bravest men I have ever met, or the most mad!"

Luke eyed the Mexican's ancient and rusty *escopeta.* "Yuh sure that thing can shoot without blowin' up?"

"It is a fine weapon! It has fought in many battles for New Mexico! It has been in my family for over a hundred years!"

Luke shook his head sadly. "It should be hangin' over the fireplace then."

214

Lupita held out a slim hand for the *escopeta*. "Federico, let me have it. You have your bow and arrows. At this short range you can be more effective with them than with the *escopeta*. Besides, I am a better shot than you are." She smiled a little.

Federico nodded. "That is true."

Quint studied the young woman as she swiftly and skillfully loaded the big-bored fusil. Despite the bruises and dust on her face, she was still beautiful. Not once had she cried out in fear in the swift retreat from Cañon Chacuaco. She had guts. As she finished reloading the musket her great eyes looked sideways deep into Quint's own.

Luke shifted his position and looked about at his companions. "The Comanches always fight on horseback if they can help it. They depend chiefly on the charge. They use short-handled lances, more like a javelin than a real lance. Only cowards need long-handled weapons, they say."

Quint nodded. "Like the Spartan mothers said to their warrior sons."

"Yuh don't say, Big Red. What tribe are they, and what part of the country they in?"

Quint smiled a little. "A long way from here, Lukie, but they were hellions in their day. None better."

"Here they come," Moccasin said quietly out of the side of his mouth.

The ground began to shake with the beating of twelve hundred hoofs. The half-wild horses plunged on in full gallop. The rising sun reflected from lowered lance points. The Kotsotekas would scorn to use their firearms in favor of their lances and bows. Garish warpaint shone on their faces and torsos—red, vermilion, ocher, white and black. Their shields, for the most part, were painted a glaring white. Feathered and horned headdresses waved in the wind of their passage. The bronzed, painted bodies glittered with polished ornaments of brass and silver. The bodies of the ponies were striped, flared and blotched with fresh bright paint. Feathers fluttered in their manes. Scalps dangled from their bridles. *Comanches!*

"Magnificent," Quint murmured, despite himself.

The woman looked quickly sideways at this strange, scar-faced man who had entered the Comanche camp alone to save her, and now, with certain death staring him in the face had admiration for those who were about to slaughter him and his companions.

215

Hears a Wolf led the charge mounted on a magnificent black stallion. His many-feathered warbonnet streamed in the wind of his passage. The sun reflected from the polished buffalo horns protruding from the front of his bonnet. His lowered lance was wrapped in shining otter fur.

"That's him," Luke murmured as though to himself. "Hears a Wolf. Now I lay me down to sleep—Lan'lord, fill the flowin' bowl."

The charge thundered closer; one hundred yards, then seventy-five yards; fifty yards, and then twenty-five. It was an overpowering, overwhelming spectacle that would freeze an ordinary person to the ground with outright fear.

"Fire!" Moccasin commanded.

Hears a Wolf's black went down wounded. The chief's head struck the hard ground. He had tied himself to his mount with his lariat. The black struggled back up onto his feet and turned back into the mass of horsemen dragging the dismounted chief under the pounding hoofs. Two other horses had gone down. The charge split at the last possible instant, flowing around the sides of the fort. Dun dust mingled with thick white powder smoke. The sun flashed from polished arrows loosed against the fort. Then the charge was past. The Comanches pulled up their excited mounts in hoof-pawing rearings and thrashings.

Quint, Luke and Lupita lay down behind the animals to face the next charge. Federico had nocked a steel-pointed arrow to his powerful hunting bow. He knelt on one knee just behind Lupita, looking over her dark head as she sighted the *escopeta*. The Delawares poured the loose powder from their left hands into the smoking muzzles of their rifles, spat in a ball, then slammed the rifle butts down hard on the ground to settle the charges, all in a matter of seconds.

The Comanches whooped and laughed as they charged. Most of them didn't know their famed war chief was already dead; he who carried a warshield that was proof against bullet and arrow. The stupid white men had fired their single-shot rifles. They were defenseless now. Lances were couched, arrow feathers were drawn back to touch the jawbone, thick buffalo-bull-neck hide shields coated with fire-hardened glue were thrust forward.

They were twenty yards away, thundering on irresistibly.

"Fire!" Quint spat out.

Two rifles and an *escopeta* cracked as one. A steel-tipped arrow was loosed. Four front-rank ponies went down in a crashing tangle, parting the furious charge. This time the racing ponies scented the full strong smell of fresh mule and horse blood from the fort, an odor that drove them crazy. The charge broke in a melee of bucking, rearing, whinnying, neighing horses and shouting warriors. The horses broke in all directions save toward the fort. Dust swirled up from the pounding hoofs. The Delawares emptied their rifles and pistols into the backs of the retreating Comanches, dropping three warriors and two horses. The warriors galloped back toward the hill and ridges leaving the plain stippled with dead, wounded or dying warriors and horses.

The top of the hill was dark with people. Those of the Kotsotekas who had not been in the pursuit that dawn had come to see the warriors ride right over the white men. They were the women, the elderly, those that were too young and those whose medicine might not be good for fighting that day.

Luke reloaded his Hawken. He looked toward the hill. "Come to watch the great victory dance," he said dryly.

"Start digging," Quint ordered.

Knives and belt hatchets bit at the hard earth. The dirt was filled in between the animals and piled on top of them. Federico knocked loose the uprights of the *carreta* and then placed them atop the earth covering the mules and horses.

Hears a Wolf lay dead about fifty yards from the fort. The wind rippled the feathers of his magnificent warbonnet. His body had been shattered and broken by the hundreds of hoofs that had struck him. His famed warshield, once said to be able to turn aside bullets and arrows, lay beside him pounded flat into the hard ground.

Luke looked at the dead chief. "He was a great one," he said.

Quint nodded. "How the mighty have fallen."

"You're sorry for him, knowing we may be next?" Lupita asked as she reloaded her *escopeta*.

"It's more respect than sorrow, Lupita."

"He was a *man*," Federico said.

"Will they attack again?" Lupita asked.

Quint looked at the Comanches. They were milling about at the base of the hill, out of long-rifle range. "Aye, that they will. It's no longer a question of gaining coups and scalps. It's a question of honor now."

Luke nodded. "There'll be a heap of wolf and *zopilote* meat afore long, certain. . . ."

The second charge came—a thundering avalanche of warriors and horses. Powder smoke foamed from the fort. The

217

charge split. The Kotsotekas reformed beyond the fort and charged, hoping the fort defenders would not have time to reload. They were wrong. Bullets struck the tough bull-hide shields with the sound of sticks hitting a board fence. Arrows swarmed like a cloud of grasshoppers and hit the dead mules and horses with a *thock,* like sticks being whipped into thick mud. Gun flashes sparked through the thick powder-smoke cloud as the charge hammered past, taking rifle and pistol bullets along with one lone arrow into the backs of the warriors and the rumps and sides of the horses.

Quint reloaded his smoking Hawken. "Everybody alive?"

They were all present and accounted for.

Minutes ticked past and tallied an hour.

The sun was up high. There was no shade on that scorching plain. The stale water left in the canteens was gone. Flies buzzed and swarmed over the bodies of the mules, horses and the lone buffalo carcass. They stung viciously at any exposed flesh. Every now and then the swollen buffalo carcass would move a little and emit a stinking, sickening effluvium that remained within the fort. There was no wind to dissipate it. The fort reeked of blood, body gas and acrid powder smoke.

The next charge was led by none other than the great medicine man Pe-arva-akup-akup, Big Red Meat. He was unarmed. He had the power to turn bullets and arrows aside as he shook his buffalo-scrotum rattle. He sang his medicine song. A half-ounce .53 caliber bullet hit him in the mouth. That broke up the charge.

The Kotsotekas gathered on the slopes of the hill and the ridges. They smoked and talked among themselves. Maybe their medicine wasn't good that day? It was a leisurely council. There was plenty of time. The white men could not last much longer.

Federico pointed toward the hill. "Look, the women," he said.

They came slowly down the hill to gather their dead and wounded. They dragged the bodies back toward the hill, but did not come too close to the fort for the bodies that stippled the ground about it. That is, all except one old crone who waddled closer and closer to within easy rifle range.

"Go home, old woman!" Luke shouted. "Do you want to die too?"

She cursed and shook a fist. "I know you, Wandering Wolf! Dog-faces! I throw shit at all of you! Cowards! Women! Wait until the council is over! Our men will ride right over you! We women will cut off your man-parts and stuff them into your mouths! We will dance on your scalps!"

Luke thumbed his nose at her. "They haven't ridden over us yet! We'll kill them all if they keep on coming! There will be howlings and wailings in your lodges! The arms and legs of your women will run red with their own blood!"

Moccasin full-cocked his Hawken. He sighted on the old woman. To kill a woman under the eyes of her men was a brave deed and considered as a coup by many tribes.

Quint reached over and gripped the barrel of the rifle just behind the rear sight. "Save the ball for the next charge, eh, old hoss?"

Moccasin studied Quint. He nodded. "All right. Her scalp too old and gray anyway. Mebbe full of lice."

The women had cleared the field of their casualties between the Comanches and the mule fort, leaving only the dead chief and the other bodies on the far side of the fort.

A young warrior rode slowly down the hill. He quirted his paint horse into full speed and hammered directly toward the fort.

Luke raised his rifle. "Wants to make a goddam hero out of hisself, does he?" he croaked.

"Wait," Quint suggested. "Let's see what he's up to. He can't hurt us."

The warrior—he was hardly more than a boy—hit the ground running carrying a coiled lariat in his hand. He noosed the lariat about one of the dead chief's ankles and was back on his horse's back in a flash. He quirted the horse and rode fast toward the hill dragging the chief's body behind him.

"I'll be goddamned," Luke murmured.

Not one of them had thought of shooting while the warrior had performed his daring feat.

The Comanches formed again. They advanced slowly toward the mule fort. A few warriors opened fire with their muskets.

Quint rolled his eyes upward. "Dear Lord, for what we are about to receive we are truly grateful."

Comanche guns flamed and cracked; arrows flashed in the sun. This time the fighting was rather halfhearted as far as the Comanches were concerned. It was really more of a dangerous exhibition of bravado on their part, showing off before their women and each other. There were no more hell-for-leather, do-or-die charges. Most of the showoffs were young warriors. They galloped around and around in circles, closing in on the fort and then pulling away, encouraged by the lack of shooting from the fort. When they neared the fort they'd throw themselves over on the far side of their racing ponies holding themselves on by means of a rope braided into the pony's mane in which they swung while hooking a heel over the pony's back. They would shoot their bows from under their pony's necks. They became a little more cautious when Moccasin shot one of them through the heel and he fell from the pony to be dragged bumping and bouncing on the hard ground.

Now and again one of the defenders would open fire to keep the Comanches at a respectful distance, but they were usually only able to kill or wound a horse. Several times, however, a rider would be thrown and would try to run to safety. Almost immediately there would be the spiteful crack of a rifle and a .53 caliber bullet would slam into his back and put him down permanently. Rarely, when one of them survived a fall and did get hit, another warrior swept in close at full speed to have the dismounted buck grip his belt or outstretched arm and swing up behind him to be galloped out of range.

Warriors circled at a respectful distance shooting arrows upward so that they seemed to vanish, seen only for a fraction of a second flashing in the sunlight as they reached the zenith of their flight and then turned over to vanish again as they dropped at speed down toward the fort. Sometimes arrows struck the earth and shattered or rebounded upward. Many times arrows struck a horse, mule or the dead buffalo. Strangely enough, or perhaps miraculously, none of the fort defenders was struck.

It was an uneasy, if not frightening, experience to see an arrow soar upward and vanish, catch an instantaneous flash from reflected sunlight as it turned over, then wait to see it strike the ground or one of the dead animals or expect to feel the flint or iron point strike into one. As arrows thudded into the carcasses with deadly regularity, the meaning of the expression "like a bolt out of the blue" had a greater significance for Quint.

By midafternoon the shooting slackened off. The mass of warriors and watching people vanished over the hill and ridges. Only a score or so of warriors kept an eye on the fort.

"Maybe they'll leave too and follow the others," Federico croaked.

Luke shook his head. "They've likely only gone for water."

The sun was sending down murderous shafts of light and

heat onto the plain. Lupita lay huddled near Quint's jacket. She did not move. It was quiet within the fort except for the perpetual buzzing of the flies and the faint sound of the escaping body gas from the carcasses.

"Maybe we could parley," Federico husked.

"With what?" Luke asked.

"The guns, packs and saddles."

Luke shook his head. "You've hunted out here for years and yuh'd believe that? They'd smile at yuh, agree with yuh, compliment yuh on your bravery and the great fight yuh put up, until they got their hands on your rifles." He quickly drew a powder-blackened forefinger across his throat and grimaced. "They'd have yore ha'r off afore yuh died. Or mebbe they'd let the wimmen get at yore privates with their skinning knives."

Quint's lips had cracked. His tongue had thickened and seemed to be trying to force its way out of his mouth. He thought of the icy streams splashing down the slopes in his valley, frothing and splashing in the clear, winy air, making tinkling fairy music. He tried to force the thought from his mind, but it was no use.

Moccasin stirred a little. "They're makin' us sweat it out," he said. "When we're weak enough, they'll be back. . . ."

The Comanches still on the hill slope squatted in the scant shade of their horses waiting for the main force to return from Cañon Chacuaco. The sun was on the wane. It was slanting toward the western mountains. When the dusk came with its attendant deceptive shadows, might the Kotsotekas not attack at speed and overwhelm the defenders of the fort?

Slowly at first and then with increasing numbers the hill and ridge slopes began to fill with the Kotsoteka men and women. It was as though the Romans were taking their seats in the Flavian Amphitheater after an intermission, waiting for the freshly strewn sands to be dyed again with the hot blood of men and animals.

A lone bareheaded rider came leisurely around the side of the hill and rode down the slope. He was followed by three other horsemen, two of whom wore hats while the hatless third man had the white slant of a bandage across his left eye. They reined in their mounts near the main body of Comanches. Quint focused his telescope on the four newcomers. The Comancheros.

The Jicarilla Apache, Jose, rode leisurely out onto the

221

plain. He raised a dirty white cloth on the end of a long stick and waved it back and forth.

"Parley!" Federico cried. "I knew it!"

Quint looked down speculatively at his Hawken.

"We might as well hear what he has to say," Federico suggested.

Quint nodded. "Wave him on. Within good rifle range." He grinned wryly.

The Jicarilla halted fifty yards from the fort. He had two heavy water bags made from the paunches of buffalos slung over the withers of his horse. They glistened with moisture and dripped slowly. Quint put the glass on him. He was grinning foolishly. His eyes wandered back and forth as though he was unable to fix them on anything. They were evidently as loose as his mind.

"What do yuh want?" Luke shouted.

"The Kotsotekas want trade water for guns," Jose shouted back.

Luke looked sideways at Quint. "We could drop him, hustle out there, grab the water bags and get back here."

"Before the Comanches would be down on ye?"

Luke shrugged. "It'd be close," he admitted. "But it might be better to go that way than to die of thirst in this stinkin' hole."

Quint eyed him. "Supposing they got ye alive, Wandering Wolf?"

There was no reply from Luke.

Federico touched his cracked lips with a swollen tongue. "Maybe one gun for one waterbag? My *escopeta* is very old. Surely it can be spared?"

"Try him," Quint suggested dryly.

Federico stood up and cupped his hands about his mouth. "My good rifle here for one waterbag? Perhaps *both* waterbags, eh, my friend?"

Jose doubled over with laughter. "Two waterbags for *all* your rifles and pistols!" he shouted.

There was no answer from the fort.

Jose rode slowly until he was a good two hundred and fifty yards from the fort. He raised one of the waterbags and poured some of its contents over his head and body. He let some of the water dribble onto the parched ground.

"Bastard," Luke husked.

The Jicarilla stood up on his horse. He turned around, flipped up his breechclout and then patted his bare rump

222

with both hands as though to imply, "Kiss my ass, white men."

A ripple of laughter cascaded down the side of the hill from the massed Comanches.

Quint eyed the Jicarilla. "How many yards?"

Luke scratched in his beard. "Two seventy-five?"

Moccasin shook his head. "Closer to two sixty-five."

"The thin air is foolin' ye. Two hundred and fifty, almost to the yard," Quint stated firmly.

Quint raised his rifle and fired almost in one motion. The powder smoke drifted off on the wind. The bellowing report seemed to roll along the flat plain until it died away. The bullet raised a puff of dust fifty yards in front of Jose and his horse.

"You see?" Federico said, "It's hopeless."

The Comanches and the three Comancheros roared with laughter. Jose splashed more water over himself.

Quint opened the smaller of his two powderhorns and poured a heavier charge into the funneled muzzle of his Hawken; almost equal in grain weight to that of the half-ounce bullet he would use. With that heavy charge the Hawken should fire flat, or nearly level at 250 yards.

Quint rested the heavy rifle on the dusty rump of one of the dead mules. He tossed a little crumbled dry grass into the air and idly watched the wind drift of it.

Jose, now that he had a highly appreciative audience, was outdoing himself. He'd splash water over himself and the horse, then turn around, bend over, flip up his breechclout and pat his bare rump with wet hands. The sun reflected from the water and his wet skin.

Quint's Hawken hammer click-clucked into full cock. He pressed the rear trigger to set the front, or firing, trigger with a faint crisp click. He looked back over his shoulder. "Well?" he asked.

Federico shook his head. "Impossible."

Quint yawned. "Any betting men around here?" He winked at Lupita.

"My Mex silver-mounted bridle against that new wool shirt yuh got at Bent's," Luke offered. "Pervided yuh wash it first."

Quint nodded. "Anyone else?"

"Quart of whiskey agin a pound of tabac," Moccasin bid.

"Done! Black Beaver?"

"Same as Moccasin."

"Joshua?"

The young Delaware thought for a moment. "Pound of tabac against a quarter pound of that English gunpowder."

Quint studied him. "Pretty sure of yourself, eh?"

Joshua shrugged. "The odds are about even, ain't they?"

Quint drew in a big breath, let out half of it and then held the rest. He allowed a mite or two for windage, lined up the silver blade front sight within the buckhorns of the rear sight and steadied the blade on the Jicarilla, who had just turned around to go through his ass-patting act again.

Quint tightened his right hand about the small of the stock and placed his finger tip on the firing trigger. The breech-clout was flapped up, revealing the bare rump to the light of the sun. The Hawken bellowed hoarsely, kicking back solidly into Quint's shoulder. The dull report flatted off across the plain.

Luke stood up. *"Wagh!* Bull's-eye!" he yelled. He jumped up and down slapping his hands against his thighs.

The bullet had given the Jicarilla a 217-grain goosing, driving him forward and off the rump of his horse. He was dead from shock before he hit the ground.

"Mother of God," Federico breathed. "I still say it's impossible."

Quint quickly reloaded with the regular powder he used. "One down and three to go," he murmured quietly to himself. If he ever got out of this scrape, he'd not rest until he made the surviving three Comancheros pay off their debt to him in their blood.

An hour passed. The Kotsotekas were talking it up again. The ignominious death of the Jicarilla clown had shocked them. They couldn't believe what they had seen.

"They'll be along soon," Luke croaked.

Federico shrugged. "We may be dead of thirst about that time."

Quint looked at Lupita. She was suffering terribly. The situation was bad enough for himself and the other mountain men, although they were used to such hardships. It must be sheer hell on her.

Federico looked at the sun. "We can't last here, companions. If the Comanches don't get us, the heat and thirst will."

Quint drew his Green River knife. He crawled to the swollen buffalo carcass, eyed it for a few seconds, then plunged his knife into the belly and drew it to one side to open the paunch. A flood of stinking, greenish water flowed out of it. He thrust his hat under it to catch some of the fluid. He crawled to the woman while the other men crowded about the buffalo to dip cupped hands into the belly for the fluid, which they sucked into their dry mouths as though it were nectar.

Lupita turned her head away from Quint's proffered hat. "Mother of God," she croaked.

"Drink," Quint ordered her.

"Never!"

She winced as he gripped her by the back of her shapely neck and forced her face into the hat. There was nothing else she could do but drink the water. When he released her she knew she was going to get sick. She looked up into his scarred face. He shook his head. "Hold it down," he said. She held it down.

The sun was low in the west.

The Comanches came on in a last desperate charge intended to go right over the top of the stubborn defenders of the fort. Surely the death of so many warriors had paid for a final Comanche victory. Delaware rifles and pistols spat flame and smoke. Comanche horses and warriors went down. The charge parted to skirt the sides of the fort. The warriors threw themselves over the off sides of their mounts to keep them in between themselves and those deadly gun muzzles while loosing arrows from under their mounts' necks.

The charge reformed beyond the fort. Dust and powder smoke swirled over the ground between the fort and the Comanches. Quint handed his loaded Hawken to Federico. He drew his pair of Paterson Colts, and cocked them, and stood up to face the coming charge. The Delawares' wiping sticks thudded home in the barrels of their rifles. They turned to stand up behind Luke, Federico and Lupita and beside Quint.

The Comanches shouted encouragement to each other. "It is a good day to die! Only the earth lives forever! Brave up! Brave up! It is a good day to die!"

The charge came on, a solid mass of feathered horsemen.

Quint presented his Colts, one in each hand, and as the others fired their rifles into the oncoming horsemen he fired each pistol alternately as fast as he could cock them and press triggers. Sixteen rounds of bullets smashed into the Comanches. Horses went down in a kicking, thrashing tangle, while others, crashed into them, leaped over them or raced around them past the fort through the thick mingled powder smoke and dust. Before they were out of range the reloaded rifles were fired at their backs.

Quint swiftly replaced an empty revolver cylinder with his one remaining spare cylinder. He reloaded an empty cylinder and replaced it in the other Colt. All about him charges were being rammed home in hot smoking weapons. Then they were ready for action again. The terrible noise of the wounded horses could not be shut out. The sickening odor of freshly spilled blood mingled with the stench within the fort.

"Mother of God," Lupita breathed. She closed her eyes and clenched her small fists. "How long will this go on?"

"Until they stop coming," Quint replied quietly.

"Or we are dead."

Quint nodded. "That too."

Luke peeled back his jacket. His right shoulder was solid black and blue from the heavy recoil of his Hawken. He grinned crookedly. "I wonder how many brass tacks I can hammer into Old Sureshot's stock for Comanche dead," he speculated idly. He didn't really expect an answer.

Quint shook his head. "*Quién sabe?* Count 'em up, divide by seven, and you've got the answer, Lukie."

"Waal, anyway, yuh kin put a tack into Auld Clootie's stock for that loco Jicarilla yuh dropped with that lovely long shot. *Wagh!*"

The sun was almost gone. A great quietness came over the plain. The dry wind shifted. Feathers on the bodies of the stiffening dead ruffled in the breeze.

They lay low in the fort, watching the rough silhouettes of the hill and the ridges against the skyline. Then the light was gone.

Quint crawled over a mule and crouched low, peering toward the hill and ridges. They were dark humps now, hardly apparent in contrast to the darkness. Moonrise would be in two hours.

Luke stood up. A spent Comanche bullet dropped from his clothing. He placed a hand here and there on one of the mules to see if he could lay it flat on a place between some of the many arrow shafts. He could not.

The ice-chip stars began to sprinkle the dark-blue blanket of the sky.

Quint and Luke moved noiselessly toward the hill. They crouched low, trying to pick up any movement or sound.

"They gone. We leave now," Moccasin whispered from behind them.

They left their possibles, costly new Mexican saddles, and well-filled packs, taking only their weapons and empty canteens. Lupita walked beside Quint as noiselessly as she could. Every now and then one of them would look back, crouching low, to listen and skyline anyone who might be on their trail. *Nothing*. . . .

A mile passed beneath their moccasined feet.

"Halt," Moccasin said.

A pony stood with head down just ahead of them. Moccasin catfooted to it, spoke to it in a low voice and then led it back to Lupita. Quint gave her a leg up onto its back and then took the hackamore to lead the pony. They went on into the empty darkness.

They looked back after a long time. The faintest touch of the rising moon was against the eastern sky.

"Where's the next water?" Quint asked.

"McNee's Creek. *Está lejos*, it is far off," Federico replied. "Thirty miles or so to the southeast. A dry bed. One must dig *pozitos* for water, holes, you know, in the stream bed to let the water seep up. If there *is* water. . . ."

Luke nodded. "He's right."

Quint looked toward the southeast. "Right past the Comanches," he said quietly.

"They might head north," Luke suggested. He didn't sound very sure of himself.

No one else spoke. They knew the risks. They knew the hell of corrosive, maddening thirst that lay ahead of them, *if* they survived the night.

Quint took the lead, settling into a steady, mile-eating dogtrot.

An hour passed.

Luke suddenly laughed.

Quint looked at him.

Luke shook his head as though at the greatest joke he had ever heard. "Saved this ol' coon's skin, but whar's my goddam mule?"

TWENTY-SEVEN

July 1838—The Santa Fe Trail

The Santa Fe–bound caravan following the Cimarron Cut-off was two months and 575 miles out of Independence, Missouri. The traders had started on the trail as soon as the grass was high enough on the plains to feed the stock. Its present position was roughly about 110 miles southwest of Bent's Fort on the Arkansas River and about 55 miles in the same direction from Cañon Chacuaco. Far to the northwestward, low on the horizon, a silvery stripe showed upon an azure base, resembling a line of chalk-white clouds—the perennially snow-capped summit of the eastern spur of the Rocky Mountains.

The caravan moved across the undulating plain in four divisions of vehicles, each under the command of a lieutenant, traveling in four parallel columns, although not always equally spaced, with sometimes many rods between vehicles. There were forty wagons, about half of which were drawn by oxen, the remaining half by mules. Six to eight oxen were yoked to each wagon, or eight big California mules costing two hundred dollars a pair and up, strong enough to haul the heavy wagons, with an equal number of teams in reserve being herded along behind the caravan. The complement of the caravan was 130 men and four women.

The freight wagons were Pittsburghs, modified versions of the older Conestogas or St. Louis–made Murphy wagons. They had one specific purpose—the efficient transportation of heavy loads on any road. Only the finest materials went into their manufacture and repair—seasoned oak, hickory and *bois d'arc,* as well as the best iron for stay and trace chains. They rolled on ponderous iron-tired three-hundred-pound wheels fifty-four to seventy inches in diameter. The wagon box and precious cargo were protected by two huge osnaburg sheets lashed tightly over the hickory bows. They were packed solidly with boxes, barrels and bales of cloth goods of every description, notions such as combs and looking glasses, ribbons, Indian trading trinkets, soap, tools of every kind, scissors, razors and Barlow knives, guns, lead, flints, gun powder and percussion caps. The average load was from three thousand to seven thousand pounds. Some of the teams hauling the wagons and their cargo were pulling four and a half tons. The teamsters were principally Missourians with a slight sprinking of French Canadians and Mexicans. These proud and independent men had two tools to enforce their authority over their teams—sixteen-foot bull whips and an extensive vocabulary of profanity. Some claimed they could strip the bark from an oak tree with their explosive, vitriolic cursing.

Authority lay with the captain, or commander, a first

228

lieutenant and second lieutenant, a clerk, and a three-judge court for the trial of trail offenses. In addition there were a commander of the guard and four sergeants of the guard and a pilot or guide. The commander of the guard was the most important officer after the captain. Every able-bodied traveler with the caravan was a member of the guard. Vigilant watch over property and lives, regulation of the order of march and defense against raiding Indians were the price of survival on the Santa Fe Trail.

The caravan moved all day long in a shroud of dust and an unceasing cacophony of sound—the unceasing crack of teamsters' whips resembling gun reports of a day-long skirmish; the thudding of thousands of hoofs, cloven and uncloven; the creaking and grinding of wheels and axles lubricated with a mixture of rosin, tar and tallow; the thudding impact of wheels bumping over countless buffalo furrows and the deep sun-baked wheel ruts left over from the exceptionally rainy year of 1834; the rattle of yokes and harness; the incessant jingling of chains; the shouting and cursing of bullwhackers and muleskinners.

A loose fan of horsemen in scattered groups moved ahead of the caravan, sometimes as much as a mile in front. The more knowing of these riders were mounted on California mules. They were more surefooted, had better staying qualities than a horse and endured the heat much better. They had an inborn sense for whiffing Indians. In short, "Mules are knowin' critters—next thing to human, if it comes to that."

Between the advance guard of horsemen, and in front of the four columns of wagons, were the traveling carriages, two rockaways and a pair of Dearborns. The rockaways each accommodated one "lady" passenger and her lighter baggage. The Dearborns each carried one maid employed by one of the ladies.

Jean Louise Allan cantered Bonnie, her Kentucky thoroughbred mare, toward the four carriages preceding the main body of the caravan. She was a pleasing and tempting sight to every man in view. She wore a riding habit composed of a long serge skirt of army blue and a tight-fitting quasi-military shell jacket of blue trimmed with the orange piping of the dragoons, with twin rows of polished brass dragoon bell buttons down the front of it. Her English riding boots were fitted with silver-plated spurs. She had topped her fine cornsilk hair with a saucy dragoon cap one size too small and tilted far to one side, held in place by a gilt leather chin strap.

The four carriages composed the rolling stock of the Allan sisters, Jean, and her elder married sister, Catherine Williston, wife to Charles Williston, the Santa Fe trader and merchant. The two Dearborns, one presided over by Bridget Shannon, Jean's strongly built and militant Irish maid, and the other by Augustin Esquivel, an employee of Charles Williston's, carried the baggage and camping equipment of the party. Each of the sisters had her own rockaway. Catherine's was driven by old Commodus, a gray-polled freed slave who had refused to leave the employ of the family. Jonas Whitlow, retired sergeant-major, First United States Dragoons, handled the ribbons of Jean's rockaway with his powerful right arm. He had left the other arm buried in a Florida swamp, lost to a Seminole arrow.

Commodus drew the rockaway to a halt as Jean swung lightly down from her saddle and mounted into the carriage, still holding the reins of her mare, who now trotted alongside the vehicle as Commodus set it into motion again.

Catherine sat buoyed up by pillows. Her big-eyed black maid, Sophronia, sat on a stool at her mistress' feet to attend to her every need. She was Commodus' granddaughter and a mute.

"Will you be riding in the van with the men again?" Catherine asked Jean.

Jean nodded. "I have every day thus far, Katie."

"But isn't it dangerous?"

Jean smiled. "The men are armed, and I doubt if any Pawnee or Comanche could catch me on my little mare."

Catherine closed her eyes and shook her head. "God forbid," she murmured. "I need you so much now, Jeannie."

"We'll soon be in Santa Fe, dear," Jean said. She looked down at her sister's swollen belly. "You can have the baby in the comfort of your home there, with the best medical attention available."

Catherine studied Jean. Jean had immense blue eyes with a quick intelligence in them, betrayed at times by a touch of mischief. Her complexion was fine and clear, tinted by the suns of the Santa Fe Trail. Her cheekbones and rather bold nose were dusted lightly with minute freckles. Her mouth was wide, full-lipped, and her teeth were excellent. She certainly wasn't a great beauty; her features, though fine individually, lacked that homogeneity required for the fashionable conception of delicate beauty. Their mother had been such a beauty, pale and transparent of skin, dark of hair and eye, one of the famous belles of Kentucky in her time. Catherine had inherited much but not quite all of her mother's dark, fragile allure. Jean, on the other hand, was her father's daughter in appearance, health, strength and spirit—perhaps as close as possible to the son he had always wanted but never had. He was Colonel Alexander Jamieson Allan, retired commanding officer, First United States Dragoons, now United States senator from Kentucky and chairman of the Military Affairs Committee of the United States Senate.

"You're such a lovely picture in that riding habit, Jeannie," Catherine said. "Especially mounted on Bonnie and riding like the wind past the caravan on one of those mad dashes of yours. Then every man in the caravan has his eyes on you."

Jean shrugged. "I don't do it for their amusement."

Catherine placed her hand on Jean's gloved hand. "I know that, dear, but you're not a skinny, long-legged child any more riding beside Father reviewing his beloved dragoons."

"I can't sit in that damned carriage hour after hour and day after day all hot and sweaty breathing dust and smelling horse manure while slapping at flies and smelling like a goat from lack of a bath."

"Like me, poppet?" Kate asked slyly.

Jean hugged her sister. "Oh no, Katie! You know I didn't mean you!"

"No matter. It's still true."

Jean studied her. "Are you not sorry you came?"

Kate looked away. "Are you not sorry you came along with the caravan just to keep me company and look after me?"

"Me?" Jean laughed with a sound of tiny silver bells. "I'm having the time of my life! I wouldn't have missed this trip for the world!"

"It must be wonderful to be just seventeen, single and in such splendid health and spirits."

"You're only four years older than I am! A mature twenty-one and married just two years. Besides, you're to have a child. Doesn't that slow any woman down a bit, Katie?"

Kate studied her sister again, "It wouldn't slow *you* down, Jeannie. Besides, even when I was your age and still single I never had your health and vigor. That's the Allan blood, pet."

The rockaway bumped into a rut and lurched, throwing Kate heavily to one side. She paled and held her forearms tightly across her swollen belly.

Jean thrust her head out the window and glared at the

231

driver. "Damn you, Commodus!" she shouted. "Watch what you're doing!"

"Yes, missie," Commodus replied.

"You drive like a goddam farmer!" Jean cried.

Kate sat up straight as Jean turned to her. "I'm all right," she insisted quietly.

"You should not have come, Katie. It's just too much, for Charles anyway. My God, do you really believe it matters to him whether you're with him or not?"

"Stop!" Kate cried. The quick tears came to her dark eyes. "You know why I had to come."

Jean shook her head in anger and frustration. "You could have had the baby back in St. Louis."

"I couldn't have joined Charles in Santa Fe then. It would have been at least a year or two after the baby's birth until I could join Charles."

"Dammit! Why couldn't he have come back to St. Louis to be with you?"

Kate looked away. "You know better than that. He couldn't leave his business," she lied. She couldn't look Jean in the eye.

"Blast him and his precious business!"

Kate smiled a little. "You've spent too much time around your beloved dragoons, Jeannie. You sound like a first sergeant at times."

Jean grinned. "Maybe that's why they asked me to leave finishing school. But we were discussing your husband, not my ladylike manners."

"We've been through this many times before, Jeannie."

Jean waggled her head. "Oh, you make me so damned mad! I worry every day and night that you'll lose the child. Not only do I worry about you, but I certainly don't want to lose my future nephew."

Kate managed a faint smile. "It could be a girl, you know."

Jean shook her head. "Absolutely not! It will be a fine bouncing baby boy I can teach to ride and shoot as father taught me."

Kate turned away again. She closed her eyes and placed a thin hand over them. The abject misery and terror of her present situation came creeping over her again. There was no place to run to; no place to hide; no one to turn to other than her beloved Jeannie.

Jean tried to pull Kate close to her, but Kate pulled back

232

from her. "Go and ride with the men, Jeannie. I wish to God I could ride with you, free and unencumbered as you are. Live that way while you can! Live fully! Forget about yesterday; live only for today; think of tomorrow only as another day of joyous life."

There was no use in trying to talk Kate out of her misery. Jean knew her sister's moods. At times there was almost a perverse quality in her in which she seemed to enjoy her depression and melancholia. It was a characteristic which Jean had never experienced.

Commodus reined in the mules to allow Jean to leave the rockaway. For a moment Jean looked into the carriage at her sister. "I know you love Charles so much, Katie. Maybe things will be different in Santa Fe. I am sure they will be!" She turned away quickly so that Kate could not see the lie on her face. "You're such a sweet angel," she flung back over her shoulder, "how can it be otherwise?"

Jean mounted the spirited bay mare and touched her smooth flanks lightly with her blunted spurs, then cantered ahead toward the line of riders ahead of the caravan. The sun was now low over the mountains to the west. Every man in the caravan who could see Jean watched her, as they always did when she rode past them. American women, at least those with her background, education and bold beauty, were few and far between along the line of the great Mississippi River from St. Louis in the north to New Orleans in the south. Beyond the Mississippi such women were nonexistent. To be sure, there was no one like her in Santa Fe and probably in all of New Mexico.

Lieutenant Shelby Calhoun of the First United States Dragoons, Virginia born and bred, was with the advance riders of the caravan that late afternoon. He was said to be traveling west for reasons of health (which was obviously in perfect condition), but in fact he had been detached from the dragoons and assigned to the Corps of Topographical Engineers in order to follow the course of the Santa Fe Trail, and thence down through the great Valley of the Rio Grande del Norte to Chihuahua, outwardly as a trader trainee for Dr. Thomas Byrne, the Santa Fe merchant. Shelby Calhoun secretly would be more than interested in the feasibility of moving troops, artillery and wagon trains to New Mexico and possibly Chihuahua in case of war. His assignment to this secretive duty was quite a plum for a young officer, in an army where a lieutenant could grow gray in the service before attaining the grade of captain—if ever—and where there was no retirement pay. It had helped his case, of course, that his uncle was a close personal friend of the secretary of war. Shelby had known all along that Miss Jean Louise Allan would be with the caravan as companion to her elder sister Catherine. There would be a great many advantages in associating himself with Miss Jean, perhaps even unto a possible marriage. Her father, Colonel Allan, now a United States senator, had been one of the most prestigious officers of the army and was now a powerful influence in Congress. Further and this was not an afterthought by any means, the colonel was an immensely wealthy man. To have a wife with high social position, powerful political connections and great wealth would fit in very well with Shelby Calhoun's carefully planned future.

Dr. Thomas Byrne rode with Shelby Calhoun that day. He was a trader and merchant of Santa Fe, Irish born and bred, educated in medicine at Trinity College, Dublin, a Catholic and a Mexican citizen who was also in the pay of the United States government as an undercover agent in New Mexico. Thomas Byrne believed fervently in the Manifest Destiny of the United States and lived for the day when the Stars and Stripes would fly over his adopted Mexican land. Before coming to New Mexico to start his trading business with funds provided by Colonel Allan, he had served briefly as a contract surgeon in the dragoons until he was incapacitated by wounds received in saving the colonel's life in action. Both Catherine and Jean Allan had been placed in his care for the long and hazardous journey to Santa Fe. He looked upon them almost as if they were his own daughters.

Jean cantered up alongside Tom Byrne. Both men turned to look at her. She was a picture straight out of *Godey's Lady's Book*.

"How is Katie bearing up, lass?" Tom asked.

Jean shook her head. "Not too well. It's the depression more than anything else."

Tom nodded. "Aye, that it is."

"Will she lose the baby?" Jean asked.

"The infant death rate is tragically high in New Mexico, Jean."

"That's not an answer, Tom!"

He looked sideways at her. "Probably, then," he said quietly.

The antelope doe was alone. Somehow she had gotten separated from her mates and now stood uncertainly in the dry bed of a draw that eventually twisted its way down toward the shallow valley of McNee's Creek. The wind was blowing from the west so that she did not at first hear the approach of the leading riders of the caravan or the caravan itself. All she could hear was the hollow, booming noise of the wind blowing over the top of the draw, drowning out all other sounds.

The lead riders reached the lip of the draw. The startled antelope sprang fifteen feet at the first reflexive bound and plunged down the narrow twisting draw.

"Dinner!" Shell Calhoun shouted.

"Tally ho!" Jean cried. She turned Bonnie and tapped her with the quirt. The mare darted down into the draw as though impelled by springs. Her dainty hoofs rattled on the hard earth and gravel in the bottom of the draw.

"She's mad! She'll break her pretty neck or the legs of the mare!" Tom shouted.

Shell Calhoun did not hear him. He had urged his fine black gelding down into the draw and was after Jean, eating the dust of her furious passage.

The rest of the outriders lined the lip of the draw, shouting encouragement after Jean and Shell. The two of them were out of sight now, leaving a thin wraith of dust floating above the draw as the only trace of their passing.

Bennett Barlow, commander of the caravan, rode up from his position just ahead of the leading wagons. "What the hell is the matter with them damned fools?" he shouted. "It's almost time to halt for the night! Go after them, Tom, and turn them back!"

Tom shook his head. "I'll never catch them now. They'll be back soon enough. They'll not catch up with that antelope, and even if they did, they've not got a rifle with which to shoot it and Shell will never get close enough to drop it with those fancy dragoon pistols of his."

Barlow looked back at the toiling wagons. "Well, it's been a damned long dry day. We'll cross the draw and make camp on the other side."

François Charbonne, who had gone back to St. Louis on a buying trip for his brother, the Taos trader, and who acted as chief scout for the caravan, came up at a hard racketing gallop. "Captain! Indians!" he shouted.

"Jesus God! What next!" Barlow snapped. "Where? Comanches? Jicarillas? How many of them?"

"Half a mile behind the wagons. Three of them. Pawnees."

Tom Byrne spat. "My God," he murmured. *"Three* of them."

"Where there are three, Tom, there will be more. They are seen only when they want to be seen. You know that," François warned.

Barlow nodded. "Charbonne is right, Tom. There will be more of them. I will not be caught in the open like this. It will soon be dusk." He spurred his horse back toward the approaching wagons.

"What about Jean and Shell?" Tom called after Barlow.

Barlow looked back over his shoulder. "My job is to protect the caravan. They knew better than to take off like that."

Whips popped and snapped as the teamsters forced their teams on at a faster pace. The flicking whips set up a fine red blood mist about the laboring beasts. The lead wagons rumbled down into the draw and the teams strained to pull their four and a half tons up the other side to the level ground beyond. The men other than the teamsters readied their rifles and rode back behind the herd following the wagons. The sun was almost gone. The dust rose high in the air to be driven and raveled by the wind. Once beyond the draw the caravan moved into its protective formation. The two exterior lines of wagons spread out and away from the two interior lines, then turned inward toward each other to meet at the front angle. The two interior lines kept close together until they reached the point of the rear angle, when they suddenly wheeled out and closed with the hind end of the two exterior lines, thus systematically concluding a right-lined quadrangle with a gap left at the rear corner so that the following herd might be driven into the interior. The ox teams were unyoked and the mule teams unharnessed, then driven into the quadrangle until they almost completely filled it. The teamsters then worked swiftly, binding the wagons together, wheel to wheel, with ropes and chains. Several ropes and chains were stretched across the gap at the rear of the quadrangle to keep the oxen, mules and horses safe within it.

It was dusk by the time the caravan was forted up for the night. Every now and then the people of the caravan would look off into the darkness to the north. Jean Allan and Shelby Calhoun were still somewhere out there. The only man of them who had become upset when refused the right to go and hunt for Jean had been Jonas Whitlow, her driver and bodyguard. No one else had been very eager to go out there into the unknown.

236

A few cookfires for coffee sprang up, dancing in the twilight. They were extinguished as soon as the coffee had been brewed. The men ate hard jerky and cold stale biscuits. After mess those who were not on guard duty stretched themselves out under the wagons with their rifles close beside them.

There would be a moon that night. Until that time the thick, velvety darkness would conceal possible enemies and unseen fears. It was not a good feeling.

An hour after darkness had fallen, and before the rising of the moon, a wolf howled from somewhere back along the trail. In a little while, and at irregular intervals, a series of long and doleful bugle notes from the throats of other wolves carried completely around the forted-up caravan. Wolves, Pawnees or Comanches? None of the silent men were willing to go and find out.

TWENTY-EIGHT

The wind brought a faint, intermittent thudding sound through the gathering dusk. Quint Kershaw sat on the dry bed of McNee's Creek with Lupita's head in his lap. He dipped a hand down into the *pozito* he had dug and dribbled some of the seep water on Lupita's cracked and swollen lips. The pony she had been riding had gone down two miles from the creek, and Quint had carried her there across his shoulders. Luke, Moccasin, Black Beaver and Joshua raised their heads from their individual *pozitos*. Only Federico still lapped greedily at the water in his hole.

"Hoofbeats," Moccasin croaked.

"Get him out of that *pozito!*" Quint ordered, jerking a thumb toward Federico. "Scatter into the brush!"

Quint lifted the girl in his arms and carried her into the shelter of the thorn brush, dusty willows and low, scraggly cottonwoods lining the north bank of the creek. Luke dragged Federico from his *pozito* and shoved him toward the brush. The Delawares kicked sand and gravel back into the waterholes, then quickly erased the footprints while backing toward cover. They moved back into the brush with Luke and Federico and then spread out, staying close enough together for mutual support in case of an attack.

The sound of the hoofbeats increased. Lupita stirred and started to speak. Quint clamped a hand over her mouth. He thrust his face close to hers. "Maybe Comanches. Can you walk?" he whispered. She nodded. "Good!" he said. "Get back into the brush. Lie low. Keep apart from the others. *Vamonos!*" She crawled swiftly away, her exhaustion miraculously forgotten in her intense fear.

The sound of the hoofbeats ceased.

Minutes ticked past.

An antelope doe broke suddenly from the brush on the south side of the creek and sprang into the creek bed. She hesitated as she scented the damp sand of the *pozitos*. Quint cocked his Hawken. It had not been the hard pattering of small antelope hoofs he had heard on the ground. It had been shod horses' hooves; more than one horse, but probably not more than two of them.

The beating of the hooves came again. This time the sound was from two different directions. Then one set died out. The other horse seemed to be moving back to the south.

The antelope pawed at the sand in one of the *pozitos*.

Now and again Quint could hear the faint, intermittent beating of hooves beyond the scrub and cottonwoods on the south side of the creek. The doe had reached water level and was lapping at the water seeping into the hole.

The unseen horse crashed through the brush. The antelope sprang directly toward Quint. He threw himself to one side to avoid her. A horse with rider jumped from the south bank and landed in the creek bed. The horse put a leg down into the hole from which the antelope had been drinking. The sudden lurch threw its rider sideways from its back. The rider fell sideways into the brush. The horse galloped off west down the creek bed.

Jean Allan struck the ground, her fall broken by the thick brush. A hand gripped her loosened hair and jerked her head back. A knife edge touched her smooth throat. She looked up into a dim bearded face.

"Jesus Christ! A *woman!* A *white* woman!" Quint blurted. He lowered his knife and squatted back on his heels.

Jean fainted.

She opened her eyes at the feel of water striking her face.

She looked up into a scarred face. "Who are you?" she asked. She wrinkled her nose at the stranger's rank smell.

"Name of Quint Kershaw. Where, in God's name, did ye come from?"

"A Santa Fe caravan on the Cimarron Cut-off. Quintin Kershaw? The name is familiar. I've heard of you from somewhere."

Quint nodded. "It's possible. I've been *somewhere*." He grinned crookedly.

She looked at him more closely. "You're a *white* man?" she asked incredulously.

"Ye ever see a yellowskin wi' a red beard?" he demanded.

"You could be a half-breed."

He shook his head. "I could be, but I'm not. Where'd ye hear about me, and what did ye hear to think I might not be a white man?"

A low, eerie whistling sound broke the quietness.

"What is it?" she whispered.

He clamped a dirty hand over her mouth.

The whistling sound came again. It was closer.

Quint drew the girl closer to him. "Indians," he whispered. "Pawnees, maybe. Now, ye crawl back into the brush and sit tight like a wee bit bump on a log, and wi' less noise than that, if possible. Whatever happens, don't move, don't cry out. Ye understand?"

He was gone quickly and noiselessly.

Minutes ticked past.

Jean could contain herself no longer. She crawled to the edge of the brush and peered cautiously around the stunted bole of a scraggly cottonwood. Something moved along the bed of the creek. A man figure showed dimly. Jean lay flat and looked sideways and up to skyline the man. Whoever it was, it was not the man she knew as Quintin Kershaw. The stranger was shorter than Quintin, and much narrower through the shoulders and chest, with a sort of upswept hairdo. The man raised his head. The eerie whistling sound came from his lips.

"Indians," Quint Kershaw had told her. *"Pawnees, most likely."*

Jean closed her eyes. Cold sweat trickled down her sides and for a moment she thought she was going to wet herself, both legs.

Pawnees. Jean had seen some of them back on the trail in the place men called Kansas. They were inveterate thieves and murderers; masters of treachery, and never to be trusted. That's all she knew about them. But this was Comanche country! How could Pawnees be here?

Jean opened her eyes. The Pawnee had vanished. It was deathly quiet again.

How far was she from the caravan? They would have missed her and Shell Calhoun by now, certainly. Perhaps they were looking for her. Where was Quintin Kershaw? Perhaps he had not wanted to be encumbered with a woman. Perhaps he had deserted her. Yes, that was it! She really couldn't blame him. In that country persons had to look out for themselves first.

The fears came noiselessly through the clinging darkness and began to gibber at her. Now and again she thought she saw some faint movement, but always out of the corner of her eye—a swiftly fleeting thing. When she looked directly toward it, there was nothing to be seen.

An overpowering thirst crept through her, aided by the intense crawling terror of her situation. She tried to think over it, but it was no use. She must have water. The antelope had evidently been drinking when she had surprised it in the creek bed. Bartolomé Esquivel had once told her how to find water in a seemingly dry stream bed. "Look for the thickest growths along the bank, señorita," he had instructed. "Dig down toward the roots. The water level may be close to the surface there, if any place."

Not a sound disturbed the sinister, brooding quietness.

Quintin Kershaw would not be coming back. She was almost sure of that. Maybe she could dig for water, at least enough to keep her alive until she could walk back to the caravan. She'd have to make her move soon. There would be a full moon that night. She'd stand out like a fly caught in amber on the barren, light-colored ground.

Damn him! Why hadn't he come back for her?

She crawled to the edge of the stream bank and looked up and down its bed. Nothing moved in the darkness. She let herself noiselessly down into the stream bed and crawled as quietly as she could toward a thick clump of growths overhanging the bank. She began to dig there.

She did not look back over a shoulder toward the east, therefore, she didn't see the faintest trace of moonlight against the dark sky.

Quint had catfooted through the darkly shadowed brush up the creek, where he had gone to cover. He imitated the eerie signal whistling of the Pawnees and then moved quickly and noiselessly farther up the creek. He lay belly-flat and looked down the dim line of the creek. He waited.

The whistling came from fifty yards down the creek.

The Pawnee, if it was truly a Pawnee, approached Quint's hiding place. He paused not twenty feet from Quint and turned his head to one side and then the other like a night-hunting cat.

They would have been trailing the caravan, Quint guessed. Their speciality was other people's horses. How many of the thieving bastards were there?

The Pawnee crossed the creek, then ascended the south bank and disappeared into the darkness.

Quint moved back from the creek. Where in the hell were his partners? He sure didn't want to walk into any of them in the dark. He'd be dead before they could identify him, unless he saw them first.

Something moved not far from Quint. He had sensed the movement rather than having heard it or seen it.

"Big Red?" Luke whispered out of the darkness.

Quint came close to Luke. "Pawnees?" he asked.

Luke nodded.

"Now many, think ye?"

"Not more than twenty."

"There's a good-looking white woman waiting for me down the creek," Quint whispered. He looked slyly sideways at Luke.

Luke looked quickly at Quint. "Yuh all right?" he asked anxiously. "Mebbe yuh got a strain or somethin' on that brain of yours walkin' all the way here from Cañon Chacuaco?"

Quint shook his head. "She's from a caravan south of McNee's Creek on the Cimarron Cut-off. Damned fool was chasing an antelope. Her horse jumped into the creek bed and threw her, then ran off west. She fell into the brush. Not long after that I heard the Pawnee whistle."

Luke grinned. "Yuh anxious to get back to her?"

Quint shrugged. "She's a looker. Damned young, though."

"For *you?*" Luke grinned again. "Mountain Woman was hardly more'n sixteen."

"Goddammit! She was Injun, wasn't she?"

Luke shrugged. "That makes a difference in women?" he asked dryly.

"Yuh keep talkin' loud like that with Pawnees in the bresh and they'll be wearin' yore head ha'r on their leggins," Moccasin said softly out of the darkness.

"Shit," Luke snorted. "They's hardly more'n twenty of 'em."

"Four apiece," Black Beaver said from behind Moccasin. "Not countin' on any help from the greaser."

"Where the hell is he, by the way?" Quint asked.

Luke jerked his head. "Hidin' back thar. I told him to stay put until we found out what this was all about. He sounds like a bull elk thrashin' through the bush."

"Moon," Joshua announced.

Quint led them single file through the brush.

Jean Allan felt her hands sink into watery sand two feet down in the *pozito*. She scrabbled hard to pull the loose sand back out of the hole and then lowered her head into it to reach the water. She slopped it up against her face and into her mouth heedless of the sand that came along with it. After a time she sat back on her heels and wiped the wet sand from her face. She looked down at her riding habit. It was a mess. Suddenly she realized she could see much better than when she had begun to dig the hole in the creek bed.

Jean felt a presence. She looked up the creek in the direction the Pawnee had gone. She could plainly see the bed of the creek and the thick brush and cottonwoods bordering the channel. The moon was rising. Best to get into cover again.

Jean slowly turned her head and looked back over her shoulder. She felt faint. Her insides churned.

They stood not thirty feet from her. Indians. There were eight of them. They wore upswept hairdos stiff with paint.

"Now ye sit tight here, like a wee bit bump on a log, and wi' less noise than that, if possible," Quint Kershaw had ordered.

Shelby Calhoun's black had gone lame after he had parted from Jean. He had dismounted and was leading the horse through the thick tangle of brush on the south bank of the creek. The caravan would be to his right, perhaps no more than a mile or two away. Where in God's name was Jeannie? He cursed himself mentally for parting from her. Still, maybe she had gone back to the caravan. They would have stopped for the night before now.

He stopped walking and listened to the faint night sounds, a rustling in the brush as some small nocturnal creature moved about; the faint and eerie-sounding whistling he had heard now and again. Some night-hunting bird, he reckoned. Still, he had never heard of any bird that called quite like that.

He tethered the black to a stunted tree and withdrew his pair of silver-mounted single-shot dragoon pistols from their pommel holsters. He half-cocked them and capped them. Now and again he would look quickly about himself. Slowly he realized that visibility was getting better. The moon was rising.

The creek would be somewhere just north of his position. Perhaps Jean had gone back to the caravan alone. But if he returned to the caravan and found out she hadn't returned, he'd be in a hell of a fix with the other men. Such things just weren't done, particularly on the wild frontier, where white women were a rare and precious species.

Shell forced his way through the brush. The thorned branches dragged at his semi-military clothing, penetrated it and stabbed mercilessly at his flesh. Sweat ran down his body and stung the many cuts. Then he saw the line of the creek, plainly marked by the willows and cottonwoods along its banks.

The faint whistling sound came from somewhere to his left. He looked in that direction. The eerie sound came from behind him. He whirled. It was quiet again. The uneasy feeling came over him that the whistling was not that of a bird, yet it didn't resemble any human sound that he had ever heard.

Shell quickly turned his head. Something moved through the brush in the area where he had left his horse. He forced his way back through the tangle. His horse was gone. The black could not have broken loose. Someone must have untethered it, but *who?*

An intense feeling of utter loneliness overcame him. He wanted to run back to the caravan, to see the strong, well-armed men there and feel the comfort of their presence. Surely Jean would have returned to the caravan by this time.

The whistling sound came clearly from behind him in the direction of the creek. He knew now that it must be human. *Indians!* They had come in behind him when he had left his horse and taken it. They must have taken Jean as well.

Shell forced his way through the brush, heedless of the thorns. "Jean! Jean! Jean!" he called. There was no answer; no echo.

The only sound was the thudding of his hurried footsteps on the hard ground and the slapping of the branches against his body. He reached the fringe of cottonwoods lining the dry creek bed. It wasn't until he pushed through the last of the brush and saw the creek before him that he saw the people standing in the creek bed. He knew who they were. He had seen Pawnees before. There were eight of them. They stood between him and Jean. She stood to one side of the creek beside a small hole filled with water. The moonlight glistened on the water. Her face was set and white.

Shell raised his two heavy pistols and aimed them at the Pawnees. He knew it was a futile gesture. He might get two of them, but they'd get him easily enough once his pistols were empty. His sacrifice would go for naught. They'd have Jean anyway.

A minute or two passed. The Pawnees were still watching Shell.

The eerie whistling came from close behind Shell.

One of the Pawnees raised his head a little. He whistled. The sound seemed to echo from the brush on the north side of the creek and then re-echo again from behind Shell and off to one side.

The tall, lean sorrelbearded man came walking noiselessly down the bed of the creek behind where Jean Allan stood. His heavy rifle rested easily in the crook of his left arm. He came to a halt beside Jean. He motioned with his head for her to get behind him. She moved quickly.

Shell narrowed his eyes. The newcomer moved like an Indian and was dressed like a half-breed, or so he thought. Who had ever seen or heard of a red-bearded Indian or half-breed? Yet he must be one of them. Why else would he have come alone from the shadows to stand in front of Jean?

"Put down those damned pistols, mister!" Quint Kershaw called. "Easy-like! Ye even look like you're going to use them and we'll all be dead as herring in this creek bed!"

Shell didn't want to lower his pistols. God knows he didn't want to, but there was an imperative quality in the voice of the red-bearded man that made Shell do as he was bid.

"There are Pawnees behind you!" Quint called.

Coo-towy-coots-oo-ter-a-oos, or Blue Hawk, had led his Pawnees down to the south to trade for horses with the Comanches, or to steal them if the opportunity presented itself. It was only by luck they had seen the caravan at the crossing of the river called Cimarron by the Mexicans. They had followed the caravan, always out of sight, but keeping in touch with it by means of three warriors, while the main body lay back during the day and closed up after darkness to wait for the chance to run off their herd of mules and horses.

244

They had been moving in toward dusk when the white man and woman had foolishly left the caravan to pursue an antelope doe. The man and woman had separated. The woman had come to the creek, but her bay mare was nowhere to be seen. Blue Hawk was more interested in their horses than he was in the man and the woman, or at least the man. The white man who had burst through the brush with his two pistols in his hands was a fool. It was the newcomer who had Blue Hawk puzzled. He knew this type of white man of old. They were more dangerous than rattlesnakes and as unpredictable, and they rarely took such a chance as this sorrel-bearded man had just taken. He probably knew there were ten more Pawnees hidden in the brush.

The two fighting men eyed each other, the tall Pawnee and the easy-standing, confident mountain man who feared no one.

"We'll all be killed," Jean whispered from behind Quint. "I'll die by my own hand before I let them take me."

Quint maintained his fixed grin. He did not take his eyes off the leader of the Pawnees. He spoke out of the side of his mouth, "Shut up! Don't be so damn melodramatic. They don't want to die any more than we do."

Quint slowly lowered his Hawken to the sand. He stood erect. He held his right hand in front of his neck, palm outward, with index and second fingers extending upward, and then raised his hand until the tips of the fingers were as high as his head, for the sign of "friend."

Blue Hawk hesitated; he handed his trade rifle to the man behind him and then returned the sign for "friend."

Despite her fear Jean was fascinated as Quint and the Pawnee conversed swiftly and fluidly in the sign language.

"What do you want?" Quint asked.

"Your horses," Blue Hawk replied.

"We have none."

"I don't believe you."

"Can you see them? Can you hear them?"

Blue Hawk shook his head. "That is true. Give me your rifle and pistol then as well as the woman."

"No."

"We are many. You are only one man. We can take them easily enough."

Quint smiled. He pursed his lips and gave an exact imitation of the eerie Pawnee signal whistle. A return signal came from behind Quint and the woman. A few seconds later, there were three more whistles from the concealment of the brush. It became deathly quiet again.

Blue Hawk knew the whistling did not come from his hidden warriors. He slanted his eyes both ways, looking at the darkly shadowed brush. He could almost feel the tension from the warriors standing bunched behind him. They did not like this business of standing out in the open, in the growing moonlight, targets for whoever was hidden in that mysterious-looking brush.

Quint whistled again. This time the four answering whistles came from areas other than the first places from which they had come. Quint had timed it so that Luke and the three Delawares had time to move to new positions.

"We'll settle for your weapons then," Blue Hawk signed.

Quint shook his head.

"All right. Let us have the woman."

Quint shook his head again. "She's not much. Too skinny and she has a terrible temper."

Blue Hawk smiled. "All right. But what can you offer?"

"I think it is you who should make an offer."

The sorrel-beard was a confident-appearing man; he was too damned confident. Blue Hawk looked beyond him and the woman. How many of them were there?

"Get on with this, you fool!" Shell Calhoun snapped.

Quint looked coolly at him. "Would ye like to dicker wi' them, man?" he asked.

Shell looked quickly away from Quint. He shook his head.

"Would you settle for the fine pistols he has?" Quint asked the Pawnee.

Blue Hawk looked speculatively at the heavy, long-barreled dragoon pistols. The moonlight shone softly on their silver mountings.

"I'll throw in his hat, clothes and boots," Quint suggested as Blue Hawk turned to look at him.

"Let's get out of here," Roan Horse urged from behind Blue Hawk. "We'll never surprise the caravan now. Let's take what we can get and get out of here!"

Blue Hawk nodded.

"The pistols, hat, clothing and boots?" Quint asked.

Blue Hawk thrust out his open right hand and moved it in a horizontal circle from right to left, breast high, then held it in front of and close to his left breast, pointing to the left. He moved the hand briskly well out to the front and to the right, keeping it in a horizontal plane. "All right," he had signaled.

Quint looked at Shelby Calhoun. "Let down the hammers on your pistols and give them to the Pawnee, butts first."

"Damn you! These were presented to me by my regiment for bravery in the field!" Shell snapped.

"Good! Now they've saved your life and that of the young woman."

"And yours as well!"

Quint shook his head. "I didn't *have* to come out here alone in the bright moonlight to dicker for your lives, mister."

"Damn you, Shell! Give them the pistols!" Jean cried.

Shell lowered the pistol hammers to let them rest on the caps. He reversed the two pistols and held them out to the Pawnee. Blue Hawk's eyes glistened as he took the magnificent weapons.

"Now can we leave?" Shell demanded of Quint.

Quint looked over his shoulder into the pale face of Jean Allan. "Isn't he the impatient one?" he asked. He winked at her.

"Come on!" Shell shouted. "He's got the pistols."

Quint turned. "You're not through yet, mister."

"Lieutenant, damn you! *Lieutenant* Shelby Calhoun!"

Quint raised his eyebrows. "I would have thought it would be Major Calhoun from your damned self-importance."

"If I still had my pistols!" Shell raged.

Quint's expression changed coldly for a fraction of a second, then he recovered, and half-smiled. "But ye *haven't*, have ye? Now, take off those fine clothes, lieutenant."

"What the hell do you mean?"

"Can't ye hear well? Take off those damned clothes, the hat and boots, and give them tae the Pawnee!" Quint roared. "That was the other part of the deal!"

"My God," Jean whispered. She shook her head.

Slowly, ever so slowly, Shell Calhoun pulled off his fine, handmade English boots. They had cost him three months' pay. He stripped off his semi-military jacket and trousers and stood there in his socks and drawers. He tossed his boots and the clothing to the Pawnees.

Someone laughed in the thick brush on the north bank of the creek. It wasn't a Pawnee. Shell Calhoun's handsome face went taut and white. Thin lines formed at the corners of his mouth. His hands trembled a little at his sides.

"All right?" Quint asked the Pawnee.

Blue Hawk shook his head. He pointed at the officer. He made the sign for "all," moving his flat right hand in a horizontal circle from right to left at breast height.

"What does he want now?" Shell demanded.

"Can't ye guess?" Quint asked. "The rest of it. Then ye can leave before the young lassie here sees ye in the altogether. Not that a *lady* wud look at ye, ye understand?"

Jean stifled a gasp. "Oh no!" She bit her lower lip to keep from laughing.

Shell Calhoun stripped to the buff. He tossed his socks and fine linen drawers to the Pawnee, glared at Quint for a moment, then turned and plunged heedlessly into the thorny brush, as naked as the day he was born.

"He'll never forgive you for that," Jean said as she stifled a giggle.

Quint turned. "Aye! Even for saving his precious life, lassie?"

"His pride is perhaps worth more than his life."

Quint shrugged. "Is that so? I wouldn't have believed it."

She studied the lean scarred face and the hard gray eyes of this strange man. "I believe you'd feel the same way, Quintin Kershaw."

Quint turned. The Pawnees were leaving. Partway down the creek bed, Blue Hawk turned. He held his left fist out from the center of his body, brought his right fist about six inches above and a little in front of it. He struck downward with the right fist by elbow action, with the second joints of the right hand passing close to the knuckles of the left. He then held his right hand at his side with the first finger extended and pointing upward and raised the hand in a gradual circle as high as the top of his head, then arched it forward and downward.

"What does that mean, Quint?" Jean asked.

Quint turned to her. He shrugged a little. "It means 'Brave Chief.'"

"So?"

"It's the highest compliment an Indian can give anyone."

"Meaning you?"

Quint nodded. "Meaning me," he replied dryly.

When Quint turned again the Pawnees were gone.

Luke, Federico and the Delawares came from the brush. Luke shook his head. "I didn't think ye'd get away with it, Big Red. I think yuh was gone beaver there, for a time."

Quint looked at the broken fingernails of his right hand. "Oh, I don't know," he said casually. He grinned at Luke.

"The Pawnees took the white man's horse," Joshua said.

"He's got a long walk through the brush then," Quint said. The faintest trace of a smile crossed his scarred face.

"Nekkid," Luke added, straight-faced.

Jean looked from one to the other of them. They were expressionless, but she knew they were laughing inside. Poor Shell! She knew Quintin Kershaw had done a brave and foolhardy thing, but she also knew that Shell would never forgive him.

Luke leaned on his Hawken rifle, eyeing Jean from head to foot. "Didn't believe it when Big Red here said he had a white woman in the bresh. Purty as a calico dress, too."

Jean looked about. "Where are your other men?" she asked curiously.

"You've seen all of them. And they're my *partners*, not my *men*, lassie. They belong to no man."

"You men, there were just six of you altogether?"

Luke nodded. He grinned. "We got the ha'r o' the ba'r in us, lady. We're all center shots, half hoss and half alligator, raised on red hump meat and Taos Lightnin'."

Jean smiled. "I certainly believe you," she said. She looked at Quint. "Where did you come from?" she asked.

"Bonnie Scotland, as a lad. Then from Canada to the United States."

"I knew that!"

"Ye detected it in my speech?"

"It is hard to miss," she admitted, "but I meant, where did you come from to this place?"

"Bent's Fort. We were on our way to Taos."

"On foot?" she asked incredulously.

Quint shook his head. "Only from Cañon Chacuaco. We had another use for our mounts back there."

"How far is that from here?"

Quint shrugged. "Thirty miles or so."

"Afoot?" she repeated.

"We needed water. This was the closest place."

She studied him. "You're not telling me the whole story."

Quint nodded. "Aye," he agreed dryly.

"You'll go on to Taos now?"

"First to Santa Fe, wi' your caravan, seems like."

Federico looked toward the thick brush on the north bank. "Where is Lupita?" he asked nervously.

Quint was a little startled. He had forgotten about Lupita, so intrigued was he with Jean Allan. "Call to her, Federico. She'll come," he said.

"Lupita?" Jean asked. "There is a woman with you too?"

Federico pushed into the brush. They could hear him calling out to Lupita.

"She led a party of *ciboleros,* buffalo hunters, ye know," Quint said. "The Comanches wiped all of them out except her. We got her back from them and brought her here with us."

She looked up into his scarred face. "Just like that? There seems to be a great deal left out in your answers to my questions, Quintin Kershaw."

Luke grinned. "Yuh don't know about ninety-nine percent of it, miss."

Lupita came from the brush with Federico. She narrowed her great dark eyes when she saw Jean Allan standing close beside Quint Kershaw. She walked slowly toward them.

The two young women studied each other, the tall, blond-haired, blue-eyed Anglo with the proud look on her lovely heart-shaped face, and the short, black-haired, dark-eyed New Mexican with the olive complexion—contrast of contrasts!

"Miss Jean Allan," Quint said courteously to Lupita, "Señorita Guadalupe Vasquez, Miss Allan."

Luke eyed the two women sideways, then looked at Quint.

"How he do it?" Moccasin said quietly from behind Luke.

Luke shrugged. "Yuh noticed it too?"

The Delaware nodded. "Their backs are up for each other already."

Quint had sensed the feeling between the two young women. "We'd best get to the caravan," he suggested.

Luke and the Delawares broke a way through the thick thorn brush, followed by Quint helping Jean and Federico helping Lupita.

"Ye said ye had heard about me, Miss Jean," Quint prompted. "May I ask where?"

"There is a French Canadian trader's agent with the caravan. A François Charbonne. A great storyteller. His cousin is a trader in Taos. François is bringing two wagons of goods to New Mexico for his cousin."

Quint smiled. "François!" he cried. "A trapping partner of ours!" He glanced at her quickly. "And what did he tell ye about me?"

"He kept us amused about the campfires many nights with tales of his adventures as a trapper. Many of his stories were about his trapping partners, a Luke, a Delaware Indian called Moccasin, but most of all about a man he called Big Red Badger most of the time, but sometimes Quint Kershaw."

Luke Connors looked back over his shoulder. He winked at Quint. "Just what *did* he tell yuh, Miss Jean?"

She slanted her big eyes archly sideways and upward at Quint. "Many things. About fighting the Blackfeet. Of how you all fought beside the Shoshonis against the Crows at the Medicine Lodge Fork of the Big Horn River and saved them from defeat and massacre. He told of how Big Red Badger became a Yellow Nose." She laughed a little. "Whatever *that* is!"

Quint shrugged. He smiled. "A great honor, at least to a Shoshoni."

Her face sobered. "He told also of how you had gone south last fall to the great Rockies to find a mysterious haunted valley that someone, whose name I can't recall, had told you about."

"Gabe Pritchett. Old Solitary."

She nodded. "Yes."

Quint looked down at her. "And?"

"That he never expected to see you again, alive or dead, if you found that valley. That misfortune would find you. He said that something, like wendygo, it was, would haunt you and then kill you."

"Windigo," Quint said quietly.

"But that was just a ghost story, wasn't it?"

Quint turned a little and looked toward the northwest. He had indeed been warned about that valley. He had not died there, but he had lost his Shoshoni woman, and a fall and spring season's trapping of the finest prime plews that he, or perhaps any other mountain man in the history of beaver trapping, had ever seen. Aye, *he* had survived! He'd never find such plews again in his lifetime, or such a woman as Mountain Woman.

"Quint?" she asked quietly. It was as though he had detached his mind from his body and it had gone somewhere into the recent past to look for something lost that it would never find again.

"Caravan!" Moccasin called out.

The moonlight shone softly on the faded white osnaburg tilts of the corraled wagons. Thin skeins of bluish-gray smoke rose about the wagons, and the glowing of the campfires reflected rosily from the white sheeting. A group of horsemen were riding swiftly toward the approaching group.

TWENTY-NINE

The advance party of the Santa Fe caravan camped the last night on the trail within the ruins of the eighteenth-century church at Pecos. The caravan itself had been left behind at El Vado de las Piedras, the Ford of the Stones, where the Cimarron Cut-off crossed the Rio Colorado about 125 miles from Santa Fe. The caravan would come to the city at its slower rate of travel, allowing the advance party of agents and traders to reach Santa Fe ahead of it, so as to employ clerks to translate their manifests. The traders would then meet their wagons at the customs house where the wagons would be off-loaded and their cargoes inspected by the Mexican customs officers. Each trader was most anxious to retrieve his goods from the customs for the earliest and thus the most profitable sales.

The advance party traveled at night to avoid two-legged predators—bandits, Comanches, Jicarilla Apaches and Utes, who as a rule avoided attacking the well-armed and protected caravan but might be tempted to attack the smaller and weaker advance party. There had been disquieting news at El Vado de las Piedras that a large party of Comanche raiders had been seen in the vicinity of Ocate Creek, about thirty miles west of the Rio Colorado, and that some Utes and renegades had raided a remote village on the Vermejo.

Dr. Thomas Byrne, the Santa Fe trader and merchant, had organized the advance party. He had hired Quint Kershaw, Luke Connors, Moccasin, Black Beaver and Joshua as guards and had supplied them with mounts from the caravan *caballada*. Guadalupe Vasquez had intended to leave the caravan at El Vado and return to Taos accompanied by Federico Casias, but upon hearing the news of raiders between El Vado and Taos she had changed her mind and decided to ride with the advance party to Santa Fe. She had relatives in the city; in fact her elder brother, Bartolomé, spent most of his time there. She could stay there for a time, recuperating from her ordeal at Cañon Chacuaco before continuing on to Taos. But it had been much more than the news of raiders that had made Lupita change her mind. Almost everyone in the caravan, and certainly everyone with the advance party, was convinced Lupita was infatuated with the Montero Americano, Quint Kershaw.

Catherine Williston and Jean Allan had been allowed to accompany the advance party because Tom Byrne had hired such a formidable group of Indian fighters as escort. Jonas Whitlow drove a rockaway carriage carrying Catherine, her quadroon maid Sophronia and Jean's maid Bridget. The other rockaway and the two Dearborn carriages were to be brought along with the caravan. Lieutenant Shelby Calhoun had added himself to the advance party, for, as he had put it to Tom Byrne, "Because of my military experience during the Seminole War, I might be of some value in commanding the escort in case of an Indian attack." There had been no comment about that interesting statement from Quint Kershaw and his partners.

The site of the Pecos ruins, called Cicuye by the Pueblo Indians, was in a quiet and lovely place of blue mountains, serene skies, a bright landscape and air that was like a tonic. Cicuye had once been the largest and strongest of all Indian towns in New Mexico, as well as being that which was the farthest east. The great pueblo had been a natural trading point between Pueblo and Plains Indians. The people had thus become rich, proud, independent and warlike.

The ruins at Pecos were safe enough from Indian attack most times, at least by the Comanches, but there was always the chance that the Jicarillas or Utes or perhaps local bandits might be tempted by the horses and mules of the advance party. Quint Kershaw had naturally taken command of the escort and the defenses of the party, despite the obvious annoyance of Shelby Calhoun. Worse than that, far worse, in fact, was the mutual interest between Jean and Quint. Since that night at McNee's Creek they had shared a campfire in the evenings in company with Luke Connors and the three Delawares. Jean was fascinated with these rough frontier characters, particularly Quint Kershaw. During the last days of the trip between the Cienequilla del Barro and El Vado de las Piedras they had hardly been out of each other's company. What was doubly annoying was the fact that it was

Jean who sought Quint's company, rather than vice versa. Shell hoped to God it was just a temporary fascination she had for him. Still, he had never seen Jean act quite like this with any man, including himself.

The trail tent of the women had been set up in the patio of the old cloister. The traders and agents bivouacked within the nine-foot-thick walls of the ancient church itself. Quint had ordered the horses and mules to be tethered to one picket line within the crumbling walls of the old livestock corral, where they could be kept under close watch by himself and his partners. Between the corral and the massive church ruins were the convent courtyard and the cloister which had been built about the patio. A series of sleeping rooms, or monk's cells, had been built around the cloister. Storerooms, weaving rooms, tanneries, a carpenter's shop and a garden area surrounded the courtyard. Quint and his partners, joined by François Charbonne, who had chosen to ride with the advance party, made their camp in the roofless ruin of a workshop adjacent to the corral.

While François cooked the evening meal, Quint and his partners scouted through the darkness around the perimeter of the ruins along the slopes below the huge rock formation upon which the pueblo and church had been built. All seemed quiet.

Quint was the last to return to the corral. The moon was just tinting the sky to the east when he passed in front of the church. Firelight swayed and postured against the walls of the roofless nave. The aroma of cooking meat and boiling coffee drifted from the ruins. The hum of voices could be heard. Men laughed. It was a good time. The last night on the trail. Tomorrow would bring them to Santa Fe, the end of the trail and of the long miles and weary days from Independence.

Quint paused and looked into the patio next to the church. A woman's laugh had caught his attention. He knew who it was—Jean Allan. There was no mistaking her laugh. It had intrigued him as no other woman's had ever done. He had been drawn to her ever since he had saved her life at McNee's Creek. The feeling seemed to be mutual, perhaps even greater on the part of Jean. Her interest in him had inflated his male ego, until he had realized it might be only a passing thing to her. He was in his element on the immense and unspoiled plains, the mighty mountains, the haunting lonely places. In her society and environment he'd be first a great curiosity, then a passing fancy, and finally a complete anachronism.

254

Perhaps he was creating something in his powerful imagination that didn't really exist. Jean laughed again. Quint passed noiseless and unseen through the cloister to the courtyard and the cheery campfire of his partners.

François filled the tin plates and passed them out. They had noticed a change in François as soon as they had seen him with the caravan, in charge of the two heavy wagons loaded with trade goods for his cousin's establishment. Gone was the always cheerful, joking, singing, storytelling mountain man Boudins that they had known. There was a seriousness about the Canadian now. Perhaps it was because he had the opportunity of becoming a man of substance in Taos—a *booshway*, a man with position and a future. Still, he had left the company of the other traders and agents to cook the last meal on the trail for his old-time partners.

Luke emptied his plate and belched politely. "Prime, Boudins," he said. "Yuh ain't lost your touch."

François shook his head. "With this poor stuff to cook? Remember the feast we had at the rendezvous with Gabe Pritchett? The night he told Big Red about his valley?" He looked reflectively into the embers of the fire. "Those were the good times, eh, partners?"

Quint filled his pipe and lighted it. He puffed it into life, and spoke around the stem. "Ye sound nostalgic, Boudins," he suggested.

"Nostalgic? What does that mean?"

"Homesickness. Melancholia. A longing for the past might be the best definition in your case."

Luke looked sideways at François. "Yuh mean yuh miss the icy streams swirling about yore man-parts while yuh set a trap?"

"A Blackfoot arrer whistling past yore ear?" Moccasin added.

"Ol' Ephraim grunting out of the brush and swiping at ye with a paw that could take your head off?" Quint asked.

The Canadian looked about at his old partners. "There were other things, my friends! The long winter yarns and the great lies. Red hump meat and sizzling *boudins*. A horn of Monongahela whiskey shared with all of you. The rendezvous. . . ."

It was very quiet. The soft dry wind whispered through the old ruins. The hum of voices came from the church. A woman laughed.

"Yuh don't like the tradin' then, Boudins?" Luke asked.

François shrugged. "No, my friend. But it is a good life. My cousin Henri promised me a full partnership if I went to St Louis and brought back trade goods. His health is not too good. He may not live long. He has a good Mexican wife and two small children, you understand. He worries about them. He has a fine house in Taos and much land."

"And he figures ye might take care of them if he passes on, eh, Boudins?" Quint asked.

François nodded. "She is fine woman. Me, I love the children."

"Then, what's the problem? Isn't that what ye wanted? Or are ye still thinking about that Shoshoni 'winter squaw' ye had on Henry's Fork of the Snake? Or was it on the Bear River?"

François looked off into the darkness. "Bear River," he replied quietly. "I saw her first on Henry's Fork of the Snake. Wintered with the Shoshonis at Bear River. Left in the spring. Never went back. I heard she had baby, little girl. Be big girl now, if she still alive."

"Ye could go back and find out," Quint suggested.

The Canadian shook his head. "The beaver trappin' is done for. Woman would be older now, maybe married. They don't wait around for mountain men to come back. Little girl wouldn't know her papa. Besides, I don't want to be squawman. Don't want to get old in yellowskin village. Then yuh ain't fish or fowl. Yellowskins don't really accept yuh. White people don't want yuh."

Quint tamped down the tobacco in his pipe and relighted it. "What's the real problem, Boudins?" he asked quietly.

François looked at Quint. "The old free life. The old friends." He looked at Luke and Moccasin.

"But we're here now. We've come to New Mexico."

"You know what I mean, Big Red. It will never be the same."

"Ye can't go home again, Boudins."

Moccasin nodded. "Only the earth lives forever."

Luke spat into the fire. "My God," he said. He rolled his eyes upward.

"Yuh don't believe that?" François asked.

"I believe in being here now, and to hell with yesterday. Tomorrow will take care of itself," Luke replied. "Which reminds me, Big Red. The 'bonnie lassie,' as yuh call her, was askin' around about yuh just before dark. Seems as though she expected yuh to *dine* with her, her sister and her friend this evenin'. Sort of a celebration it was to be, the last night on the trail and all."

256

Quint shrugged. "I knew about it, Luke."

"Yuh could have gone over there, Big Red. Seems like they had some wine for the celebration. She was kind of disappointed from what I could tell."

Quint looked slowly sideways at Luke. "I've got enough problems ahead of me without getting mixed up with that one. She thinks I saved her life at McNee's Creek, and is grateful, I suppose. That's all there is to it."

Luke studied Quint. "That so?" he asked dryly.

Quint nodded. "Aye." He looked around at the others. "None of ye believe me. I can see it in your faces. She's but a child, little more than eighteen years of age."

"Seems to me yuh once said the same thing about Mountain Woman," Luke reminded him.

"Aye, that I did. But I want no more entanglements with women. At least at this time. When I get to Santa Fe I'll be looking around for something to do; something with a future. I'll have little time for women, ye ken."

Black Beaver filled his coffee cup. "Man smart, he'd pay attention to that Taos woman." He nodded his head in agreement with himself. "Federico say her father got money, lots of land, horses, mules, sheep and everything."

"Lupita?" Quint asked. "Another child; little more, Beaver."

"He's actin' surprised again, like he don't know what we're talkin' about," Luke said dryly.

Joshua grinned at Quint. "That white woman got hair like sun; eyes like mornin' sky. *Wagh!*"

Luke lay down and rested on one elbow. "Too damned bad Big Red Badger couldn't take *both* of 'em. Good-lookin' wimmen. One bright like sunlight; one dark like moonlight. Sunlight got lots of money; moonlight got lots of land. Both mebbe got lots of lovin'. Make tipi nice and warm on cold winter nights. *Wagh!*"

"I said I didn't want any entanglements!" Quint snapped.

Luke shrugged. "Who said anything about *entanglements?* Mebbe *they* don't want entanglements either."

"You're suggesting just a roll in the feathers then?"

Luke widened his green eyes in simulated surprise. "Now, what made yuh think of a nasty thing like that?"

Quint grinned at him. "Because I know *ye,* ye sinful bastard!"

Moccasin spat into the fire. "Mebbe they found a real man in their lives, for a change," he suggested. "That sunlight one, anyways."

Quint knocked the dottle from his pipe. "She's got Mr.

257

Calhoun sniffing at her sign heap like a stud beaver, Moc."

Luke nodded. "Yuh don't need a crystal ball to figger out what he's after. Her old man is a big chief in Washington. Colonel, now Senator Allan, no less. Some of the traders told me the old bastard is richer than, than . . . who the hell is that coon yuh once told us about, Big Red? The one who had all the money in the world once?"

"Croesus, Luke."

"Yeah—Creesus. Waal, that ought to be enough to get Mr. Calhoun more than just interested in Miss Jean Allan. Besides, she is purtier than a calico dress."

François stirred the fire. "The story is that he'd come west for his health. Got leave from the army. He looks as healthy as a bull buffler to me."

"We heard at Bent's Fort that the Republic of Texas claims the Rio Grande del Norte rather than the Nueces as its western boundary," Quint said. "And that it might be only a matter of time before the United States annexes the Republic of Texas, with the approval of Texas, of course. If that happens, and Texas insists that the Rio Grande is their western boundary, the very land we're on right now could be claimed by the United States, and that would include Santa Fe, Albuquerque and El Paso del Norte. Ceran St. Vrain said that it might be a matter of between five and seven years or perhaps ten at the very most until that happens. If that is so, then the United States government will be deeply interested in military installations and the number of Mexican troops in New Mexico. I personally think that's why Shelby Calhoun came with the caravan. Tom Byrne told me Calhoun plans to continue south into Chihuahua, at least, with those merchants and traders who will travel that way after they are through with their business in Santa Fe."

François looked about at the impassive faces of his friends. "Is that why yuh came here, Quint? To be part of New Mexico when and if it becomes part of the United States?"

"Aye, Quint, that's a damned good question Boudins has asked yuh," Luke said.

Quint shook his head. "I didn't know about it until we were at Bent's Fort. I had intended coming here anyway with the stake I would have by selling my plews at Bent's. Seems like I'll not get that stake now, partners. But there's no use crying about it. No, the fact that the United States may own New Mexico someday had nothing to do with my coming here, but what Bent and St. Vrain told us at the fort confirmed my feeling that there is a future here for the right men."

Luke was puzzled. "So? All we've got is our Hawken rifles. Even the horses we been ridin' here don't belong to us. All we know is beaver trappin' first, and Indian fighting second. The beaver trappin' is done, and there sure as hell ain't much profit and one helluva risk in fightin' the yellowskins."

"When the day comes that the United States owns New Mexico we'll be established here, one way or another. That day will surely come, Lukie. Meanwhile, we can work toward it."

"But we'll have to become Mex citizens."

"So?"

Luke shook his head. "I ain't so sure I want to do that, Big Red. I don't fancy myself as a spic citizen."

"Ye won't get anywhere here unless ye do."

Luke shook his head. "No," he said firmly.

"Then what's the future for ye?" Quint demanded. "Ye can't go back to the beaverin'. Within a year or two that will be past history. What else is there? Meat hunting? A dollar and a half a day and powder and ball. My God!"

"Well, there's other things!" Luke said defensively.

"Name them," Quint challenged.

Luke opened and then slowly closed his mouth. After a time he spoke. "Quint, I ain't cut out to be a trader. Business ain't for me. I can't read or write."

"There's the *land,* ye damned fool! Can ye reckon how much the land here in New Mexico will be worth when that day comes when this will be part of the United States?"

"Yuh've no money, yuh jackass! Yuh need money to buy land, even if yuh *are* a Mex citizen! Yuh said so yourself when we was up north and yuh wanted to trap old Gabe's valley. Well, yuh can remember what happened to yuh there. Yuh lost everything, including that Shoshoni squaw. Those Comancheros are out of yore reach. You'll never see your money out of that deal."

It seemed to become quieter after Luke's statement. Quint narrowed his eyes and his big right hand closed tightly around the wood and metal of his Hawken. He looked slowly sideways at Luke. His scarred face was set and grim.

"So, yuh got one of 'em. Didn't do yuh a damned bit of good profit-wise, did it? The others are gone out of yore reach like last night's drinkin' likker."

"I bide my time," Quint said quietly. "I'll find those others somewhere, sometime. I expect no profit now, but if not in value, in blood alone. They will not escape me."

Quint stood up and reached for his Hawken rifle. "I'll take a look-see around the place. Work it out among yourselves to see who takes first guard. About a two-hour shift should be right." He walked off and out of sight among the cloister ruins.

François filled his coffee cup. "How long has he been like that?" he asked.

Luke shrugged. "Ever since he left that damned valley of his."

"He ain't the same Big Red."

Moccasin shook his head. "He should never go to that valley. Ol' Solitary warned him."

"Lost his plews and his woman," Luke said.

François sipped at his coffee. "No more plews, looks like."

"What about woman?" Black Beaver asked.

Luke began to fill his pipe. "*What* woman? He's got *two* of 'em after him now."

THIRTY

The moon was well up, shedding a clear pale light throughout the valley, softening the stark coloration and angular lines of the massive ruins. Bluish wraiths of smoke drifted upward from the church and patio to form a slowly drifting scarf in the windless air. Voices sounded faintly hollow from within the roofless church.

Some of the ladders still stood leaning against the pueblo terraces. Quint reached the north pueblo, a massive, five-story rectangular village that had probably housed some 2,500 Pueblo Indians in its day. Now the immense ruins were inhabited only by the owls and the pack rats.

Quint climbed the rickety ladders to the top terrace of the north pueblo, where he had a splendid view of the moonlit valley and the adjoining mountains. He filled his pipe and struck flint and steel to light it. As he puffed at the pipe to get the tobacco ignited he looked down toward the base of the pueblo. A slender white-shawled figure showed in contrast to the light-colored ground. He watched Jean Allan as she looked about uncertainly as though seeking something, or someone.

"Ye shouldn't be wandering around alone in this place, Miss Jean!" Quint called down to her.

She looked up at him. The moonlight was fair on her cornsilk hair and oval face. She was wearing a dress, in honor of the last night on the trail and the celebration at the church. Wine had flowed freely, and she had drunk her share of it. She placed a small slippered foot on the lowest rung of the bottom ladder and looked up at him.

"Be careful of the ladders," Quint called.

She came slowly up the ladders, encumbered somewhat by the long skirts of the dress she wore. She hitched the skirts up with her hand while climbing, revealing trim ankles in fine hose. She smiled at Quint as she reached the uppermost terrace. A twinge of nostalgia flowed through him. There had been a lassie who lived at the Red River Settlement. Elspeth MacBeth, a cornsilk blonde with immense blue eyes and a complexion like peaches and cream, much like Jean Allan. Quint had been hard smitten by bonnie Elsie MacBeth. She had been about Quint's age, not quite sixteen though, as he was when he left the settlement forever. She had been promised to another. Maybe she would have waited for Quint to return and claim her. During his first years of beaver trapping he thought he might return for her, but there had always been another rendezvous and another season and yet another. The lure of the mountains and the freedom of the life had been stronger than the cornsilk hair and blue eyes of bonnie Elsie MacBeth.

"What a view!" Jean cried exultantly.

Quint nodded. "Aye, that it is."

"It's beautiful! Such a lovely place to live! But why did the people leave such a paradise?"

Quint shrugged. "Perhaps it wasn't the paradise it seems to be. The life here declined in the past four hundred years, or so Tom Byrne told me. Tom is quite the local historian."

"They were here that long?"

"The original pueblo was built on this great rock about the fourteenth century. Coronado, the Spanish explorer, subdued the people about 1540. The Pueblos worshiped a great living snake god who supposedly lived in an underground temple,

261

or kiva. An eternal sacred fire had burned there for many years before the arrival of the Spaniards. Young children were sacrificed regularly to the snake god for good fortune.

"The Spanish padres built the church Nuestra Señora de Los Angeles, or Our Lady of the Angels, about 1617. The Pueblos drifted into Christianity. The sacred fire was allowed to die out. The human sacrifices were abandoned. Many of the children died in an epidemic shortly after the sacrifices were discontinued. In time the snake god left the kiva and crawled toward the Rio Grande del Norte, leaving as its track the present Galisteo River. It crawled down the Rio Grande to the Gulf of Mexico, about a thousand miles from here. It disappeared into the sea. Thereafter one disaster after another overtook the Pueblos. That's the legend of Cicuye."

"One of the traders told me there might have been as many as two thousand people living here at one time or another."

"There likely was, from the number of rooms in the two pueblos. There might have been more than that. About eighty-five years ago they made the mistake of marching out of here to try the might of the Comanches. The Comanches, as is their custom, allowed just one Pueblo warrior to survive in order to carry the news of the disaster back here. Some years after that a smallpox epidemic left less than two hundred survivors. A little over thirty years ago an epidemic of mountain fever wiped out about half of them."

Jean looked up into Quint's face. He was looking over her head into the distance, as though he saw or imagined the disastrous events that had destroyed forever the many people who had once populated Cicuye. She had noticed this introspective characteristic of his before; as though there was a part of him that he kept shielded from the searching eyes of others, even those he liked, or perhaps even loved.

Quint looked down at Jean. "The last of these people left here just a few months ago, driven from here by means of witchcraft from the Mexican villagers nearby. There were just seventeen survivors."

"Will they not return?"

Quint shook his head. "Their way of life was destroyed forever by the coming of the conquering Spaniards with their swords, armor and horses, and their padres with their crosses and Catholic doctrine."

"As the New Mexicans will have their old way of life destroyed forever by the coming of the Americans."

He eyed her thoughtfully. "Ye realize that?"

"Of course. It's really only a matter of time, isn't it?"

Quint nodded. "It was the mountain men who were the first invaders. Then came the traders. They formed the advance guard for what is inevitable—the American domination of the Southwest. The Santa Fe Trail is a spearhead that will stab the sovereignty of Mexico to the heart."

"I've been told that before."

"Who told you?"

"My father. Shelby Calhoun. Tom Byrne. Others."

"Ye understand much, for a woman."

The wine had been working on her. "Why, damn you for no gentleman!" she snapped.

He smiled a little. "Forgive me. I did not mean it as a slight. It is the Highland Scots way of speech, direct and ofttimes blunt, but usually to the point."

"You're not in the Highlands now!"

He nodded. "Aye, that's true. But is it not much the same with the men of your class?"

She reached up and placed a cool hand against the terrible scar on his left cheek. "Forgive me," she said quietly. "I am apt to be my father's daughter too often. He always wanted a son to carry on his name and ambitions."

He pressed his left hand against her hand resting against his cheek, and as she withdrew her hand he held it. He looked deep into her eyes. She held his gaze for a fraction of a minute.

"Your father wanted a son and he got you and your sister," Quint said. "Two beautiful, intelligent women. Was that not enough?"

"Would it have satisfied you?"

Quint shrugged. "I've not had the experience—yet. . . ." He smiled down at her.

Jean withdrew her hand from Quint's and walked to the terrace wall overlooking the lower slopes of the base rock foundation of the pueblo. "Catherine doesn't concern herself much with such matters as the eventual American conquest of the Southwest," she said.

"But you do."

She turned and rested her back against the wall. "Very much. I could hardly avoid it, being my father's daughter."

"Your father could conceivably have had a son who was not interested in his ambitions. It has happened many times in history and it will continue to happen."

263

"Did it happen to you?" she asked bluntly.

He was still looking at her, but it was as though a shadow, the very faintest of shadows, seemed to cross his face. Then it seemed again as though he was looking at something she could never see, and perhaps understand.

"I asked you a question, Quint," she said, to bring him back to the present.

He shrugged. "My father was an educated man. A gentle man. A fine teacher. He wasn't fitted for the frontier. He never quite fitted into the frontier life at Kildonan, our home in the Red River Valley of Canada. He had lost his only daughter to cholera on the ship that brought us to Canada. He lost his wife, my mother, hardly a year after we settled at Kildonan. He tried hard to polish me; to prepare me for the future, perhaps as a teacher. He wanted the future for me that he had never been able to achieve. It was not for me. The life there was too hard; the rewards far too little. When he died, a broken man, there was nothing to hold me there. That was over seven years ago. I've never been back."

Elspeth MacBeth would be long married by now, with children of her own. Her lovely face seemed to drift through the mists of time and memory until Quint realized with a start that he was looking at the face of Jean Allan.

"And now that you're through with beaver trapping, you plan to settle here in New Mexico and make a future for yourself?" she asked.

"Who told ye that?"

"It's obvious, isn't it? What future is there for you in Canada? The States? The north?" She shook her head. "The future for you is here in New Mexico, Quintin Ker-Shaw."

He half smiled. "Ye may be a witch at that, lassie. Or perhaps a gypsy?"

She smiled back. "My grandmother Allan was said to have the second sight."

"And ye inherited it? Is that how ye can foresee my future?"

"I doubt anyone would need the second sight to foresee that, Quint. All the signs are there, plain to be seen."

"And ye? What is the future for ye, lassie?" he asked quietly.

She turned away from him and leaned her arms on the wall to look out over the moonlit slopes. "I will be returning to the States once Catherine is settled in Santa Fe and has her child."

"With her new baby and devoted husband?" he asked dryly.

Her back stiffened a little.

"She'll likely be needing ye for some time, Jean."

She turned quickly. He was closer than she had expected him to be. Her loins pressed against his. He didn't move back. She made no effort to move. "Why do you say that about Katie?" she demanded.

"She's a lovely, fragile flower; one that requires the right conditions to survive, and tender loving care as well. She's not much like ye, Jean."

"You've had too much to drink!"

He smiled. "Never enough, lassie."

"Just what did you mean by that last remark!"

He held her by her arms. "Nothing that is not true." The almost overpowering urge came over him to draw her close and crush his mouth against hers. She made no effort to be free of him.

"Catherine will be happy enough in Santa Fe," Quint said. "She'll have her husband and her baby. Nothing else will matter. But ye are something else. This is a foreign country whose ways of life are as different as night from day from the way of life to which ye are accustomed. Ye don't know this country, nor the people. There are only a handful of Americans and a few foreigners living here now, and they are for the most part not in your class socially and financially. They are hardworking, hard-driving, money-grubbing and unpolished. Most of them have Mexican wives or at least concubines."

"Like Charles?" she asked coldly.

"I know nothing of that."

"You don't have to evade the issue!"

"I'm not evading the issue. I've heard rumors; I've not investigated the facts. Further, I'm not interested in the matter. If the story is true, there is nothing ye can do to change it now. What's done is done. There are two things your sister can do—she can return to the States and forget the man, or she can stay here in New Mexico with him and her child and make the best of it. Either way, she'll need your help. But we were not discussing Catherine. We were discussing ye."

"It's really none of your affair, is it?"

He shook his head. He released her arms and stepped back a little. "I didn't mean to be tactless and abrupt, lassie."

"The Highland Scots way of speech, direct and oftentimes blunt, but usually to the point," she parroted him.

He grinned at her. *"Touché,* Jean."

She smiled a little. "No harm done. What you said was just about what my father would have said under the same circumstances. You think and act much as he does." She studied the lean, scarred face of this mountain man who seemed to have moved into her every thought ever since he had saved her life at McNee's Creek. She owed him for that, at least. "Yes," she added slowly, "there is a great deal both you and my father have in common, the good *and* the bad."

"Tell me about the good," he suggested.

She shook her head. "Another time, perhaps, when we know each other better."

Was she playing with him now? Was she a tease? It would be easy enough to be charmed by this capable, self-reliant girl with her beauty, her fresh, vibrant youth and great vitality. God, what fine-blooded stock could be bred from such a woman. She'd have to have the right stud, of course. It was not for Quintin Kershaw; not now, at any rate. He was penniless and footloose, and *young.* Aye, that was it! He had youth, and with that vital youth a love of personal freedom and the ability to go when and where he chose, without considering the wishes and desires of a woman.

"Ye'd best get back, Jean Allan," Quint suggested. "It's getting late. We've yet a good ride ahead of us to Santa Fe. Ye'll be needing your rest."

"It will be difficult, if not impossible, to sleep this night," she said.

He nodded. He helped her get started on the ladder. She looked up at him as she descended the ladder. "Will you be standing guard up there all night?" she asked.

He shook his head. "I only came up for the view by moonlight."

She paused at the foot of the first ladder. The moonlight was full on him, a tall, lean lath of a man with a beak of a nose and two hard gray eyes that seemed to look right through her. The night wind ruffled his sorrel beard and lifted the otterskin-wrapped braids from his shoulders.

"Are you coming?" she asked.

Quint studied her for a fraction of a second. The soft moonlight was gentle on her fine yellow hair and lovely features. A sudden and insistent craving for a woman, particularly this one, came swiftly and insidiously over him. He descended the ladder and helped her get started on the next one down. She held his left forearm with her right hand and looked directly up into his eyes. He could have sworn there was the slightest and unnecessary pressure on his forearm, and then she was descending the ladder.

She waited for him on the next terrace, the second above ground level. "Is there no one here anymore?" she asked.

He looked up and swung an arm outward. "Gone, all gone. Like the snows of yesteryear, never to return."

"Can I see the interior of one of the rooms then?"

"Why not?"

As she passed Quint he looked toward the church. There was no sign of anyone outside of the walls, although he knew the traders and others would still be celebrating the last night on the trail. Quint entered the low-ceilinged room and struck flint and steel to light a twist of corn shucks he found on the floor. Jean came into the room and stood close beside him. The faint flickering light revealed the few pitiful objects the former occupants had left behind, a ragged blanket, a large heap of corn husks, a broken *metate* on which they had ground their corn with a *mano,* or hand stone shaped like a blunt spindle. A few broken pots lay in a corner.

"And this is how they lived," she said quietly.

"Aye, for almost five hundred years."

"Before Columbus discovered America," she said in awe. "What's in the next room?"

She was so close to him he could smell the perfume of her lovely hair and the faint scent of the wine on her breath.

He lighted another torch and thrust it into the next room. The only artifact in the room was a low, trundlelike bed thickly covered with corn husks and dried leaves.

Jean pressed close against Quint to enter the low, narrow doorway. She turned slowly to face Quint. An unspoken challenge seemed to show in her eyes.

"Damn!" Quint dropped the burning corn husks as they seared his fingers. As they struck the floor he stamped out the fire in them. The room was in darkness except for the faint outline of moonlight limned on the floor by the outer door.

"Quint," Jean said softly.

They met in the center of the room. Her arms went up and around his neck as he encircled her slim waist and crushed her close against his hard body. Their lips met. He bent her backward. She struggled a little, knowing and perhaps not caring that there was literally nothing she could do to protect herself from this pantherlike stud of a man. She could appeal to his honor. She did not appeal; her soft mouth was closed with his hard lips.

His big fingers fumbled with the tiny buttons fastening the back of her dress. The liquor he had drunk and the contact with her body and the scent of her made him bold. He gripped the neck of the dress at the back and ripped it down to her buttocks. The buttons pattered on the hard floor.

"Wait, Quint!" she whispered. "Give me some time!"

He peeled the dress from her shoulders down to her waist and stripped the brassiere from her upthrust breasts. They were a pair of creamy, cherry-tipped beauties. She struck him across the eyes with the edge of her hand and staggered back toward the wall, pulling her ruined dress up about her body. For a long moment the two of them eyed each other. She made no effort to evade him as he came closer to her. He reached out for her. She shook her head and turned it aside.

He tilted his head to one side and studied her. "Ye didna say no," he said quietly. "Ye said to wait and to give ye some time. How much time? Or was it just a ruse, lassie?"

Minutes ticked past. She started toward him.

The faint calling voices came to them. Quint catfooted to the door. "They're looking for ye, lass," he said over his shoulder.

"Fasten the back of my dress as best you can," she said hurriedly.

He did the best he could with the remaining buttons and then draped the shawl over her shoulders. She quickly touched her hair here and there, then slid her arms up about his neck and drew his head down so that their mouths met and molded together. Then suddenly she was gone from the room.

Quint walked toward his rifle. The tiny buttons rolled under the soles of his moccasins.

"What are you doing up there, Jean?" Shelby Calhoun called from the ground level.

"Admiring the moonlight, Shell," she replied.

"It's dangerous to come out here alone. You knew that. You've gotten everyone worried."

The ladders creaked as she made her careful way down them to the ground level.

Quint waited a reasonable time. He left the room and looked toward the massive church ruins. There was no one in sight. He walked along the terrace in front of the second story until he reached the end wall. He swung himself easily over the parapet and hung by one hand, then dropped lightly to the ground.

"Was it an entanglement or a dalliance, Big Red?" Luke asked from the shadows.

Quint turned. "Ye've a big nose, Lukie."

Luke grinned. "Sure enough, but Calhoun was lookin' around for her on the other side of the church. I told Moccasin to keep him occupied until I got over here. Didn't have time to warn yuh, but I knowed where yuh was. So I showed myself a little and Calhoun went for the bait. He came down this way calling for the woman. Like as not, he didn't see her come out of the same room you came out from later."

Quint leaned back against the wall. "Like as not?"

Luke shrugged. *"Quién sabe?* Anyway, he's got no claim on her, has he?"

"I doubt it."

Luke shifted his chew and spat. "Wal, how will yore stick float now, Big Red?"

"I haven't changed my mind, Lukie."

They walked together back toward the church.

When they were gone from sight, Lupita came out of the room in which she had hidden herself when she had seen Jean and Quint enter a dwelling close by together. She had walked noiselessly to the outer doorway and listened to what was going on in the inner room. Her lovely face had been set and hard when she heard Shelby Calhoun calling for the *gringa* woman. She had just enough time to hide herself in the next dwelling when Jean had walked out on the terrace to respond to Shelby's calling.

No matter, Lupita thought. Let the yellow-haired *gringa* keep her hold on him at least until they reached Santa Fe. Lupita couldn't compete with her now, but in her own environment she would have all the advantages. She knew such men as Quintin Kershaw. He was a true Montero Americano.

What was it the mountain men would say? "Taos! White likker and brown women! *Wagh!*"

THIRTY-ONE

July 1838—Santa Fe

The advance party was up before dawn light and left the
ruins at Pecos. They rode past the Mexican village with its
rushing torrent and green gardens set among the shaggy
piñon-covered hills. The road ascended the slopes to the pass
at Glorieta and then turned left at the white church of
Cañoncito to pass through a canyon of colored rock where the
trailworn hoofs of the horses and mules were washed by the
clear cold rivulet that rippled across the road. They climbed
again to the northwest over the Glorieta range, through
rough shaggy hills and across dry arroyos on the final twelve
miles to Santa Fe. Here and there along the road were
white-painted crosses to the memory of travelers murdered
there by the *ladrones*, the highwaymen, who at times in
fested the approaches to the city. But they only attacked the
lone traveler or those who were weak or poorly armed. They
knew better than to attack the advance party of the expected
caravan that clear morning. They knew and recognized for
what they were the sharp-eyed, well-armed mountain men
who rode as escort. The Montero Americanos were never to
be trifled with at any time.

The travelers reached the rise from which they could see in
the distance the Royal City of the Holy Faith of St. Francis of
Assisi lying displayed before them at seven thousand feet
altitude below the massive green and drab bulk of the Sangre
de Cristo Mountains, so named by the padres of old because of
the roseate pinkish hue the setting sun gave to the snow
capped mountain peaks. The bold rocky foothills thrust them
selves out toward the city. They and the looming backdrop of
the mountains seemed close enough to touch in the thin air
Here lay Santa Fe, capital of so large a province its bound
aries had never been explored, and administrative center of
settlements from El Vado de San Miguel near Las Vegas to

Jemez. Like the Rome of the ancient world, all roads led to Santa Fe, the Hub of Trails. The Chihuahua Trail extended from Vera Cruz on the Gulf of Mexico two thousand miles to Santa Fe. The Spanish Trail reached from Santa Fe to Los Angeles on the Pacific Coast about nine hundred miles westerly. It was about fifteen hundred miles from Missouri to Santa Fe on the Santa Fe Trail.

Below on the left hand lay the city spread out in a maze of brown, golden and white box-shaped houses, low and flat-roofed, on the edge of a vast plateau sweeping away westward toward the Valley of the Rio Grande del Norte. The plateau was dotted with green herbage and studded with pointed hills, the atmosphere showing certain lights from the rising sun that gave the impression that one was looking along the bottom of some immense ocean deep, an unreal and mysterious sensation to the newcomer to that land of enchantment. To the far west across the great valley were the blue ranges of the Jemez and Sandia mountains.

The travelers now moved along the base of a huge, flat-topped mesa studded with huge piñon trees. The city was straight ahead, due north beyond scattering groves of piñons and junipers. The fresh morning wind brought the faint sound of ringing bells. There was an extended valley to the northwest dotted with occasional clumps of trees. Large fields without fences and walls were verdant *labores* and *milpas,* cultivated areas of dwarf corn and shallow wheat, interspersed with plantings of peas, beans, onions, and red peppers.

Jean Allan had been riding a horse beside the rockaway carrying her sister and the maids. Now she cantered her mount up beside Quint Kershaw and Tom Byrne at the head of the cavalcade. She pointed toward square, blocklike protuberances here and there amid the fields. "What are those? Brick kilns?" she asked innocently.

Quint looked sideways at her, with her youthful freshness and vigor, an overflowing of vibrant life; a woman so much like bonnie Elsie MacBeth. It was the first time she had spoken to him since she had left him in the pueblo room. He half smiled at the memory of those last words, "Fasten the back of my dress as best you can." Then she had kissed him and was gone.

"Quint?" she asked, looking at him curiously.

"*Casas*, Miss Allan," Tom Byrne answered her question. "Farmhouses, ye might call them back in the States."

"And that ahead," she asked, pointing toward irregular cubelike clusters beyond the spreading fields.

The Irishman smiled. "The Royal City of the Holy Faith of St. Francis of Assisi. It's not much to look at but it may be an antidote for those of us who hate the smugness, hypocrisy and overfastidiousness of the American civilization we once lived in. Still, some of us may hope it will be your place of residence for some time to come, Miss Allan."

The city had been irregularly laid out with most of its streets like common highways traversing scattered settlements of surrounding villages interspersed with the ubiquitous corn, wheat and produce fields aThe road into the city wound downhill between endless adobe walls as high as the horses' heads, behind which were gardens and orchards. The green-leaved tracery of peach, apple and apricot trees showed above the walls. The walls of the houses themselves were continuous and forbidding, sometimes portaled or arcaded to keep out the sun and the rain, with tiny mica-paned and barred windows. The large bolt-studded doors of heavy planking were usually securely closed and barred, although here and there where a door had been opened or left ajar, a sunny *placita* or patio could be seen.

Santa Fe, despite its resounding name and importance was close to a slum in reality; merely a small town huddled hit-or-miss about a bare sun-baked plaza. It probably numbered no more than three thousand inhabitants in the city proper, with the surrounding villages embraced in corporate jurisdiction adding perhaps another three thousand souls. The winding streets beyond the central plaza were narrow, unpaved, unlighted, unswept and littered with garbage in varying stages of decomposition. There was no sewer system. Travelers and passersby rode through a haze of dust, scattering half-naked children, squalling chickens and barking dogs. Cats, dogs, pigs, goats, chickens and burros wandered at large rooting through the piles of garbage in the public lanes. Pure, clear cold water was brought down from the snow peaked mountains by means of *acequias,* irrigation ditches which were fouled with manure and garbage. Women washed clothing in the ditches; children played and splashed in them; cats drowned in the murky water; other animals waded in the shallow water, dropping manure and urinating in it even as they drank the water.

Many of the houses were drab, small, dingy and forbidding but here and there were sun-struck houses of a brilliant

272

dazzling whiteness, mica-limewashed with finely crushed soft white gypsum spread on by means of sheepskin mops with the final smoothing done by the hands of women whose dried palm marks still showed. Despite these contrasting houses the town in general beyond the central plaza wore a primitive and shabby air of cheapness, dirt and sheer nastiness.

"There are no newspapers here," Tom Byrne said quietly. "No schools, theaters, libraries except for my modest private collection, museums, free government or religious tolerance. The Three R's seem to be vice, superstition and dirt."

"Then why do you stay here?" Jean demanded to know.

The Irishman shrugged. "I came here ten years ago, an *extranjero*, a stranger to these people and their ways, without a living relative in Ireland or the States. My people in Ireland had all died of the famine. These people accepted me for what I was, asking no questions. I have been successful here, far more than I would have been back in the States and certainly far more than back in my native Ireland. There is a future for me here. There is a future here in New Mexico for anyone with ambition and drive." Here the Irishman slanted his blue eyes sideways at Quintin Kershaw. Quint missed it; Jean Allan did not.

The *plaza publica*, or public square, called La Plaza de la Constitución since 1821, when the flag of the new Republic of Mexico was raised over the Palace of the Governors, was the only area throughout the city with any architectural compactness and precision. It was treeless, flowerless and shadeless, an expanse of hard-packed adobe in the dry season, a sea of mud in the wet. An *acequia* ran on both sides of it. From this central plaza radiated the streets in which dwelt the *pobres*, the poorer people. The sundial in the center of the plaza had the maxim inscribed on it: *Vita fugit sicut umbra*— Life flees like a shadow.

The Palacio, or Governor's Palace, dominated the north side of the plaza for about four hundred feet. It formed the southern side of a dusty compound of ten acres surrounded by a crumbling eight-foot-high wall that extended eight hundred feet to the north. It had originally been planned as a *presidio* and place of defense. Within the walls, and sometimes forming part of the walls themselves were the governor's palace and quarters for the military garrison to which was attached the fearsome, filthy *calabozo*, or prison. Within the compound were corrals, a small *campo santo* or cemetery, a *plaza de armas*, or drill ground, and a chapel. A *zaguán*, a

273

gateway fitted with heavy wooden double doors studded with bolts was the only entrance into the compound. The buildings within it were known in Spanish times as the Casas Reales, or Royal Houses.

The Casa Consitorial of the Alcaldes, or mayors, was on the south side of the plaza. Facing the palace was the Castrense, the Capilla de los Soldados, the Chapel of the Soldiers, with its two low bell towers. On the west side of the plaza was an oratorio, or small chapel. The customhouse was situated at the northeast corner of the plaza. The *parroquía,* or parish church, dominated the east side of the plaza. The houses of affluent citizens and some shops stood wall to wall around the plaza filling in the gaps between the public buildings. They were sheltered by a fringe of wooden *portales* or *corredores* beneath which the citizenry could walk in comfort protected from sun and rain.

The open-air *mercado,* or market, was situated along the outside of the western wall of the palace and extended the full length of the compound behind the palace to the open fields where the horse traders met to dicker, trade and sell. Beside the walls were the *puestos,* or stalls protected from sun and rain by square white canopies. Here the country folk sold their produce and the city folk sold their wares.

The citizenry of the city, the Santafeanos, crowded the plaza and the *mercado.* There the gracefully moving daughters of Mexico could be seen to full advantage—unstayed, unpadded and barelegged, with full voluptuous figures. They wore skimpy *camisas,* a loose sort of blouse with abbreviated sleeves which left their arms bare. Their costumes were exciting and colorful with gayly colored shawls and short red skirts revealing trim well-turned ankles and tiny feet in silver-buckled slippers. They had never heard of hose, underwear, petticoats, bodices, long sleeves and high-necked gowns. It was unheard of to bind up their lush bodies in the American style. Their hair was a glossy blue-black under filmy rebozos. Brilliant eyes and flashing teeth made up for any other facial deficiencies. Some of them were rather startling to see, at least by American standards, for they had covered their faces with a bleaching agent of flour paste or a heavy white powder made of ground bones which sometimes imparted a ghastly pale-lavender hue as though one from the tomb. Others had applied the brilliant bloodlike smears of scarlet *alegría* juice to their faces for the same purpose.

"Coquetry is an instinct and not a trick with these Mexican

women, Miss Jean," Tom Byrne said. "They are relentlessly coquettish, engaging and flirtatious."

A bold-eyed woman called out to Quint Kershaw, giving her name and address, "Rosita, 17 Calle Castillo!" she cried.

"Do you know her, Quint?" Jean asked quickly.

Quint shook his head.

"She seemed to know you."

Tom Byrne smiled. "She wants to know *every* Americano."

The young mèn of Santa Fe lounged around the plaza. They were lithe-figured and sober-eyed under their great sombreros. They wore braided *chaquetas,* or jackets, trousers laced or buttoned up the sides but left partway open to show their white drawers, which often were more of a dingy grayish color, and beautifully embossed leather boots. Their narrow, colorful *serapes,* a streaking of bright colors, hung from their shoulders. Their dark smoldering eyes watched the big Americans as they rode past, shouting and calling to the responsive Mexican women.

Most of the Indians in the streets and plaza were Pueblos. They were not allowed to stay in the city after dusk. Off-duty soldiers idled about the plaza. There were many padres in somber black or brown robes. Swarms of beggars and *léperos,* or vagabonds, hovered about the crowded plaza on the chance of pilfering or snatching up something of value.

Man and boy, girl and woman, the Santafeanos smoked incessantly. Fine-cut tobacco was carried in a *gague,* a small canteen of leather or metal. To many Americans the casual cigarette smoking enhanced the foreign charm of the coquettish New Mexican women.

Quint gave Jean his hand to help her down from her horse. She squeezed his hand hard as she dismounted. "Will you be staying long in Santa Fe?" she asked.

Quint shrugged. *"Quién sabe?* More likely Taos will be a better field for me to try my fortune, I suppose." He smiled. "Whatever *that* may be."

"But I will see you again?" she asked hopefully.

"I'll be here for a time. I may apply for Mexican citizenship while here."

"But doesn't that mean you must convert to Catholicism?" she asked, with the faintest touch of the acid in her tone of voice.

He looked down at her with a slightly amused look. She was pure white, an Anglo-Saxon Protestant, a true daughter of the America of that time. "My mother was a Catholic," he said. "I was baptized in the Catholic Church, perhaps against my father's wishes, but he had agreed to allow my mother to raise the children of their union within the church. She did not press the matter. My sister and I were baptized in the church, but that was all. In Canada the Red River Settlement was almost purely Protestant. In the Scotland of my youth, and even in Canada, Catholicism wasn't too popular."

There was almost a smile of relief on her lovely face.

"So, ye see," he added dryly, "I have at least *one* facet of the Holy Trinity of America."

She narrowed her eyes. "What do you mean?"

He smiled. "I am *white*, of Celtic ancestry, but never an Anglo-Saxon, and a Protestant only by the faith of my father."

She tilted her head back a little and studied him. "You're a strange man, Quintin Ker-Shaw."

"I could have told yuh that, Miss Jean," Luke Connors said from behind them. "The lootenant, ol' Shell Calhoun, has his eye on the pair o' yuh," he warned.

Passersby had been looking curiously at the pair of them, with good reason of course, for they stood out in that foreign plaza and among the New Mexicans—the lovely blond young *gringa* and the tall, redheaded, scar-faced Montero Americano.

The rockaway bearing Catherine Williston had been driven into the plaza and halted before the house of her husband. The remainder of the advance party were dismounting and scattering about their business with a driving urgency. Shelby Calhoun was looking toward the little group about Jean Allan. He started toward them.

Tom Byrne pointed toward the Palacio. "It was started in 1610, Miss Jean." He looked over her head at Quint and moved his head ever so slightly to indicate he should stand aside. "That was about three years after the founding of Jamestown," the trader continued his impromptu lecture on the city he loved. "The bravest Spaniards massed there for the defense of the city in the Pueblo Revolution of 1680. Sad council was held there to determine the evacuation of the city. It was the scene of triumph for the rebel Pueblo chieftains as they ordered the destruction of the Spanish Archives and church ornaments in one grand conflagration. Here De Varga gave thanks to the Virgin Mary, to whose aid he attributed the triumphant recapture of the city. Forty-seven Pueblos were executed right over there in front of the Palacio.

"Lieutenant Zebulon Pike was brought here before Governor Alencaster as an invader of Spanish soil. Just sixteen years ago the new eagle-and-cactus standard of the Mexican Republic was raised here in token that New Mexico was no longer a dependency of Spain."

Shelby paused beside Jean and Tom. "What are those brown things strung from pillar to pillar in front of the palace? Dried fruit?"

Tom shook his head. "As you know, there was another Pueblo Revolution in New Mexico almost a year ago. Governor Perez had started to subdue the insurrection in the north only to meet his death near Agua Fria. The very next day the insurrectionists installed Jose Gonzalez, a Pueblo Indian of Taos, as governor of New Mexico. Soon thereafter, Manuel Armijo, the present governor of New Mexico, executed Gonzalez and many of his supporters. That drying fruit, as ye call it, Shell, is the ears of those Indians who were executed, as well as the ears of hostile Indians who raided here in the vicinity of the city and were captured. Ye might call the ears a tally of victory like the scalps garnered by the Comanches and others of the Plains tribes."

Jean paled. "My God," she murmured. "What kind of a place *is* this?"

"Something like the Dark and Bloody Ground of Kentucky, not too many years past," the trader replied dryly. There was no expression on his face.

Shell Calhoun looked over the head of Jean toward Quint and Luke, who had stepped back to lean against the pillars upholding the portal in front of Tom Byrne's big casa facing the plaza. He looked directly at Quint, who gave him hard eye for hard eye. Finally the officer turned away.

The Williston casa was adjacent to Byrne's own. Charles Williston was greeting his wife. He was a handsome man, but there was something of the feminine about him. His blond hair was as fine as that of a baby. His eyes were hazel, and very large, with a somewhat luminous quality about them and an emptiness behind them as though one were looking through a pair of windows into a vacant room. His mouth was soft and rather petulant. Catherine rested her head against his chest. Her eyes were closed and moist with tears and her slim shoulders trembled a little. Jean Allan had hurried to her sister's side.

"Touching, is it not?" Tom Byrne asked dryly.

"She's been through hell, Tom," Quint reminded him.

"That I know. The lass should have never taken this trip, at least in the condition she's in. Besides, she'll soon have to

277

face his 'housekeepers,' sometimes mere children bought and paid for. Charley Williston likes 'em young and virginal. He pays top dollar to have them in that condition. Still, it's common practice among many prominent men in New Mexico, Mexicans and Americans alike."

"Yuh think he'd move 'em out, now that his wife is here," Luke suggested.

Tom shook his head. "If Miss Jean were to stay with her sister he might be forced into it. He'd never get away with it with Miss Jean in the same household. There's a lass with everything a man could want in a woman—looks, figure, spirit, vitality, position and wealth. A damned fine catch for any man." He sneaked a look at Quint as he spoke.

"Such a man would have Shell Calhoun in his way," Quint countered.

"Aye, but she's got her eye on *ye*, Quint."

"Seems to me, Tom, yuh might angle a bit toward her yourself," Luke put in lazily.

Tom looked slowly at Luke. "I've speculated on the matter. But I'm not sure I'd want her in my casa. It would only be a matter of time before she'd be tryin' to wear the pantaloons on those long legs of hers. She may be tryin' to be both a woman and a man in a man's world. She might get away with it in Kentucky, or even in Washington, where she's her father's daughter. But here, in New Mexico, as both of ye know, it just won't set right. She's *got* to be a woman here."

Luke shrugged. "Ain't always true, Tom. Lupita Vasquez seems to be makin' a halfway good job of both, according to Federico."

"Aye, but out of sheer necessity. Her brother Bartolomé is hopeless as far as taking control of the Vasquez family holdings. He's wasted much of their former wealth in gambling and living here in Santa Fe rather than on their holdings. Quite a few Santa Fe merchants and traders hold notes from him. If they foreclosed on him all at the same time, the Vasquezes would lose everything and be plunged into bottomless debt. Don Francisco is slowly dying, an old man with but a short time left in his life. If a *real* man married Lupita, he'd do well for himself, *if* he could handle her, that is."

"But he'd still have Don Bartolomé in the way, wouldn't he?" Luke asked.

"Aye, but maybe not for long. The man is a fool, a hothead with a pride that bears not the slightest prick. He's already killed three men, fairly enough, 'tis true—there was nothing

278

murderous about the acts, but none of the three could be considered real fighting men."

Jose, Tom Byrne's half-breed Comanche stableboy, came to get Jean's and Tom's horses. He looked hesitantly at the horses of Quint, Luke and the Delawares.

"Take my roan, the sorrel and the pinto, Jose," Tom ordered. "Quint, ye and Luke will stay with me, along with Jean Allan, of course. There's not enough room in the Williston casa for the lass." He slanted his eyes a little at Quint. "Ye might find her pleasurable company. Then too, there's a business proposition I might have for the two of ye."

"Gracias, Tom, but what about the Delawares?" Quint asked.

"Indians are not allowed to stay in the city after dusk. I've no objection to them, as ye know, but here in Santa Fe it is the law."

"They're Delawares, dammit!" Quint snapped.

"And *Indians,* dammit!" Tom snapped back. "It's not my choosing! It may be all right at places like Bent's Fort, but this is New Mexico! When in Rome, one does as the Romans do!"

Moccasin nodded. "It's all right, Big Red. We understand."

"I've got a small ranchito just outside of town," Tom said. "Estebán, an old *mozo* of mine, stays there and raises my fruits and vegetables, and takes care of my horses and mules. The Delawares can stay there with him."

"Good enough," Moccasin agreed. "How long yuh stay here, Big Red?"

Quint shrugged, *"Quién sabe?* We've no money. There's no trapping to do."

"Colonel Bent at the Big Lodge said we might work for Brother Charley at Taos," the Delaware reminded him.

"In trade? We'd be flunkies. Engagees. Moc, we're *mountain men!*"

"Ye lads can make your minds up once ye get around to it," Tom Byrne suggested. "Meanwhile, ye are my guests for as long as ye like. I have not forgotten ye saved the life of Jean Allan and that of Shell Calhoun. They would have been lost otherwise, and I'd never have been able to explain that away to Colonel Allan. 'Twill be a great pleasure to have ye and Luke as my guests here in the city, and the Delawares as well at the ranchito. It's not easy for foreigners without funds to get by in the city and New Mexico in general. I can outfit ye from my stores. Your credit is ace-high with me. Come now, Quint, I can add the promise of the hottest bath ye've had in years as an added lure. What say ye?"

279

"I can't resist, Tom," Quint replied. "I'll speak for me and the Wandering Wolf here beside me."

"Jose, guide the Delawares out to the ranchito," Tom instructed. "Tell Esteban they are to stay as long as they like and can take advantage of the full facilities of the place."

"Come back into the city tomorrow, Moc," Quint suggested. "We'll have a council to decide what we plan to do."

The Delaware nodded. "Me, Black Beaver and Joshua no plan to stay here too long, Big Red. Roof and walls for wintertime only." He studied Quint closely for a moment, then turned on a heel and walked away.

"He doesn't seem to think ye'll be in a hurry to leave Santa Fe," Tom suggested.

"I'll not be here long, Tom," Quint said.

The Irishman smiled. "What will be, will be," he said mysteriously.

"Señor Quint!" Federico called.

Quint turned to see the *cibolero* leading the two horses Tom Byrne had loaned to Guadalupe and Federico.

Federico handed the reins to Jose. *"Gracias, mil gracias,* Señor Byrne," he said.

The trader waved a hand. *"Por nada,* Federico."

Federico turned to Quint. "My *patrona,* the Señorita Guadalupe Vasquez, invites you to dinner this coming Friday evening, Señor Quint. It will be at the home of her cousin. Shall I tell her you will come?"

"You're almighty formal all of a sudden, *compañero,*" Quint said dryly.

The *cibolero* shrugged. "We are in Santa Fe now. You will come?"

"Aye, Federico."

Quint watched the Mexican stride across the teeming plaza. A small female figure stood between two of the pillars supporting the portale of the Governor's Palace. Federico approached her. He spoke to her. Lupita looked across the plaza toward Quint. She raised her right hand a little, as though to acknowledge Quint's acceptance of her invitation, and then she and Federico were gone in the crowd.

"She doesn't seem to know yuh don't plan to be in Santy Fee very long," Luke said dryly.

Quint turned. "What will be, will be, Lukie. Let's go get those baths Tom promised us."

Together, arm in arm, they sauntered toward the trader's big casa.

THIRTY-TWO

Tierra Encantada—The Land of Enchantment

Land of desert, mesa and mountain. The Province of New Mexico. La Tierra Encantada—the Land of Enchantment; the "Northern Borderlands" of Mexico, an enchanted land remote from Mexico proper with clear, winelike air under a brilliant sky more luminescent than the finest turquoise. Here, space was seemingly limitless, with vast stretches of plain, desert and lofty mountains whose peaks touched thirteen thousand feet; with towering buttes and mesas amid far purple distances. A land of many mountain ranges and semiarid plateaus with bare-earth-color tones, where the scenery ranged from brilliantly colored mesas of startling beauty, deep brooding canyons and great expanses of desert in the south to the snow-crested mountains of the north with their swift-rushing streams and immense forests of grave and towering pines.

Quint Kershaw knew something of the people, much of the terrain, but little enough of the history and background. Thus he allowed himself to come under the skilled tutelage of Dr. Thomas Byrne and the spell of his study with its book-lined walls and massive, dark Spanish Colonial furniture brought by oxcart from Chihuahua or made by skilled local artisans. The study probably contained the best private library north of Chihuahua, Mexico, if not Mexico City itself, and west of St. Louis, Missouri. Here, in addition to volumes of history, theology, medicine, geology, philosophy and many other disciplines, were old friends and companions of Quint— Shakespeare, Burns, Scott, Milton, Chaucer and many others.

It had been Tom Byrne's earnest advice to Quint that he thoroughly ground himself in the history both secular and sacred of the Province of New Mexico in order to assure himself a future of some importance in this, his soon-to-be-adopted home. Long cool summer evenings passed pleasantly within the study. Jean Allan used them to satisfy her curiosity and thirst for knowledge of New Mexico; besides, Quint Kershaw was there every evening. Shelby Calhoun was also a regular attendant, principally as part of his mission—he was soon due to leave with a caravan for Chihuahua. But he also wanted to keep an eye on Jean and her growing relationship with Quint. Although Luke Connors had but the most fundamental teaching in reading and writing, taught to him by Quint during the long winter months they had *hivernaned* together, he had an absorbing interest in New Mexico, particularly the terrain; few men to Quint's knowledge had Luke's feeling for terrain, as good or better than most Indians and damned near as good as that of the buffalo. Luke had little to say during these long sessions, but he learned much. Besides, Tom Byrne, a drinking man himself, had as fine a stock of whiskey, wines and brandies as any *rico* in New Mexico, as well as the best Havana tobaccos.

There was one other constant attendant at the impromptu meetings—Luz García, fifteen years old, a female of startling and somber beauty with almost a Madonna-like quality about her. She was never far away from Tom Byrne, spoke little, but her great dark eyes followed him constantly. Luz was not her real name, nor was García for that matter. Her mother, a New Mexican from Abiquiu, northwest of Santa Fe on the Chama, had been captured by Comanches. Her father had been a Kotsoteka Comanche. Her mother had died during childbirth in the village of the Kotsotekas. Her father had been killed in battle with the New Mexicans, and she had been brought back by her saviors. Other New Mexicans retaken from the Kotsotekas had told her story. She was a *genízara*, or one begotten by parents of different nations. The *genízaros* were captives ransomed from the Apaches or Comanches. They might be Indians, Mexicans or mixed bloods. The authorities had provided settlements for them—Tome, Abiquiu and Belém. Until recently they had been known as towns of grief and fear, because of constant Indian raids on them. The Towns of Terror, they were called.

Luz had been the name Tom Byrne had given to the girl child he had bought from the people of Abiquiu who had taken her in. Luz, "light," for she had indeed brought light into his empty, lonely life. No matter that she did not know her parentage; no matter that on the church lists at Abiquiu the word "coyote" was listed next to her name, meaning mixed blood. Now the genizaro towns were more Spanish than Indian or mixed blood, but that fact had not changed the cruel listing of the church—*coyote*. . . .

As the days passed, the contents of the many volumes in the library as well as the vast and detailed knowledge Tom Byrne had of New Mexico opened the pages of history to Jean, Shelby, Quint and Luke.

One evening talk turned to the border dispute between Mexico and the Texans.

Quint said, "If the Texans insist on the Rio Grande as the western boundary, that means half the Province of New Mexico, including both Albuquerque and Santa Fe, as well as Taos, of course, will then become part of the United States."

Luke leaned forward. "And if that happens it's only a matter of time before the United States will push on all the way to the Pacific Coast."

"Manifest Destiny," Tom said quietly, almost as though to himself. He looked up at his guests. "And war," he added.

Shelby snorted. "These greasers won't fight, Tom."

"Perhaps. Do not underestimate them. New Mexico was always the frontier province, with its attendant and always present dangers, hard labor just to exist, privations and rough edges, just like any other frontier. Terror was constant, spread by nomadic Indians. Sometimes it was the Utes; quite often the Navajos; always the Apaches and Comanches. Almost every family has lost members to Indian warfare through generations. The raids came out of every mountain chain or shadowed canyon encircling this remote province on the far northernmost border of New Spain. No settlement is so large as to be secure against these raids. Eighty years ago the Comanches attacked Taos and carried away fifty women and children, who were never recovered. Less than twenty years ago the Navajos raided there and carried off some women and children who were never heard of again.

"Generation after generation of New Mexicans have lived in a constant state of insecurity, developing not weakness and fear but rather a sort of fatalism coupled with an inner toughness and resiliency. These people are frontiersmen. In reality a brave, tenacious and hardy people, who, if well led, will fight well to defend their province and homes." Tom smiled at Shelby. "Have I added to your understanding of these New Mexicans?"

"You said, *if* well led. Who'd lead them, Tom?"

"Governor Armijo," Quint suggested dryly.

"A powerful man," Tom said.

"Politically," Quint added.

"He's no coward," Tom countered.

"It takes more than bravery to be a leader," Shelby insisted. "Besides, what kind of troops would he have for defense? We've seen some of his 'soldiers' hanging around the plaza. That seems to be their principal duty."

"The officers are inexperienced and, in most cases, totally ignorant of their duty. Most of them are in the army for its social and political value. I have it on good authority that there are maybe as many as twenty percent more officers in the Mexican Army than there are enlisted men. However, most of them are on half pay or detached service."

"And the enlisted men?" Quint queried.

"Conscripts. Few educated or upper-class men serve in the ranks. The result is that the Mexican Army is hardly an organization. The private soldier is picked from the lower classes. No one bothers to ask him his opinion on the matter. He is poorly uniformed, worse fed, and seldom, if ever, paid. He is turned adrift when maimed, or severely ill, or when no longer wanted. Still, they can and will fight well. I repeat— they are a brave, tenacious and hardy people, and, despite their manifold disadvantages, they are just as intensely proud of their Snake-and-Cactus insignia as the Americans are of their Stars and Stripes or the British of their Union Jack. Do not, I beg of you, underestimate their patriotism."

It was very quiet. The piñon fire was but a thick bed of embers through which a secretive red eye of fire peeped now and again. A faint chill had crept into the room. Luz, who had been sitting on a small stool at Tom's feet, glanced at his guests, then stood up and pressed close against his side. He slid a strong arm about her slender waist and drew her close. She rested her head against his.

The candles were guttering low. Quint studied the earnest young dragoon officer. There was no reason he should dislike the Virginian. Shelby had more reason to dislike Quint than Quint had to dislike him. He was a man of undoubted courage. He had proved that at McNee's Creek when he had faced the Pawnees, armed only with his pair of single-shot pistols. He was a first-class soldier with a fine war record and had been wounded in action. He would not have been selected for the secret and dangerous mission he was now undertaking unless he was highly qualified, although Tom Byrne had hinted that the young officer had some political connections. There was no question that Shelby Calhoun had a fine military career in his future, *if* he lived to see it.

Shelby glanced at Quint, as though he sensed the man was studying him surreptitiously and thinking about him. Their eyes met, as they usually did, like those of two duelists feeling for weaknesses in their opponent's defense before they got down to the serious business of maiming or killing each other over some trivial point of honor.

"It's getting late," Tom Byrne said quietly. He had been watching Quint and Shelby—two first-class fighting men, if he had ever seen any. They would be of inestimable use to him, and, of course, the United States, when and if the United States went to war with Mexico. They might work well together if handled with care and tact.

Quint Kershaw was too proud and independent a man to work for Tom, or any other man, Anglo or Mexican, in New Mexico. He might accept work temporarily but only with the purpose of attaining his own independence again. But in order to be of value to Tom Byrne, and, of course, the United States, Quint must become a man of means, of property, of importance. If not in trade, it must be in the land and the flocks and herds. The Vasquez fortunes were at a low ebb. A combination of Quint Kershaw and Guadalupe Vasquez could be a keystone in the underlying structure Tom Byrne was determined to build in northern New Mexico—Taos, to be exact, with Charles Bent, Ceran St. Vrain and others. He would have to see to that.

Shelby Calhoun stood up. "I thank you, Thomas Byrne, for a most informative and pleasurable evening," he said.

Tom stood up. "My pleasure. You're leaving for Chihuahua tomorrow?"

"Yes, with the advance party, before dawn light. I had originally planned to wait for the caravan, but it will be too slow for my purposes."

Tom nodded. "Ye might like Chihuahua, Shell," he suggested.

Shell shrugged. "I doubt it, from what I've seen here in New Mexico."

"It can grow on one," Tom warned.

"No chance."

Shelby turned and extended his hand to Luke. "We'll meet again, Luke Connors." He smiled. "Always a pleasure."

Luke bent his head a little. "Likewise," he murmured.

Shelby held out his hand to Quint. "I'll see you on my return, Quint Kershaw." His grip was strong. The man had

285

been well trained and was skilled in the use of the dragoon saber, "the wristbreaker." His hand met the hand of a man whose grip could be likened to that of a vise. Their eyes held for a fraction of a second.

"Good luck, Shell," Quint said. He sincerely meant it.

Shell turned to Jean. "I may not see you until I return. May I see you alone for a moment or two?"

Jean nodded. "Of course, Shell." The two of them walked out onto the moonlit patio.

Luke glanced sideways at Quint with his strange green eyes. "Yuh gonna miss ol' Shell?" he asked dryly.

Quint grinned. "Of course."

Luke headed for his room and probably the buxom and amorous Rafaela. Tom Byrne walked with Luz to the inner door. He turned. "Ye understand, certainly, that all that was spoken here this night is in the strictest confidence?"

"I'm not ordinarily a talkative man, and certainly not a damned fool, Tom."

The door closed behind Tom and Luz.

Quint refilled his brandy glass and lit a fresh cigar.

He blew out the candles and walked to the patio door. It was slightly ajar. Jean and Shelby stood close together by the fountain. She was looking up into his earnest face. She shook her head slightly, placed her hands one on each side of his face and kissed him lightly.

Quint had the hearing of a hunting wolf. It served him well now.

"But it need only be a promise, Jean," Shelby pleaded.

"I'll be here when you return," she said.

"You'll consider my proposal?"

She smiled. "Of course. It's a great honor."

"Then why not accept it now?"

"Shell, I'm just not sure, that's all."

"There's someone else?"

She shrugged a little. "Perhaps."

"There was no one back in the States. It has to be that damned mountain man. Isn't that the truth?"

She turned away from him. She had no need to reply. The answer was plain on her lovely face.

Shell turned on a heel and strode from the patio. The front door banged shut and echoed hollowly throughout the big *casa.*

For a moment Jean stood there in the faint moonlight. She looked down into the splashing fountain and dabbled a hand carelessly in the water. She turned quickly and walked toward the door behind which Quint was standing. There was no time for him to leave the room. nor did he try.

She pushed the door open and walked directly into him. She looked up into his shadowed features. "Were you listening?" she demanded.

"Inadvertently," he admitted without a trace of shame.

"You could have closed the door."

He shrugged. "I thought of it."

"But you didn't close it. Why?"

He reached over her shoulder and pushed the door shut. The latch clicked into position. "It's closed now, lassie."

She walked to the fireplace and stirred the embers. She placed several small piñon branches atop the embers and turned toward Quint.

"Are you considering his proposal?" Quint asked.

"I may be."

"He's a catch, perhaps, as they say in the States. Of good family. A career officer. Handsome. Dashing."

She smiled a little. "But incredibly dull and almost penniless."

"That last makes a difference to you?"

She shook her head. "Only in the matter of having someone marry me for my money."

"Speaking of catches," Quint said dryly.

"You're interested, aren't you?"

He drained his brandy glass. "Wine?" he asked her.

"Brandy," she said.

He filled the glasses. "Am I the reason ye would not accept his proposal?"

"Is that conceit or arrogance?"

Quint smiled a little wryly. "It was Shell Calhoun who mentioned it, not I. And ye didn't answer him. I flatter myself that your silence was an agreement with his statement."

"You didn't answer my question as to the matter of your interest in me, Quint."

He came closer to her. She sipped at the strong brandy and looked up into his face. She expected him to take her in his arms and try his way with her. He turned away from her and looked uselessly at the flaring piñon branches. She thought she had him going.

"Quint?" she asked quietly.

He turned. "Aye, lassie, I *am* interested in ye."

"You don't make it very obvious. I think of you as a direct

man, an egotistical male, who strikes out after what h
wants, whatever it may be."

He shrugged. "It's the way of the mountain man."

"Is it another woman? That Mexican woman? Lupita,
they call her?"

Quint shook his head.

"Then who?" she demanded.

This time it was not the face and phantom of Elspet
MacBeth that came into the shadowed room to haunt him
Dotawipe, Mountain Woman, had taken her place.

"Is it the Indian woman then?" Jean demanded.

"Ye know about her?"

She nodded. "The story got around the caravan."

His face changed and became fixed. "I am not ashamed," h
said coldly.

"I am not accusing you, Quint. But isn't she dead?"

He looked into the strange, flickering patterns in the thic
bed of embers.

"Quint?" she queried quietly. She held out a hand i
sympathy toward him, but he did not turn toward her i
recognition of it.

"I don't know, Jean; I just don't know." His voice broke
little.

It was the first time she had seen this monolith of a ma
show any softness of emotion.

Quint drained his brandy glass and refilled it. "As long as
don't know for sure, ye ken, I can't commit myself to an
other woman."

"That's not usually the way of the mountain men wit
Indian women, is it?"

"There have been rare instances."

"Such as yours."

He held her eyes with his. "I am not sure. She meant muc
to me at the time, although I tried to think otherwise. I neve
had any intention of keeping her with me after two season
trapping."

"Could you have left her even then?"

He shook his head. "I had no plans for her in my future
She knew that. It's the way of things when Indian wome
become 'winter' squaws."

"Then you *used* her, didn't you?"

Quint raised a big hand, almost as though to strike out a
her. "Damn ye! I said it was the way of things!"

"But not for a man such as yourself. That's the problem

that you brought with you from the mountains, is it not?"

He studied her. She was wise for her years. "Ye know much for a woman," he admitted. "My own mother had that innate wisdom in the ways of people. The second sight they called it in Scotland."

"Then there can be no understanding between us until the matter of the Indian woman is settled, is that it?"

He tilted his head to one side and half smiled. "The lassie is aye direct," he murmured. "I'm not so sure I'd want a female around me for future years who is quite so direct."

"Perhaps such a woman would make a fit mate for you, Quint."

He shook his head a little. "No," he said quietly, "I can't quite see it that way, lassie. Ye'd want to return to your life in the States, to stand beside your father, with his power and great wealth. Where would a man such as myself fit in there?"

"You're much like my father, Quint."

"Aye, but that's perhaps the rub, Jeannie. Do ye ken?"

She studied him closely. He was right. He had seen through her and placed his finger directly on her innermost, perhaps subconscious need.

"But if I stayed here in New Mexico . . ." she suggested.

He shook his head again. "No, Jean. This will be my home. I plan to build my future here. Someday I will marry, but it must be a woman of the country, who accepts it, and me as well, for what we are. I do not believe that you are that woman."

It was very quiet in the shadowed room. The hearth was thick with embers buried in feathery ashes, affording very little light. Jean came close to this panther of a man, drawn to him by a mental and animal magnetism she had never known in her lifetime before meeting Quintin Kershaw that moonlit night at McNee's Creek.

He cupped his big rough hands on each side of her lovely oval face and tilted her head back ever so gently. "Don't speak," he whispered. He kissed her lightly, then released her.

She looked up into his shadowed face for a moment, then turned on a heel and left the study.

"*Vaya*," Quint said softly.

Somewhere in the depths of the great dark house he heard her bedroom door close.

THIRTY-THREE

The select and exclusive monte gambling sala of Señora María Gertrudis de Barcelo, or La Tules, as she was more commonly called, ran through the entire block from San Francisco Street to Palace Avenue bordering on Burro Alley and facing on the road to Tesuque. The gambling sala was open only to those whom La Tules invited. It had the distinction of having a plank floor, sawed and planed by hand—one of two in the entire province. A board floor in New Mexico was like walking on gold pavement. The sala was divided by a long beam and posts to hold up the heavy roof. One end was used for the gambling, principally monte, chuza—which was like roulette—faro and various dice games. The other end was used for dancing and held the bar. One of the largest mirrors in the province, if not the largest, was hung behind the bar, reflecting the glitter of light from hundreds of candles. A high platform for the three-piece orchestra—fiddle, guitar and violin—flanked the long bar. Near it was the high seat for the "stool pigeon" or spotter who watched for crooked gamblers and fights.

Long, narrow mirrors rose from low white marble shelves, reaching almost to the rafters. The polished glass reflected the deep-red curtains at the windows—which were paned with real glass brought by caravan from St. Louis instead of the usual mica—and the ornately carved chairs, tables, *trasteros,* or cupboards, the other furnishings of the long sala and the packed humanity within the room. A great chandelier holding a hundred candles of perfumed wax hung from the center of the ceiling, toward which the heavy blue haze of tobacco smoke drifted or hung in rifted layers from wall to wall. The establishment was thronged with humanity—dancers, drinkers, gamblers and onlookers. The spicy aroma of *mistela,* a fragrant brew of brandy, spices, sugar and chimaja leaves sealed in a jar, covered with thick dough and simmered for hours, mingled with the tantalizing odor of *empanaditas* or small hot mince pies, and fine spongecake. Mixed with the scent of the food and liquors was that of tobacco smoke, perfume and perspiration, forming an atmosphere that was at once exciting, earthy and sensuous.

Quint Kershaw withdrew a twist of raw cotton from its tin tube and dexterously struck a spark from flint and steel to ignite the charred end of the cotton. He held the smoldering end to the thin tip of Luke's *cigarrito*, lighted his own, then drew the burning cotton within the tube and placed a finger tip on the end of it to cut off the air supply and extinguish the fire. He picked up his double glass of brandy and drained the fiery *aguardiente* from it in one gulp. "Yore gettin' mighty good at that sleight-o'-hand, Big Red Badger," Luke observed dryly. "Mebbe as good as ary greaser here in Santy Fe."

"Santa Fe," Quint corrected easily. "So? When in Rome, as Tom Byrne always says, to make a point of local customs."

"In the weeks we been here yuh seem to be makin' a fair imitation of Don Grande Rubio, the Big Redhead, as the *pelados* call yuh behind yore back. One of these days, God forbid, yore old trappin' friends might mistake yuh for a greaser yoreself."

Quint grinned as he refilled his glass. "With my size, gray eyes and sorrel hair and mustache, Wandering Wolf?"

"Yuh looked at yoreself much lately?"

Quint looked down at his "costume" as Luke usually called it unkindly. He wore a gray *charro*-type jacket embellished with swirls and arabesques of black braid. He had on black leather pants split from the knee down and loosely laced to reveal his fine linen drawers. His saddle-yellow boots were of the finest leather and workmanship.

"Yuh see what I mean?" Luke demanded.

"Ye didn't expect me to stay here in Santa Fe wearing that stinking trapping outfit, did ye? It was so bad the servants burned it while holding their noses, and *yours* as well, old hoss, if my memory serves me right."

"Waal, gawddammit! Yuh could have gotten a *white* man's outfit like I done from Tom Byrne, instead of that damned greaser costume, Big Red."

"When in Rome," Quint repeated.

"I ain't never been there, wherever it is, and neither have you!" Luke snapped disgustedly.

"Just what the hell is the matter with ye, anyway?"

Quint demanded hotly. "What do ye think I owe ye now?"

"I don't want nothin' from you, Big Red, and I never did, 'cep'n friendship, and that yuh know right well. Whatever we owed each other over the years I never kept account of and neither did you. Mebbe we're even up over the years and mebbe we ain't. I ain't talkin' about that. I'm talkin' about what's to come, not what has passed. We been here weeks now doin' nothin' but eatin', drinkin', gamblin' and livin' off Tom Byrne like a couple of damned parasites."

"Ye forgot fornicatin', Lukie." Quint grinned.

"That too! A *real* man can have enough of that too after a time."

Quint rested an arm about the shoulders of his partner. "What's really botherin' ye, Luke?"

Luke looked about the packed sala. "Walls are for wintertime, Quint," he murmured cryptically.

"Ye came to New Mexico with me to try to start a new life, didn't ye?"

Luke looked sideways at Quint. "Not really. Tradin' ain't for the likes of us. Yuh said so yourself back at Bent's Big Lodge."

"That was in reference to working for Bent, St. Vrain and Company. It wasn't meant to mean we couldn't strike out for ourselves. What else is there for us to do here? The beaver trapping is about done."

"There's other game—bear, deer, buffalo. The trade in their hides and peltries ain't too bad. They's a good market for them here and in Taos."

"Just enough profit for buying more powder, caps, lead and traps, then back to the goddam mountains again, with a weepin' in your pants, a monumental hangover and dead broke, holding your rifle in one hand and your life in the other."

"Well, leastways a man is about as free as he'll ever get in this damned life," Luke said quietly.

"Even if we did want to make a try at the tradin'," he argued, "we ain't got a copper tlaco of our own to invest in goods, not with the credit prices these established local traders are askin' for their goods. By God, Big Red, the very clothes we got on our backs we got on credit from Tom Byrne! The food we eat, the likker we drink, the women we screw, and the money we gamble with we get from him. We haven't paid him back a centavo even from our winnings."

Quint shrugged as he refilled their glasses. "Old Tom ain't

throwing his money away on us just because he likes the cut of our hair, Lukie. Ye know he wants us to stay here in the province. Ye know I've applied for Mexican citizenship."

"And been turned down, ain't yuh?"

Quint shrugged. "It's just a matter of time."

Luke rolled his eyes upward. *"Dios mío!* My best friend and trappin' partner a gawddam Mexkin."

"Ye mind what Bill Bent and Ceran St. Vrain said about that, and Tom Byrne as well. Maybe only a matter of a few years, Lukie."

Luke drained his glass. He looked squarely at Quint. "I'm an American and so are you despite yore Scots ancestry and Canadian boyhood. Ain't nothin' can change that in my book."

"I said it was only a matter of time."

Luke nodded. "Aye, but mebbe it's more than that. Are yuh becomin a Mexkin because yuh *want* to be one, or only because yuh can work from within to make New Mexico part of the United States?"

Luke, with his usual demanding directness, had placed his finger squarely on the problem that had been bothering Quint of late. His innate honesty rebelled against the thought of becoming a Mexican citizen merely to mark time until the day New Mexico became part of the United States. Was that what he really wanted? The years in trapping had made many other trappers and perhaps himself into men without a country. He was Scots by birth, Canadian by upbringing and American by choice, but was that last really his choice? He had spent more than a third of his life in the mountains. A wild, unsettled, independent life with perfect freedom from nearly every kind of social dependence as an absolute necessity for his being. Daily, hourly exposure of his life and property to complete loss had developed the innate habit of relying only on himself and his rifle, both for protection and support. If he was wronged, there were no courts or juries he could call upon to adjudicate his disputes or abuses, save his conscience. There were no powers he could invoke to redress his wrongs, save those which the God of Nature had endowed him. He knew no government, no laws, save those of his own creation and adoption. He lived in no society which he must look up to or propitiate. His was truly a sovereign independence.

A murmur went through the sala. "La Tules!" The nickname was passed from one to the other of the people crowding the long room, and even the intent gamblers turned from their games to look at the famous, or rather notorious, Señora María Gertrudis Barcelo, owner of the gambling establishment, with the favor and backing of the governor, Manuel Armijo, who always had a room reserved for himself in her imposing casa behind the gambling hall, which he ruled as though it were his own.

La Tules was a real *rubia,* a coppery-gold redhead with flashing wide green eyes. She was not a great beauty in the true sense. There was almost a handsome masculinity about her strong features. Her nose was too long, her mouth was too wide, and the formation of her face wasn't quite right for beauty. But there was a feline feminine quality about her that could draw the eyes of any lusty man. Her red hair was daubed with sugared water to hold it in position in high shining coils on top of her head and tight firm ringlets that hung down to her bronzed arched and plucked eyebrows. A magnificent tortoiseshell comb had been thrust into the hair at the back of her shapely head, over which had been draped a black mantilla of the finest and most delicate lace. Her face was thickly powdered white, and her rather thin lips were scarlet with thick carmine. Her gown was of black taffeta, the mark of intense respectability, fastened with buttons of polished jet, and there were blond lace ruffles at her throat and wrists. A gold locket was dependent about her neck, while within the confines of the locket chain a tiny gold cross shone in the brilliant candlelight. A bowknot of pearls with an emerald pendant held the high throat of the gown closed. She wore a number of gold and silver bracelets on her shapely wrists and innumerable rings on her slender, supple white fingers. An exquisite lace handkerchief had been thrust up within the left wristband to hang just below her long red-painted fingernails. Her earrings were long and hung almost to her shoulders and were made of the very finest Mexican filigree from Taxco. Black satin slippers with high gold heels were on her feet. Over her shoulders she wore a *manton de Manila,* a mantle of finest Chinese silk by way of Manila lavishly embroidered in crimson roses and flying white birds within an extremely long fringe. She used the finest French perfume. *La Tules!*

La Tules! Orphaned baby daughter of Joaquín Barcelo, a soldier killed by Indians, and Luz, a Sonoran peon, a so-called *soldadera,* a woman who followed her soldier on campaigns, to cook and wash for him and at times even to join him in battle. La Tules' heritage from her father had been her red hair and green eyes. He had been of Andalusian stock and born with the blood of the Right People. Christened Maria Gertrudis Barcelo, but always called "Tu-les" for short, she had been raised by her widowed mother, who served as a bound peon to Don Miguel Salazar of Taos. A survivor was La Tules, the barefoot *pelada* born into a harsh and tumultuous existence of cold, hunger and the constant menace of Navajo raiders. Married young, and widowed young, she had become a vendor of *jaboncillos,* or small perfumed cakes of garishly colored soap, in the *mercado* next to the Governor's Palace. She had been highly successful, more for trading her sexual favors to soldiers and politicians than selling her soaps, until she had reached the heights and become the *querida* of Governor Manuel Armijo. She was a born gambler and queen of the monte tables. Today, in a town where she had once been despised and ridiculed, she was a power, and a woman of wealth and position. Her motto? "With silver, nothing fails." *La Tules!*

The sharp green eyes surveyed the crowd and then met the gray eyes of Quintin Kershaw. Something passed between them.

"Dios te salve! God save yuh," Luke murmured. "She's got her eyes on yuh, Quint."

Quint shrugged. "So? She's seen us in here every night for the past two weeks or so."

Luke slanted his green eyes toward Quint. "Not *us,* Big Red. *You....* What happened that night a week or so ago when Armijo was down in Albuquerque and she invited yuh back to her casa for wine and cakes?"

Quint looked sideways at Luke. "We were just getting acquainted when she was tipped off the governor had returned a day early, leaving his wife in Albuquerque, because he was anxious to see his *querida.*"

"And you went out the back door when he came in the front?"

Quint looked casually at his fingernails. "Actually, I had to go over the damned wall." He grinned.

"Jesus! You know how Armijo feels toward her!"

"Who doesn't?" Quint asked carelessly.

"Armijo runs her house as though it was his own. He might be back there even now keepin' away from that horse-faced wife of his'n. Can't say that I blame him at that."

La Tules moved graciously through the throng. She would

not approach Quint directly. He was a gringo, an *extranjero,* a stranger in Santa Fe. He was the friend of Tomás Byrne, a respected merchant and somewhat of a confidant of Manuel, giving him good advice on many occasions, as well as substantial loans for which he never dunned the governor. La Tules stopped beside the monte table, deciding whether or not she would deal that night. She glanced back over her shoulder at Quint Kershaw. He stood with his broad back toward her but looked into the huge polished mirror behind the bar, and their eyes met again. That same vibrant charge seemed to pass between them. She *must* meet this *rubio* alone again. It had been some time since a man had vaguely excited her like this. *Madre de Dios!* To have such a stud in bed with her! Manuel, despite his bulk and appearance, was not a great performer in the feathers. But what could one do? She would not have achieved her amazing success in Santa Fe without his patronage. She knew that to show favor to another man, particularly this Yanqui *extranjero,* might very well result in the displeasure of Manuel, or something worse. This Quint Kershaw (it really was a ridiculous name, wasn't it?) had applied for Mexican citizenship under the sponsorship of Tomás Byrne, and he was known to be a friend of Carlos and Guillermo Bent, as well as Ceran Sambrano, all powerful men in high favor with Manuel. She knew too that Manuel was debating whether or not he should have citizenship granted to Quintin Kershaw. If she was to show the slightest further interest in Quint, that much would be enough to turn Manuel against him. She *wanted* Quint to stay in New Mexico and become a citizen. After all, Manuel wasn't too popular with the people, and his life was in constant danger from malcontents and assassins. La Tules had to think of the future. Like many prominent New Mexicans, particularly those in business, she felt that it might be only a matter of time before New Mexico became part of the United States. Already the upstart Texans were claiming the Rio Grande del Norte as their western boundary instead of the Nueces. If the Texas Republic became part of the United States and the United States claimed that same boundary ... With a man such as Quintin Kershaw beside her she felt that the two of them could conquer the province.

"Jesus, what a woman," Luke murmured.

Quint nodded as he filled their glasses. The potent *aguardiente* was working deep within him, giving him a solid feeling of well-being and power and the lust of a rutting stag or a doe, in this particular case that of a green-eyed *rubia*. *Verdad, hombre,*" he murmured. "That's the truth, man."

"Your *amigo* Don Bartolomé Vasquez just walked in," Luke said out of the side of his mouth.

"I thought La Tules had barred him from this place."

Luke shrugged. "Who's to enforce it? Even the governor is careful around Don Bartolomé. The Vasquezes are in a decline, as Tom Byrne says, but they still got a lot of power, at least in the north country around Taos. Tom says Don Bartolomé is the head of a secret faction plotting to overthrow Armijo."

Quint looked up into the mirror behind the bar. His eyes met the cold hard stare of Don Bartolomé. The man was ox-faced, his aristocratic features narrow and triangular, nose somewhat aquiline and lips so thin as to be almost nonexistent. There was an arrogance about the man that might cover a deep-seated lack of confidence in himself, or perhaps a wavering mental unbalance. In either case, it made him dangerous. Quint had met him just twice—the first time through Lupita, who had told Bartolomé about Quint and how he had saved her life. There had been little or no gratitude from Bartolomé. He hated gringos with a passion, almost as much as he hated Manuel Armijo and the authorities of the province, as well as La Tules. Further, Lupita had invited this unmannerly boor of a gringo to dine at Bartolomé's house in Santa Fe the week the caravan had arrived. Despite the fact that Bartolomé had deeply resented the invitation without his permission, it had rankled much deeper, almost to the core, when the gringo had not shown up. He had not even bothered to send his regrets, before or after the act. Bartolomé had learned later that Kershaw had gotten drunk that night and had been seen in the company of La Tules at Tomás Byrne's house. Lupita had left shortly thereafter for Taos. Lupita herself meant little to Bartolomé; nor did the rest of his family matter to him in the slightest, except for what he could wrench out of them to pay his exorbitant gambling debts. It was the matter of family honor that had been sullied; such honor was a fetish, almost a mania, with Bartolomé Vasquez, a not uncommon thing among the *gente fina* and *ricos* of New Mexico.

Don Bartolomé was indeed a dangerous man. What was it Tom Byrne, a keen student and analytical observer of the vagaries of human behavior, had said about Don Bartolomé? *The man is a fool, a hothead with a pride that bears not the*

297

slightest prick. He's already killed three men, fairly enoug
'tis true—there was nothing murderous about the acts, b
none of the three could be considered as real fighting men.

Jaime Salazar, a garrulous employee in Tom Byrne
merchant establishment, sidled up beside Quint. Quint didn
particularly like the man, but he was a fount of informatio
about the seamy side of life in Santa Fe. "It's said that L
Tules paid for that bowknot of pearls and the emerald pen
dant with her winnings from Don Bartolomé," Jaime said ov
of the side of his mouth. "That was months ago, of cours
Don Bartolomé constantly challenges her at monte in orde
to regain his losses. It's said, on good authority, that he ha
hardly a tostón, a half-peso, in cash, left to himself. H
father, good Don Francisco, has fallen on hard times payin
Don Bartolomé's debts. Don Francisco is an honest man;
man with great family pride and honor. Some say already
large number of the Vasquez holdings in the Taos Valley ar
heavily mortgaged because of those debts. That includes Do
Bartolomé's fine casa here in town, which is, or was, reall
his father's, of course. The fact that Don Francisco onc
opposed Manuel Armijo in his rise to power here in th
province has not been forgotten by Don Manuel. Believe m
he forgets nothing like that! Don Manuel too bears
hatred toward Don Manuel, but it is much worse than tha
which his father bears toward the governor. There are r
mors that Don Bartolomé plots against the governor. .
dangerous game. But there are many such rumors, an
many such plotters, so one hardly takes them into accoun
Ay, qué caray, hombres! What the hell! That is simply th
way of life here in the province, Don Quintin."

Luke drained his glass. "Who holds the mortgage, Jaime'
he asked.

Jaime narrowed his bushy eyebrows. "What mortgage?"

"The one for much of Don Francisco's holdings in the Tac
Valley?"

Jaime looked back over both shoulders. "It was La Tule
but she made a deal with Don Tomás, my *patrón*. For cash. L
Tules likes cash in hand, as the saying goes. They say she ha
black alpaca bags full of pesos in a locked wooden chest in he
casas. Many of them, fellows. *Many. . . .*"

Luke looked casually at Quint as Jaime headed for a gam
of chuza. "A large part of the Vasquez holdings," he sai
quietly. "It's said to be prime land, heavily stocked. Rur
down, sure, but nothing a good man couldn't rebuild. Say

nan was to get his hands on that land, then take that little
Lupita to wife. . . ."

"Ye forget Don Francisco and Don Bartolomé," Quint reminded him.

Luke grimaced like a hunting wolf. "Don Francisco is old,
very old, and in poor health. Don Bartolomé lives dangerous-
ly. *Quién sabe?* Some dark night, on his way home, he might
trip and run into a handy knife blade stuck out toward him."

"Ye murderous bastard!" Quint cried.

Luke raised his eyebrows and held out his lean hands,
palms upward. "Who? *Me?*" he asked innocently.

They grinned at each other.

Quint looked toward Don Bartolomé. "I have a fey feeling,"
he said quietly, almost as though to himself, "that Don
Bartolomé will find his own quick death, and that soon, if he
carries on his present style of life."

It was late, but there was no cessation of the gambling,
drinking and dancing. It was this way every night not only in
La Tules' place, but in every gambling sala, dance hall and
cantina in Santa Fe. It was the way of life, a ceaseless pursuit
of pleasure and amusement; a passion, an obsession, a perpetual carnival and ball, and to hell with tomorrow.

"La Tules is going to deal," the murmur went quickly
through the long sala. It was to be the same this night as it
had been for many other nights—La Tules virtually alone
against Don Bartolomé. There would be other players, of
course, but all knew it was a personal duel between the *rico*
and the low-caste woman. The other players would drop out
as the stakes rose.

"Bien, caballeros!" La Tules cried. "Let's see what the
future holds for us!"

Monte was played with a thin deck of forty narrow Spanish
cards, the eights, nines and tens having been removed from
the deck. The green tablecloth was marked in squares for the
placing of the bets. Jose Vaca, the "lookout," sat opposite La
Tules, prepared to take in the losing bets, pay the few
winners, watch for cheats and keep his pistol handy in case of
trouble. There were two cash drawers, one on each side of the
dealer's chair, filled with bright silver pesos. La Tules always
played for the highest stakes.

La Tules' slim hands and tapered fingers with their rings
and red sharp-tipped nails worked the forty cards effortless-
ly, faster than the eye could follow. Hers was fabulous good
fortune in the game of monte. Some said she was a *bruja,* a

299

witch, and so was able to make the cards fall at her will. N
one really knew; many suspected. Away from the mont
table, La Tules was a study in charm and vivacity, but whe
she was seated in the dealer's chair her green eyes seemed t
become sharper and clearer in an absolutely expressionles
face. She knew Don Bartolomé would be her principal oppo
nent that night. She hated the man personally, not so muc
for himself but for what he stood for—a *rico,* one of the *gent*
fina whose type had kept her peon mother in bondage fo
much of her life until La Tules had become rich herself. L
Tules herself had worked for her *patrón* at the wage of fort
pennies a year, until she had fled from that slavery. The
there had been the hard, cold, impersonal rapes when sh
had been a mere child, by the *galanes,* the gallants, so calle
the young drunken sons of her *patrón* and their friends a
well. She had never forgotten; she would never forget.

La Tules looked about at the onlookers and players aroun
the monte table. "To good luck, señores!" she cried.

Some of the onlookers and players called back, almost i
unison:

> "*Salud y pesetas,*
> *Mujeres y muletas,*
> *Ay, qué caray!*"
> "Health and wealth,
> Women and she-mules,
> Oh, what the hell!"

La Tules snapped down the first quartet of cards for th
layout on the green cloth and called, "*Alza!* Place your bet
caballeros! To have money and not to play is a sin!"

The bets were placed. La Tules then drew the cards fror
the bottom of the pack and placed them face up. Don Federic
Baca had dropped a stack of silver on the queen of cups. Th
matching card had come out of the gate, and Jose Vaca, th
lookout, pushed a pile of pesos toward Don Federico, payin
the bet four to one. There was no expression on the face of L
Tules. She knew Don Federico's favorite cards, his bettin
habits and the size of his purse. She wasn't interested in Do
Federico; although she had almost as little use for him as sh
did for Don Bartolomé, she did not have the same hatred fo
him. She would be patient.

The game went on, a winner here, a loser there, with Do
Bartolomé winning just enough to draw him on, until at las

he alone faced La Tules. It was very late now, almost the usual closing time, but the crowd had not diminished. The orchestra had quit playing to join the onlookers.

Don Bartolomé lost all his winnings that night. Time and time again he looked at the inscrutable face of La Tules and learned nothing. Tiny pearl-like drops of sweat ran down his lean face. Now and again he held his thin lower lip between his fine white teeth. He bet the last of his money on the knave against La Tules' three-spot. La Tules deftly drew the winning three. Don Bartolomé paled as his money was raked in. He looked about at the spectators. Their faces were blank. Don Bartolomé was not a particular social favorite in Santa Fe.

La Tules waited patiently, tapping a fingernail on the winning three-spot. *"Alza!* Place your bet, *caballero!"* she cried.

Don Bartolomé turned slowly to face La Tules. "You drew that three-spot from the top of the deck instead of the bottom," he accused in a low hard voice.

La Tules stood up. "The bank is closed," she said firmly.

Quint stood just behind Don Bartolomé. He knew the man carried a pearl-handled pistol in the sash about his narrow waist. Quint glanced at Luke and moved his head a little to position him on the other side of Don Bartolomé and closer to Don Federico, a friend of Don Bartolomé's and said to be involved in his shadowy plotting against the governor.

Don Bartolomé shook his head slowly. "No. The bank is not closed until I have a final chance to win back my losses."

La Tules looked about herself. She had to be careful, keeping the goodwill of the crowd at all times. She could read their faces like an open book, testing their mercurial temperament. This night she knew she must continue to play against Don Bartolomé. The crowd might not be fully behind Don Bartolomé, but she also knew they might not be fully with her. She could take no chances.

"Well?" Don Bartolomé demanded.

"You have something left with which to bet, Don Bartolomé?" La Tules asked quietly.

"No money," Don Bartolomé replied.

La Tules shrugged. "Then what? I doubt if you can gamble away more of your father's holdings."

The door opened and Manuel Armijo walked in, followed by several of his armed retainers. A long blue cape of finest material hung from his broad shoulders, barely showing the

301

red-and-gold stripes on the collar of his uniform. He was a large and handsome man in his late thirties, with an arrogant nose, dark inscrutable eyes and full sensuous lips. There was a dominating virility about the man; an air of shrewdness and power. His face clouded with annoyance as he saw La Tules still seated in the dealer's chair at the crowded monte table. He was tired after his long journey from Albuquerque and wanted only to be alone with his *querida,* but he quickly sensed something dramatic, perhaps even dangerous, was in the close air of the sala.

Don Bartolomé had turned a little at the entrance of the governor. "A double brandy," he said to the waiter.

"Amigo," Don Federico said in a low voice, "you've already had too much to drink. You forget yourself."

Don Bartolomé waved an impatient hand. "This is my affair, Federico. Stay close by my side and watch for cheating on the part of this woman."

"Be careful, Don Bartolomé," Manuel Armijo warned.

"What will you bet?" La Tules asked impatiently.

Don Bartolomé looked about the crowded sala. "The Vasquez Grant," he said quietly.

The crowd was instantly hushed. Everyone there, with the exceptions of Quint and Luke, knew all about the famous Vasquez Grant, east of the Sangre de Cristo Mountains, a royal Spanish grant, one of five which encompassed vast areas of land in northern New Mexico. Don Bartolomé's grandfather had attempted to settle the grant and had failed because of Indian depredations and severe wounds which had eventually caused his death. Don Francisco too had tried and failed. There was a saying, "No Vasquez will ever settle that land and make it prosper." Still, it was a land of great possibilities, with many fine streams, the finest of grazing, good soil and much timber. That, of course, was still there, but then too, so was the Indian menace. A strong man, such as Don Bartolomé's grandfather had been, might possibly settle the land in these times, possibly. . . .

La Tules raised her bronzed eyebrows. "We can't accept such a bet, Don Bartolomé, unless we have some authority from Don Francisco."

Don Bartolomé slowly shook his head. "That is no longer necessary, La Tules. My father passed away last night. He left the remainder of the Taos Valley holdings to my sister, which, of course, I can also demand as my right. He left the grant to me, as sole owner."

302

The governor narrowed his dark eyes. "And you are here gambling on the day after his death? For shame, Don Bartolomé!"

A low murmur of polite horror passed through the crowd. Gamblers though all of them were, even to the few padres among their number, to do such a thing as Don Bartolomé had done was the next thing to sacrilege.

Don Bartolomé looked at La Tules. "Well?" he demanded.

La Tules looked past the young *rico* at Manuel Armijo. The governor half-closed his eyes. If La Tules drew the right cards this night, she could accomplish much, perhaps a minor miracle. Most of the Vasquez holdings in the Taos Valley were heavily mortgaged to Tomás Byrne. True, the estate was much run-down, but there was great potential there. The merchant was always looking for good investments, and although there were some laws preventing a foreigner, even a naturalized citizen such as Tomás Byrne, from owning such a land grant, there were certain devious legal ways well known to Manuel Armijo to circumvent those laws, and with a neat profit to the governor himself. True, also, if Don Bartolomé lost the Vasquez Grant, that might eliminate him as a powerful factor in the enemy's camp. Ay, but La Tules must not lose! Manuel nodded. La Tules could read him like an open book. She knew what he meant. *She must not lose,* under any circumstances.

The thought of Lupita passed quickly through Quint's mind. He remembered her out on the *llano,* hunting for meat and hides with the *ciboleros,* when Don Bartolomé should have been leading them. To Quint's way of reckoning, Don Bartolomé didn't have long to live. He was a natural to get killed, and then Lupita would inherit the Vasquez Grant. But not if he lost it first by drawing the wrong cards this night.

La Tules nodded at last. "How will you bet, Don Bartolomé?" she asked quietly.

Don Bartolomé leaned forward and placed his hands flat on the table. "The entire Vasquez Grant against the bank and your monte sala, La Tules."

It was very quiet.

"You are mad," Federico Baca said out of the side of his mouth.

Don Bartolomé paid no attention to his friend. "Well, La Tules?" he sneered.

La Tules looked at the governor. Again he nodded.

"The bank is here with the sala," La Tules said. "Where is your security on the bet?"

"Is not the word of a Vasquez enough security?" the *rico* cried.

Manuel Armijo came to stand beside Don Bartolomé. He smiled. "Under ordinary circumstances your word is enough. A little chit, say, with the terms of the bet written thereon, and witnessed by your friend Don Federico and myself, is necessary because of the size of the stakes. Your word and honor are not at stake here tonight, Don Bartolomé."

Jose Vaca placed pen and paper in front of Don Bartolomé. He hesitated, then hastily scribbled on the paper. He shoved it toward La Tules but Manuel intercepted it, read it quickly, nodded, then placed it back on the monte table beside the layout squares. La Tules swiftly shuffled the cards and dealt two.

"I bet the Vasquez Grant on the ace of swords, against the bank and the monte sala," Don Bartolomé said steadily.

The card opposite the ace of swords was the gold five. The bet, of course, depended on which card was paired first by drawing two cards. La Tules half-closed her eyes. Her long memory ran over the cards in the deck. She was almost sure the ace Don Bartolomé needed to match his ace was near the bottom of the deck, but not certain about her matching five to win.

"Draw," Don Bartolomé said hoarsely. "San Augustín help me."

La Tules, without hesitation, turned up a four and a deuce.

The tension could be felt throughout the crowded sala.

The first card in the next draw was the blond queen, followed by a four.

Don Bartolomé paled. A tiny bead of cold sweat ran down his face. He narrowed his eyes and clenched his lower lip between his teeth.

La Tules looked up at Don Bartolomé, then drew a deuce. She hesitated, then quickly drew the next card from the bottom of the deck. It was a five.

"Maldita puta! Cursed bitch!" Don Bartolomé shouted. "You drew that five from the top of the deck!"

"Damn you, de Vasquez, can't you lose like a gentleman?" Manuel roared.

Don Bartolomé whirled. He thrust his right hand into his sash and drew a double-barreled pistol which he pointed at the governor as he cocked it. A powerful hand came over his ight shoulder and gripped his pistol wrist to raise it. The pistol exploded into flame and smoke. The bullet whipped through the governor's hat crown. Don Bartolomé turned to face Quint Kershaw. His left hand was thrust inside his jacket and as quickly withdrawn. The candlelight reflected from a thin shining blade of finest Toledo steel. The knife was thrust firmly and surely toward Quint's belly. He stiffened and grunted almost inaudibly as the keen steel went home.

The governor went down on his knees, white-faced, but unharmed. Don Bartolomé darted toward the door through the swirling powder smoke with reddened blade in one hand and pistol in the other. Onlookers broke to one side or the other to give him free passage.

"Death to all tyrants!" Don Bartolomé shouted dramatically. He disappeared into the darkness beyond the door.

Quint gripped the edge of the monte table with his right hand and held his side with his left. His face had paled. For a moment he stood swaying back and forth under the awed eyes of the onlookers and then he fell sideways, dragging the cloth from the table with him. Pesos and cards were scattered over the floor, the silver coins jingling against the wood or rolling about under the feet of the crowd.

The last thing Quint remembered was the horrified face of La Tules bending close over him, and the firm pressure of her full breasts against his chest while she murmured over and over again, *"Don Grande Rubio, Don Grande Rubio . . ."*

THIRTY-FOUR

October 1838—A Fire of Piñon Logs.

Quintin Kershaw was alone in the moonlit patio of the great casa of Thomas Byrne. He reclined on a cowhide chair Tom had ordered constructed especially for Quint when he had recovered sufficiently to be able to get out of bed after so many long weeks. His wound bothered him at times. In the days that had followed the stabbing, he had suffered from great fevers and wild deliriums that required someone to stay at his bedside around the clock. At times it had been Tom Byrne himself, or the gentle, silent Luz, or a deeply worried Luke Connors; and one memorable night he had been quite sure it was La Tules and not a dream beside his sweat-soaked bed. But it was Jean Allan he remembered most vividly. There had been times when her lovely features had melted, distorted and run together like melting wax only to cool and shape the face of Elspeth MacBeth, and once it had been his own gentle mother, but only for a fraction of time.

Despite Manuel Armijo's raging orders that he be run down and summarily executed, Don Bartolomé had made good his escape from Santa Fe and New Mexico as well; but he still had many friends in the province as well as in Mexico proper. News came that he had reached Mexico City, and in some circles it was said that he was held in high esteem there for his courage in trying to rid New Mexico of the tyrant and dictator Armijo. There was little doubt among many Santafeanos that he would be back one day.

Tom Byrne had made a deal with La Tules—actually with Manuel Armijo—to take over the Vasquez Grant. The governor had been granted a one-fourth interest in the vast tract. Tom was a kind man, but a shrewd businessman. He could have taken over much of the Taos Valley holdings of the Vasquezes. Lupita Vasquez still held the great casa and the land surrounding it, free and clear, but there was hardly enough land to sustain the shrunken estate for long. It would only be a matter of time before she would be forced to sell the remainder of the estate in order to survive. Tom and his Luz, Luke Connors, Moccasin, Black Beaver and young Joshua were at present in the north inspecting the Taos Valley holdings and part of the Vasquez Grant.

Manuel Armijo, in deep appreciation for Quint's saving his life in La Tules' sala, had immediately pushed through his application for Mexican citizenship, thus avoiding the legal two years' residence required of all applicants. If he knew of La Tules' interest in Quint he had not mentioned or even hinted at it.

Shelby Calhoun had returned at last from Chihuahua. He had even gone as far as Mexico City, with a side trip to Vera Cruz. On his return he had immediately laid suit to Jean Allan again. He was due to return to the States within the week. One of his self-imposed duties was to provide escort for the tiny girl child of Catherine Williston. Frail, gentle Katie had died in childbirth within two weeks of arriving in Santa Fe. Charles Williston, despite his apparent coldness toward his wife, seemed to have been hard hit by the tragedy and had taken heavily to drink. A mental breakdown had followed. It had been Jean Allan's decision that the child should be taken to the United States for better care and upbringing. Charles had not debated that point with his sister-in-law. He knew better. There were some keen observers who said his drinking and mental problems were but an elaborate sham to get rid of his unwanted child. Those who knew him well would not have put it past him.

As Quint recovered from the wound a vague restlessness came over him, growing stronger every day as his strength returned. The old mountain man saying came back to him time and again, "Walls are for wintertime." The hides of the buffalo and the plews of the beaver would be starting to thicken for the approaching winter. The turning leaves of the aspens would be minting their gold. The ducks and geese would be starting to follow their great air trails to the south.

There was a chill in the night air of Santa Fe. Quint drew a blanket up over his long legs, poured a brandy for himself and then shaped and lighted a *cigarrito*. The casa was empty that night. Everyone had gone to a great fiesta nearby.

It was only a matter of a week or so before Quint was able to get about in his customary manner. He had to think of the approaching winter and, more important, his future in New Mexico now that he was a citizen of Mexico. Tom Byrne had made him an offer of one-fourth interest in the Vasquez Grant in exchange for superintending future colonization activities there, with a long-term option to buy half of the Taos Valley estate. But was Quint willing to tie himself down to such an enterprise; to put down roots, so to speak, in his new country? His mind and hands itched to get out of the stultifying confines of Santa Fe and into the distant purple mountains to the far north. The very food of New Mexico had begun to pall on him. He thought often of buffalo hump and *boudins*.

He drank, and drank again, until a soft warm glow was within him. He looked about the moonlit patio with its tinkling crystal fountain and potted plants. It was a good life for a man such as Tom Byrne, but far too confining for a mountain man. Still, if he did take up either one or both of

Tom's generous offers, he would be able to live a comparatively active outdoor life.

A chill grew in the night air. Quint draped the blanket about his shoulders and picked up the bottle of brandy. He entered the quiet, darkened house and went to his room. He stacked piñon branches vertically in the beehive fireplace in a corner of the room and lighted them. A fiery crackling filled the room as he stripped off his clothing. He lighted a fat candle and lay on the wide bed with the brandy bottle close at hand on a small table. The room filled with a grateful warmth. He had just dozed off when his ears picked up the sounds of the front door lock being opened and the heavy door creaking as it swung back. He heard the door close and the hard heels clicking on the packed earthen floor of the hallway. He glanced sideways to the end table. One of his loaded Patersons was in the drawer, the other under the mattress at the head of the bed. Quint took no chances even in the comparative security of the Byrne casa.

Someone was in the hallway just outside his bedroom door. Then the door lock turned. "Quint?" a woman called in a low voice. It was Jean Allan.

"Come in, Jean," Quint invited. He hastily pulled a sheet over his nakedness.

She entered the room and stood just without the deep-set doorway. The hood of her dark-blue cape lay on her shoulders. The flickering fire and candlelight picked up the high lights of her golden hair. She wore a red silk dress with a rather daring neckline for the times. Her fine firm breasts were outthrust against the thin silk of the gown. He remembered that pair of cherry-tipped beauties from seeing them revealed in Pecos Ruins.

"How do you feel?" she asked.

"Better, much better, almost fit to leave this place and head for the mountains," he replied.

"So soon? Is that all you really want to do?"

He shrugged as he rose up on one elbow. "It's my life, lassie. What are ye doing back here? In that dress ye could be the belle o' the fiesta."

"I pleaded headache and left early."

"Ye've a headache?"

She shook her head. "I knew you were alone. I wanted to see you; talk with you."

He held out his hands palms upward. "I'm here. Talk." He smiled. "It's about Shell Calhoun, isn't it?"

She came closer to the bed. "Yes," she admitted.

"He came from Mexico for the answer to his proposal of marriage."

She nodded.

"So?"

She studied him in the soft flickering light—the scarred face, the other scars and puckered bullet holes on his muscular torso. "You don't know?" she asked quietly. "I can't believe that.'e

He pointed to a chair. "Brandy or wine?"

She dropped her cape on the floor and sat down on the chair. "You're drinking brandy?"

"Aye, the best."

"Then I'll do the same."

He eyed her. "It's unco strong, lassie."

"I may need it."

He shrugged as he filled the glasses. He handed one to her. "Why?" he asked guilelessly.

"Damn you!" she cried. "Don't you understand even now?"

Quint nodded. "Aye, I do. I understand ye wish to return to the States with your wee bit of a niece and that Shell Calhoun has offered ye escort back home and marriage into the bargain."

"So?" she asked coolly.

He studied her. "Ye want me to tell ye that I love ye and that I want ye for my wife. That I'll return to the States with ye. That there can be no other way."

"You charge into a problem like a wild bull."

"It's the Highland way of speech. Direct and to the point."

"Tell me the truth then. What is it you want?"

He shrugged. "If it's love ye want, lassie, I'll be direct again. I've never been sure of the meaning of the word. It's true I have a great attraction to ye, and you're often in my mind. Perhaps too often. But whether that is love, I can't say."

She couldn't help but smile at his logic. "But if you don't know it's love, how will you *ever* know unless you give it a try?"

"It's nothing to gamble with," he said cautiously. "But I'll tell ye this—I do want ye for my wife when and if I get established here in New Mexico."

"With or without love?" she said dryly. "Can't we learn to love each other?"

He eyed her. "Ye don't sound so sure yourself," he suggested.

"Perhaps. But, I do know this—if you come back to the States with me as your wife you could have a splendid career there. You have all the possibilities—intelligence, courage, breeding and a driving ambition to achieve success. I'm not even sure you're fully aware of that last. We could make a great team, Quint. My father has great influence. The choice of career can be yours. I would suggest the military. You'd make a fine soldier. It might be possible to arrange a commission for you in the dragoons."

Quint smiled wryly. "Like Shell Calhoun?" He shook his head. "I'm too free a soul to submit to rigid regular army discipline. I'm a guerrilla fighter at heart."

She shrugged. "No matter. There are other careers."

"Aye, but they require two things, one of which I do not have and the other of which I will not submit to," he countered.

"Go on," she urged. "Tell me about them."

"The first is money. The only wealth I have at present is a strong body and a sense of humor, plus my skill to live on the frontier. Other than those qualities, I don't have a centavo to my name."

"My father is a wealthy man. I have money and property left to me by my mother."

He shook his head. "The money must be mine, money that I have earned myself. I want no handouts."

"And the other thing you mentioned?" she queried.

He looked fully into her eyes. "A discipline to which I would have to submit if I were to be dependent on the first item. A discipline I could never abide."

"Meaning?" she demanded tartly.

"The discipline you would try to maintain over me as my wife whose wealth I would be dependent on for my career. The discipline my prospective father-in-law would try to wield over me as his son-in-law."

She quickly shook her head in frustration. "You're a stubborn fool! We all have to submit to some form of discipline in order to achieve success. Don't you understand that!"

He grinned faintly. "Ye simply canna understand the discipline that is required of every mountain man to live, and moreover simply to *survive,* on the frontier."

"You're a stubborn fool! An untamed half-civilized human being! So help me, Quint! If I didn't know better I'd swear that in all but complexion and that red hair of yours you were an Indian!"

Quint shrugged. "I take that as a compliment, lassie. In

310

your heart ye know I'm right. Washington and the East is no a place for this untamed child. I've taken Mexican citizenship, as ye know. My future is here now."

The soft warm firelight shone on her fine golden hair and reflected from her great blue eyes. It brought out the velvety flesh tones of her skin and the beautifully molded mounds of her upheld breasts. It shone on the brandy that moistened her full, almost sensuous red lips.

Jesucristo, Quint thought to himself. An intense desire for this tempting young female creature flooded through him.

"You're sure about this?" she asked.

Quint came back to cold reality. "You yourself told me my future was here in New Mexico. It was at the Pecos ruins. Don't you remember? Your words were something like this, as I recall: 'It's obvious, isn't it? What future is there for you in Canada? The States? The north? The future for you is here in New Mexico, Quintin Ker-Shaw.' "

She drained her glass and held it out to him. He refilled their glasses. They were moodily silent for a time; two strong, self-willed people who might or might not be in love with each other, yet each of them determined that *their* way would come first, above all.

Jean swirled the brandy in her glass and studied the rich amber fluid, shot through with the light of the fire. "We could come back to New Mexico someday," she suggested. "Perhaps when it is part of the United States. My father has great influence within the government. He could have you appointed to some official position."

"But *when,* lassie? *When?* It might be within a few years, a decade at most, and perhaps never."

"You know it will come to pass. Is there no way I can persuade you to come with me, to marry me and build a future together?" she asked quietly.

Was there an unspoken challenge in her meaning? An insidious craving for this young woman returned to Quint. There was an urging for her in his loins, an intense burning sensation that could only be satisfied in one way. He looked into her eyes, seeking the vaguest of invitations. He remembered her response to him in the cramped and musty little room at Pecos. What was it she had said when he had stripped her dress down to her waist? "Wait, Quint! Give me some time!" She had not refused him, in a sense. All she had asked for was time to consider the act. At that moment he had asked her how much time she wanted, and whether or not her asking for time was just a ruse to keep him away. But then, she had started for him, only to be interrupted by the voices of those who were searching for her.

"I asked for time to consider, there at Pecos Ruins," she said quietly. "Do you remember?"

It was almost as though she had read his mind. He nodded.

"I've considered," she said. She stood up.

He looked up at her. "And?"

Her answer was to drain her glass and place it on the table.

Quint stood up, naked as a jaybird. "There will be no going back this time," he warned her.

"I know," she whispered.

They came together in a crushing embrace, lips molded together. She thrust her loins hard against his. He swiftly unbuttoned the back of her dress and peeled it down to her waist. He unfastened her brassiere. She took it from his hands and threw it across the room. He pushed the close fitting gown down over her rounded hips, and it fell to the floor about her ankles. She stepped out of it and kicked it aside. He knelt before her and stripped her fine cambric drawers from her long, beautiful legs. He touched his lips to the firm mound of her belly and worked her fine silk hose down about her ankles, then removed her high-heeled black satin shoes. He stood up and drew her close. She sought his lips with a hungry passion that surprised and delighted him. He placed her on the bed and lay down beside her, resting on an elbow to look at her white body, the rose-tipped creamy mounds of her breasts and the soft mat of golden curly hair at her crotch.

"Do I please you?" she whispered.

"You're not much more than a child, at least in age. The body is that of a young woman."

She laughed softly. "Don't *I* know? Kiss me."

"Are ye sure this is what ye really want?"

"Have you ever asked any of your squaws that stupid question?" she retorted.

He grinned down at her like a hunting wolf.

"Or your New Mexican women?" Jean asked. The brandy was working well within her.

Quint shook his head.

"Or La Tules?" she added as a final thrust.

He shrugged. "Never got around to it with La Tules." He filled the brandy glasses, and as he turned again toward her she gripped his privates with a strong little hand. He dropped he glasses to the floor and rolled over on top of her, molding er breasts in his rough hands, passing his hands down her at belly to that inviting golden mat of hair. She spread her gs and wrapped her arms around his neck. They came)gether with a passion and a hunger that blotted out everyning but their desire to satisfy themselves and each other. he was good at the act, and no virgin. Quint let himself go ith a driving force that had been amiss since Don Bartolomé's nife thrust had penetrated his belly.

"My God," she murmured as Quint flung himself sideways om her and stood up beside the bed while reaching for the randy bottle. "There's breeding-stallion blood in you, Quint."

He grinned down at her. "You're nae sae bad yersel, ssie," he said in broad Scots. "Ye've been along this road efore."

She covered her eyes with a forearm. "A lost lover," she urmured. "Killed by the Seminoles."

"Aye? Another dragoon?"

"Yes."

He filled the glasses and sat down at the edge of the bed. Ye wouldn't be lying to Don Grande Rubio, eh, lass?"

She withdrew her arm and studied him. "You're no gen-.eman," she accused.

He handed her a glass. "Perhaps, but say merely an obserant lover."

She sat up and rested her back against the head of the bed. I didn't convince you then?" She sipped at the brandy.

He nodded. "Positively."

"To return with me to Washington?"

He shook his head. "That ye are a lover."

"Then this is the way it is to be? No more?"

Quint shrugged. "How can it be otherwise? With ye in Jashington and myself here in New Mexico."

"You never had any intention of going with me!" she cried.

"Is that the only reason you came to my room in the dead of ie night, knowing the casa was empty and that I was lone?"

There was no answer from Jean.

There was a new closeness between the two of them, a eeling of mutual comfort and perhaps of better understandig. Somehow both of them knew that this was only the ginning of a relationship that would last through the ears, if not in a physical sense, then one of the memory.

Jean eyed Quint's muscular torso with the thick mat of

red-golden hair on his chest and at his crotch. She looked
the livid scar that disfigured the left side of his face. S
reached out a slim and lovely hand and traced the faint li
of the bullet track that had creased him and nearly kill
him. She looked into his eyes with an unspoken question.

"A Comanchero," he said quietly.

"You killed him?"

He shook his head. "Not yet."

"But you will some day?"

"Aye."

She traced the parallel scars on his left shoulder. "These
she asked.

"Old Ephraim donated those to me; and the scar on my le
cheek."

"Old Ephraim?"

He nodded. *"Ursus horriblis,* horrible bear; the great gri
zly."

"Why do they call them that?"

He grinned crookedly. "From the Bible—Ephraim is we
ded to his idols; *leave him alone.*"

"You killed him?"

"Aye, but not alone."

"One of your partners helped you?" she asked innocentl

Quint stood up. The fire had died out. He stacked piñ
branches and logs within the fireplace and lighted the
They caught fire immediately. He stood looking down in
the crackling flames.

"Quint? What are you thinking about?" Jean asked.

He looked back at her over a shoulder. "They have
superstition here that if the piñon log fire blazes up whe
first lit and the logs stand upright against the chimney un
they are charred, sweethearts will be true."

She smiled a little. "Us?"

He came back to the bed. "Perhaps, but the logs are n
charred yet."

"You didn't answer my question."

He narrowed his eyes. "What question?"

"Who helped you kill Old Ephraim after he put his mark
you?"

He turned silently and opened a chest. He rooted through
and withdrew the grizzly-claw necklace Mountain Woma
had made for him seemingly so long ago. He had refused
for she had done as much, perhaps more, in killing the be
than he had done. He showed the necklace to Jean.

"Those are the claws that marked you?" she asked in awe.

"Aye," he replied quietly. He remembered all too well the vage battle Mountain Woman and he had fought against d Ephraim. He had been as close to death as at any her time in his dangerous way of life. He had not thought of ountain Woman for many long weeks. Her memory was ding with him. But it had been she who had saved him from rtain death that twilight in the woods.

Jean knew when to change the subject. She touched a ckered bullet hole just below his right ribs. "This?" she asked.

He threw the necklace into the chest. "Blackfoot."

"And this?" She touched a two-inch knife scar on his right cep.

He placed a hand over hers and pressed it close against his re arm. "Ab-sá-ro-ke. A Crow-Hears-with-His-Ears. He anted a red-haired scalp to show off. He didn't get it." He inned wolfishly, and Jean felt a faint chill of fear run rough her.

"You're cold?" he asked solicitously.

She looked up into his eyes. "I can easily be warmed."

He lay down beside her and drew her into his arms. This ne their lovemaking had none of the passion and wildness it of the first act. Perhaps they realized it might be the last ne together for them.

The candle guttered low.

"They'll be coming home soon," Jean whispered.

"Aye, lassie."

He helped her dress.

"When do ye leave?" he asked.

"The day after tomorrow, Quint."

They stood looking at each other. He placed his hands on ther side of her lovely face, tilted her head a little and ssed her gently. She placed a cool hand against the terrible ar on his left cheek and stroked it downward, then she rned quickly on a heel and walked to the door.

Jean turned and looked at the fireplace. "The logs are arred and still upright," she said.

She turned quickly, opened the door and left the room, osing the door softly behind her.

"Vaya," he said softly. Neither of them, impulsively or liberately, had said, "I love you." Still, there was a powerful traction between the two of them. They had not seen e last of each other.

He reached for the brandy bottle and raised it to his lips.

THIRTY-FIVE

October 1838—El Valle de Taos

The Rio Grande cut its way by means of a black tumbl'
gorge through an immense mesa in northern New Mexi
There lay the sage-brushed Taos Plain, extending for fo
miles. To the west of the river sprawled a great plateau,
Otra Banda, the free haunt of wild horses. El Valle de Taos
seven thousand feet altitude ran north and south in a nea
circular shape hemmed in by mountains flanked by the I
Grande to the west and the Sangre de Cristo Mountains
the south, east and north. The valley was seventy-five mi
north of Santa Fe and was reached from there through t
Canyon of the Rio Grande with its huge cliffs of igneous roc

The plateau was noted for the freshness and purity of
rarefied atmosphere and an illimitable clarity of light maki
all colors pure and luminous—a space so great, with vision
plain and such clear air, that human activities and mo
ment could be seen from afar and sound carried great d
tances. Here in this lovely valley little villages lay peaceful
seemingly asleep, with the tall blue mountains forming
magnificent background.

The area of Taos was in reality not one but three commur
ties. Two and a half miles northeasterly of Don Fernando
Taos was the rather dismal-looking Indian Pueblo de Taos,
the base of a contiguous mountain.

As the Pueblo de Taos was to the northeast of Taos prop
so the old Indian farming center Ranchos de Taos was to t
southwest of Taos, in the foothills of the Sangre de Crist
where the members of the Taos Pueblo had sought bett
fields for their crops.

Between the pueblo and the farming center lay the thi
and most dominant of the three communities—Don Fernan
de Taos, named after one of its leading citizens of the seve
teenth century, but simply called Taos, or "Touse" by t

ountain men who had been coming there for more than
venty years to trade in their furs.

Taos had long been a trading center, an agricultural set-
ement with an annual trade fair; a meeting place of Plains
nd Pueblo Indians, and traders from Mexico and even Old
pain itself. Here *hacendados* and villagers from all over the
rovince came to trade and do business. It was the northern-
ost town of New Mexico, nearest to the teeming beaver
reams of the looming mountains. Since 1815, the mountain
en, a race of men apart, had sooner or later come to Taos
ke buffalo to a salt lick. They had done much for the
evelopment of Taos. The town became famous to them, or
erhaps notorious as the place of "brown wimmen and white
kker." *Aguardiente de Taos*, a whiskey made from wheat,
ecame the mind-blasting "Taos Lightnin'."

In Taos, as in Santa Fe, a man could buy a Mexican woman
r twenty dollars and Indian women for less. Some bold
ntrepreneurs established a thriving trade by capturing Ute
nd Digger women and driving them to Taos or Santa Fe like
heep, forcing them to forage for their own food on the
urney. They were sold for what the traders could get. Many
f them were bought and forced into prostitution by their
asters, or kept as concubines until no longer wanted, then
rced out into the streets to beg or adopt prostitution. Others
ere bought and sold like horses or mules.

The houses hid behind great expanses of mud walls with a
w tiny windows almost concealed by thick wooden cross-
ars. There was nothing inviting about those walls. The
arsh grip of poverty was on that land. The peons were
ppressed and helpless to do anything about it. The majority
f them lived in tiny adobe houses or shacks, some of them
aving but one room. They subsisted mainly on beans, chiles
nd tortillas and seldom saw a whole peso. They were com-
letely at the mercy of their masters; some of them worked a
fetime without ever getting out of debt to their *patrón*.
lany couples lived in sin because they could not pay the
hurch fees. Young daughters were sometimes sold to help
ie remainder of the family survive.

The mountain men, trappers and traders did not, as a rule,
old the inhabitants of the Valley of Taos in high esteem,
onsidering them depraved, indolent, untrustworthy, dishon-
st, cowardly, servile, ignorant, superstitious and dirty. Some
ven considered the Indians superior to the Mexicans. The
wo things the trappers and traders did admire about the

317

Taosenos, whatever their vices, were their hospitality a
their women, despite their lack of "modesty." The pries
were considered immoral, avaricious and unduly influenti
in politics. The officials were corrupt, ignorant and rep
sented a political system that was undemocratic and ar
trary. To the Americans the Mexican government w
infinitely worse than none.

Taos had early become a center for foreigners and Ame
cans who wanted to avoid the grafting Santa Fe officials a
used Taos as a supply base because of its proximity to t
beaver-trapping mountains and streams. As such, it w
ideal. Thus it became the center for foreign-born residents
New Mexico. They became so influential they could intin
date, bribe and influence the local *alcalde* for special favo
In short, Taos had become quite "Americanized," althou
illicit trade had become well established long before t
arrival of the first gringos. Taos was more "cosmopolita
than Santa Fe, and many of the foreigners became naturaliz
citizens.

Many of these naturalized citizens had remained Ame
cans at heart. Even now they were concerned about t
administration of justice and the protection of their proper
rights as they settled into careers more sedentary tha
trapping. They resented the fact that such a fine land, aboun
ing in nature's favors, was occupied by men who appeared
be incapable of either moral or political advancement. The
was a strong undercurrent in favor of American acquisiti
of New Mexico.

Quintin Kershaw, Luke Connors and their three Delawa
partners had left Santa Fe for Taos late in October, the
principal objective being to winter on the immense Vasqu
Grant east of the Sangre de Cristos. Thomas Byrne h
previously arranged for some of the peons, servants and oth
employees of the former Vasquez holdings in El Valle de Ta
to form the core of the old Vasquez settlement that Tor
Governor Armijo and Quint Kershaw planned to reinhab
and restore to prosperity. The first contingent had alrea
left Taos, and the remainder were even then preparing
leave. A number of them had been longtime peons ar
servitors on the Vasquez land which still remained in Vasqu
hands—those of Guadalupe "Lupita" Vasquez. She had go
into an extended period of mourning after the death of h
father and had refused to see anyone other than close rel
tives.

318

The Vasquez hacienda, El Cerrillo de Vasquez, stood alone
a a low flat-crowned hill sloping down toward the town some
iles to the west. It was a great house, seemingly a fragment
Old Spain transplanted to northern New Mexico. Sun,
ind, rain and snow, cobiined with the passage of many
ars and the effects of many past Indian attacks, had soft-
ied the huge sprawling casa into a moundlike structure of
Iden-brown adobe. It stood just short of a huge bosque of
nerable cottonwoods whose restless leaves dappled the
re earth with lights and shadows. On the other side of the
ove an icy racing stream had been captured into an *acequia
adre,* or mother irrigation ditch, from whose sides, like the
ng teats of a bitch hound, there stretched branch *acequias*
water the many fields surrounding the hacienda.

The fortresslike walls of the house were two feet thick for
armth in winter and coolness in summer. Tiny bits of mica
inted from the walls of the house as the sun struck them.
here were only a few tiny windows with oiled paper panes
irred with wood or iron. A long narrow veranda on the front
Id a thick double door, studded with nails and heavily
irred within like the gate of a medieval keep. Behind the
use was a huge corral with walls ten feet high, their tops
iked with vicious cactus plants. There was only one way in
id out, a solid ten-foot-high carriage gate swung on massive
ind-forged hinges. The house itself was said to contain
tween twenty-five and thirty rooms, but only those who
ved in it, or were permitted to visit, such as relatives and
ose friends, knew the exact number, and some of them were
t even sure about it. Beyond the house and the corral were
itbuildings, sheds, servants' quarters and several corrals
naller than that which was really part of the hacienda
use.

Quintin Kershaw rode alone from Taos to the Vasquez
acienda one early morning late in October mounted on
andy, a coyote dun gelding seventeen hands high, with re-
rves of speed and power which never ceased to amaze him.
had been the parting gift of La Tules, who had won it in a
ime of monte. Quint wore a well-tailored suit of finest
ack-dyed buckskin with silver buttons molded on order for
m by Matias Lucero, the best of the Santa Fe silversmiths,
the shape of a badger with teeth bared as in battle. His
mbrero was heavy and banded with silver. His boots were
the finest leather, with silver-chased spurs, which he wore
ore for effect than use. In New Mexico of that day a man

had to dress to fit the role he played. That had been t
advice of both Tom Byrne and Manuel Armijo. His sad
was of California style and make with a saucer-shaped ho
On each side of the pommel there hung two embossed leath
holsters with covering flaps in which he sometimes carri
his pair of matched Paterson Colts. If afoot, he usually thr
one of the Colts through his sash. His Hawken rifle w
encased in a leather scabbard and slung alongside the sad
and under his right thigh.

Federico Casias came around the side of the casa when
saw the lone rider approaching. He narrowed his eyes a
shaded them with a hand until he recognized Quint. *"Ma*
Santisima!" he cried. "Holy Mary! *Qué hombrón!* What
man! Is it indeed Quint Kershaw?" He grinned widely.

Quint reined in the dun and extended a hand. "How does
go, *compadre?"*

Federico shrugged. "Not well, Quint." He flung out an a
to indicate the hacienda and its environs. "You can see
yourself."

Quint dismounted. He winced a little and paled as t
healing wound drew up a little. "Lupita, she's home t
day?" he asked.

Federico nodded. "As always. She has not left the hou
since the death of Don Francisco. She'll likely be in de
mourning for a year, possibly longer."

Quint leaned back against the side of the dun and shap
two *cigarritos.* He placed one between Federico's lips a
lighted it, then lighted his own. He looked about himself.
Cerrillo de Vasquez was indeed a beautiful place, with a p
of violence and blood to sustain its very existence, and now
seemed as though it would soon pass from the hands of t
Vasquez family who had lived there for 185 years.

"You seem to have recovered from your wound," Federi
suggested.

Quint nodded. "Aye, to some extent. The steel was sha
and fairly clean. The wound was not too deep, otherwis
would not be here."

The vaquero crossed himself. *"Gracias a Dios.* And that
should be Don Bartolomé! Would to God that it had be
another!"

Quint shook his head. "The ways of God are sometim
inscrutable, my friend."

Federico was puzzled. "How do you mean?"

"If I had not been standing close behind Don Bartolo

hat night, Governor Armijo would be dead, and Don Bartolomé executed and his lands confiscated."

"And you would not have become a citizen overnight and a *hacendado* of the Vasquez Grant, partners with Governor Armijo and Dr. Tomás Byrne."

Quint half smiled. "You've got the idea. However, Don Bartolomé is a fugitive with a price on his head, and Lupita sits there in that great casa in deep mourning with a rather bleak future."

"That is so?" Federico studied Quint. "Is that why you are here?"

Quint nodded. He looked at the blank facade of the house. "If she'll see me," he said quietly.

"To ask her hand in marriage?"

Quint looked quickly at Federico. "No! Just to offer my assistance and sympathy to her."

"She knows about that gringa woman with the yellow hair, friend," Federico warned.

"She's gone back to the States."

Federico tilted his head to one side. "But with some arrangement with you, perhaps?"

Quint shook his head. "She married Lieutenant Shelby Calhoun in Santa Fe the day before they left to return to the States."

Federico studied the expressionless scarred face. "You loved her?" he asked sympathetically.

Quint shrugged.

"She loved you then?"

"Who knows the way of a woman's heart?"

Federico nodded sympathetically. "But she was rich and beautiful, Quint."

"Aye, but such a one must wear the trousers in one's family. *That* I cannot abide."

"Where will you ride when you leave here?"

Quint pointed. "Beyond the mountains."

"The Vasquez Grant?"

"Yes. I plan to winter there. In the spring there will be much work to do on the land, but now we must get ready for the winter. The settlement on the Rio Brioso must be rebuilt and the houses readied for the winter."

"And fortified against the Indians," Federico added dryly. He shook his head. "Men have tried for fifty years to settle that place, and all have failed."

"Vasquezes," Quint said quietly. *"I am not a Vasquez."*

Federico opened and then closed his mouth. He had seen the set of Quint's jaw and the look in those glacial eyes of his.

"I can use a man like you, Federico," Quint suggested.

The *vaquero* smiled quickly. "I'm your man!" His face changed. "But, Lupita . . . Before God, Quint, she needs me."

"There is no future here for you."

"That is true." There was a note of indecision in Federico's voice.

Quint looked at the house again. "This is a lovely place. The land is fine and productive. Coupled with the rest of the former Vasquez land here in El Valle de Taos, a man could do well."

"What do you mean?"

"You know this land. Thomas Byrne has control of the portion Don Bartolomé threw away on the monte tables. In time, you understand, his land could be rejoined to that of El Cerrillo and once again it would flourish and be productive."

Federico studied Quint. "You mean there is a chance that you might eventually take over El Cerrillo?"

"It is in the back of my mind, once I reestablish the Rio Brioso settlement and make it successful."

"But Lupita, what of her?"

"That is why I am here, Federico."

"To offer her sympathy and assistance, as I've said."

"But not marriage?"

"This is not the time. After her period of mourning, when the loss of her father has dimmed a little, perhaps she'll consider such a proposal."

Federico nodded. "You are learning the ways of our people, Don Quintin. What is you want me to do?"

"Wait until I've seen her. If she agrees to consider marriage with me in time, I want you to stay here with her and help her as much as you can. I'll pay your wages. In fact, I'll double them from what you now earn."

Federico half smiled. "Such munificence! I haven't seen even one cuartillo this past year."

"Whatever your wage scale is, I'll pay your due wages, and double those that will be forthcoming."

Federico thrust out a hand to meet that of Quint. "And if she does not agree to wait for you?"

"You are your own man. You can join me at the Rio Brioso if you wish."

"It's a deal! I didn't want to leave her anyway."

Federico took Quint's dun. Quint walked slowly toward the

322

house accompanied by the sound of his boot heels on the hard earth and the faint musical tinkling of his silver inlaid Chihuahua spurs.

A silent Indian woman opened the door. She padded noiselessly into the dark, quiet interior of the huge house. He stood in the great sala, a room which extended across the entire front of the house. The ceiling was low, supported by heavy beams between which colored willow withes had been laid in herringbone fashion. The walls were covered with snow-white gypsum plaster. The lower part of the walls had been hung with light-red cotton cloth to protect clothing against contact with the gypsum. There were two large beehive fireplaces in opposite corners, each stacked with fragrant piñon faggots. Folded mattresses had been placed against the walls for couches and covered with Navajo blankets in bright colors and varying patterns. There were two low tables of excellent native craftsmanship and a few chairs with rawhide seats. The floor was of packed earth as hard as rock after the footfalls of generations. Crucifixes and saints' images hung on the walls, while in niches about the room the stolid wooden faces of *bultos* and *santos* stared back at Quint. A niche had been cut into the thick wall beside one of the fireplaces, and therein stood a severe-faced *santo* made by the Franciscan Third Order and therefore a representation of St. Francis. He wore hand-sewn clothing fashioned after the best style of the day.

She came noiselessly to the door that opened into the interior of the house. Lupita was dressed in funereal black and wore a heavy black lace mantilla over a comb thrust into the back of her thick hair. She held the mantilla across the lower part of her face to reveal only her great luminous eyes, darkly shadowed from grief.

"My sympathies, señorita," Quint said quietly.

Lupita nodded. "Thank you, señor. Please be seated."

Quint waited until she had seated herself on a large Spanish chest covered with ornamental carving and fitted with ancient cumbrous hand-forged fittings and a huge lock. He seated himself on one of the rawhide chairs.

"Your wound, it troubles you?" she asked quietly.

Quint shrugged. "Only when I laugh," he said. He wanted to see her smile, but she did not. He realized then that it hadn't been quite the proper thing to say.

"I have great sorrow that such a terrible thing was done to you by my brother."

323

Quint waved a hand. "It was quite accidental, I assur you." The lie fell flat.

"You are staying here in New Mexico?"

"Yes." Did she not know about his role as *hacendado* of th former Vasquez Grant?

She studied his clothing and then lifted her great eyes t meet his. Was there the faintest trace of a smile on her lovel face? "As *hacendado*, señor?" she asked dryly.

He nodded. "You knew about it then?"

"Yes. News travels fast about either good fortune or bad."

"Which of those do you consider that news to be?"

She looked away. "Good for you, señor."

"My name is Quintin. My friends call me Quint."

She looked back at him. "Or Big Red? Perhaps Big Re Badger? Or is it Don Grande Rubio?"

"That is unkind," he gently chided her.

"I meant no offense. My apologies."

"We're very formal with each other," he said dryly. "I thinl I know why. I apologize for not coming to your home in Sant Fe. I have no excuse. I drank too much."

"With La Tules."

"Aye, the same."

"A notorious woman."

Quint shrugged.

"But she likes you. All women seem to like you."

Quint waved a deprecating hand. "Not all, surely!"

"Most," she said. This time she really smiled.

"Jean Allan is now Señora Shelby Calhoun," he said. "*I* you're interested."

"Why should I be?"

He shrugged. "No reason."

"Why are you really here, other than to offer me condo lences on the passing of my father?" she asked pointedly.

Quint stood up. This was the way he liked to do things— direct and to the point. "I'm leaving this day for the settle ment on the Rio Brioso. I will not propose marriage at thi time, but I want you to think about it when you have completed your period of mourning. I know it might be a long time, perhaps a year, but I'm willing to wait. When you are through mourning, please notify me, and I'll return here a once."

She looked up at him. She seemed so small and fragile with those outsize eyes in her small oval face.

He bent his head a little. "Lupita?" he asked quietly.

She stood up quickly and came to him. She rested her head against his chest. *"Gracias a Dios,"* she murmured through her tears.

As he rode from El Cerrillo, he looked back from the first turn in the road. A small figure clad in funereal black stood beneath the long portal in front of the main house. From somewhere in the past a faint recollection came to him—in the bright clear light of an early summer morning in the valley of the Popo Agie. A slight woman figure had stood on a low hilltop near the village looking in his direction.

The faint metallic sound of copper bells came from Taos on the morning wind as Quint Kershaw rode around the first turn in the road and out of sight.

THIRTY-SIX

Fall, winter and spring, 1838–1839.
Don Quintin Kershaw, *hacendado.*

The Vasquez Grant was situated on the watershed of the Rio Brioso, or Lively River, on the eastern slope of the Sangre de Cristo Range. The Brioso flowed for over thirty-five miles after rising in a little gem of a lake which nestled close to the foot of a towering naked peak just above the timberline. As it gained volume, speed and strength it plunged into a long, narrow, twisting canyon of dark rock, foamed and splashed its dashing way through rocky gorges and then vanished into thick forests of blue spruce at eight thousand to ten thousand feet, thence through a box canyon to emerge into a valley which widened toward the distant hazy plains, with the ridges parting and dwindling in size and height. Here the river passed from the spruce forest into stands of ponderosa, or Western yellow pine, tall stately trees with red-brown bark and huge crowns. The river passed through open meadows, shielded from distant view by its willow-lined banks. Here and there on the meadows lone pines stood as stately sentinels.

The land was alive with game. It was a fertile land ripe and ready for the hand of man. There was timber enough to build a small city, great stands of virgin pine, and unlimited supplies of firewood for the cold winters. Thousands of acres of rich bottomland and flatland were tinted with the purple of ripe grama grass, the richest forage in the world. The range on the lower ridges and flats could support thousands of cattle, sheep and horses. Along the lower reaches of the Brioso on the flatlands, well protected from prevailing winds by close ridges, were the semi-ruins of the old settlement started by two generations of the Vasquez family. Just beyond the lower slopes of the ridges was the trace of the Mountain Branch of the Santa Fe Trail, and 35 miles to the south it joined up with the Cimarron Cut-off. Beyond the Vasquez Grant to the north another royal land grant extended for perhaps 100 miles. To the south other land grants coupled together reached as far as the Capitán Mountains, about 250 miles away.

The Vasquez Grant along the Rio Brioso was therefore a frontier to the east of the central line of settlement of New Mexico, a narrow strip of civilization following the course of the Rio Grande del Norte and some of its northern tributary streams where tiny settlements clung along the watercourses. Beyond this central line of Spanish settlement the colonists were surrounded on both sides and to the north by hostile tribes—the Moache Utes and Jicarilla Apaches to the north, the Navajos to the west, the fierce and predatory Comanches, Kiowas and Faraon Apaches to the east and the Mescalero Apaches to the south. There was absolutely no military protection available in the northeast, and the owners of the various land grants had given them up as hopeless. Perhaps that was why Don Bartolomé Vasquez had been so quick to bet his inheritance against a sure thing—La Tules' bank and monte sala, which was indeed a veritable gold mine.

The Jicarillas and Moache Utes were comparatively peaceful at this time. The Utes, supremely Mountain Indians, relatives of the Shoshoni and the Comanches, had been fierce raiders in the earlier days of the land grants and had allied themselves with the Comanches. In the middle of the eighteenth century they had joined with the Jicarillas and had later fought with the Spaniards against the Comanche and Kiowa raiders from the plains. The Faraon Apaches, who lived far out on the plains, still raided the Jicarillas, the Moache Utes and the Pueblo groups of the northeast.

In late October the Taos justice of the peace, one Cornelio Vigil, came to the embryo Rio Brioso settlement, and in the presence of five witnesses confirmed the possession of the Vasquez Grant by the new owners—Thomas Byrne, Governor Manuel Armijo and Quintin Kershaw. Governor Armijo was represented by one of his aides. Cornelio Vigil followed the ancient procedure of possession by having erected a series of seven mounds to mark the somewhat vague boundaries. He then took Thomas Byrne and Quintin Kershaw by the hand, the aide holding the hand of Thomas Byrne, and walked on the land with them, causing them to throw earth, pull up weeds and show other evidences of possession. After that he declared them in "perfect and personal possession," and he immediately returned to Taos to file the new document of possession.

No time had been wasted by Luke Connors in getting the settlement started. Timber had been cut to temporarily roof over the stone buildings for the approaching winter, and a great deal more had been cut, barked and left to season for more permanent repairs to be made in the spring. The Delawares spent most of their time hunting, bringing in great quantities of buffalo meat and hides, mountain sheep, venison and bear meat. Quantities of corn and wheat meal were brought from Taos. Santiago Zaldivar, a *viejo*, an old one, who had lived on the Brioso in the days of Don Francisco and whose age was great for the dangerous life he had lived on the frontier, served as Luke's *segundo* and had crossed the Rio Grande to the west to trade for horses and mules with the Utes. He had also managed to make a good trade deal with the Apaches, a right dangerous business, for mules and horses they had stolen in Sonora. Thomas Byrne sent up wagonloads of tools, seed for the spring planting, cheap coarse yard goods for clothing and bedding, trade rifles, gunpowder, caps and flints, bullet molds and lead. Luke made certain that each reconstructed building had additional loopholes cut through the thick walls. Now and again scouts were sent to the east out on the plains to keep an eye out for wandering bands of Apaches, Kiowas, Comanches and perhaps Pawnees as well, although this area was nearly beyond the farthermost boundaries of their almost limitless raiding range.

By the time the first snows whitened the tips of the towering peaks the little settlement of Rio Brioso was fairly well set for the winter. Those women and children who had been left behind in the safety of Taos Valley were brought to the settlement. There would be no Indian raiding during the long cold winter, but in the spring, when the grass sprouted thick enough for the ponies, they would surely come.

Soft spring was on the land when Antonio Ochoa came in from Tequesquite Creek, where he had left a westward raiding party of Comanches and his two erstwhile "partners," Jake Stow and Kiowa. News had drifted eastward from the Rio Brioso country that once again colonists had reestablished a settlement on the old Vasquez Grant. It was probably more curiosity than cupidity that brought him back. When much younger he had participated in the last raid on the Brioso, the one that had driven the few survivors back through Mora Canyon to Taos. It had been Antonio himself who had put a bullet in the left knee of old Don Francisco rather than killing him. It gave Antonio great pleasure to cripple his enemies. Before God, what fun was it to kill a man forthwith? He had once been a bound peon in the employ of Don Francisco. He had never forgotten that humiliation. Was it the old man himself who had reestablished the settlement on the Brioso? Antonio smiled. This time he'd kill the old sonofabitch. There was really no great reason to raid the Brioso this spring as far as Antonio was concerned. The Kotsotekas had supplied gold in dust and tiny nuggets in exchange for the trade goods Antonio and his partners had brought from Bent's Fort.

Antonio cautiously moved to the southwest and crossed the Canadian at Cañon Largo, then swung up northerly again after he reached the Gallinas, as though he was coming from Santa Fe by way of Vegas Grandes. It was wise to be cautious; some people might recognize him for what he was—a Comanchero, an outcast, a pariah.

It was Joshua the Delaware who first saw Antonio Ochoa in the vicinity of Rio Brioso. He was on outpost duty, established by Luke Connors as soon as the first sprouts of grass heralded the coming spring. Joshua had a remarkable memory; he rode at great speed to Quintin Kershaw and described the man he had seen approaching the valley.

Quint saddled his dun, grabbed his telescope and rode to just below the crest of a ridge overlooking the trail from Vegas Grandes. There he dropped flat and adjusted his telescope to focus it on the lone traveler riding leisurely not more than two hundred yards down the long slope. He narrowed his eyes. Then he nodded. It was one of the Comancheros.

Quint rode swiftly back to the settlement and dismounted before the dun came to a full halt. "Luke!" he shouted. "Goddammit! Where the hell are ye?"

"Right behind yuh, Big Red," Luke said.

Quint whirled. "I think it's one of the four Comancheros who stole my plews—the one called Antonio."

Luke raised his eyebrows. "Within rifle range and yuh back to tell me about it?"

Quint shook his head. "Ye ever stop to think if he's still with the Kotsotekas he might be scoutin' out the layout here for a raid?"

Luke shrugged. "Possible," he murmured. "But, I still can't figger out why yuh didn't kill him."

Quint shook his head. "Ye ain't too bright, Luke, but ye have a good heart anyway." He looked about at the settlers who had gathered about him and Luke. *"Escuche!* Listen! This man who comes here is a Comanchero. A man who robbed me of a small fortune in beaver plews and other furs. I don't know if he's still with the Comanches, but we'll take no chances. He's here to spy us out, I wager. Let him look around. Act stupid. Let him leave when he's ready. Some of our men will follow him to see where he goes. If he goes to the camp of the Comanches, which I suspect will not be far off, he'll bring them back to raid us. We'll be ready for them. We'll teach them a lesson they'll never forget and safeguard the future of your homes, Rio Brioso and this land grant."

"And if he does not go back to the Comanches?" Santiago Zaldivar asked quietly. "Shall we kill this Comanchero?"

"No! Gawddammit! He's *mine!*" Quint spat out. "If he comes back here with the Kotsotekas I want no one to kill him. He's mine! Ye understand, damn ye all? *He's mine!*"

"Maybe his two partners will come too, Quint," Luke suggested quietly. "Are they yours too, or can we get in on a little of the killin'?"

Quint laughed. "Be my guest," he said, "but only after I get first crack at them, and if I miss, they're yours."

"The Comanchero comes," Joshua murmured.

Quint entered his quarters and watched through the slit in the wooden shutter of one of the loopholed windows. The Comanchero came closer up the single street of the little settlement, smiling affably and shouting greetings to one and all.

Antonio spent that night in Brioso as guest of Santiago

Zaldivar and his fifteen-year-old half-breed wife. She wasn't bad, Antonio thought. He'd see to it that she wasn't harmed in the raid. There were plenty of other women and many children in the settlement, as well as many fine horses and mules, enough to satisfy the Kotsotekas. He had noted the fine herds of horses and cattle, the flocks of sheep on the distant hills, and although the settlement was in an early formative stage there was an air of productivity and permanency about it. He had noted the few weapons in sight—rusty old *escopetas* that might blow up at the first firing, doing more damage to the shooter than the target, a number of *cibolero* lances that were of little use unless the wielders were mounted, and some *carcages* of bows and arrows for buffalo hunting. He did not see the racked shining new trade rifles in the improvised armory, nor the stone magazine hidden at the edge of the village, holding many kegs of gunpowder and cases of percussion caps. He did not see Quint Kershaw, Luke Connors, the deadly Delawares or any of the tough young New Mexicans who had been well trained during the winter in the use of the rifle.

When Antonio Ochoa left Brioso early one morning, ostensibly to travel to the north, he did not see the three horsemen paralleling his course out of sight beyond the next ridge. Black Beaver, Joshua and Jesus Martinez, a *genízaro* whose father had been a Moache Ute, were still on his trail by late morning when he turned toward the east and rode to the Canadian River, following it toward Vermejo Creek, which he reached long after dark on a worn-out horse.

The Kotsoteka raiding party was not a large one, some thirty warriors in all, mostly young men, some of whom were on their first raid. When the grim Kotsotekas heard the Comanchero's news they nodded in satisfaction. It was as they had suspected. The stupid Mexicans had walked into a trap of their own devising.

Jake Stow squatted on his heels sifting fine earth through his fingers as he listened to Antonio's glowing account of the new settlement. He looked sideways at Kiowa. "What do you think?" he asked.

Kiowa shrugged. "Easy pickings."

"Any soldiers around, Antonio?" Jake asked.

Antonio shook his head. He grinned. "The government can't afford to keep a garrison in that country, and besides even if they did, you know how they are armed and trained

330

These settlers have only a few rust-eaten *escopetas* and a few horns full of rotten Mexican gunpowder."

Jake looked up toward the western sky. "Seems too damned simple to me, *amigos*."

Kiowa grinned. "You afraid?" he asked.

"You know what happened when them damned mountain men raided the Kotsoteka camp at Cañon Chacuaco, and what happened when the full weight of the Kotsotekas was thrown against them right out on the open ground. Them bastards defeated the Kotsotekas on their own ground!"

"And likely died of thirst escaping that night," Antonio added.

Kiowa turned slowly and looked at the New Mexican with his one eye. "No," he said quietly. "I want that goddam red-headed sonofabitch—the one that stole that woman from me and put out my eye."

"He's dead, I tell you," Antonio insisted.

A hand shot out and gripped the New Mexican's left wrist. Kiowa drew Antonio closer to himself and looked into his eyes with an unblinking stare that almost unnerved the tough Comanchero. "No," Kiowa hissed. "He's mine. He can't be dead. *He's mine.*"

"What's the plan here?" Jake asked to change the subject.

Antonio rubbed his wrist. "They ride tonight and get in position on the ridge just to the south of the settlement. The horses will be left there and the warriors will go in just before dawn on foot to get mounts from the horse herd. Then they'll sweep back through the village and catch the people in their beds. It shouldn't take long."

"What about us?"

Antonio shrugged. "If you want to stay in good with the Kotsotekas you'll go in with them, at least into the village." He grinned. "Some nice women there. Grab them off before the bucks get to them and claim them, then trade them off for the horses and mules. That'll be our chance to get to hell away from these people. We can drive the horses down to Albuquerque maybe and get rid of them for money. Shit! With the gold we got from the Kotsotekas and the money from the horses we can live like *gente fina,* for a time at least. I'm damned tired of this life anyway. It was fun and profitable while it lasted, but I'm getting too damned old to live out on the plains like a Comanche or Kiowa."

Jake nodded. He looked at the mixed breed. "Kiowa?"

"Count me in," the breed said. An eerie look drifted across

his rough face. "Mebbe that red-headed Montero Americano' here somewhere."

It was in that cold and dark period just before the dawn when man's spirits are at their lowest ebb. Brioso was hardly visible in the clinging darkness of the valley. All doors were barred; all windows were shuttered; not a light showed.

The Kotsotekas left their trail horses in charge of three untried braves on the reverse side of the ridge crest, just to the east of the village, with the open land stretching down almost imperceptibly to the distant and unseen valley of the Canadian. The raiders moved against the faint intermittent wind like hunting cats down the long easy ridge slope. Soon they were between the quiet horse herd and the sleeping village. Antonio, Kiowa and Jake loitered far in the rear with Antonio the closest behind the warriors. In that case, they would be closer to the village and the women than the bucks

It was very quiet.

The noiseless flitting figures of the raiders were almost upon the outlying horses of the big herd.

Quint Kershaw swung himself up into the saddle of his coyote dun. "Now," he said over his shoulder.

Ten splendidly mounted horsemen, New Mexicans all, followed Quint down the long slope on the far side of the horse herd from the raiders. The faint drumming of forty-four hoofs on the soft ground came to the startled Comanches They turned to run.

Quint held his reins between his teeth, guiding Dandy by the pressure of thighs and knees, as he unholstered his twin Paterson Colts in a swift cross-arm draw. He raised them overhead and fired them in rotation toward the night sky Each of his followers emptied the pair of single-shot pistols with which they were armed. As they charged they shouted like madmen. The drumming hoofs, staccato pistol explosions and flashes and the fierce yelling of the horsemen stampeded the horses and mules down the gentle slope of the valley directly toward the main street of Brioso. The rear warriors of the Kotsotekas were overtaken by the thundering herd. A few of them darted to either side. A few more waited until the horses were upon them, gripped them by their manes and swung up on their backs to race along with the herd.

All along both sides of the one street of Brioso, rifles were thrust through loopholes. As the fleeing warriors raced through the village a ripple of concentrated riflefire tore into their flanks. Slugs that missed ricocheted from the stone buildings and sang eerily into space or whined off between the close-set buildings.

The handful of raiders who reached the end of the street thought they had won free. The sky was faintly graying. The growing light made the stampeded raiders fair targets for Luke Connors, Moccasin and five of the best shots of the settlement. It was like shooting fish in a barrel.

The three untried braves who were the horseholders of the Comanche herd beyond the ridge crest had heard the gun reports, wild shouting, and thundering of hoofs. They did not panic—they were *Kotsotekas!* They mounted their horses to lead the remainder of the horses down the slope to the raiders. In so doing, they sharply silhouetted themselves against the faintly graying sky. Three Hawken rifles flashed. Three braves were knocked from their horses' backs. Black Beaver, Joshua and Jesus Martinez trotted down the slope reloading as they ran. They did not see Jake Stow and Kiowa run through the semidarkness leading their horses, to vanish over the next ridge and race out toward the graying plains to the east.

Here and there along the single street of Brioso a gun cracked as the last of the raiders were ignished off. Horsemen galloped off to round up the stampeded herd. Quint Kershaw leaned against the side of his dun reloading his twin Patersons.

"Don Quintin!" Santiago Zaldivar shouted. "We have something for you!"

Quint looked up. The old one held his rifle at waist height with the muzzle touching the back of the Comanchero Antonio. Antonio narrowed his eyes as the tall man dressed like one of the *gente fina* walked quickly toward him with a catlike stride. He had seen someone who walked like that somewhere.

Quint halted ten feet from the Comanchero. "You know me, Comanchero?" he asked quietly.

Antonio slowly shook his head, but there was doubt in his hard dark eyes.

"Well?" Quint asked.

Antonio shook his head. "You have the advantage of me, sir." He smiled a little.

Quint pointed to the north. "There was a Montero Americano who found a lost valley not far from the headwaters of the Rio Grande del Norte. He had a Shoshoni woman with him. He trapped for two seasons and amassed many prime beaver plews and other furs. Four men came to that valley. They

333

killed the woman, and thought they killed the mountain man. They stole all of his goods and his plews. They took them to Bent's Fort, claiming them as their own, then took the trade goods out on the *llano* to trade for horses and mules, and maybe gold, with the Kotsotekas at Cañon Chacuaco."

The people of Rio Brioso had gathered behind the Comanchero. He looked back over both shoulders. Their faces were expressionless. There was a Montero Americano among the people, a man with strange green eyes like bottle glass, and just as cold. There were three Indians standing beside him. Delawares?

Antonio faced Quint. "Is it possible *you* are that Montero Americano?" he asked.

"You're gettin' close, yuh sonofabitch," Luke commented dryly.

Quint nodded. "What happened to the woman?"

Antonio shrugged. "She's dead, I think."

"You don't know?"

"She was alive the last I saw her."

"When you raped her."

Antonio nodded. "That is the way of things, señor."

"*Your* way; the way of the Comancheros."

"I was not the last one with her."

"Who was?"

"The 'rough-face,' he who is named Kiowa. The one I think you put out his bad eye at Cañon Chacuaco. Yes, it must have been you!"

Quint looked beyond Antonio at Luke.

Luke shook his head. "This bastard is the only one we found, Quint."

Antonio wet his lips. "Kiowa was the last one with the woman. He liked it that way. He had his own way with her. After that, no man would want her, you understand? I wanted to take her with us, but they would not." He smiled. "After all, she was only an Indian."

"Only an Indian," Quint repeated mechanically. He looked directly at the Comanchero, but it was as though he did not really see him or was looking right through him.

"The lodge was in flames when we left," Antonio added. "No one could live in there."

"He's right," Luke said.

Antonio held out his hands. "Let me go," he pleaded. "I didn't kill her. As for the furs, here, I'll pay you my share of the loot for my freedom." He reached inside his jacket and

334

withdrew a buckskin pouch. He untied the draw strings and poured gold dust mingled with tiny nuggets and what the Mexicans call *chispas,* or sparks, into the cup of his left hand. He held it out toward Quint.

Quint took three strides forward and struck the hand of the Mexican with the edge of his hand. The gold flew glittering through the air and fell to the ground.

Antonio slowly rubbed the hand against the side of his thigh. "You are a fool," he murmured. He knew then he was going to die. He looked about. "The brave Montero Americano," he sneered. "Facing down a lone unarmed man." He spat on the ground at Quint's feet. *"Cobarde!"* he shouted.

The scar on Quint's left cheek tightened almost imperceptibly. "How do you want to fight?" he asked. "Pistols, rifles, knives, boots and fists? Name it, *cobarde. . . ."*

Antonio smiled mechanically. He was a master of knife fighting. "Knives," he said.

"Be careful, *patrón,*" Santiago warned.

Quint shook his head. During the long winter months he had whiled away the time learning some of the intricacies of fighting Mexican-style with the knife. There was no better master of the art than Santiago Zaldivar. Even Santiago had been forced to admit Quint had possibilities, for a gringo.

The sun was tinting the eastern sky as Quint and Antonio stripped off their jackets and shirts to stand bare from the waist up. Thoei villagers who had never seen Quint's bare torso looked in awe at the manifold scars on the firm flesh.

A ring was formed by the people in the center of the street. The two combatants circled each other slowly, keeping their eyes on each other's eyes. The blades were extended and tapped together to feel for strength and weakness. The faint clinking together of the blades, the shuffling of feet on the ground and the harsh breathing of the knife fighters was all that could be heard.

Antonio thrust hard. Quint parried. The blades rose up, locked together, as the two powerful men struggled for the advantage. Antonio brought up a knee toward Quint's crotch, but a hard left fist glanced off his jaw as Quint threw him backward. They circled.

The very tip of the New Mexican's blade traced a faint course across Quint's chest. Tiny droplets like ruby beads on a string rose to the surface and then began to run down into the thick mat of reddish hair on Quint's chest.

The blades constantly locked, rose, and then one or the

other of the two opponents threw the other back. Again Antonio scored. This time it was a traced fine line across Quint's powerful left biceps.

Antonio grinned. "Enough?" he asked.

Quint shook his head.

"I can kill you, gringo," the Comanchero boasted.

Quint nodded. "Go ahead," he suggested.

Antonio charged, throwing caution to the winds, thrusting for Quint's guts. But the big red-headed mountain man was no longer in front of him. He leaped to one side and extended a long right leg. Antonio fell over it and hit the ground.

"Now, *patrón!*" the settlers shouted.

Quint waited, slightly crouched, blade extended. "Get up, you sonofabitch," he said in a lwa voice.

The man was good, perhaps much better than Quint. He jumped to his feet. His strength was still there. He had sensed a weakening in the gringo. He did not know, of course, of the wound Quint had suffered at the hands of Don Bartolomé. Antonio charged. His reddened blade did not meet a metallic parry, but rather an outthrust left arm and solid muscle and bone. The blade sank into the forearm between the two bones. The people gasped as blood spurted. Quint dragged the Comanchero aside with his hooked left arm. Antonio would not release the knife. That was his mistake. Quint's blade was plunged deep into Antonio's belly low and to one side. A powerful hand and arm dragged the keen steel first to the left across the pit of the stomach, then back again on an upward course and then hard right again in an exaggerated Z shape, completely disemboweling the Comanchero.

Quint raised his head and looked about himself with an unseeing stare. He quickly withdrew the knife from his left forearm and threw it down on the body of Antonio. "Luke," he said quietly. Luke darted forward and caught Quint before he hit the ground.

Santiago Zaldivar looked at Quint as Luke helped him to his quarters. "He has created a legend in his own time," he said proudly.

THIRTY-SEVEN

It was Federico Casias who came to Rio Brioso late in August with a message for Quint Kershaw. Lupita Vasquez had at last finished her period of mourning for her father. Quint and Federico rode for El Cerrillo the next day at dawn.

Lupita wore a short-sleeved white linen bodice that left her smooth shoulders and arms bare and revealed perhaps a mite too much cleavage. She wore a short woolen skirt of bright red that hung just below her shapely knees. Her legs were bare. Silver-buckled black slippers were on her feet. The faint and delicate scent of imported French perfume was about her. She had a silver-mounted comb of finest tortoise-shell thrust into her blue-black hair. Her earrings of soft pure gold had been sent to her by Quint earlier that summer. He had not told her where he had obtained the gold. The interior of the thick-walled casa was cool that sunny August, so she wore a shawl, one of bright-yellow silk worked with an intricate design of red flowers.

The contrast with the last time Quint had seen her, wearing the funereal black of mourning, was remarkable. By God but she was desirable! Now and again one of her slim hands would rise to touch her hair. The shawl seemed more of an accouterment to coquetry than a mere garment. As Lupita and Quint talked in broad generalities, skillfully avoiding the real purpose of her invitation and his presence, she shifted the shawl almost constantly, at times drawing it about her, then flinging it off or rearranging it and smoothing it while all the time studying Quint with catlike eyes. Invitation, teasing or challenge? Which was it? Or, perhaps none of them at all. *Quién sabe?*

"It is said you are now a legend east of the mountains, Don Quintin," she said.

Quint shrugged. "More or less," he admitted. He studied her. "You know why I am here," he added.

337

She looked coquettishly away from him.

"I am a direct man, Lupita. I did not propose marriage you last fall because of your sorrow, but I did ask you to thin about it. I was willing to wait for your decision. I asked you notify me when you were through mourning. That you ha done. What is your decision?"

She studied him. "There are no other women in yo heart?" she asked quietly.

"None."

It was very quiet in the big sala.

"It is said that when you fought that Comanchero to th death this last spring you tried to get information from hi about a certain Indian woman," Lupita said.

Quint shrugged. "She was only an Indian," he said car lessly. He instantly regretted it.

Lupita slowly shook her head. "I can't believe you. If w were to marry, might not this Indian woman always b between us until you are sure she *is* dead? Isn't that true?

"You make my heart big, En-Hone," Mountain Woma used to say.

"Quint? Are your thoughts really here in El Cerrillo? A you here with me? Your Lupita? Or are you with someon else in your imagination?"

Quint looked at her. "What do you want me to do?" h asked quietly.

"Nothing, other than marry me. I'm not thinking of myse now, but rather of you. Quintin, you must assure yourself th Indian woman is truly dead, or you'll never find rest in ou house or bed."

Minutes ticked past.

Quint stood up at last. "It's a long way to go. *Más allá—o* beyond, as the saying goes. It will be dangerous. I might no come back."

"You don't have to go if you don't want to. The decision i yours."

They looked steadily at each other.

Quint picked up his hat. He drew her close with one arr and kissed her gently. He turned on a heel and left the roor The faint musical sound of his fine spurs died away. The ho tears did not come quickly to Lupita but rather when sh heard the last hoof-falls of his great dun horse.

THIRTY-EIGHT

Return to Kershaw's Valley

Quintin Kershaw had crested the towering pass by late morning. The valley where he had spent a winter and two trapping seasons lay spread out toward the north.

He lighted a *cigarrito* as he sat in his California saddle with the Hawken across his thighs. He eisted his crossed forearms on the saucer-shaped saddlehorn. The bright fall sunlight slanted beneath the upturned brim of his heavy felt sombrero and picked out the welted cicatrice on his left cheek that stood out white against the saddle-leather hue of his weathered skin. Nothing in a full lifetime could ever darken that mark of Old Ephraim.

Quint focused his telescope and scanned the huge trough set amid those mighty guardians of the stillness, the towering nameless peaks. There seemed to be no change in the valley. It was almost exactly as he had first seen it that cold September morning seemingly so long past, even to the remnants of the first heavy snow of the season.

He could not see the far, or northern, end of the valley from his position just above the timberline, for great mountain shoulders thrust themselves out into the valley to block his view. There was only one way for him to see the northern end, but something deep within him held him back.

"Turn back," the mind voice seemed to say. "She's dead. Naught but a passing shadow; a fading memory. Gone forever."

It would be easy enough to turn back. He thought of Lupita. He thought of her perfume, a scent that aroused him more than any other such feminine wile had ever managed to do.

"Jesus," Quint murmured softly.

"You make my heart big, En-Hone."

He touched the coyote dun with his heels and tugged on the lead rope of his pack mule. He rode down the pass into the valley.

339

He paused for a time beside one of the bigger beaver ponds. He remembered it well. As he watched, a whiskered nose came gently to the surface, followed by a hump of glossy black. The beaver swam toward the far bank, leaving a spreading V of ripples that eventually lapped up against the bank with a sound of fairy music. The young beaver waddled out of the pond and vanished into the quiet woods. Faint shufflings and rustlings came back to Quint.

Quint turned his back on the pond. "Ye're safe enough from me, laddie," he said. "My trapping days are o'er." There was a faint tone of nostalgia in his voice. Hard and hazardous as the life had been, there had been an element of freedom in it, a freedom he kne ehe would never experience again.

Once, as he rode to the north, he caught a glimpse of a gray slinking shape within the moving cover of shade from the leaves of a bosque of cottonwoods. He remembered then the secretive population of huge wolves dwelling in the valley. He recalled the sharp clear night of hard frost, the faint howlings within the shadowed woods, the swift killing rush of six great wolves.

He reined in the dun at the edge of the large meadow where he had killed the six wolves in a matter of minutes. The leaning tree where Mountain Woman had sought escape from them had long since fallen to the ground, probably from the great weight of the winter snows. She had fallen in a dead faint from that very tree into his arms, and he had ridden with her through the quiet woods to the warmth and safety of their lodge.

The huge skeleton and thick broad skull of Old Ephraim lay half-buried in a thick mat of fallen leaves. Scavengers had scattered some of the bones and separated the skull from the skeleton frame. There was a healed scar on a nearby tree—the mark of the grizzly. He had missed a murderous swipe at Quint and neatly barked the tree instead. Quint left hand raised to touch the scar.

The dun and the mule shied and blew at the faint odor coming from the massive skeleton. Quint led them on a way and then dismounted. He walked back to the bony relics of the grizzly. He poked about within the great ribcage and picked up three flattened 217-grain bullets. One had been from his North pistol fired with the muzzle almost touching the bear's tough belly; the other balls had been one each from Quint's Hawken and Mountain Woman's Leman, fired by her into the bear's back at about one-foot range. Even then th

owerful beast had not died at once. It had taken numerous
hrusts of Quint's knife up to Green River to finish the job.

"Aye, ye were a fit opponent, Old Ephraim," Quint said
oftly.

He rode through the woods toward the old campsite. He
eined in at the edge of the wide meadow. On the far, or
orth, side was the blackened oval hole where the lodge had
een. Twice stout winter lodges had been built on that site,
nd twice they had been deliberately destroyed by fire, possi-
ly by the same Comancheros.

It was very quiet in the woods. The chirpings of the birds
nd the angry chatterings of the disturbed squirrels had died
way along with the faint Aeolian harping of the wind
hrough the leaves of the trees. It was almost deathly quiet; a
raveyard stillness.

The peeled-pole corral Quint had fashioned now sagged to
he ground. The roof of the pony shed had collapsed. A jaybird
wung in low over the meadow and then saw the man figure
itting motionless on his horse. It was startled into an angry
hrill chattering as it tilted up on one wing and fled swiftly
ver the still treetops.

He crossed the meadow and swung down from the saddle.
Ie set the butt of his Hawken on the ground and rested an
lbow on the muzzle while he surveyed the ruins of his lodge
nd camp. The lodge hole was thick with blackened ashes
nd bits of charred wood packed down tightly by the weight
f winter snows and spring and fall rains.

*"That's a bad way to live. There is no medicine power in a
quare or rectangle,"* Mountain Woman had told Quint when
e had squared out the hole old Gabe Pritchett had originally
ug here for his lodge. *"Everything the People do is done in a
ircle. That's because the power of the world always works in
ircles and everything in nature tries to be round. It's the* right
ay. Everything the Power of the World does is in a circle. . .

*"Even the seasons form great circles in their changings.
'hey always come back to where they were."*

Now he knew why he had to come back to the valley—*full
ircle.*

He unsaddled the dun and unpacked the mule, then turned
em loose in the meadow, where they rolled on the ground to
ase their sore sweating backs. He propped up the roof of the
ony shed. A fieldmouse scuttled from what was left of the
rass and cottonwood bark strips Mountain Woman had
ocked in there as horse fodder. He stripped off his jacket

and shirt and cut firewood from a fallen pine. The music ringing of the ax echoed from the far side of the valley an died away in the distance.

He cooked his meal as the shadows grew across the valle When he finished eating he lighted a *cigarrito* and sat on th same stump he had sat upon while cleaning his rifle ju before he had left the valley in pursuit of the Comanchero He sipped a little now and then from his pewter flask of Pa brandy. He knew he had searched the campsite as thorough as he could have done. He had hunted through the qui woods for her. He had scoured the woods on both sides of th stream and had probed the deeper pools for her body. He ha done everything possible to find her. He had made the nor end of the valley echo with the sound of his voice calling o to her.

Had he *really* taken enough time? Had he been meticulo in his searching for her? Or had he been in too much of hurry to pursue the Comancheros and regain his value plews? Perhaps she had still been alive and unable to answ him. Supposing that were so, and she had heard him b could not respond? Perhaps she had been conscious, or sem conscious, left alone in the darkening valley she had alway feared to die alone, wounds untended, slowly bleeding death. Or if she had survived that first day, had she been ab to fend for herself?

Quint stood up suddenly. "Mother of God," he murmure She could have starved, or perhaps died of thirst, if th wolves had not found her first. Or had they found her whe she was still alive? They liked to eat from living flesh.

He would allow himself a week to prove conclusively th she was dead. But supposing he could not find that proof?

He spent the last hours of daylight digging into the thic bed of damp ashes in the lodge pit, trying to keep from h memory the thoughts and scenes that had taken place rig where he was working. He could almost see her sitting on robe beside the warming fire slowly and methodically bea ing the fine deerskin hunting shirt she had made for hin while she listened thoughtfully to his reading of the Bible her.

He found no traces of human bones in the ashes. He ha known all along they wouldn't be in there. If she had bee left within the lodge to die, or was already dead, he woul have found her burned corpse there the first time he ha looked for her. Still, he could leave no stone unturned.

Quint sat for a long time beside his campfire smoking his
pe and looking into the dying, flickering flames with their
range and eerie pictures. It was a small circle of light in the
eat pool of darkness that was the valley. Now and again he
ould look up and out into the blackness, a lean, hawk-faced
an, looking older than his years, with eyes the color of
acial ice and a terrible scar from just below his left eye that
sappeared into his short reddish beard like a seaworm
riggling into kelp.

He fell lightly asleep within the shelter of the shed lying on
thick serape and covered with a closely woven Chimayo
anket. Now and again he awoke to lock his big hands at the
ape of his neck and look up through the holes and cracks in
e shed roof to see the tiny ice-chip stars against the dark
arine blue of the night sky. Then he would rise up on an
bow and look out into the darkness. He had little fear of
ing surprised, at least by Indians. A mule was better than
y dog in scenting Indians. In any case, as Gabe Pritchett
d insisted, the Eutaws or Utes wouldn't come near the
lley. It was bad medicine for them. *"Ain't no place for a
an alone,"* he had warned Quint. *"Got to have someone to
atch his back."* There would be no need for the Comancheros
return. There was no lure for them now—no unsuspecting
apper piling up a small fortune in prime winter-thick
aver plews. But supposing, just supposing now, they *did*
me back? Quint moved his right hand a little and rested it
the cold wood and metal of Auld Clootie. His pair of
aterson Colts were just under the edge of his blanket. He
inned like a winter-hungry wolf in the darkness.

In the days that followed his reaching the valley he hunted
d searched from dawn to dusk. He could not find the
ightest trace of Mountain Woman. He quartered the area
thin a quarter of a mile each way from the campsite and
ok a day apiece to thoroughly search each quarter. He
turned to the stream and worked the banks on both sides,
obing the bottom yard by yard with a long sapling. Noth-
g. . . . He stripped and plunged into the icy waters of the
ep churning pool at the bottom of the waterfall. Noth-
g. . . . He worked up the stream against the current, know-
g full well though that if she had been thrown into the
ater or had fallen into it she would have either drifted
wnstream or perhaps become wedged in the rocks or tan-
ed in driftwood. Nothing. . . .

The Comancheros had not taken her with them. That was certainty.

His last night in the valley he sat at his campfire while th new moon rose slowly from behind the eastern mountain He had done his duty. Morally he was in the right. Now h could return to Lupita and marry her.

"But, supposing, just supposing," he mused aloud, "sh might have made it out of the valley somehow." It was almos as though someone else had spoken. After a time he sai slowly and with great reluctance, "Aye, it's possible."

He stood up and walked to where he could see the towerin notch of the north pass. After a time he nodded. He dran deeply and went to bed. He did not awaken once that nigh nor did he dream.

He started his climb just at daylight. By the time th sunlight flowed into the valley he was already well up int the pass. When he reached the crest he turned to look bac down into the great valley—Kershaw's Valley. He grimace wryly at the conceit and self-confidence he had had at th time he named the valley. There had always been the though half-formed in the back of his mind, that he might retur there someday after he had sold his plews and made hi "fortune" in New Mexico. It might not have been for year but it had been a strong possibility. Now he wasn't so sur

There was everything a man might want for the res of his natural life—game of all kinds, wood for fires an timber for building, limitless water and excellent pasturag

"There is somethin' evil about that place, Big Red. Somethin that is not for men. Stay away from it. Go and trap Bayo Salade or the San Juans, but not that valley," Old Gabe ha warned Quint. When he had left Quint and Mountain Woma twenty-five miles to the north and east of the pass his las words had been *"Vaya con Dios*—Go with God." If Old Sol tary believed in God, any god, no one had ever heard him sa so. Old Gabe had turned to look back after he had ridden little way. *"Acaso!"* he had called out. "Maybe. . . ." Go wit God, maybe. . . .

Aye, the valley was a good place for a man, *at least by sigh* But old Abe Walker and Pawnee Jack Stearns had died ther in cold blood, shot down likely from ambush. Gabe Pritche had almost unhinged his mind there; he had never been th same after the winter he had spent alone there. He had los two seasons' harvest of prime plews, as Quint had done. Hi lodge and possibles had been burned, and Quint had suffere

he same fate. Old Ephraim had nearly killed Gabe and had
marked him for life, as Quint had been marked for life.
Mountain Woman might have died there as well. Its pleas-
antness was a deception; a perilous Eden.

Quint lit a *cigarrito*. He looked to the north. Had she
survived and gone north to return to her people? When he
had first searched for the valley he had left her behind,
warning her to return to her people if he did not come back
within three to five days. Still, he was deeply puzzled. If she
had been alive after the attack by the Comancheros she
likely would have responded to Quint calling to her. "Likely,"
he mused aloud. He had thought he knew her well enough to
believe that if she had not been able to contact him, she
would have figured he would head either south to Taos, or
southeasterly to Bent's Fort. She could have trailed him if
he was able. *If* she was able. . . .

It was about 350 miles to the Popo Agie and the Shoshonis
of the Wind River country. That was as the crow flies. It was
some of the ruggedest, if not the most rugged, mountain
terrain Quint had ever traveled through. Even if she had
started out on the trail she might not have made it back to
her people. She could have died anywhere within that 350
miles. She might have been captured by tribal Utes. She
might have been caught by the Cochetopa Utes who haunted
parts of that country. They were renegades and killers, a
mixture of Utes, JicarillaAgpaches, Navajos and Mexicans,
with a bad American or two thrown in for good measure to
further poison the brew. She would not have lasted long with
them. They used captive women only until they were no
longer usable and then got rid of them.

"Turn back. She's dead. A passing shadow. A fading
memory," the insistent thought drifted through Quint's mind.

He passed a hand across his eyes and shook his head.

"You make my heart big."

Quint picked up the dun's reins and looked once more down
into his valley.

He turned and led the animals down the steep descent of
the path toward the distant north.

THIRTY-NINE

November 1839—David Kershaw

Quintin Kershaw was fifty miles north of the River o'
Stinking Water and almost within sight of the Yellowstone
yet he had not seen a single Crow warrior from the band o.
Medicine Wolf, whose village was near the river at The
Cliff-That-Has-No-Pass. It was early afternoon, but it was
darkening fast from the low swift-moving clouds that had
moved in from the northeast, bringing with them the smell o.
approaching rain.

During his long ride from the village of the Shoshonis or
the Popo Agie he had holed up during the days, moving or
only from dusk to just before dawn. He came in peace with
trade goods packed on his mule. He might be able to bargain
with the Crows for the woman and child. Had he not fought
so hard with the Shoshonis against the Crows on the Medicine
Lodge Fork of the Big Horn it would have been far less
dangerous for him to enter the country of the Crows. He
knew the Crows. He had lived with them for a time and had
grown to like them.

He had reached the Shoshoni band of Washakie in October
An enemy greater than the Blackfeet or the Crows had been
there that fall. The stinking spotted sickness, the Red Death
of smallpox, had struck at the Shoshonis. He heard rumors o'
the plague while on his way north to the Popo Agie. It had
been a recurrence of the ravaging attack of the disease which
had struck the Indians with such devastation two years past
The American Fur Company steamer *St. Peter* up the Missouri
River from St. Louis had brought it to Fort Union on the rive
above the mouth of the Yellowstone. One hundred and fifty
miles to the southeast of Fort Union, on the Missouri, the
Mandans had flourished in two towns. Of sixteen hundred
people in the two towns only thirty-one had survived. Of al
the Mandan tribe there were hardly one hundred left. Rumor

ad it that 60,000 to 150,000 Indians in all had been wiped
ut that terrible year, perhaps an exaggeration, but even so
he loss of life had been devastating.

The smallpox had been brought to the Shoshonis by half-
breed traders from the Missouri. The Shoshonis had suffered
ome losses, but nothing like those suffered by the Mandans,
Crows and Sioux. Purcose, Buffalo Leggings, one of the two
eaders of the Yellow Noses, was gone. Pon-Sooke, the Otter, a
eader of the Logs, had died. Zawipe, Good Woman, one of the
vives of Buffalo Bellowing, the medicine man, had died
espite all his efforts. Good Woman had been the aunt of
Mountain Woman. Bareyagat, Elk Calling, she who had once
een the close friend of Mountain Woman, had almost died,
ut had recovered, a "rough-face" with her pretty features
avaged and pitted by the disease.

But what of Mountain Woman? The Shoshonis knew little
bout her. A Taoseno half-breed trader by the name of
Etienne Provost who had been in the country of the Eutaws, far
outh of the Popo Agie, had found her weak and emaciated,
ut still stubbornly heading north to return to her people.
Provost's mother had been a Crow of the band of Medicine
Wolf, whose village was usually on the Yellowstone, called
y the Crows the Elk River, at a place named The-Cliff-
That-Has-No-Pass. He had taken Mountain Woman with
im to that village. Whether or not she had gone willingly
vith him none of the elders knew. After all, she was only a
voman. If En-Hone was looking for another winter squaw
e'd have no trouble finding another one among the people.
Yes, Mountain Woman was said to be among the Crows. The
hoshonis had learned that at the last rendezvous held on the
Seeds-kee-dee Agie. But Etienne Provost had been captured
y the Par-keeh, the murderous Blackfeet. He had been
calped and tortured to death.

Elk Calling had come to Quint's lodge one dark night. She
ad refused to enter, not wanting him to see her ravaged face
n the firelight. She had told him Mountain Woman had a
oy child, but by whom she didn't know. How old was the
hild? She wasn't sure, but the rumor had been that the child
ad been born ahead of his time early during the Moon of the
Changing Season. That would be October of 1838. Thus the
hild, if he was still alive, would be about fourteen months
ld. Quint had wasted no time. He left the camp of the
hoshonis within fifteen minutes after Elk Calling had told

347

him of the boy child. It would be a long and hazardous ride to the Yellowstone.

The Crows should know by now that he was in their country. He now rode boldly in the open, to avoid an ambush, of course, but also to make sure he was seen. They would know who he was. In any case it was too late to turn back now.

The darkling plain was empty. Nothing moved except the low racing clouds and the wind-blown grass. The course of the Yellowstone was defined by low bluffs ahead. The village should be there. There was no vast herd of ponies dotting the hills and the plain. No smoke rose from the village. No dogs barked. The only sound was the faint moaning of the rising, rain-laden wind.

Scavenging ravens flew up at Quint's approach to the silent village. They hung on the wind with outstretched wings, hovering not very high over his head. Nothing else moved except the flaps of the tipis fluttering in the wind. No smoke rose from the tipis. No dog barked. It literally seemed to be a village of the dead. Quint halted the dun and the skittery pack mule at the very edge of the village. Here and there, sprawled corpses dotted the hard-packed bare earth in the center of the great double circle of the lodges facing the east. The stench of rotting death was stirred by the freshening wind, but it was not to be dissipated; it was too strong for that.

"Our tipis are round like the nests of the birds, and these are always set in a circle within the village, like a nest of many nests, where the Great Spirit Tamapah, the Sun-Father and Father of us all, even you, En-Hone, meant for us to hatch our children," Mountain Woman had said, seemingly so long ago.

One tipi stood apart from all the others on the far side of the village. It was small, no more than eleven skins at the most. Quint rode toward it. The thudding of the hooves on the hard ground seemed inordinately loud. As he neared the small lodge he noted that it was not quite like the others in the pattern of the Crows. Then he recognized it for what it was—Shoshoni.

He suddenly looked back over his shoulder. Nothing had changed except that the ravens were swinging low to the ground and landing near to or on the stiffened corpses. He wondered idly if they might be susceptible to smallpox.

Quint turned suddenly. Just as he did so he thought he saw a quick, shadowy movement inside the open door hole of the mall tipi. He dismounted and led the dun toward the tipi.

"Dotawipe!" Quint called.

There was no answer. Nothing moved.

"Dotawipe!"

Nothing.

He walked forward in his Ute moccasins as noiselessly as a
unting cat. He stopped close beside the door hole and just
ut of sight of anyone who might be looking out. Minutes
cked past. The dun suddenly shied and blew. Quint's left
and shot out and closed on living flesh. He drew a little boy
ato the open. The child was about fourteen months old and big
r his age. He was dressedihn a miniature pair of leggings
nd deerskin shirt. A deerskin harness was fastened to his
hest, and a long plaited thong trailed back into the dimness
f the tipi. His face was dirty and greasy and his nose was
nning. He stank!

Quint got down on one knee. He placed his big hands one
n each side of the boy's face and tilted his head back. He
oked into a pair of big gray eyes. His hair was filthy, and it
as difficult to detect the true color, but there was a dark-
eddish tinge to it. The little lad did not seem afraid of Quint.

"My God," Quint breathed.

Something stirred within the darkened tipi.

Quint peered into the tipi. The sickening stench that
manated from it made him hold his big nose. Something
irred again. He released the boy, who promptly whirled and
an back into the interior. It was deathly quiet again.

The ravens were cawing as they scuttled about scraping
eir claws on the hard ground. The wind shifted a little and
lew harder.

"Dotawipe?" Quint queried.

He'd have to enter the tipi. If she was alive he'd have to
elp her as best he could; if she was dead or dying, he'd have
) take care of the boy whether it was his son or not.

He entered the tipi. The stench was overpowering, that of
ingled human waste, rotting food and the indefinable decay
f a powerful disease. There was a heap of robes at the rear of
ie lodge. The little boy squatted near the door on the
ard-packed earth floor beside the big peg that had been
riven into the ground and to which his harness thong was
ttached. He had just enough leeway to reach the door, but
ot enough to reach the bed in the rear of the tipi.

"Go away," the woman's muffled voice came faintly from
ie bed. She had spoken in English.

"It's Quint," he said quietly.

There was a long pause. "I know," she said at last.

"I've come to help you and the boy."

Another long pause. "It's too late for me," she said.

"I didn't know."

What didn't he know? That she had smallpox? That she ha[d] been living with the Crows? That she was alive at all? Whe[n] had he been in the months since he had left his valley alone[?]

Guilt and stinging remorse flowed through him, and yet h[e] knew deep within himself that he would have done the sam[e] thing over again if the occasion rose. All he had really don[e] in coming north from New Mexico on his long and hazardou[s] journey, was to attempt to expiate his guilt; to make sure sh[e] *was* dead. *Now what?*

"The boy? He's mine?" Quint asked.

She moved a little but did not reply.

"The eyes? The hair?" he asked desperately.

"Yes," she replied softly at last. I hope so, she thought.

Quint picked up the little boy. "Jesus, you stink," he sai[d.] He grinned into the moppet's dirty face.

"Does he have the spotted sickness yet?" she asked tensel[y.]

My God! He hadn't thought about that! He placed the b[oy] on the floor and went out to his horse. He took his possibl[es] sack from the saddle cantle and brought it back into the tip[i.] He struck flint and firesteel and lighted some buffalo-fa[t] candles while watched by the fascinated eyes of the chil[d.] He took a copper kettle and left the tipi, removing his b[ig] gourd canteen from his saddle. He hurried to the rive[r] passing some decaying sweat lodges. He paused on the ban[k.] Several naked bloated corpses swirled slowly in an edd[y.] Their skins were blotched with great pustules. Quint shoo[k] his head. The last thing the suffering Crows should have don[e] was to take sweat baths and then plunge into the cold wate[r] of the river. He went upstream and thoroughly washed ou[t] the kettle. He filled the kettle and the canteen with fres[h] water and hurried back to the tipi. He started a fire to bo[il] water.

Quint stripped the little lad, grimacing at the stench of th[e] fully packed diaperlike loincloth he wore. He wiped awa[y] most of the accumulated filth and closely examined the so[ft] brown skin. Not a telltale red mark was visible.

"He's clean," Quint said, as though to himself. "How, [I] don't know. Still, there's a chance he might have contracte[d] it. I'll likely know within the next four or five days."

"I prayed to your God," she said simply. "Take him from here, En-Hone."

"Aye, and ye too, lassie!"

She knew better.

"He's a bonnie wee laddie!" Quint cried in delight. "What's his name?"

"The Crows call him Little Red Badger."

"And ye?"

"David. You said that was your father's name."

"Bueno! I couldn't have done better myself! We'll leave at dawn. I'll rig a travois for ye. We can be miles away from this place of stinking death by noon. I'll make a camp near good water and nurse ye back to health. Aye, that's the ticket! Dr. Kershaw, M.D. Does that not tickle your fancy, lassie?"

"Go tonight, En-Hone. Go now! *Leave at once!*"

"I can't leave ye like this."

"Go! Take nothing from this tipi with you!"

Quint stripped off his jacket and wrapped it around the boy, girding it with a leather thong. The fire was dying in a bed of ashes. The buffalo-fat candles were guttering low.

"Dotawipe," Quint said, "we're ready."

She did not speak.

Quint stood there, a lean panther of a man holding the tiny hand of his son, wanting with all his heart and soul to leave that stinking place of death, yet held there by a fascination, perhaps not morbid, but still having a powerful hold on him.

"Dotawipe?" Quint queried softly.

The wind moaned down the smoke vent. The first drops of rain pattered against the taut sides of the tipi.

Quint reached out to turn back the buffalo robe that covered Mountain Woman, but something stayed his hand. Pictures of her as she had been flooded through his memory. He must leave with the boy, and yet he must make sure there was no chance of survival for her.

Quint slid a hand under the robe. He felt her soft naked breasts and pressed his hand down over her heart. He could feel the large weeping pustules that covered her soft skin. Her heart was still. He withdrew his hand and wiped it hard on the buffalo robe. For some long moments he looked down on the robe where it conformed to her face.

Quint turned suddenly. He plunged his hands into the kettle and washed them thoroughly. He rubbed them hard against the dirt of the floor and then washed them again. He carried the boy to the dun and placed him in the saddle. He

351

returned to the tipi and threw wood on the fire. The kindling caught, snapping and crackling. He placed any kind of combustibles he could find on the fire and then fanned the flames until they roared. He then kicked the fire apart, spreading the burning materials over the robes and blankets. He held the end of a flaming faggot to the side of the tipi. A runnel of fire quickly raced upward. He stepped outside and dropped the door flap.

The wind caught at him. A wraith of smoke laden with fat sparks rose from the vent flap and was driven by the wind. Quint moved the boy forward on the saddle and then mounted behind him. He lifted the boy up into his lap and kicked the dun with his heels. The hooves of the animals thudded on the hard ground. The ravens rose into the air and scattered into flight, cawing angrily, as Quint galloped his dun and the mule through the village. Beyond the village he reined in on a rise and looked back. The lodge was flaring like a torch. The wind was carrying burning fragments throughout the village. Some of the tipis were beginning to smolder.

"*Vaya!*" Quint shouted into the wind.

None but the ravens heard him.

He rode to the south. The cold rain began to be driven hard by the wind as the twilight came on, hardly distinguishable from the darkling light of the late afternoon.

Quint did not look back again. He had a long way to go, for much stretched before him.

Más allá—On beyond. . . .